MICHE

"*Boneyard* is a winner! A ... attention to the human heart. It'll keep you up ... And don't we just love Special Agent Kelly Jones!"
—Jeffery Deaver, author of *The Sleeping Doll*

"*The Tunnels* starts out scary and only gets worse— or, if you like frightening thrillers— ... Michelle Gagnon is a fresh and confident new ... ime fiction, and *The Tunnels* marks ... ... Jebut."
—John Lescroart, *New York* ... ...ing author of *The Suspect* a... ...Club

"Michelle Gagnon's stellar debut is ... .dge-of-your-seat story of suspense and intrigue. FBI agent Kelly Jones is in a race against time to stop a series of gruesome murders on a pristine eastern college campus. With a deftly crafted plot and a winning protagonist, Gagnon spins a fast-moving yarn that is certain to keep you up late. We will hear more from this talented newcomer. Highly recommended."
—Sheldon Siegel, *New York Times* bestselling author of *The Confession*

"Michelle Gagnon has written a tremendously fine debut novel that's as dark, twisty and thrilling as the tunnels she so hauntingly describes therein. Expect to sleep with the lights on for at least a week after you've relished the final page."
—Cornelia Read, Edgar Award nominee for best debut novel, *A Field of Darkness*

"A great read. Scarily good. *The Tunnels* takes you into some very dark places, as a bright new talent takes on old-world horrors and scares the living daylights out of you. It's *The Wicker Man* meets *Silence of the Lambs*."
—Tony Broadbent, author of *The Smoke* and *Spectres in the Smoke*, named by *Booklist* as one of the best spy novels of 2006

"A fast-paced, heart-fluttering run of a novel that taps into primal fears as it unfolds in real tunnels as well as in the labyrinth of the human mind. Things go down fast, decisions have to be made, and Michelle Gagnon has written characters who are up to it. Don't read this one when you're alone in the house."
—Kirk Russell, author of *Dead Game*, named by *Booklist* as one of the Top Ten Crime Novels of 2006

"A tantalizing premise, brilliantly executed. *The Tunnels* is a powerful Gothic-tinged thriller that hits the ground running and doesn't let up until the final page. So slick and polished it's hard to believe this is Michelle Gagnon's first book."
—Denise Hamilton, contributor to *Thriller*, edited by James Patterson

"Beware: Michelle Gagnon will pull you into a crime as dark, dangerous and twisted as those subterranean tunnels. Better lock the doors and windows before you start reading!"
—Gillian Roberts, author of the Amanda Pepper Mystery series

"From its harrowing prologue to its haunting last paragraph, Michelle Gagnon masterfully crafts a stellar work of mounting suspense and terror. Ritual murder, ancient magic and buried secrets...all blend seamlessly in this debut mystery by a major new talent. Not to be missed!"
—James Rollins, *New York Times* bestselling author of *Black Order*

BONE YARD

MICHELLE GAGNON

MIRA®

ISBN-13: 978-0-7783-2539-0
ISBN-10:　　0-7783-2539-3

BONEYARD

www.MIRABooks.com

Printed in U.S.A.

To Callaghan

Prologue

Cougar flipped through the trail log. He found the name "Chaz" two pages back from where he'd just signed, and checked the date. Damn, the bastard was a full day ahead of him. At this rate he'd never catch up. Letting the logbook fall back into place, he unscrewed the cap of his Nalgene bottle and took a long swig of water. It was his own damn fault. Last night he'd partied at a dive bar in Bennington instead of getting to bed early. He'd planned on hiking twenty miles today, all the way to Bascom Lodge at the top of Mount Greylock. He glanced at his watch: it was already four o'clock, there were only a few hours of daylight left. Between the hangover and his late start, he was lucky to have made it this far. He'd have to find somewhere to stay in North Adams tonight, maybe even stealth camp next to the trail if the motels were too expensive.

He looked around for a place to set his camera. Carefully perching it in the crux of two branches, Cougar squinted through the viewfinder at a sign proclaiming, in bold white letters, "Welcome to Massachusetts. Pine Cobble Trail: 1.3 miles. Sherman Brook Campsite: 2.3 miles." He quickly ran a hand through tousled brown hair while the self-timer's red light flashed. Posing, he grinned and flashed a double thumbs-up sign, then resumed his scowl as soon as the shutter clicked.

Fuckin' Chaz, he thought. He should never have signed up for this trip with that competitive bastard. The Appalachian Trail was a huge undertaking, one he would never have done on his own. It involved hiking for months across fourteen states, starting in Maine and ending in Georgia, a total of over two thousand miles. Chaz had talked about nothing else their senior year, wearing Cougar down until he finally agreed to come along. They'd spent Christmas and spring breaks poring over maps, planning every detail.

"Dude, it'll be totally awesome," Chaz had said, gnawing on his usual nasty wad of chew. "Last hurrah before we become slaves to the man."

And he was right, the first few weeks had been awesome. By the time they left Maine, the initial soreness had worn off and they'd grown accustomed to the weight of their backpacks. The mountains in New Hampshire had been challenging but rewarding. Every night they ate under the stars and either slept in a trail hut or out in the open. For Cougar, a city boy born and bred, it was his first real camping experience, and he loved it. He and Chaz had spent long hours around the campfire discussing everything: politics, philosophy, what the future might hold for them. Chaz had brought along some amazing weed, and they'd get high and stare up at the night sky. Despite his initial misgivings, it was turning out to be the best time of Cougar's life.

Then a few nights ago, after a particularly grueling stretch of the Green Mountains in Vermont, they drank too much and fought over who ate the last piece of turkey jerky. Cougar awoke the next morning to find that Chaz had already taken off, and now he was busting ass trying to catch him. It was the end of August. They'd started late enough in the season that they hadn't hit many other southbound thru-hikers, but he should be hitting the northbounders soon. There would probably be lots of other cool people to hang with, maybe even some hot chicks. It would serve the antisocial bastard right, Cougar thought as he shrugged the backpack onto his shoulders and marched through delicate stands of white birches. His fifty-pound pack felt like nothing now; after the mountains of Maine, New Hampshire and Vermont, the rest of the trail through New England should be a cakewalk.

The forest was thinning the farther south he got, densely packed fir and spruce trees giving way to cedar. Some sections were steep and plunged sharply, forcing him to skitter down sideways, loose stones cascading under his feet. Now, as he entered Massachusetts, the trail finally leveled out. Small beaver ponds dotted either side of the trail, the wind kicking up small whitecaps on their surface. It was quiet; Cougar paused for a minute. He was still a little spooked by that weird guy he and some others had hitched a ride with last night. Most locals who lived near the trail understood that hikers went by a handle; out here he was known as Cougar, which was far superior to his real name. He loved the way it looked when he signed it in the trail logs, loved the fact that no one (besides Chaz, of course) knew that in the real world he was just Jeff Feldman from Boston, a nerdy kid who deferred dentistry school to make this trip. But the creep driving the shitty Tercel kept pressing for his real name, making him wish he hadn't called shotgun. Something about the way he eyed him, too, just hadn't felt right. But the guy had dropped them at the trailhead as promised, and Cougar completely forgot about him during the drunken stumble back to Congdon Shelter.

He paused and cocked his head to the side. Shouldn't there be more birds? He had become attuned to a certain level of wilderness background noise, yet as soon as he crossed the state line everything became still. A blackfly landed on his neck; he swatted it away absentmindedly and made a mental note to buy more deet in the next town. He started walking again, more briskly even though he was probably just being paranoid. What kind of asshole would have followed him seven miles down a trail? If the guy had wanted something, he could just as easily have tried it last night, or snuck up to the shelter when they were all crashed out. The other hikers wouldn't have suspected anything if they'd woken in the morning and found him gone. Happened all the time, people decided to get a jump on the day and left without saying goodbye. The thought sent a chill down his spine; he tugged at his bandanna in aggravation, swiped at the sweat pooling in the nape of his neck. This was all stupid; he was just freaking himself out. *Fucking Chaz,* he thought again angrily. Chaz was six-three and weighed in at two-fifty. If they'd stuck together, no one would consider messing with him.

A loud crash to his left made him stop short. He heard the sound of branches breaking. Something large was lumbering his way. Cougar froze, then slowly turned toward the source of the noise. It was coming closer. He debated running, but where the hell to? As far as he knew there was nothing but woods for miles in every direction, and he hadn't seen another hiker all day. He backed up a few steps, the hairs on the back of his neck rising. He scooped a stick off the ground; bark crumbled away in his hand, but it felt like it had some heft to it. His pack scraped against something and he spun around. He was up against a tree, a good-size sugar maple. Whatever was coming, it was getting closer, splashing through the pond he'd just passed. As it emerged from the bushes a few yards away, Cougar's breath caught in his throat and his grip on the stick tightened.

It was a brown bear, and a big one, several hundred pounds of matted fur. As it turned toward him, he saw a branch dangling from its mouth. It eyed him curiously. Cougar's mind raced; the *Thru Hiker's Guide* provided instructions on how to handle a bear encounter, but damned if he could remember any of them now. All he knew was that you weren't supposed to run. The bear opened its jaws and the stick fell out, then it lumbered closer. Cougar's breath was coming in short gasps, it felt like his lungs had withdrawn deep into his chest and refused to expand. A trickle of urine ran down his leg, soaking his inner thigh. The bear's head tilted upward, snout raised toward the sky as it whiffed the air, then issued a loud chuffing noise. After a moment, its head lowered and their eyes met. Cougar's breath snagged in his chest as the bear gazed at him, eyes dark pits that seemed to be measuring him, trying to decide whether or not to charge. With a loud grunt, the bear suddenly shifted left and ambled back into the woods, passing within a few feet of Cougar.

Just then, Cougar heard voices. Other hikers were heading up the trail. His knees buckled, and his body slid haltingly down the tree until he landed with a thump on the dirt. As his breath slowly returned to normal, the sense of overwhelming relief quickly changed to embarrassment at the telltale damp stain on his shorts. He definitely didn't want to gain a rep as the guy who pissed himself when he saw a bear, that would hound him all the way to Georgia. He leaned forward and awkwardly shrugged out of his pack, then hurriedly dug inside it. By the time the group emerged on the path behind him, he'd managed to cover the stain by knotting a flannel shirt around his waist.

Just in time, because it turned out to be a group of girls. Judging by their small packs they were day-hikers, and not unattractive. He jerked his head toward them and said, "Hey."

"Hey, what's up," answered the blonde in the lead. Her hair wound down from a red scarf in two ponytails, she wore a matching red jog bra and tight black shorts. She looked him over. "You a SOBO or a NOBO?"

"SOBO," he answered. SOBO was trail jargon for "southbound." A day-hiker who knew that was probably local, he surmised. If he played his cards right, he might have a bed to sleep in tonight after all.

"Yeah? Still got a ways to go then, huh?"

He shrugged casually. "Yeah, but the hardest part is over. The White Mountains, those were rough."

"Yeah, I've heard that," answered one of the brunettes, cute but not a looker like the blonde. They had stopped about ten feet away from him, almost exactly where he'd had the showdown with the bear. He was already framing the story in his mind, only in this version he scared the bear off, when she glanced at the ground, "What's that?"

She was pointing at the stick the bear had dropped. Cougar strolled forward with exaggerated nonchalance. "Oh yeah, you guys just missed…" His voice trailed off as they all stared at the object. It wasn't a stick, after all.

"Omigod, is that…" The blonde took a step back, then glanced up at him in horror.

Bile flooded his mouth; he choked it back. "I think…" His voice faltered, and he cleared his throat. "I think we better hike into town and call the cops."

One

Kelly Jones strode across the Quantico campus, pausing briefly to let a contingent of new trainees walk by. The hint of a smile danced across her face as they passed, heading toward a brown, barrack-like classroom building. She had hated wearing that uniform—the navy golf shirts and khakis. It always looked as if they'd been sidetracked en route to the ninth hole. But in retrospect, those sixteen weeks of training had been some of her best, she mused as she continued walking. She'd loved the classroom time, the weapons training, and her daily runs along "The Yellow Brick Road," named for the saffron-colored rocks marking the trail. Ever since then her life had been a tangle of failed relationships and dead bodies, she thought ruefully as she hauled open the door leading into one of the nondescript buildings.

She paused briefly in the foyer, trying to remember the route to her supervisor's office. The Behavioral Science Unit was housed in the basement and was comprised of a confusing warren of hallways painted a cheerful color to mask the fact that there were no windows. Even after six months she still managed to get lost in here, mainly because she'd spent most of that time crisscrossing the country to assist on cases. Going by her gut, Kelly took a right and headed down a long, narrow passage, her footsteps loud on the sterile white tiles. After a few more turns she stood outside a door marked, Special Agent in Charge Gerald McLarty. She knocked and entered. The room stood in stark contrast to the hall outside. The floor was plushly carpeted in thick, slate-gray Berber wool. The wood-paneled walls were covered with framed antique maps, and a few plants sprouted unobtrusively in the corners. Kelly smiled at the woman behind the desk at the far side of the room, who gestured to the phone against her ear and pointed to the navy couch facing her. Kelly resisted the urge to grit her teeth—she hated to be kept waiting. Especially today, when there were a million things to do before she headed home to pack. As she settled against the cushions, she started composing a list in her head. She'd have to finish the piles of paperwork from her last case, and make sure copies were sent to the appropriate departments. She desperately needed to stop by the dry cleaners before they closed, and despite the fact that she loathed shopping, she needed to find a good sunhat. Her red hair and fair skin weren't going to take kindly to the Caribbean sun, especially at this time of year. And back home she'd have to deal with her fridge, since some of the food was threatening to crawl off the shelves.

Her train of thought was interrupted by a door opening at the opposite end of the room. Gerry McLarty's voice boomed out, and Kelly smiled to herself. Her new boss was infinitely superior to her old one. He was one of the main reasons she'd decided to accept the promotion when they'd offered it to her. The difference between the two men was stark. While Assistant Special Agent in Charge Bowen had been a wormy pencil-pusher with no field experience who compensated by bullying subordinates, Gerry McLarty was a highly decorated field agent who had risen through the ranks by virtue of his own guts and brains, and was highly respected by everyone fortunate enough to work with him. Though he chafed at driving a desk, the mind that had helped capture some of the nation's most elusive serial killers had proved to be equally adept at managing the agents serving under him.

Kelly had initially been leery of joining the Behavioral Science Unit. She'd spent a good chunk of her career rolling her eyes at the composites compiled by BSU profilers, and the invitation to join their ranks had not been appealing. A phone call from McLarty had changed all that. He'd been impressed with her work on a case that garnered a lot of national attention, one that dealt with a series of murders in the tunnels beneath a college campus. He'd been persuasive, arguing that her style of investigation would fit in perfectly with the philosophy of the BSU. After considerable arm-twisting, she agreed to the transfer on a provisional basis.

McLarty's ruddy face poked around the corner of the door and immediately lit up. "Agent Jones! They told me you were back. Get in here, I want to hear all about it." He summoned her with a beefy hand and she followed him into his office. Here the nautical theme continued, maps now interspersed with photos of McLarty with various dignitaries including the president, the attorney general, and Bono from the band U2.

"So." He plopped into an enormous leather swivel chair

and folded his hands together on the desk. "How did every-thing turn out in Cleveland?"

Kelly gave him the rundown on how she'd helped the local homicide unit track down a man suspected of abducting over a dozen children in the past decade. They had him in custody now, and were hoping to extract a confession based on evidence tying him directly to at least two of the killings. As she spoke, however, she got the sense that her boss's mind was somewhere else. "Everything okay?" she asked, when there was a long pause after she'd concluded her report.

"Sure, sure." McLarty tapped a finger on his desk in a quick staccato. His edgy energy was an office joke, but he seemed even jumpier than normal today. His enormous frame was contained in an impeccably tailored suit, and the fluores-cent lights reflected off his thinning blond hair. He examined her with sharp green eyes and said, "You're due to take vacation time?"

Kelly nodded. "Yes, I'm all set to leave tomorrow."

His gaze dropped to the floor, and a pit formed in Kelly's stomach. "What's going on, Gerry?" she asked, already dreading the answer.

"We might need you. Just for a few weeks..." he contin-ued hurriedly when he caught the expression on her face. "Thing is, I'd send Manolo, but he and Jennifer are stuck doing the antiterrorism-training thing, and everyone else is on active assignment. You're the only one in the unit that's quali-fied and free right now."

Kelly bit her lower lip. She should have known. The first vacation she'd planned in five years and work got in the way once again. Her longest break since joining the FBI had been the week she took off to settle her mother's affairs after her death. How typical that a case would come along just as she was getting ready to board a plane. For a moment she questioned again her decision to remain at the Bureau. Instead of transferring, maybe she should have left altogether.

Gerry caught the look in her eyes and shook his head. "Jones, I feel terrible about this. How about I tack on a few extra vacation days when you get back? After all your hard work, you deserve it."

Kelly wanted to point out that she already had months' worth of vacation time accrued, but asked instead, "What's the case?"

"Ever been to the Berkshires?" When she shook her head, he continued, "On the bright side it'll be kind of a mini-vacation for you anyway, it's gorgeous there this time of year. Lot of New Yorkers keep a second home there. In the summers they've got the Boston Symphony, theater, you name it. The wife even dragged me to a dance festival there once, didn't take to the people rolling around in tights but the spot was pretty…" His voice trailed off at her raised eyebrows. "Anyway, they've found a boneyard there."

"What, like the ones Bundy left?" Kelly asked. Any agent who'd dealt with serial crime knew the stories of how Bundy had used a few different dump sites in Washington State for his victims, places he came back to time and again with fresh bodies.

McLarty shrugged. "Maybe. It's not clear yet, all they've found is skeletal remains. Five bodies confirmed so far, possibly six, and they're still looking."

Inwardly Kelly groaned. "Skeletal? How old are they?"

McLarty shook his head. "Don't know that yet either, but I'm sending along a forensic anthropologist, he should be able to help. You'll be leading a task force of officers from Massachusetts and Vermont. And Jones, tread carefully. Unless you can find any evidence of a federal statute being broken, you're there in a strictly advisory capacity."

"So the bodies are spread across two states? Sounds like a jurisdictional nightmare," Kelly said, not even bothering to keep the despondency from her voice. For this she had to miss her vacation.

"I know," McLarty answered sympathetically. "So far the search area spans a couple of miles on either side of the state line, which is why we're being called in. Apparently animal trails might open it up even further."

"Five bodies is a lot to stumble across all at once," Kelly noted. "Were they buried?"

McLarty shook his head. "Apparently not."

"Strange that no one smelled them decomposing," Kelly said, intrigued in spite of herself.

"See? It could prove interesting." McLarty settled onto the edge of the desk, facing her. "And honestly, Jones, you get in there and nothing seems to be happening, after a few weeks with no leads I'll pull you in. We'll tell them you'll go back if new evidence materializes. I just need you to run interference until then." He hesitated briefly before continuing. "From what I understand, so far the task force members haven't exactly been getting along."

"Fantastic," Kelly muttered. "When do I leave?"

"Tomorrow morning. As a special favor, I've arranged to have a Massachusetts State Police chopper pick you up in Boston to shuttle you the rest of the way. Thought that might cushion the blow."

Kelly smiled weakly with what she hoped looked like gratitude. "Thanks, Gerry."

He waved her off. "Don't thank me, I know if I were you

I'd be cursing my name the whole way there. But I won't forget this, Jones. Next time a cherry assignment comes along, I'll see you're first in line."

"Great," Kelly said with marginally more enthusiasm. Which was curious, she pondered ten minutes later as she settled in behind her own desk. A year ago she would have jumped at the promise of first dibs on important assignments. Hell, she would have chosen nearly any assignment over a vacation; the thought of lounging on a beach would have been completely unappealing. Funny how things change, she mused. Of course, the murder of her partner last year had hit her hard, making her question for the first time in her life the path she'd chosen. During her decade-long career at the Bureau she'd been driven, single-minded in her need to hunt down killers like the one who stole her brother's life when they were children. But despite all of the interesting cases the transfer to BSU had brought her, she'd felt her enthusiasm flagging lately. When it came right down to it, she was tired of being surrounded by death.

Her eyes drifted across the matte-gray walls of her cubicle. To call it spartan would be putting it kindly. The only evidence that she'd ever used the space was a university mug on her desk that held a handful of pens. Not a single photo or news-paper clipping decorated the walls, and her computer monitor was set to the default image. Of course she'd barely spent any time there, she reasoned, knowing full well that even if she never left the office she probably wouldn't have been tempted to add anything personal. That just wasn't her style.

She gnawed her lip in agitation, eyeing the desk phone as if it might bite her. After a minute she picked it up, muttering, "Might as well get this over with."

It rang twice before someone answered and asked, "All packed?"

Her eyes squeezed shut as she responded, "I've got some bad news."

"Great to see you," the bald man exclaimed, shaking his hand heartily. "How are the wife and kids?"

He matched the enthusiasm of the grip. "Doing great, enjoying the last bit of summer." He smiled widely, casting through his memory for baldy's name. Finally, it came to him. "How about you, Allen? Haven't seen you folks at services lately."

"Oh, you know…" Allen's voice trailed off and his gaze shifted to the ground.

Belatedly, he recalled a rumor he'd heard at the church potluck, something about Allen's wife and a gardener. His ratcheted his grin up a few notches. "How about this weather, huh? Unbelievable!"

"It sure is. No better place to spend the dog days of summer." Allen's expression brightened again. They were standing outside the Wal-Mart in North Adams, Massachusetts. The enormous white-block building looked particularly incongruous set against the backdrop of rolling hills and trees. "Planning on taking full advantage," Allen continued, holding up his shopping bag and nodding toward the fishing pole jutting out the top. "How about you, what you got there?"

"Nothing much, just doing a little work around the house," he said, keeping his own bag down, handles firmly closed.

"I hear you. Hey, how about those bodies they found up by the border? I hear there were a dozen of them, maybe more."

Allen lowered his voice. "I've got half a mind to take the kids back to the city early this year, cut the summer a little short."

"No need for that." The man scoffed. "Probably just some lost hikers. Half those assholes on the Appalachian Trail have no right being there."

"Maybe." Allen sounded doubtful. "Still, we're heading out a little early this year. So if I don't see you again…"

"Absolutely, have a good one!" His grin vanished as soon as Allen lumbered away across the parking lot. His truck was parked in the opposite direction and he strolled toward it, keeping his head down. Once there, he opened the doors to the king cab back seat and dropped the bag into the wheel well. It landed with a clank. He draped an old blanket across, concealing it, then slid into the driver's seat. He pulled the hat brim down low over his eyes as he pulled out of the lot, ruminating on what Allen had said. So people were frightened to the extent of leaving early, which was a shame. This time of year the Berkshires were so lovely, he thought ruefully. Chasing away good churchgoers had certainly never been his intent.

Strange that his boys had been found after all this time. Strange, and inconvenient. But then he was due to switch things up a little, he mused, flicking on his turn signal and executing a sharp right toward home. After all, in these hills there was no shortage of places to bury a body.

Two

Kelly Jones peered out the window of the helicopter as it circled the site. Through the dense foliage below she could make out a long line of people hunched shoulder to shoulder, slowly forcing their way through the underbrush.

She tapped the button activating her mike. "Are those state police down there?"

The helicopter pilot shook his head. "From what I hear, local search and rescue is handling it. Berkshire State Police couldn't spare the manpower."

Kelly made a motion for him to drop down and circle. The chopper banked right. Sunlight glistened off the tops of the waves kicked up by their rotors as they dove past small beaver ponds. A few heads in the line tilted up to stare at them.

"Are we landing soon?" another voice chimed in.

Kelly half turned in her seat to regard the passenger behind her. Despite the fact that they were the only three in the chopper, Dr. Howard Stuart was perched dead center in the back, clutching the seat belts strapping him in, eyes squeezed tightly shut.

Kelly switched her mike back on. "My apologies, Doctor. Thought you'd want to see the scene, since you've come all this way."

One eye cracked open a notch. "I'm not much for flying, I'm afraid."

"Understood. One more pass and we land."

Kelly settled back into her seat and sighed. Personally, she'd really enjoyed the chopper. They had left Boston forty-five minutes ago and were already arriving at the opposite end of the state. It had been a beautiful ride, too. All of Massachusetts appeared carpeted in green, a never-ending stream of trees gliding past below. As they approached the Berkshires the terrain started to roll in waves, hills rising up to lap at them as they passed overhead. It had temporarily made her forget about the grim job she was heading toward, and she made a mental note to thank McLarty for arranging it. Dr. Stuart was clearly not feeling the same way. She sincerely hoped the forensic anthropologist would prove useful so that they could get out of here quickly. He certainly looked as if he knew his way around a lab—judging by his pallor he hadn't been out of a Smithsonian bunker in years.

They set down by a small picnic area, next to an open pavilion that swept to the edge of a large pond. It reminded her of a summer camp she had gone to as a kid. Gorgeous day like this, Clarksburg State Park should have been packed with people enjoying the last gasp of summer, Kelly thought. It was closed now, had been for a week, ever since the first remains were discovered. Today the picnic tables and deserted boat launch played host to a squadron of police cars and green forest service SUVs.

Kelly jumped lightly from her seat as the rotors slowed and

strode forward. A group of Massachusetts state troopers were perched on the edge of one of the tables, sipping from Dunkin' Donuts cups. Their chatter stilled as she approached.

"Special Agent Kelly Jones, FBI," she said, flashing her badge. They gazed at her in silence. Inwardly she sighed. McLarty was right, she was probably going to have a turf war on her hands. "Mind pointing out who's in charge?"

One of the troopers jerked his head toward the woods. "The L.T. is in there, supervising the search and rescue unit."

"Just follow the trail," offered one of the younger troopers, eyes glued to her chest.

She nodded briskly and turned toward the woods. As she walked off, the first cop called after her, "Mind asking when we can break for lunch?"

Yeah, because you've worked up such an appetite, Kelly thought to herself, already annoyed. This was her least favorite type of assignment, dealing with old remains when the killer's trail had long since gone cold. Not to mention she'd be leading a task force comprised of cops from different jurisdictions in neighboring states. In cases like this the cops frequently split into warring camps, with everyone hoarding information and eyeing one another with distrust. Added to that was the fact that the murders had taken place in the Berkshires, a summer resort for old Manhattan money, so the media pressure was intense. Worst-case scenario, the investigation could drag on for months, years even. And, on top of everything else, she had a forensic anthropologist to babysit.

"Um, Agent Jones?"

She stopped and turned to find Dr. Stuart nervously tugging at the chin strap on his hat. Despite the fact that over the phone she'd advised him to dress for fieldwork, he was wearing suit pants, a short-sleeve shirt, tie and dress shoes. Apparently fieldwork for him carried different connotations.

"Yes, Doctor?"

"Would you mind terribly if I waited here? I neglected to bring bug repellent, and I understand the ticks can be quite vicious this time of year."

"Why don't you see if they have anything in transition from the site to the lab." She nodded back toward the picnic tables. "I'm sure those officers would be happy to help you."

The woods were oddly silent. It was a beautiful day, a slight breeze stirring the leaves as she strolled down the path, knotting her hair in a ponytail as she went. The scent of pine and cedar coated the humid air. A half mile down the trail she came across two men. Hands on their hips, they watched the search and rescue line's slow progress.

"Detective Lieutenant Doyle?" Kelly asked.

The taller man turned to face her. He was in his mid-forties with steel-gray hair boxed in a crew cut, sporting the standard-issue state trooper Ray-Bans and mustache. Instead of a uniform, he was dressed in khaki slacks and a white polo shirt. "You the Feds?" he asked through the piece of gum he was working over.

She nodded and extended a hand. "Fed singular, I'm afraid. My understanding is that you just need someone to help co-ordinate the task force. Special Agent Kelly Jones. How's the search going?"

Doyle shook hands reluctantly and shrugged. "Just dandy, considering the animal activity, beavers rerouting the river and all. Most of what we're finding is damned old—could be from an Indian burial ground for all we know. For the record,

I think a task force is a waste of time. I figure we got a lost hiker on our hands."

Kelly ignored the last part and turned toward the other man. He was dressed in an expensive pair of hiking shorts and an expedition shirt. He'd removed his sunglasses and was peering at her through warm brown eyes. "Nice to meet you, Agent Jones. I'm Sam Morgan. I'm helping Bill and Monica coordinate the search."

"Are you a trooper?"

He laughed and waved a hand dismissively. "Me? Afraid I'm just a civilian. I'm a stockbroker who moonlights as president of the Berkshire Search and Rescue Unit." Sam gestured toward the line of people retreating steadily away from them. "We're an all-volunteer group, usually called in when a day-hiker doesn't show up for dinner. This is pretty much the most exciting thing we've ever done, at least since I've been around."

Kelly half smiled at his enthusiasm. "And you've been out here for about a week?"

"Six days. The first few days we were working the quadrant closest to the campground—that's where we found most of the bones. Now we're working known animal trails. They have standard routes to and from the lake to their dens. No luck today, though. If you'd like, I could show you on the topo map—"

"We got another one!" a voice called out excitedly.

Kelly glanced at the men. "Shall we?"

She led the way off the trail in the direction of the voice. The ground was slightly marshy underfoot, her hiking boots sinking into the lush carpet of needles blanketing the forest floor. The farther from the trail she got, the more the trees thickened until she was dodging branches. *Not the easiest place to dump a body,* Kelly thought to herself. Factoring in the hike from the parking lot and the terrain, it would have to be done at night, by someone who knew the woods fairly well.

The line of searchers had stopped a hundred yards off the path. A few of them stood silently to the side. They looked exhausted, Kelly thought sympathetically. Most were middle-aged men in sweat-soaked shorts and T-shirts. They probably never imagined when they signed up for the SAR unit that they'd be spending days searching for scattered human remains.

She squatted down and peered at the spot they were staring at. A small finger bone protruded from the moss; brownish-white, it pointed accusingly toward the sky. "All right. Let's mark this one and get a few shots of it. You're recording these on a central map?"

"Not my first dump site, miss," Doyle mumbled at her shoulder.

"No, I'm sure it's not. Just double-checking. When you're finished, I'll send my guy in for collection." Kelly straightened up.

"Uh-uh." Doyle shook his head vigorously from side to side. "We're still on our side of the state line. Anything found in Massachusetts, stays in Massachusetts. I'm under orders to send all we get to the state lab."

Despite the fact that he was right, she found his condescending tone grating. Unfortunately, she had no authority to order the remains sent anywhere until there was proof that something other than a bear had dragged the victim across the border. "I see. And where's that?"

A smile played about his lips. "Sudbury."

"Sudbury? Outside Boston?"

"That's the only Sudbury I know of, miss." Doyle rocked back on his heels, clearly enjoying himself.

"You swinging that dick around again, Bill?" asked a female voice.

The lieutenant's smile instantly faded. "Thought we'd agreed to stick to our respective borders."

A petite woman with blond hair cut in a bob had emerged from the woods and was standing behind them. Also in her mid-forties, her green eyes matched her uniform and shone through a healthy tan. She grinned at Kelly while waving a hand dismissively at Doyle. "Borders, schmorders. Don't worry, honey, we saved some bones for you. Ignore Doyle, just this morning I caught him pissing on some bushes to mark his territory."

"Bullshit." A red flush rose up Doyle's neck. "You know damn well…"

"Yeah, yeah." She rolled her eyes and her grin widened. "Morning, Sam. Sam's one of the good ones, aren't you, Sam?"

Sam Morgan was hanging back, watching the exchange. "Awfully nice of you to say so, Monica."

"Shame he lives on this side of the state line, that's all I can say." Monica turned to Kelly and explained, "Sam and I took a spelunking class together a while back and, let me tell you, this guy put the rest of us to shame. Sam, you belong in Vermont, you and that nice family of yours should look into property there. The schools are a damn sight better, not to mention the people."

"Please, Monica, you were the star of that class," Sam replied, grinning. "There was this one tunnel, it was just a foot high and went back a hundred yards before opening into a chamber. She was the only one of us to make it through."

"Too bad she didn't stay there," Doyle grumbled under his breath.

Monica glared at him before shifting her attention back to Kelly. "Welcome to the party, honey, and about time you got here. Doyle has nearly driven me to my last nerve."

Monica gripped Kelly's hand firmly, almost crushing it. Kelly winced slightly.

"Oops, sorry about that, just so happy to see you. Lieutenant Monica Lauer, Vermont State Police, Bureau of Criminal Investigation. So, we found another one?"

"Looks like a finger bone," Kelly said.

"Like a jigsaw puzzle, isn't it? We got parts of one body in our lab, which—" she raised an eyebrow pointedly in Doyle's direction "—is in Bennington, just a hop, skip and jump away. Ours is missing an arm, so we figure it might be the rest of the John Doe that hiker stumbled across. Massachusetts is sitting on four or five more, near as I can figure, but it's hard to know what we've got when everything is scattered to the four corners."

"Massachusetts has one of the top forensics facilities in the country," Doyle snorted.

"Yeah? 'Cause last I heard your lab screwed the pooch on a whole bunch of DNA samples," Monica retorted.

Noting the flare of Doyle's nostrils, Kelly interceded. "I'd like to get a better sense of what we're dealing with before we discuss the jurisdictional issues." She was suddenly aware of the weight of dozens of eyes. The entire SAR team had stopped and was watching the discussion with interest. "Mr. Morgan, perhaps…"

"Call me Sam, please." He raised his voice and clapped his hands together. "All right, everyone, why don't we take a break for lunch, start up again in a half hour?" He led the team back toward the trail, leaving the three of them standing alone. Kelly looked from one to the other. Monica stood with her hands on her hips, while Doyle had locked his jaw in a grimace.

"So it looks like we have a lot to talk about," Kelly said, leading them away as a forensics technician materialized and began taking photographs of the bone in situ. "Things here seem pretty much under control. Lieutenant, I'm guessing you can suggest a place in town for us to have lunch?"

They piled into Doyle's squad car and slowly edged out of the lot. Monica Lauer was simmering in the back seat. Kelly could sense the waves of dislike emanating from her. She repressed the urge to gnaw her lip, which was already starting to feel raw. Obviously these two were clashing, and so far she hadn't been impressed with the level of professionalism demonstrated by either of them. None of which boded well for the investigation.

A uniform up ahead eased a sawhorse to the side of the road and waved them through. Instantly, they were swarmed by a herd of reporters; four television station vans were parked along the road. Doyle brushed them off like gnats, but slowed as they approached a blond reporter at the far edge of the scrum.

"What are you doing?" Kelly asked, puzzled.

Doyle rolled down his window and smiled at the blonde, who leaned forward just enough to reveal a hint of cleavage. "Afternoon, Jan," he said, grin widening.

"Lieutenant Doyle, good to see you!" Jan responded in a honeyed voice. "Anything new?"

In the back seat Monica muttered, "For Pete's sake."

"Lieutenant Doyle..." Kelly said warningly.

He ignored her. "Same as I told you earlier, we're thinking maybe an Indian burial ground, or a couple of lost hikers."

"Really?" Jan glanced at the other reporters, who had surged forward with their mikes and were pressing in on her. She shoved back at them with her hip and leaned in closer. "Because there are rumors that a serial killer might be responsible."

"Serial killer! Now, who's been—"

"Lieutenant Doyle, we really need to get going," Kelly said sharply. The blonde's attention flicked over to her, taking inventory, and her eyes narrowed.

"Excuse me, ma'am, which unit are you with? Are you part of the task force?" Jan asked, shoving her microphone forward.

Kelly ignored her, and Doyle finally eased the car forward. Jan stepped back as he drove away.

"What the hell was that?" Kelly asked through gritted teeth.

"Just issuing a statement to the press," Doyle said without taking his eyes off the rearview mirror.

"Oh, is that what they're calling it these days?" Monica asked.

Kelly repressed a sigh and sank back into her seat. In a parallel universe she'd be lying on a beach right now drinking a piña colada, not babysitting these two. She could already tell this was going to be a long case.

Dwight's leg jiggled nervously as he tapped out a cadence on the bar with his fingers, humming along to the jukebox. *Before I was born, late one night, my papa said everything's all right...* Catchy tune, "Hand Jive"; he'd always liked it.

Charlie the bartender shuffled over and squinted at his arm. "Looks like you got a new tat."

Dwight glowed at the attention, held his arm up and tilted

it forward to catch the light emanating from the TV set. "Yup, got it done yesterday." The letters were black, the skin around them an angry red. The tattoo stood out in bold relief against his pale skin, squeezed into the space between a Navy Seal logo and a Coast Guard skiff.

Charlie leaned forward and peered at it. "CIA, huh? So you got in?"

"Just going through the final security check," Dwight answered proudly, missing the dubious tone of voice. "You know, to get top clearance takes a while. They gotta talk to everyone—Ma, the guys at work, maybe even you." Something suddenly occurred to Dwight, and he leaned forward eagerly. "Hey, anyone come by asking questions about me?"

Charlie slowly shook his head, avoiding his eyes. "Not on my shift."

"That's all right." He waved an arm and settled back on his stool, took a big gulp of tepid tap beer. "Sure they'll be in soon."

"Sure they will," Charlie said. "Hey, you should probably keep that covered, first few days after inking it can get infected."

Dwight ignored him, distracted by what was happening onscreen. On the television a chopper was circling a line of searchers barely visible through the trees. The camera cut back to the blond reporter who looked like she had a real pole up her ass. Her pursed lips murmured silently into the microphone.

"Hey, Charlie, hit the volume, would ya?"

The bartender followed his gaze, grunted and reached up to press the button. The blonde's voice, sharp as her looks, gradually increased in volume but was periodically drowned out by the jukebox.

"*...no word yet on...task force has arranged to meet... more developments later...*"

The station cut back to the anchors, sitting at their usual cheap-ass plywood desk. Terrible studio set they had, they'd been using the same one since the seventies. *"Any word, Jan...dealing with a..."*

Jan's head was cocked to the side, her expression of concern as carefully tailored as her suit. She listened as the other anchor uttered the words Dwight had been waiting to hear.

"Police won't confirm or deny, but all indications are that's exactly what..."

The bartender shook his head. "You believe that? A freakin' serial killer, here?"

Dwight smiled into his beer. "Yeah, I believe it. Lot of sick fucks in the world, Charlie."

"Sure are," the bartender agreed. "Good thing the season's almost over. Hate to think what this'll do to business."

Dwight stood, slid the pile of pennies he'd been playing with off the counter and into his pocket, then dug out a five and slid it across the bar. "Yeah, time to get back to the grind. Keep it." He jiggled the change absentmindedly as he strode out into the blazing sun.

Three

"I don't give a goddamn what you want, you're not getting it!" Doyle fumed.

Kelly leaned against the edge of the desk, regarding them silently. The three of them were crammed in a windowless conference room at the Berkshire State Police barracks in Pittsfield, Massachusetts. A battered desk in the far corner held a lamp and a black phone on a ragged blotter. In the center of the room, the conference table had one noticeably shorter leg bolstered by a piece of shredded cardboard, with four rickety folding chairs holding court around it. Just inside the door a fake ficus plant was doing a poor job of hiding the large water stain on the grayish wall, while next to it a large piece of corkboard was mounted clumsily with thumbtacks. On top of it all, with no AC, the room was like an oven. All in all, this was easily one of the worst command centers she'd ever been stuck in.

Lieutenants Doyle and Lauer glared at each other across the table. Their feuding had started at lunch with barbed comments about the relative incompetence of their respective departments, and had escalated to the point where Kelly recommended they pack up their sandwiches and head over to the office. It was either that or chance having everyone in the diner hear the full extent of the investigation. Not that there appeared to be much progress. Aside from the actual recovery of the remains, most of which had been located by the volunteer search and rescue team, remarkably little investigative work had been accomplished. Kelly generally resisted the prevailing Bureau belief that cops were bumbling hacks who'd rather shoot someone than use their brains. Over the years she'd met plenty of talented detectives in police departments across the country. But based on first impressions, these weren't two of them. Kelly wondered how they'd managed to scramble so far up the career ladder.

Every time they descended into another spat, Kelly gently coaxed them back to civility. She was already exhausted. Hard to believe these two had only been acquainted for a week, Kelly mused as she watched them peck away at each other. If she hadn't known better, she would have taken them for a couple married twenty years too long.

"Well, why don't we just find out what the FBI has to say about it?" Monica snapped. They both turned toward her, faces expectant.

Kelly smiled thinly. "Keep in mind that so far no federal statutes have been violated so, officially, I'm only here in an advisory capacity."

"So advise," Doyle sneered.

"I don't think that tone is necessary, Lieutenant." Kelly raised an eyebrow at him, and his eyes dropped. Silently he unwrapped another piece of gum and popped it in his mouth.

Typical bully, she thought to herself—once confronted he backed right down. "Why don't we start by reviewing what we know so far, then we can work on the jurisdictional issues."

Doyle grumbled something that she took for acquiescence; Monica just shrugged.

"Great," Kelly continued. "Let's start with what the hiker found. First recovery was the forearm and part of a hand, just over the state line in Massach—"

"We got the rest of that body in Vermont," Monica interrupted, casting a scathing look across the table.

Kelly peered at her notes, then glanced up at the corkboard where she had mounted photographs of the body parts lying in situ. "Right, I see that a partial skeleton was found a half mile away in the Green Mountain National Forest."

"Would have had all of him if it weren't for that damn bear," Monica finished.

"Wouldn't have found him without the bear," Doyle retorted.

"Much as I appreciate your level of enthusiasm for the case, could we keep this civil?" Kelly chided them again. "Time of death is still being determined, but based on the fact that we're dealing with skeletal remains, the body was dumped at least a month ago. All the victims appear to be males, but no luck yet on an ID."

"Your guy's working on that though, right?" Monica said.

Kelly had sent Dr. Stuart over to the morgue in Bennington, Vermont, to examine the John Doe being stored there. McLarty claimed that Stuart was the top forensic anthropologist in the field, capable of extracting evidence from the most scattered of remains. She was fervently hoping that he lived up to that reputation. Based on the expression of anxiety on his face when she sent him off in a Vermont state cruiser, she had her doubts.

"How much longer we gotta keep Sam and his crew out there? You know, some of those people have jobs to get back to…" Doyle said.

"We'll get to that later," Kelly said. "But let's discuss the SAR team. Why were they called in?"

Doyle shrugged. "Our unit didn't have the manpower to handle that kind of search, and they volunteered to do the job. Why?"

"It just seems to me that whoever dumped these bodies had to have some outdoor experience and familiarity with the area."

"And a member of the SAR unit would fit the bill," Monica chimed in, finishing her thought.

Doyle rolled his eyes. "Great theory—if half those guys weren't bankers and stockbrokers. I can just see them running around the woods at night dumping bodies."

"Could happen," Monica said, "Maybe one of them decided to try blue-collar crime for a change. Problem is, we got a lot of groups like that up in Vermont. At least a dozen I can think of offhand. Camping and hiking are what folks do for fun around here. Hell, even I know most of these trails like the back of my hand."

"Then I'd like each of you to compile a list of all the outdoor groups on your side of the border," Kelly said firmly. "See if you can get membership rosters, some of them might be posted online. Based on what was found at the site in Vermont, we can be reasonably certain we're dealing with a homicide."

Doyle scoffed. "Yeah, or some guy that got lost in the woods."

Monica raised an eyebrow. "And I suppose he just got rid of all his clothes and lay down there? Not to mention the evidence of wounds on the bones."

"Animals could've done that."

"Not any that I've ever—"

"The Vermont medical examiner has ruled the death of John Doe number one a homicide. Until I hear otherwise, we'll continue on that assumption," Kelly interrupted. "So far we have five bodies confirmed, and other remains that haven't yet been matched to the bodies. Doyle, when will your lab finish dating and running DNA on what you've got?"

Doyle shrugged. "They get to it when they get to it."

"Well, have them put a rush on it."

He rolled his eyes. "I'm not going to make my guys work on a weekend for a stack of bones that've probably been there for years."

Kelly said firmly, "You will, or I'll pull some strings and get samples sent to the FBI lab."

He glowered at her. She matched his gaze and cocked her head to the side. After a minute, he looked away. In truth, this was an empty threat on her part. There was still no evidence that any federal statutes had been broken, so she didn't have the authority to move the bodies anywhere. But Doyle was clearly territorial, and she'd already gleaned that her best bet for keeping him in line was implying that with one word from her, a swarm of FBI agents would descend on his precious homicide unit. Kelly knew that among cops of all stripes, the fear of having the Feds steal "their" case was universal.

The United States has one of the most decentralized policing systems in the world, with every city, county and state maintaining their own force, each with their own way of dealing with crimes. Which was why in cases like this one, where similar victims were found across state borders, there tended to be a lot of jockeying for position. Sometimes when that happened, the respective head honchos agreed to pool resources and create a task force. Putting an FBI agent in charge was a great way to shift the blame to the federal government if the case was never solved, and it also kept their department's homicide stats in the black.

Kelly let her eyes trail across the corkboard. It contained a jigsaw of photos, some of nearly complete skeletons, others just a few fragments of bone. Each photo was marked as a John Doe, with a number and a rough estimate of how many months the victim had been dead. The bones in the photos were brown and moldered. It was almost impossible for Kelly to imagine them as people who had laughed and danced and loved, never dreaming that one day they'd end up as so much detritus scattered across a forest floor. "So do we have any leads on who these victims may be? This is a small region. I can't imagine many people go missing without being reported."

"You'd be surprised," Monica said. "We get a big influx of people in the summertime for all the festivals, then another group in the fall for the foliage. Plus there's the Appalachian Trail hikers—no record of them but the logbooks. It could be months before anyone realizes they never came back from the hike."

"What about those logs? Anyone check those against missing-persons reports?" Kelly asked.

"Hikers go by handles instead of their real names, so we won't have much luck there. In addition to them we got the drifters, former deadheads—"

"Not in Massachusetts," Doyle muttered.

"Forgive me for implying that such—undesirables—might cross state lines," Monica scoffed. "Anyway, I went through our missing-persons reports, and there's not much. If they were locals they would've been·missed."

"What about you, Lieutenant?" Kelly asked.

"Same here," Doyle conceded grudgingly. "Most of what we've got is older men skipping out on their families, that sort of thing. We're at the tail end of the season, lots of tourists still around." He raised an eyebrow and smirked at her. "So looks like it's up to your forensics guy to figure out who our arm belongs to."

"Looks like it," Kelly said, straightening out the papers in the file in front of her and silently praying that Dr. Stuart wouldn't let her down; otherwise, she could be stuck here indefinitely. "As far as jurisdiction goes, here in the command center we'll keep a record of all evidence corresponding to the remains, including the map marking where they were found. As long as your respective labs are processing the finds in a timely manner, I'm fine with the remains staying where they are. If in the future I feel that everything needs to be consolidated at one central location, I'll let you know. Agreed?"

They both nodded.

"For now, the SAR team keeps going." She held up a hand to stave off Doyle, who had opened his mouth in protest. "At least for a few more days—we'll see where we are then. I've also called in a K-9 unit to go over the sites where most of the remains were found. And I think we should post warning signs at the trailheads recommending that hikers travel in pairs, and listing a number they can call to report suspicious behavior. Any questions?"

"Yeah, what the hell are we supposed to do?" Doyle said.

"Lieutenant Doyle, please contact your lab and tell them I'd like those DNA results back ASAP. Then head back to the boneyard, keep an eye on the search, and assemble that list of all active outdoor groups in this area. Lieutenant Lauer, I need your list as well. And why don't you check the ViCAP database for young males found in remote areas."

Doyle scoffed. "ViCAP is a waste of time. Do you Feds really expect us to fill out forms with a couple hundred questions every time a body falls into our laps? We put our ViCAP forms in a round file." He jerked his head toward the trash can.

Kelly's eyes narrowed, but before she could respond Monica said, "I gotta say, Doyle, I'm shocked. I figured someone with your work ethic would welcome the chance to sit on his ass all day filling out forms." She turned back to Kelly, "Don't worry, Agent Jones, I'm on it."

Doyle stormed out, slamming the door shut behind him. Kelly felt her temples starting to throb and yearned for an aspirin. She knew from experience that a lot of cops didn't bother filling out their ViCAP forms, but it was still disheartening to hear of a whole department throwing them away. The Violent Criminal Apprehension Program was a national database used to track MOs, so if a similar crime had been committed in another jurisdiction or state, a match would pop up. It was one of the only ways to track active killers who crossed state borders to commit crimes. Especially in a case like this one, that information could prove crucial. But since the creation of ViCAP in the 1980s, few police departments bothered to take the time to fill out the lengthy questionnaires detailing every aspect of a crime. *Which just helped the bad guys get away with more murders,* Kelly thought despondently, *and made her job a lot harder.*

As they were leaving, Monica grabbed her elbow and held her back. "Can I talk to you for a second?" she said in a low voice.

Doyle had already stormed off down the corridor, no doubt

to bitch about them to the other detectives in his unit. He was on his home turf here, a situation Kelly hadn't wanted to encourage, but the Berkshire cops were the first on site and were due some privileges because of it. Kelly stepped back into the room and closed the door.

Monica faced her, gnawing a fingernail. She had a guilty expression on her face. "Listen, I don't usually hold back, but Doyle is such a piece of work…."

Kelly waited, arms crossed.

"There was another thing, about the body in Vermont. Stuff we found around it."

"Like what?"

"Like a pile of change. Pennies, ten of them, stacked neat as can be right by the head. And the marks on the skull, by the eyes…" She paused.

"Yes?" Kelly pressed after a minute.

"Well, it looks like the eyes might've been gouged out. Tough to say, maybe your guy will be able to tell us more, but that's how it looked to our M.E."

"What about the animals? The skull could've been dragged, the pennies might have not have been near it when it was dumped."

Monica shrugged. "Yep, that's all true. But I gotta say, my gut tells me that body was dumped right there. It was too weird, finding a pile of change out there in the middle of nowhere. And the eyes—well, your guy will be able to tell us for sure, but I got a feeling about this, you know?"

Kelly nodded. Sometimes you had to go by your gut. "Thanks for filling me in. But in the future…"

Monica waved an arm. "Yeah, I know, gotta keep Lieutenant Unpleasant in the loop. I'll work on it."

* * *

"I don't like it."

Doyle shrugged. "Doesn't really matter if you like it or not—she's here. Not much we can do about it now." He leaned forward and spit in the sand at the base of the picnic table, then glanced over his shoulder to make sure their conversation wasn't overheard. In the distance, he could hear one of the K-9 dogs yapping as the search for body parts continued.

"Does she know anything?"

Doyle squinted at the other officer. They'd shared a desk in the Homicide unit for almost a decade now. Doyle had never really liked Kaplan, he'd always been a little squirrelly. Couldn't trust someone like that to watch your back when the chips were down, Doyle thought as he scrutinized him. The guy's bug eyes were jumping around, beads of sweat creeping out from the sides of his Berkshire State P.D. cap. "Just keep your mouth shut, Kaplan. I'm handling it."

"Easy for you to say, you're a year away from your pension and got no family," Kaplan grumbled. "Me, I lose this job my wife'll kill me."

"You're not going to lose your job." Doyle rubbed his eyes with a thumb and forefinger. Thanks to those two broads he'd been stuck with, he had a migraine coming on, which was making it hard to resist the urge to smack Kaplan. "I got a guy at the lab in Sudbury, he's handling things. Another week, all this—" he waved toward the woods "—will die down, and the Feds will be out of our hair. So relax."

"I hope you're right, Doyle."

Doyle snorted. "When the hell have I been wrong before?"

"I can think of a few times," Kaplan said. "Matter of fact, I think that's what got us in this mess in the first place."

Doyle's eyes narrowed. Kaplan shrank visibly under his gaze. "You better think long and hard before running that mouth off at me again," he said after a lengthy moment.

"Or what?" Kaplan demanded, although the bravado had largely faded from his voice.

Doyle didn't answer, but shifted his focus toward the tree line. Just past the police tape he could see Jan Waters, that hot blond reporter, leaning against her van. He raised a hand in greeting, and she smiled and wiggled her fingers in return. Kaplan followed his eyes and let out a low whistle. "Man, would I like to tap that."

"That's a surefire way to lose your wife," Doyle said.

"Bet she'd be worth it, though." Kaplan stared at her longingly. "She can probably crack nuts with those legs."

Doyle guffawed at the image. "She can crack more than that."

"Yeah?" Kaplan scrutinized him. "Sounds like you might know."

Doyle smirked in response. A patrolman was coming down the trail with a Belgian Malinois panting on the end of a leash. Two other officers followed him. Doyle stood and smacked Kaplan on the arm. "C'mon, boy," he said, grinning. "It's your turn to get in there."

Four

"Ready to go?"

Kelly glanced up from the stack of reports she'd been sifting through. Monica stood in the doorway, jiggling her car keys in one hand.

"Sure, I'll be right there." Kelly tapped the papers, straightening them into a pile, then rose to join her.

It was a short drive across the border to Bennington, a picturesque Vermont town complete with a village green. A strange obelisk dominated the landscape, stone sides sloping three-hundred feet up to a point at the top. Monica nodded to it as they drove past. "Commemorates the Battle of Bennington, when they drove the Brits back up to Canada during the revolution. Butt-ass ugly, isn't it? Me and my friends call it the 'mighty gray dildo.'"

Kelly laughed. Despite her brash nature, Monica exuded a warmth and spirit that was hard to resist. She was feeling better about the case today. After getting a good night's sleep at a local bed-and-breakfast, she felt lighter, more able to handle a daunting stack of cold cases. The fact that it was a gorgeous day outside didn't hurt, either.

They crossed a covered wooden bridge and passed rows of fields and rolling green meadows. It was almost unbelievably lush. After a few minutes they turned into the parking lot at the Southwestern Vermont Medical Center, a stately Georgian building of brick and marble that looked more like a college library than a hospital. Monica slid into one of the spaces reserved for emergency personnel.

As Kelly turned to get out of the car Monica stopped her with one hand. "Listen," she said firmly, "I know that so far we've been making the Keystone Cops look like pros, and you must think we're a bunch of Podunks dead set on bungling this case for you. But what you've seen so far today—well, let's just say I didn't put my best foot forward. You gotta understand, Doyle has been driving me bananas. I feel like he interferes every time I try to get something done."

Kelly started to reply, but Monica waved a hand, cutting her off. "You don't have to say anything. I know we all gotta get along, and I'm really going to try. Just wanted to apologize to you first."

"Okay," Kelly said, unsure how to respond. After a second she added, "Thanks."

"No problem. Now, let's go see what a forensic anthropologist from the Smithsonian looks like. I'm ready to be impressed," Monica chirped, throwing her car door open.

Dr. Stuart barely looked up when they entered the room. He was bent over a laptop, tapping furiously. The morgue was located in the hospital basement. Clearly the casualty rate in Bennington was low, the room barely large enough to hold all three of them. Laid out on a stainless steel table behind him was a fragmented skeleton: a tibia and foot on one side, femur on the other, pelvic girdle above them. Then a few assorted ribs, vertebrae, a piece of sternum, sections of a right arm and hand, with a skull at the top that was missing the lower jawbone. Behind the table, three metal sliding drawers were set into the wall. The fluorescent bulb overhead needed to be changed; it buzzed intermittently.

Kelly watched him for a moment, then said, "Dr. Stuart…"

He whipped a finger up, silencing her. She raised her eyebrows.

Monica nudged her, repressing a smile. "He's kinda cute," she muttered in Kelly's ear. "Not what I was expecting."

Kelly glanced at her, surprised. Honestly, she couldn't see it. He wasn't unattractive in any obvious way—he reminded her of Bill Gates's younger, dorkier brother. He did appear to have regained his confidence, which helped. Dr. Stuart continued typing, unaware of being appraised. Clearly the man was now in his element, no trace of the bundle of nerves he'd been on the chopper. A lock of brown hair fell forward as he hunched over the keyboard. Finally straightening, he removed his wire-rimmed glasses and began urgently polishing them on a corner of his untucked shirt.

"So sorry, Agent Jones, but I really wanted to finish inputting the numbers before I lost my train of thought." His eyes widened at the sight of Monica. "Oh, and you've brought someone else along…."

Kelly said, "Monica, this is Dr. Howard Stuart from the Smithsonian."

Dr. Stuart carefully perched the glasses back across the bridge of his nose and smiled faintly. "Hello…"

Monica thrust out her hand, shaking his vigorously.

Dr. Stuart winced. "Lieutenant Monica Lauer, Homicide Division, Vermont State Police. Wow, the Smithsonian. I took my kid there a few years back."

"Oh, really?" Dr. Stuart had regained his expression of slight dismay tinged with fear.

"Yep. Love those ruby slippers, and Lincoln's hat. Didn't see any skeletons there, though."

"Yes, well." He cleared his throat. "We're housed in a different building. The Smithsonian has a long and storied tradition of consulting with the FBI on forensic anthropology."

"Haven't had many cases dealing with bones myself, we usually find our victims before the critters get to them." Monica gazed down at the bones splayed across the table and rapped her knuckle against the surface. "Any word on our guy here?"

"Word? Um, yes, I suppose there is. I just finished running the numbers, and I can say for certain that he's Caucasian."

"Yeah? Computer told you that, huh?" Monica peered at the laptop.

Dr. Stuart pointed at the upper jaw. "It was difficult without a complete set of dental features, but the program compared what we did have to measurements gleaned from known populations, Asian versus Caucasian, for example. And I can state with ninety-percent certainty that we're dealing with a white male."

He straightened again, looking pleased with himself. Monica cocked her head to the side. "Well, Professor, I'm afraid that in this neck of the woods, you're looking at ninety-five percent."

"Really? Based on what?"

"Based on that's how many white people we got here, ninety-five percent of the region. You got anything else?

'Cause I went to a lot of trouble to get these bones back from the State Medical Examiner up in Burlington. They gave me a hell of a time over it, but I told them the FBI was bringing in some hotshot. You're not going to make me a liar, are you, Professor?"

The doctor appeared miffed. "I'm not technically a professor…."

Kelly sighed. "I think what Lieutenant Lauer means to say, Doctor, is that you've had a day with the remains now— how long until you can tell us something?"

The doctor sniffed to illustrate his pique. "Well, I was just beginning my debriefing. I also have an approximate age, based on the stage of epiphyseal union in the vertebral centra—"

"The what?" Monica interrupted.

Dr. Stuart gestured toward the table. "The backbone. It takes much longer for a skeleton to reach maturity than some people realize. Until the epiphysis, or shaft of the bone, has completely united with the main body of it, a skeleton is not considered mature. And vertebrae fuse later in life than other bones, not until the late twenties in some cases. I'd estimate this young man's age at twenty-three or twenty-four. He was also approximately five foot eight inches tall. Most likely an ectomorphic body type."

"Ectomorph?" Monica asked, puzzled.

"Slight, thin, not a large person," Dr. Stuart clarified. "And at some point he broke his right femur."

"During the attack?" Kelly asked.

Stuart shook his head. "It's an old break, at least five years. It doesn't appear to have healed properly. So whatever medical attention he received was somewhat inadequate. There's also something odd about his teeth."

"Odd in what way?" Kelly asked.

"If you'll look, here…" Using a tongue depressor, he gently tilted the skull back so they had a clear visual of the remaining upper set of teeth. "You see the amount of cavities here? Significant, particularly for a young man."

"Yup, lots of fillings." Monica agreed.

"But that's just the thing," Dr. Stuart said, easing the skull back down. "These are composite resin fillings, and a few porcelain inlays as well, all notably high-end work. I'd have to draw a sample from each, but by observation alone I'd say they appear to have been done at the same time, and fairly recently."

"So our boy here had bad teeth for years, and someone recently took him to the dentist," Kelly said slowly.

"Exactly." Dr. Stuart's cheeks glowed slightly. "It'll take a few days to get the results, but just in case I drew a DNA sample."

"Didn't think you could get DNA from bones," Monica commented.

"Oh yes, in fact generally they provide the best samples. I've been using a relatively new isolation method that combines the use of a cetyltrimethylammonium bromide buffer and isoamyl alcohol…" Catching the expressions on their faces, Dr. Stuart concluded, "Anyway, it's very effective."

"Won't do us much good unless our boy is in the system," Monica noted.

"True, but there you might be fortunate. Massachusetts and Vermont have two of the largest DNA databases in the country. If he's ever been arrested for a felony, you have a good chance of a match."

"How long for the DNA results?" Kelly asked.

Stuart cast a glance at Monica. "I sent a sample to the FBI lab for processing, I hope that's all right. I was uncertain of the protocol, and they tend to be the quickest. I can't speak for Vermont, but I know that Massachusetts has a backlog of thousands of cases."

"Fine by me. The sooner we find out who our boy here is, the better, far as I'm concerned." Monica waved a hand dismissively while smiling broadly at Dr. Stuart. He shifted self-consciously under her gaze.

Kelly directed their attention back to the skull. "Lieutenant Lauer mentioned some marks on the body."

"Right, those." He pointed toward the gaping eye sockets with the tongue depressor. "Difficult to determine if these were administered ante- or post-mortem."

"But they're not animal related?"

He shook his head. "Decidedly not. These were administered by a sharp blade of some sort. There were also similar marks here—" he pointed to the sternum "—and here," he finished, noting an indentation of the pelvic girdle.

"A knife?"

He tilted his head to the side. "Probably. Difficult to say for certain."

"And how long was he out there?"

Dr. Stuart shrugged. "If we knew exactly where he had fallen, we could take soil samples, try to determine the level of volatile fatty acids present. But if these bones were removed from the original site by animals…"

Monica glanced sideways at Kelly. "I think we might have some idea where he was dumped."

Kelly nodded. "I'll send a tech out to gather soil samples."

"Fantastic." Dr. Stuart perked up, excited. "If the lab finds evidence of decomposition in the surrounding soil, I could possible narrow the time of death to days."

"And if you don't find that?"

"Unfortunately, in the wild, at this time of year, we're looking at a range of anywhere from twelve days to a few months. Any longer, I believe we would have seen more of an environmental impact on the bones."

"No hair or fibers?"

"I'm afraid he was too far along in the decomposition process." Dr. Stuart paused and glanced back down at the body.

"Anything else?" Kelly pressed, watching his face.

Dr. Stuart slowly shook his head from side to side. "No, it's just…it's a shame, to be missing the arm from this sample. Not to mention the other remains…examining them together would be helpful. Without having something to compare to, it's difficult to say if there is any relationship between the victims."

"I'll speak to someone in Massachusetts, see what we can arrange. Maybe I can get them to let you examine the bodies tomorrow."

He looked up anxiously. "Perhaps this time I could travel by car?"

Kelly grinned. "It'll take a lot longer than a chopper ride, but I suppose we can manage that. Would you like a lift back tonight?"

"I have a few more tests to run, if you don't mind." He checked his watch.

"I can hang out. My kid's on a camping trip, so I've got nothing on my plate other than pizza and a hot bath," Monica said. "Maybe the professor can give me a crash course on this bone stuff."

A look of mild panic crossed Dr. Stuart's face again; he nervously ran a hand through his hair, shoving the lock back. It immediately fell forward again across his eyes. "Um, I suppose—"

"That's settled, then. See you both tomorrow." Kelly nodded at them and gathered up her purse.

As Kelly left, she heard Monica say, "So you specialize in bones, huh?" She smiled to herself. At last a few members of the task force seemed to be getting along.

The kid flicked his cigarette into the gutter and exhaled a long stream of smoke from his nose. He stood just inside the circle of light cast by a lamp mounted above the club door. The rest of the street was pitch-black. Inside, the drag show was finishing up, and the DJ was getting ready to take over, same as every other Wednesday night. Northampton was a college town, one of the few places where bars and clubs stayed open late. It was sixty miles southeast of the Vermont border, far enough from home that he never worried about anyone recognizing him. It would be difficult to explain himself if he did encounter someone he knew; Northampton was famous above all else for its thriving gay scene, a Gomorrah nestled in the heart of Massachusetts.

His truck was parked across the street, a few doors down from the club. From his vantage point he had a clear view of the entrance, where a velvet rope stood watch forlornly. This late in the season Club Metro would only be half-full, there was no need to keep anyone waiting outside. Aside from the boy, there was no one else around. A couple emerged, arms intertwined, weaving slightly and laughing. Too many apple-tinis, the man thought with disdain. How he despised them, with their tight jeans and mustaches. He ducked a little lower behind the steering wheel and pulled the brim of his cap down as the couple passed within five feet of his truck.

The boy stayed where he was, the light making his pale

skin glow iridescent. He glanced up every time the door opened, waiting for someone who was leaving alone— someone lonely enough to purchase his company for a few hours. The kid was slight, around five-six, with light brown hair worked into complicated spikes that made his head appear even smaller than it was. His ragged jeans drooped low on his waist and fell into folds over beat-up sneakers, a black T-shirt hid a concave chest that barely rose with each inhale. He would be an easy one to take. The man had watched him for weeks. Like migrating birds the other boys had vanished, heading south to New York or further, to South Beach. But not this boy. He had nowhere else to go.

The man's finger tapped the steering wheel. It had been almost a month now since he had taken one—too long, really. Yet he still wasn't feeling the urgency that the act required. He needed at least another few days to prepare, especially with the recent discovery of the other bodies. It would be smart to let things calm down a little. After all, the police weren't going to waste much time over an old pile of bones, but a fresh victim might keep them engaged. And that was the last thing he needed, especially now.

But leaving now meant waiting another full week, and enduring another long night of driving, his car chewing up the freeway centerline as dark trees whipped past, the radio chatter goading him on until morning. He couldn't have another of those nights, wandering across hundreds of miles only to end up back at the same place, right back where he started. Plus by next week the boy might have disappeared, gone with the rest of them. Stranger things had happened, maybe one of the other fags would take pity on him and whisk him away. And then he'd be stuck, nursing the urge through all those long months. It was difficult enough waiting out the winters, unable to take one because of the inherent difficulties in disposing of the bodies. But stopping now would be like quitting smoking with one cigarette left in the pack.

He felt himself slipping into the right frame of mind. His grip tightened on the steering wheel, eyes narrowed as he watched the boy struggling with his lighter, tapping it to summon enough juice to light another cigarette. No, it had to be tonight, and with that thought a wave of relief washed over him. It was when he was at his most calm, just before possessing them. Everything came to one focal point, his mind went into a kind of fugue state when everything felt right, when he felt invincible. The panic would come later, much later, as he scoured the walls with bleach, wondering if he'd left anything behind, made any mistakes.

But right now he was the master, and the boy was waiting. He twisted, groping across the back seat until he felt the handles of the duffel bag. He tugged it forward and checked the contents. Everything he needed was right here. All he had to do was approach the kid and offer him enough money to get in the car without asking any questions. The rest would be easy.

Five

Kelly set the phone down and finished scribbling a name on the pad in front of her.

"Good news?" Monica asked, raising an eyebrow. It was Thursday. Over the past week they'd settled into a routine at their command center in the Berkshire State Police barracks. Monica had set up a post at the main table, while Kelly had taken the desk. The two of them were digging through the ViCAP results. The search parameters, *murdered young males found in the woods,* had elicited an enormous stack of similar cases, and they'd spent days filtering out those that were way off mark. Doyle still worked from his cubicle in the main detective unit, periodically gracing them with his presence. He would stand in the door smirking while reporting the inconclusive results of tests on the other bones. For all his talk of the crack forensics team at the Massachusetts State Police lab, Kelly was starting to have her doubts. Odder still was his smugness about their lack of leads. Kelly had worked with plenty of lazy cops who did the bare minimum while waiting for their pensions to kick in, but they usually made at least a nominal effort to look busy. Doyle didn't seem to fit that mold—if anything he flaunted the fact that he wasn't participating. If they didn't turn up anything in the next few days, she'd have McLarty petition for the unidentified remains, or maybe see if she could get Massachusetts to assign a different cop to the task force. Even if neither move worked, it might motivate Doyle to become more involved.

Kelly grinned at Monica. "We got lucky. There was a hit on the DNA sample Dr. Stuart sent to the Bureau lab, from John Doe number one." She looked down at the notepad. "His name was Randy Jacobs, age twenty-four. Northampton is faxing over a copy of his sheet."

"Yeah? So he's got a record?"

Kelly nodded. "Solicitation, shoplifting, nothing too serious."

"Nothing you'd think would get him killed." Monica noted.

"Maybe he stepped it up a notch." And maybe this wouldn't turn out to be a serial case, Kelly thought hopefully, which meant she could pack her bags and head home. If the kid had had a dispute with a partner in crime, and the other John Does weren't identified, she might be off the hook. It still wasn't too late to start her vacation.

"I'll grab the fax." Monica pushed back from the desk. "Should I fill in Little Mary Sunshine, or should we let him sweat it out a bit?"

"Bring him in," Kelly said. "Let's show him what a real lab can do."

As Kelly waited, her phone rang. She picked it up and glanced at the screen. When she saw the number she frowned and shook her head slightly. She couldn't deal with that conversation, not right now. She'd been putting it off for days already, a few more hours couldn't hurt. Kelly raised her arms above her head, arching her back in a stretch.

As Doyle shuffled in behind Monica, she quickly assumed a more formal pose. "What now?" he complained. "I was on my way to lunch."

Monica brandished a sheaf of papers in one hand. She rolled her eyes and said, "Yeah, I heard it was 'bonehead day' at Bennigans—two appetizers for the price of one, right?" Doyle started to respond but she cut him off. "Man, record is right. This kid Randy got around." She handed the papers to Kelly.

The kid's mug shots glared up at her accusingly. He was sullen looking but attractive, with big doe eyes and a cowlick. He looked to be about eighteen in the photo, hair bleached blond, eyebrows thick and bushy. Slight, like Dr. Stuart had surmised. His stats were five foot eight, just a hundred and forty pounds. He looked like a kid who'd never known anything but hard times. Kelly flipped quickly through the rap sheet—lots of arrests, mainly for solicitation. Some days he was released from jail, then thrown back in the same night. Each arrest form listed him as living at a different address.

Doyle peered over her shoulder and grunted. "Looks like a little punk."

"So he deserved to die? And to get dumped in the woods like yesterday's garbage?" Monica said reproachfully.

Doyle rolled his eyes. "Check out Ms. P.C. I'm just saying, a kid that's gone in and out of the system like this, don't expect me to shed any tears."

Kelly furrowed her brows. "No arrests since April, so apparently he started behaving himself."

"Or left town," Doyle noted.

"Let's do a national search for any arrests. We might as well start trying the local dentists, too, see if we can find out who paid for Mr. Jacobs's pricey dental work."

"There's probably a hundred dentists in a twenty-mile radius," Doyle protested.

"Now that we've got a name, it shouldn't take too long. We'll divide them up."

"I still think this is a waste of time," Doyle grumbled.

Kelly frowned at him. "Yes, Lieutenant, you've made that abundantly clear over the past week. But until you get reassigned, you're still a member of this task force, and you might as well make yourself useful for a change."

"I'll get the list of dentists together," Monica chirped, pleased to see Kelly put Doyle in his place.

"So Doyle, you handle the search of prior arrests. I'll add this information to our profile, that should help us get a better sense of our killer. Let's meet again at four-thirty, see what we've got."

Doyle stormed out, slamming the door shut behind him.

Monica said, "How's that profile coming, anyway?"

Kelly shrugged. "It's still pretty vague." That was an understatement: the truth was that due to the extreme decomposition of the bodies and the remoteness of the dump site, so far her profile looked like a serial killer 101 primer. She knew they were probably looking for a man in his thirties or forties, based on the fact that some of the bodies appeared to be at least a decade old, and most serial killers began killing in their twenties. Also, he had some familiarity with the outdoors, and was most likely physically fit. Gouging out the eyes was an odd act. It could indicate either that he experienced a moment of shame at being watched by his victims, or that he was trying to erase the things they'd seen. And according to a friend she'd conferred with at the Bureau, stacking objects like pennies next to the bodies was a sure sign that at some point or other, their killer had been institutionalized. Since that could range from a foster-care facility to prison, however, it still didn't give her much to go on.

The fact that one of their victims had engaged in gay prostitution added an interesting angle to the case. A lot of serial killers targeted prostitutes, mainly because they'd get in a car with just about anyone and were rarely missed when they vanished. Then there was the gay angle: it was possible they were dealing with a repressed homosexual. Many killers turned their inner rage outward, absolving their own gay impulses by punishing others. Alternatively, they could have a religious nut on their hands who thought he was doing "God's work" by murdering male hustlers. Sadly, that was a common excuse for many serial killers.

Monica cocked her head to the side. "I'm going to grab a soda from the vending machine, can I get you anything?"

"No thanks, I'm fine."

"All right. And hey, I think this is a solid break. We ID a few more vics, that profile of yours will shape up nicely." She tapped Kelly's shoulder and left the room.

Finally she'd have something to report during her daily briefing to McLarty, Kelly thought with a smile as she clicked her laptop open and initiated a search for prior arrests under the name Randy Jacobs. Usually she'd trust an officer to carry out their assignments, but with Doyle she thought it wise to check his work. It would be interesting to see if he brought her the same results. There was a tentative rap on the door. "Come in," she called out.

The door opened, and a sheepish looking Sam Morgan

ducked his head inside. "Hope I'm not interrupting, Agent Jones. Just thought I'd stop by, since I haven't heard from you for a few days."

"Oh, hello, Mr. Morgan." She followed his eyes to the whiteboard she'd bought and mounted on the near wall. In addition to the photos, each of the six columns now held a few notations, the results of Dr. Stuart's lab work. Kelly quickly stood and moved to the door, blocking his view. "Why don't we talk in one of the interrogation rooms."

She led him down the hall and opened the door to a bare cell. A closed circuit camera was mounted in one corner, and the battered chairs and table were matches to the ones in the command center. The carpet stank of sweat and fear. At least the department was consistent with their decorating scheme, Kelly thought as she gestured for him to take the chair across from her.

Sam grinned as he sat down. "Wow, I have to say being in here makes me nervous. I feel like I should confess to the candy bar I stole back in fourth grade."

She laughed. "I'm pretty sure the statute of limitations ran out on that. I apologize for the inconvenience, Mr. Morgan, but we're not allowed to bring civilians into the command center."

"Sure, I get it, sensitive material and all that. You could tell me, but you'd have to kill me, right?" He winked at her. "I've gotta insist you call me Sam, though. Every time I hear Mr. Morgan, I look around for my dad."

"All right, Sam. What can I do for you?"

"I just wanted to see if you were ready to pull my SAR guys out of the woods yet. I mean, in all honesty," he continued apologetically, turning his palms to face the ceiling, "I'm down to my last ten guys, anyway. It's turning into more of a social club."

"Didn't Lieutenant Doyle call you?" Kelly asked, her brows knitting together. She'd told Doyle to discontinue the search the day before.

Sam shook his head. "Not that I know of. I can check at home, maybe I just didn't get the message…" His voice trailed off.

She gritted her teeth. Apparently Doyle wasn't just unpleasant, he was also incompetent. "I'm so sorry, Sam, this is a huge oversight. Please apologize to your unit for the inconvenience."

He shrugged and held up both hands in protest. "Seriously, don't worry about it. Like I said, most of them like having an excuse to skip out on yardwork at home. But I'll let them know."

"Thanks for being so understanding." She stood and extended her hand for him to shake.

"Are you making any progress?"

"Some," she replied cautiously. "Nothing I can discuss, unfortunately."

"That's great news. Love to see those families get some closure." As he was leaving, he snapped his fingers together and turned back toward her. "Almost forgot. You like Albee?"

"Sorry, what?" she asked, confused.

"Edward Albee, the playwright? They're closing out the season at the Williamstown Theatre with *Three Tall Women,* and I've got two tickets for tonight."

Kelly cocked an eyebrow. "I thought you were married," she said hesitantly.

His eyes crinkled up at the sides as he smiled. "Oh, I am. Sorry, you misunderstood me. I was offering you both tickets."

"Oh." Kelly flushed bright red. "Of course. Um, I really have too much to do, I'm afraid."

He waved a hand. "No need to explain, I'm sure you're swamped. Just thought I'd ask."

"You should ask Monica, she might want them," Kelly said. Over the past few days Monica had alluded several times to the fact that she and Dr. Stuart were fast becoming an "item," as she put it. Apparently they'd already gone out for dinner a few times, and had something planned for the weekend. They made an odd couple, but then who was she to offer anyone advice, Kelly thought ruefully. And as long as the relationship didn't interfere with their work, she had no problem with it.

"That's a great idea, I'll find Monica on my way out." And with a final wave, he was gone.

Kelly returned to the command center, settled behind her desk and tried to concentrate on the search again. It was odd that she'd made that mistake, she was usually pretty good at reading men. She idly wondered how strong Sam Morgan's marriage was, caught herself and frowned. She wasn't heading down that road again, no way. She bit her lower lip and tapped away at her keyboard.

The kid woke up slowly. It was cold in here, too cold. He was shivering, which was strange because it was still summertime, wasn't it? Summers were the easy time. Summers he could crash outside, no worries, or sometimes a trick would even let him spend the night in hopes of a freebie in the morning. Not him though, no way—he didn't work for free.

But where was he? Man, he felt groggy. Didn't remember taking anything the night before, but he must've. It was a weird fuzziness, though. He tried to pinpoint it. Didn't feel like coming down off meth, or special k, or ex. What the fuck had he taken? He reached for his forehead and felt his hand snap back, then the sound of metal on concrete. *What the...* He tried again, extending his arms in front of him in the darkness. Halfway up they stopped, and now he recognized the cold steel of manacles encircling his wrists. He tried to stand, but only managed to crouch before his knees gave out against the resistance of more chains. His mind suddenly snapped to, wide-awake. He dimly remembered an older guy in a pickup—not bad looking—and the wad of hundreds he'd flashed. The sick fuck had chained him up, which he never agreed to; S & M wasn't his thing. He squinted into the darkness. "Hey? Hello?"

No one answered. It was pitch-black, and he felt the walls starting to press in. Just like when he was a kid, when his mom used to lock him in the closet while she entertained "boyfriends." Only at least then there was a slit of light at the bottom of the door and he had the warm press of clothes around him. He shivered again, more forcefully, teeth starting to chatter. He was naked, he realized, and the concrete floor below him was hard and cold. He groped in every direction, as far as the chains allowed, feeling his way up the wall until he located the bolts the chains were attached to. He tugged with all his strength, arching his back, bracing his foot against the wall as he tried first one side, then the other. The chains clanked slightly but didn't give. After a few minutes he gave up, panting.

"Motherfucker!" It came out as a choked sob and he tried again, louder this time. "You sonofabitch! Let me go, you crazy bastard! I'll kill you, I swear it!"

He strained his ears, listening hard for some response, part of him knowing the whole time that he was all alone in the room. He sank back to the floor, tears streaming down his face, as the horror of what was happening to him grew. He started to pray, babbling and sputtering through the words, promising things he didn't have, anything if he could just be out of this place.

Suddenly the room was flooded with light from above. He tilted his head up toward the ceiling, involuntarily lifting a hand to shield his eyes, momentarily blinded. "What are you…" His voice trailed off as the figure slowly descended. "Listen," he started to plead, but the man held up a hand to silence him, then flicked on a light in the corner. The boy's eyes widened as the real meaning of the room was revealed. The hatch above slammed down, stifling his scream.

Dwight gnawed an energy bar as he waited. The tattoo on his arm still throbbed, and he scratched it absentmindedly with his pinkie finger. Charlie had probably been right, he should field dress it when he got home. Worst thing that could happen right now would be to get some sort of infection. That kind of delay could throw off his whole plan, and he'd been working on this for too long. Digging up all those bodies, scattering the parts next to the campground had taken weeks. Then the waiting. It took longer than he expected for the first bones to be found. He'd planned on having the whole thing done by now. He tore off another chunk of chocolate-covered nougat with his teeth and chewed enthusiastically. He just hoped it all came together before he headed into training at Langley. In all honesty, he was a little disappointed with the progress so far. He figured once the FBI got involved it would speed things along.

Dwight was perched in the blind he had constructed in the

woods on the edge of the Captain's property. The foliage was still thick enough to render the camouflage netting surrounding it redundant, but he'd rather not take any chances. He of all people knew how dangerous the Captain could be if provoked.

He raised the infra-red binoculars to his eyes once again and peered through them.

Ten minutes earlier he'd watched as the Captain crossed the yard, heading toward the hatch. In spite of himself he shook his head with admiration at the thought of what would happen next. He had to give it to him, the Captain had it where it counted. Dwight heard a muffled sound and tilted his head to the side. Maybe he should have bugged the room, might have made it easier to tell what was going on. Without realizing it his hand drifted down toward his crotch. Had to be a good feeling, he reflected, doing those things to another person. Lately he'd caught himself daydreaming about it, picturing what he'd do if he was in the Captain's shoes, how he'd make them beg, how even if they did it wouldn't make any difference…

Dwight shook his head to clear the thoughts away. Time to focus. This was day one, which meant the Captain would be down there for an hour at least. He clicked on a penlight and made a note in his log, then clicked it off and waited for his eyes to readjust to the darkness. Day six, he thought to himself, allowing his mind to drift again as a little smile danced across his features: now that was his favorite day of all.

Six

"Dr. Glendale told us you paid for Randy Jacobs's dental work, sir," Kelly said.

"So what if I did? Since when is helping someone a crime?" Calvin Sommers was clearly perturbed by the questioning, running a hand through thinning hair dyed a shade too black, sporting one of those expensive spray tans. Bleached teeth, Kelly noted, and clothing straight from the Versace summer line. This was a man with cash to spare.

"We're not accusing you of anything, Mr. Sommers," she explained again, patiently. "Just trying to find out more about Randy."

"I hardly knew the boy, so whatever he's telling you is a lie."

"May we come in?" Kelly asked, stepping forward. It had taken almost a week to track down Randy's dentist, and it was the best lead they had so far. She was determined not to leave empty-handed.

Sommers's eyes flicked from side to side as he considered the request, and Kelly wondered what was inside that he was so afraid of them seeing. His grip was tight on the door handle. The house was a sprawling colonial painted bright yellow with a red door and matching shutters. His front lawn swept down to the street, shaded by mature maple and cherry trees. A brass plaque proclaimed it a historic landmark built in 1737. Even by the standards of Williamstown the house was a stunner, tucked along a quiet lane surrounded by other mansions. *Hard to picture a kid like Randy Jacobs at home here,* Kelly thought to herself.

Reluctantly, Sommers stepped back and motioned for them to enter. The house had been extensively renovated, she noted; what should have been a tiny foyer leading to a warren of small rooms had been redesigned to create an open floor plan. There was a large living room with an ornate stone fireplace on one side, a dining area leading to a kitchen with cherry and stainless steel accents on the other. Despite the exterior of the house, Sommers's tastes were contemporary; the artwork on the walls was primarily avant-garde and postmodern.

Sommers leaned against the sofa armrest without inviting them to sit down. Kelly cast a glance at Monica, who stepped forward and plopped down on the nearest armchair. Sommers winced slightly as she lifted a stone statue off the end table. "Whatcha got here?" she asked curiously, turning it over in her hand.

"Could you not…" he said, attempting to retrieve it.

Monica examined it closely; it was a phallus with a mounted pair of wings. "Now that's something you don't see every day, huh?"

"It's a Dionysian fertility symbol, and quite a valuable one," Sommers snapped, snatching it back.

"Whoa, easy." Monica held both hands up. "I wasn't going to break it."

Kelly sighed. She definitely didn't regret leaving Doyle behind—she could only imagine his reaction to Sommers. But bringing Monica might have been a mistake, too. However, interviewing a suspect alone was a strict Bureau no-no, both for her own safety and to guard against any claims of brutality or corruption. Normally, she'd be partnered with another FBI agent by this point in an investigation, but these days the Bureau was spread thin investigating thousands of accusations from people convinced their neighbors were terrorists. In the current political landscape, the discovery of five skeletons that might have been buried for years was a low priority, especially if most of them turned out to be young gay hustlers. "Mr. Sommers, when was the last time you saw Randy Jacobs?"

"I can't say for certain," he hedged.

"It's important that you try," she pressed.

"What's this all about, anyway?" he asked. "What's Randy done now?"

"He went and got himself killed," Monica piped up.

"What?" Sommers seemed to fold into himself as he reached for the armrest and lowered himself slowly onto the couch. Kelly scrutinized the shocked expression on his face. If he was acting, it was a good show.

"Calvin? Everything okay?"

Kelly turned. There was a good-looking kid standing in the doorway, clad only in white board shorts that hung low on his pelvis, exposing a glimpse of plaid boxers. His hair was bleached blond, skin deeply tanned with a smattering of freckles. He was barefoot and looked as if he'd just woken from a nap.

"It's nothing, Jim. Go on out to the pool, it needs to be skimmed again." Sommers flicked a hand toward the boy.

The kid's gaze drifted over Kelly and Monica, sizing them up as a smile spread across his face. He scratched himself absentmindedly and stayed where he was.

"Jim, please." Sommers's voice assumed a pleading tone.

Jim rolled his eyes and mock-saluted. "Yeah, right. Skim the pool. I'll get right on that." He turned on his heel and sauntered away. A door slammed at the rear of the house. Through the wide-paneled windows across the back of the room, Kelly watched as Jim pulled on a pair of sunglasses and flopped down on a cushioned chaise longue next to the pool.

She glanced back at Sommers, who looked wildly uncomfortable. A small bead of sweat worked its way down his forehead. It was hard for her to believe that in this day and age he was still so frantic to keep up appearances—for God's sake, wasn't gay marriage even legal in Massachusetts? Unless he was hiding something else. "Mr. Sommers, your sexual orientation isn't really my concern. We're here to find out about your relationship to Randy Jacobs, and when you last saw him alive."

"Looks like you already found a new friend," Monica noted, arching an eyebrow.

Sommers looked defeated. "I can't believe he's dead," he murmured, examining his hands, then running them across his face and through his hair. "God, he was just a child. How did it happen? Drugs?"

"I'd rather not get into that just yet," Kelly said before Monica could disclose any more information. When questioning potential suspects, she preferred to keep them in the dark as much as possible to see what they let slip.

Sommers stood and went to the rear window, facing away from them as he crossed his arms over his chest. "I met Randy in the spring, at Club Metro in Northampton. They have a… special night on Wednesdays."

"A gay night?" Monica asked.

"I suppose you could call it that. Anyway, he was a little rough around the edges, but sweet. I ended up taking him in. His teeth were a mess, Dr. Glendale really worked wonders with him. And it wasn't cheap, let me assure you. He lived here until about a month ago."

"So what happened?" Monica asked.

"I had to go to Manhattan for a show—I own a gallery there. My assistant generally manages things in the summers, but we had an artist emergency." He waved a hand in the air and started pacing. "When I got home, Randy had clearly had other…guests here. That was one of my rules, no company when I was out of town, I'd made that clear from the beginning. Anyway, I threw him out."

"Huh. He must've liked that," Monica said.

"He was extremely upset. We'd discussed having him come to New York with me in the fall, perhaps going back to school…" Sommers's voice trailed off.

"Did he become violent?" Kelly asked.

"Randy? No, he was hardly the type. He begged for a second chance, but…you should've seen the state the house was in, not to mention what they did to the Mapplethorpe… no, it was truly unforgivable. He left reluctantly, but quietly. I changed the locks the next day and haven't seen him since."

"And this was…"

"Ah, let's see." He tapped a finger against his forehead.

"The opening was on the seventeenth, it must have been the twentieth of July, sometime around then."

"Anyone we can verify that with?" Kelly asked.

"You can speak with my maid, she'll be here tomorrow morning, or you can try her at home. Here, I'll get you the number." He went to a credenza in the corner of the room and slid open a drawer, flipped through an address book and scrawled a number on a scrap of paper.

Kelly accepted it. "Anything else you can let us know about Randy? Friends he might have had, or where he went after he left? Or did he leave anything here?"

"No, nothing. And as far as I know, Randy had no other friends. He was a lonely boy, a sad case, really. He ran away from home when he was thirteen, and from what little he told me I gathered that his family situation was not ideal. Now, unless there's something else…" He moved toward the front door.

"You won't be leaving town anytime soon, will you, sir?" Monica asked as they followed him out.

His shoulders tensed again. "Why, am I a suspect? Because if so, I can also get you the number of my attorney."

"Please just let us know if you decide to head back to the city," Kelly interjected. She'd like to keep pressing him for information, but without more evidence linking him to Randy she didn't have grounds, plus he was already threatening to lawyer up. Better to come back once she'd dug further into his background.

The door closed behind them with a slam. As they walked back to the car, Kelly heard a raised voice coming from the backyard. They both stopped to listen. It sounded as though Sommers was dressing down Jim.

"Someone's got a bit of a temper, huh?" Monica said in a low voice.

"Sounds like it. I want a full workup on him, see if he's got a record here or in New York. We should also try to find out who some of his other charity cases have been, and if any of them are still around. Also, let's confirm the dates of Randy's departure. Would you mind calling the maid?"

"Nope, if you drive I'll try her on the way. I'd like to catch her before Sommers does," Monica said. "Be an interesting coincidence if more of his boys have gone missing."

Kelly looked at her watch. "We should head back to the office, see if Doyle has dug up anything else."

"Doubtful," Monica snorted. "Best he can do is give you an update on the doughnut situation in the break room. What about this Club Metro?"

"I was thinking the same thing. Tomorrow night is Wednesday, we'll go see what we can turn up. If Randy was turning tricks there, someone might have seen something."

"Are we taking Doyle?"

Kelly smiled slightly. "Northampton is in his jurisdiction. I'm sure he'd be offended if we didn't invite him."

"Oh boy." Monica slapped a hand on the dashboard. "Doyle at a gay club. This could make my whole week."

He heaved the last bag into the open truck bed and slammed the hatch. Taking a moment, he leaned against the bumper and wiped a bead of sweat from his forehead. It was still unbelievably hot, despite the late hour. On a night like this it was hard to believe that fall was just around the corner, but any day now he'd wake up shivering, wishing he hadn't left the AC on. He checked his watch: time to get going, there were only a few hours left until dawn.

Leaving the driveway, he automatically started to turn left,

swore under his breath and corrected the wheel, yanking it to
the right. His forehead crinkled with annoyance. It wasn't like
him to make a mistake like that, heading to the old site. He
was getting rusty. Which would have been fine, before; now
that the others had been found, he'd have to be more careful.
The discovery of the bones was puzzling. Based on what he'd
managed to glean through various sources, the body that initially set off the search was probably his last, the boy with the
big sad eyes. Which was surprising, he'd taken his time with
that one, buried him deeply. And more perturbingly, he'd been
found in the wrong place.

Animals, probably, he thought, shrugging it off. And it
hardly mattered, that site was pretty much tapped out for him
now. He rarely used it in the summers anyway, too many
campers, lots more than there used to be. It irked him that they
swarmed his forest, trampling over his graves. He sighed. He
was getting too old for this, when it really came down to it.
It took a toll on him, staying up late. The killing was fine, he
still had the energy for that. More than that it gave him energy,
stripped the years away.

But the aftermath of dealing with the body, painstakingly
removing the eyes, hauling it out to the woods and burying
it; he winced slightly as he circled his left shoulder and felt a
twinge. He'd reinjured it, just as he'd feared. He'd better ice
it when he got home. Maybe it was time to schedule that
surgery the doctor had recommended.

He glanced over his shoulder at the pile of bags in the truck
bed. This had been a good one, satisfying. The boy had even
made the mistake of spitting on him at the outset. Not by the
end, though, by then he could have gotten him to do pretty
much anything. He recalled the boy's small voice, begging for

his life, and repressed a smile. His eyes slid across the paneled interior to the clock: 3:00 a.m. If he hurried, he'd get enough sleep to make the church's pancake breakfast in the morning.

Seven

"Stop pouting, Doyle. I'm sure someone'll ask you to dance if you just give 'em a minute." Monica tapped him playfully on the arm.

"They better not," Doyle grumbled, gnawing a wad of gum. He appeared physically uncomfortable, as though he was trying to shrink into himself. He was rhythmically wincing in time to the driving bass that pulsed through the nightclub. Club Metro was situated on Pleasant Street, a few blocks off Main, in the section of Northampton where quaint antique stores and church spires ceded to industrial warehouses. The hour-long drive from Pittsfield had been oppressive for Kelly, thanks to the palpable tension between Monica and Doyle. Doyle had initially been reluctant to join them but Kelly had insisted, threatening once again to pull rank. She would have preferred going without him, but the club was in a different jurisdiction and they'd be joined by another Massachusetts cop. Kelly was hoping that having Doyle along would smooth over any turf battles.

"What, your dance card full, Doyle?" Monica said. "Shame. In that outfit, you could be the belle of the ball. I didn't know they still sold Members Only jackets."

Doyle stormed off in the direction of the bar. Kelly's eyes panned across the crowd as she followed him. She should've reined in Monica, but she had to admit to deriving pleasure from seeing Doyle so out of place, especially after the way he'd been treating her for the past two weeks. Despite the loud music, the club was relatively quiet. There were only a few dozen patrons, mostly older men in tight jeans and Izod shirts. Most held a cocktail in one hand as they shifted their weight slightly from side to side, eyes continually roaming the room as if someone new might materialize if they just kept looking. Kelly felt some of those eyes settle on her and Monica, and she self-consciously tugged at her shirt collar. They were dressed plainclothes so that they wouldn't stick out like sore thumbs, but Kelly had the feeling they'd been spotted anyway. She and Monica were both wearing jeans and T-shirts, and Doyle had on khakis and a jacket despite the warmth of the night. The Northampton officer, Bennett, had done the best job of blending in, wearing a pair of ironed board shorts and a tank top. He was in his late twenties, with a square jaw and black hair shorn close to his head. Of all of them, he seemed most at home here.

"Slow night," he commented, glancing around the room. "Season's winding down, doesn't look like many of the boys are around."

"How many are there, usually?" Kelly asked as they approached the bar.

Bennett grinned at the bartender and nodded. "What's up,

Tony. Can I get three Sam Adams?" The bartender eyed them a second longer than necessary, then went to retrieve their order. Turning back to Kelly, he shrugged. "Depends. Height of the summer, anywhere from thirty to fifty of them work the crowd."

"Didn't know there was such a scene here," Monica said. She looked bemused as a drag queen in four-inch stilettos sashayed past.

"Oh, absolutely. The women's college down the road has a lot to do with it. Northampton is known for being an enclave of tolerance in what is still a pretty conservative part of the state." His eyes fixed on Doyle, who stood a little apart from them. Bennett dropped his voice to say, "I'm sure you've probably noticed the attitude of the other units."

"Yeah, it's pretty hard to miss," Monica said. Doyle glanced over at them, then focused back on his beer.

Bennett sounded bitter as he continued. "Truth is, there have been rumors for years about these boys going missing. Every once in a while we put up flyers, send out alerts to other departments. But a bunch of gay hustlers…"

"Most cops figure why bother, they won't be missed," Kelly said, finishing his thought. He nodded in agreement.

"What, we're going to just sit here all night?" Doyle snarled from down the bar. A few heads in the crowd swiveled toward him. "Christ, let's get this show on the road. Ever seen this kid?" Doyle shoved a copy of Randy Jacobs's mug shot at the bartender as he swung past. The bartender's eyes skimmed over him as he kept going, heading for the taps. "Buddy, you hear me? I asked you a goddamn question!" Doyle raised his voice at the end, drowning out the music. Conversation around them stilled. A few men put their drinks down and edged toward the door.

"Nice, Doyle. Subtle," Monica muttered.

"Lieutenant Doyle, if you'll just give me a minute," Bennett said, putting a hand on his forearm. Doyle jerked, shaking it off as if it was contaminated, and glowered at the officer.

Kelly flipped open her badge with a sigh, any chance of keeping a low profile utterly blown. "Hi, Tony. Special Agent Kelly Jones with the FBI. We're looking for information on this kid."

The bartender reluctantly approached and took the picture in one hand. "Never seen him," he said decisively.

"You sure? You barely looked at it," Monica pressed.

"Listen, I can haul you down right now…" Doyle spoke over her.

"Lieutenants, why don't you canvass the club, see what you can find out?" Kelly said. They both looked at her. Monica appeared hurt, but complied. Doyle opened his mouth to protest, then snapped it shut and shuffled away. Kelly watched as he approached an enormous man who was wearing a manacle around his neck, and hoped this wasn't going to get any uglier. She turned back to the bartender.

Bennett was speaking to him in a low voice. Tony's eyes shifted back and forth from him to her, indecisive. Kelly waited for them to finish.

"Tony thinks he might remember the kid," Bennett said in a low voice.

"Yeah?" Kelly raised an eyebrow.

The bartender slowly nodded. "Name's Randy," he mumbled.

"Right, Randy Jacobs. He met someone here earlier this summer, an art dealer, and probably disappeared from the scene for a while. I'm thinking he showed up again, around the end of July. I need to know who he went home with."

"Why? What'd the kid do?" The bartender's brow furrowed. He was pushing thirty, T-shirt straining across his belly. With one hand he rubbed a carefully maintained five-o'clock shadow.

"He turned up dead." Kelly held up the picture again.

"Damn." The bartender whistled. "He wasn't one of them in the woods, was he? Papers are saying you found a bunch of them."

Bennett and she exchanged a glance. "I can't confirm anything until we've tracked down his next of kin."

"Won't be easy to find them," Tony said to himself. His gaze shifted back to Bennett. "You think this might be a gay thing?"

Bennett said, "Hard to say yet, but maybe."

"Like the other ones, huh?" Tony bit his lower lip and shook his head. "With these kids you never know, figure they might have OD'd or something. One night they're here, then no one ever hears from them again."

"How many boys have disappeared?" Kelly asked.

Tony shrugged. "Man, over the years, who could say. Dozens of them. But again, these boys don't go missed you know? Could be they got lucky and found someone to take care of them, straightened out."

"Or they might be John Does in another jurisdiction," Bennett concluded. "We've put up posters—I don't know, what, five, maybe six times? Other boys reported them missing, said they never showed up somewhere they were expected. But again…"

"Yeah, I know. They could have gone anywhere." Kelly sighed. "What about Randy?"

"Randy kicked around here for the past few years. Always managed to find someone, but then showed up alone again start of the next season." Tony leaned across the bar and lowered his voice. "He was back, just about a month ago. Came in for the Wednesday night party."

"Did he leave with anyone?" Kelly asked.

"Not that I saw. Sorry—wish I could tell you more." He glanced across the room. "Tell you who could, though..."

Kelly followed his eyes. A tall, skinny boy was standing in the corner with a middle-aged man who had one arm slung around his waist. He was sipping a drink and regarding Kelly warily. Their eyes met, and he leaned over and murmured something to his companion. They started walking toward the door.

Kelly nodded to Bennett, who abruptly turned and walked to the far side of the room. Kelly strolled in the other direction, making as if she were going to the ladies' room. At the last moment she veered, and the two of them cut off the couple near the exit. "Evening," she said, flashing her badge. "Could we have a word?"

She directed the question to the boy. His older companion was already backing away, waving both hands. "Honestly, officers, he told me he was twenty."

"Yeah, right." The kid rolled his eyes. "Like then it would be legal. Freakin' fool." With a sigh of resignation he turned toward the wall, placing both palms flat against it and spreading his legs. "Whatever. It's a warm bed and three squares, right? And my lawyer'll have me out for the weekend."

Bennett raised an eyebrow and jerked his head toward the older man trying to edge past him. "He can go," Kelly said, then turned back to the kid. "I'm not arresting you."

The kid turned back toward her. "You're not?" She shook her head. "So what, then?" He leaned against the wall and dug through his shirt pocket for a pack of cigarettes.

"This." She held the photo of Randy out to him.

He took it, squinting in the darkness. "What about him?"

"You know him?"

The kid shrugged.

"What's your name?"

"Danny."

"Danny what?"

"Smith."

"All right, Danny Smith. It's not too late for me to change my mind about arresting you."

"Do what you want, lady." His eyes wandered past her and he stiffened as Doyle approached. Kelly waved him off.

"Look, I just want to find out if you ever saw Randy leave here with someone."

"There was the art guy…" the kid hedged.

"Other than him. It would've been after that, about a month ago.

"He's dead, huh?" Danny asked. Kelly nodded in response. The kid shifted his weight to the other foot and lowered his eyes to the floor. "Figures. Randy always was a fuckup."

"In what way?"

He twitched a hand through his hair, tugging it out from the roots nervously. "Always thought he'd find someone to take care of him, then every time he did, he'd blow it. Last time he was in here he said he was skipping town. Was going to head down to New York, humiliate his ex-boyfriend somehow. He was going to turn one trick to cover bus fare and…expenses," he said the last with a slow smile.

"But he didn't say how?"

"Nope. That was the last time I saw him, though."

"And you didn't see the trick?"

Danny shook his head. "Saw him leave around last call, alone. Pissed off about it, too."

"Okay. Has anyone else gone missing, or had a problem with a trick getting too rough?"

"What, I gotta keep track of every dick in town now?" He chuckled as he scratched at one arm.

Kelly glanced down: track marks. "So that's a no?"

"Let's just say I take care of myself. Am I free to go, lady?"

"Yeah, you're free to go." She watched as he shuffled back to the bar and wrapped an arm around another middle-aged man.

"What do you think?" Monica asked, coming up behind her. Doyle was standing by the door, sulking as he waited for them.

Bennett joined them. "Kid tell you anything?"

"Not much that we didn't already know. And I don't think we're going to get anything else here tonight."

"Amen to that," Monica muttered. "If I hear one more techno song, my head will explode. Let's blow this joint."

Dwight gnawed a nail as he watched the cops leave the club. They were finally getting somewhere, must have figured out where the boy got taken. Which meant it was time for stage two of his plan. He glanced at his watch, experiencing a flush of pride as he gazed at the face. It was an MTM, the same kind special ops guys wore, it said so right on the Web site. Shatterproof glass set in an indestructible case of stainless steel and titanium—cost him two weeks' salary, but it was worth it. *Most important thing in the field,* he thought, *gotta know what time it is.* He'd read that somewhere once, or saw it on TV. The glow-in-the-dark hands read 11:30 p.m. Too early still for what he had to do. Dwight jiggled the pennies nervously in one hand as he sifted through various options. Not a good idea to hang around here, someone might take notice. Ma was at home, and she'd be pissed if he went out again. And the bars would be closing soon—he was no good at bars when he was like this anyway, so jittery he always spilled something and the last thing he needed was to call attention to himself.

Dwight wondered if he'd always be like this, jumpy out in the field. The Captain never seemed nervous at all, he thought resentfully, seeing him again in his mind's eye. He'd been cool as ice, digging that hole, dropping in the bag, covering the mound with brush so it looked like the rest of the woods. Too cool to even notice someone watching from a hundred feet back. Dwight had to hand it to those night-vision goggles, man, they'd been worth every dime. Lately the urges were getting stronger, until he was almost overwhelmed by the need to find out what it felt like to be working on one of them. Watching the Captain, he'd felt all tingly, almost like he was turned-on. He'd pressed on the gauze covering his forearm, but the pain actually made the feeling more intense, not less.

He could pass the time by shuttling some hikers from the bars back to the trail, Dwight mused. Except he was in the company cruiser tonight, so they might assume he was a narc. 'Course, he could try to shake them down instead. Those kids were always carrying pot, if they were drunk enough they might figure him for a cop and would pay to be let off with a warning. He'd done it before, and it would be a shame to waste the cruiser, the boss didn't trust him with it very often. Dwight had claimed that his own car was in the shop, not wanting to chance the Captain recognizing his Tercel if he was staking out the club, too.

Dwight was struck by a thought: maybe he could stop by

the house in North Adams, see if any of the other fag boys were around. That could be a lot of fun, messing with one of them. And they would definitely be high, they always were. He tucked the pennies back in his right pocket as he started the car. *Who knows,* he thought, lips curling back over his teeth in a grim smile. *Maybe this would be his lucky night.*

"Where were you?" Sommers asked, arms folded across his chest. He was standing at the top of the stairs in a robe.

Jim stifled a yawn. "Out."

"Obviously you were out, but who the hell were you out with?"

"Dude, chill. I was at Metro. Just felt like dancing."

"Bullshit." Sommers's voice lowered a register, heavy with menace. "Larry called me, said you didn't show. Don't think you can dick me around, boy."

"Whatever. You're like my fuckin' ma, you know that? It's getting to be a real fucking drag."

Sommers charged down the stairs, not bothering to close the folds of his robe as they flapped open. "You don't like it, you little pissant punk, you can go sleep in the fuckin' dump I found you in."

"Fine." Jim ran a hand through his hair and shrugged. "This was getting old anyway. Peace out, asshole." He slouched toward the door.

Sommers paused at the bottom of the staircase, staring at the door as it slammed shut. He took a few faltering steps forward, stopped and went into the living room. He sank down on the arm of the couch. A breeze swept down the chimney flue, and he absentmindedly closed his robe and retied it.

His eyes lit on the end table and his brow furrowed. He

stood and executed a quick turn, panning the room as his face darkened with rage. "Why, the little bastard…" he growled, fists clenched. The Dionysian figurine was gone, as was the Nan Goldin photograph he'd just acquired. Those two alone were worth close to a hundred grand. He marched into the kitchen, yanked the phone from its stand, then hesitated. What would the cops do in a situation like this? He could picture their faces, smug and disdainful, thinking to themselves that the old pervert got what he deserved. The Berkshire cops were known for not giving a damn, particularly when it came to offenses against the gay community. If he was lucky they'd fill out a report and bury it in a filing cabinet.

Sommers pursed his lips and slowly set the phone back down, crossed the kitchen and opened the basement door. The gloom at the bottom of the stairs lapped at his slippers. He'd hidden it well, in a Ferragamo box marked "photos" that was buried under the Christmas ornaments. At least he'd been smart enough to keep some of his things where the punks would never think to look, he thought angrily. It had been years since he'd used it. He'd better give it a good oiling first, he thought, as he flicked on the lights and descended. He'd make that little bastard pay for making a fool of him, if it was the last thing he did.

Eight

"So have you made any more progress?"

Kelly held the phone away from her ear as McLarty's voice boomed through the receiver, then moved it back to her mouth. "Not much, thanks to the usual jurisdictional nonsense. Lots of red tape, the lab work is taking forever, and the two lieutenants assigned to me are still in a blood feud. But we have an ID on one of the victims, a young gay hustler named Randy Jacobs. We're combing through the background of the last guy he hooked up with to see if there's anything there. Apparently this isn't the first kid from the gay scene to go missing."

"Any chance the other victims were turning tricks, too?"

"It's possible," Kelly answered. "It would explain why we don't have any missing-persons' reports to match the vics we've found. We should know more when the rest of the DNA results come in. If you wouldn't mind placing a call to the state lab in Sudbury, sir—"

"Absolutely, I'll light a fire under their ass." He paused

before continuing, "You know, if you can prove any of these boys crossed the state line to turn tricks—"

"The Mann Act kicks in, and this becomes a federal case. I was thinking the same thing. The hate-crime statute might turn out to be relevant, too," Kelly said, finishing his thought for him. The Mann Act made it illegal to cross state lines to engage in prostitution. If they could prove any of these boys had picked up a john in Massachusetts, then serviced him in Vermont, Kelly could claim jurisdiction. Or if evidence appeared that the boys were being targeted simply for being gay, that would count as a violation of the hate-crime statute. Both were tough to prove, but if she managed to gather enough pertinent evidence, she could relinquish her advisory status and assume full control of the case. Even though that would grant her more power over Doyle, it also meant she'd be staying here for a while. She felt as though she could see the shores of her vacation getaway drifting farther away by the minute.

"Probably not your favorite option, but at least then we could process everything in our lab." McLarty heaved a sigh that Kelly swore shook the phone. "If it does go federal, just let me know what you need and I'll make sure you get it."

"Thanks, sir. I appreciate that."

"Oh, and, Jones? Try not to let the other task force members get to you."

"Thanks sir. I'll try." There was a heavy silence on the other end of the line. Kelly could picture McLarty sitting with his forehead scrunched up, debating whether or not to tell her something. "What's up, sir?" she asked, concerned.

He hesitated before replying. "Don't take this personally, Jones, but I know people skills aren't your strong suit. You're a great agent, but maybe you should relax a little bit, try some humor to put them at ease."

"Some humor?" Kelly asked dubiously, trying to picture Doyle's reaction to her telling a joke. Her cheeks smarted with indignation.

McLarty spoke in a rush. "Sure. Listen, an Irish cousin told me a great one the other day. Late one night a Dublin cop pulls over a guy driving erratically and asks if he's been drinking. The guy says, 'Aye, so I have. 'Tis Friday, you know, so me and the lads stopped by the pub where I had six or seven pints. Then I had to drive me friend Mike home and o' course I had to go in for a couple of Guinness—couldn't be rude, ye know. Then I stopped on the way home to get another bottle for later…' The guy fumbles around in his coat, then holds up a bottle of Bushmills. So the cop sighs and says, 'Sir, I need you to step out of the car and take a breathalyzer test.' And the guy gets indignant and asks, 'Why? Don't ye believe me?'"

Kelly sat in stony silence. After a minute McLarty coughed awkwardly, then said, "Listen, Jones, I didn't mean anything personal by that. It was just a suggestion, you know."

"Of course, sir. I'll take it under advisement." She took a few deep breaths after hanging up, then pushed back from the desk and headed to the water cooler. She couldn't believe that McLarty had automatically assumed the problems with her team were a direct result of her people skills. Sure, she wasn't someone who went out for drinks with co-workers, or cracked jokes, but she'd always gotten along fine with her partners. Morrow, the one who was killed last year, seemed to even really like her. She tilted a Dixie cup under the pump, filled it and drank deeply. After draining it she refilled it. Problem was, she mused, that no matter where she went in the Bureau, she always seemed to run into a boys' club. She'd thought the BSU under McLarty was different, but this conversation served as a reminder that even though he acknowledged her capabilities, the gender gap persisted. As she headed back into the command center, she wondered yet again if staying with the Bureau had been the right decision.

"Captain stopped me today," Kaplan said. "Asked me about your task force."

"Yeah? What'd you tell him?" Doyle squinted at Kaplan. They were sitting in front of a hamburger joint that was popular with the force. Four patrol cars were parked in the lot, and blue uniforms sat scattered among the Formica tables sunken into the patio.

Kaplan shrugged and took another bite of burger. Ketchup dribbled down his chin. His mouth full, he said, "Told him you were cooperating, but you said the FBI chick was a waste of space."

"Keep your voice down." Doyle's eyes darted around the lot, but no one was paying any attention. A few radios bleated in the background. "What'd he say?"

"He laughed. You know him, he doesn't think skirts should be allowed to own guns." Kaplan shrugged, focused on the oozing handful. "Damn, I love these burgers. Don't tell my wife we came here, my cholesterol is through the roof."

"Your secret's safe with me," Doyle said drily. He rubbed his chin thoughtfully. "Wonder why he's talking to you. I just reported to him yesterday."

"Dunno. Figured maybe he got some heat from the Feds, wanted to make sure everything was okay. You still sitting on those lab reports?"

Doyle nodded in response. The DNA results for the other victims had been processed a few days ago, but he'd held off on submitting them to the rest of the task force.

"I'd hand it over soon, if I were you. Captain catches you stalling, he's going to start asking questions. Besides, the labs don't prove anything, right?"

"Doesn't matter what they prove, they could give her control of the case." Doyle pushed away his food.

"You gonna finish that?" Kaplan asked eagerly. When Doyle shook his head, he pulled the wrapper toward him. "So what?"

"So if she gets jurisdiction, she can start digging deeper. She'll be able to use her own lab, and things won't take as long. Then she might start making connections that none of us want her to make," Doyle said meaningfully, keeping his voice down.

"So keep doing what you gotta do." Kaplan shrugged. His eyes narrowed as two men walked past, hand in hand. "Buncha fags," he said, loud enough for them to hear. They glanced over, saw the uniform and hurried to their car.

Doyle watched Kaplan shove a stack of fries in his mouth. Morons like him were too stupid to see the bigger picture, to see the boulder waiting at the top of the mountain, ready to sweep down and crush them all. Doyle knew better, knew exactly what was coming. And the closer it got, the clearer it was that only a miracle would help him avoid it.

His wife sat next to him on the couch, legs folded beneath her. He let his eyes wander over her clinically. She was doing a nice job of concealing the gray infiltrating her hair, after his comment last week she'd immediately gone to the salon to address the problem. Botox treatments had eased the fine lines on her brow and around her eyes, and regular Pilates sessions in combination with a tummy tuck had erased any sign of her pregnancies. She had wanted to wait, suggested they try for another one, perhaps a boy this time, but he had mandated the tubal ligation. Funny, she had such difficulty believing that he had no interest in a son, poor thing assumed that was all any man wanted. He repressed a shudder at the thought of a filthy little boy in their midst. He wouldn't have permitted it, if either of the amnios had indicated a male he would have insisted on aborting. No, he loved his perfect little girls. Boys were nothing but trouble.

They were watching the news on television. The lead story continued to deal with the boneyard found in Clarksburg State Park. The station had run out of new footage and was simply panning through earlier recordings: police ducking under yellow crime-scene tape; emergency vehicles stacked along the sides of the road five deep; that redheaded FBI agent holding up a hand to block the cameras as she marched past. His grip reflexively tightened on his beer bottle at the sight of a gurney being rolled toward a waiting van. *How dare they,* he thought to himself, rage flushing his cheeks. Those bodies belonged to him and no one else.

"Feeling okay, dear?" his wife asked with concern, pressing a cool hand to his face.

"Think I got a little sunburned out there today," he grumbled, before shaking off her hand and sipping his beer.

"It's all my fault, letting you run out of sunblock," she said, brow furrowing. "If you'd like I could go to the store right now, make sure you have some for tomorrow?"

He glanced at the clock, then replied reprovingly, "That wouldn't leave you much time to get dinner on the table by six-thirty, would it? No, it'd be better if you went first thing tomorrow."

"You're right," she agreed. Her eyes shifted back to the television and she shook her head. "I just can't believe this is happening here. Those poor families."

He considered responding, but thought better of it and watched along in silence. The picture switched over to a blond reporter conducting man in the street interviews. She was talking to an obese guy leaning against a minivan piled high with bags. He nodded along to her questions: yes, he was scared, had packed his family up early. *"Won't let my kids outside by themselves anymore,"* he said. *"Not until they catch this weirdo."*

"That's so sad," his wife said. "What do you think, dear? Maybe we should keep a closer eye on the girls?"

He looked at his watch. "I thought you said the chicken would take twenty minutes to cook."

She jumped off the couch. "You're right, I'm getting side-tracked. I'll go put it in the oven."

He reached over and grabbed the remote, listening to her footsteps retreat toward the kitchen. The blonde was talking to a hiker now, grubby from weeks on the trail. The hiker shook his head. *"Nah, I'm not worried. Those bodies were hella old, man. I doubt whoever did it is still around."*

He clicked off the television and stared into space for a minute, reviewing his most recent conquest. He'd been extra careful, had buried him deep, far off any trail and miles from here. Still, it had been a risk, taking another one. At this point it was probably best to wait until next year—by then things should have settled down. And he had his tokens to comfort him through the long winter ahead.

* * *

"So, what'd you think?" Monica asked, looping her arm through his.

Howard Stuart shrugged. "Completely implausible. I'll never understand why they don't even make an attempt to get their facts straight."

Monica chortled. "Howie, it was a film about aliens. How exactly were they supposed to get their facts straight?"

"The laws of physics would still apply. I can't believe people are willing to spend ten dollars to sit through such drivel."

"Well, I liked it," Monica said.

They walked the rest of the way to the car in silence. Monica's arm now felt awkward draped through his, but disentangling it might send the wrong message. It was a relief when they arrived at the passenger-side door and separated. She waited as he opened the door for her, then slid inside.

As he started the engine Monica searched her mind for something to say. Lately she'd been censoring herself before speaking, trying to tone down her persona. She hated herself for it, but she'd seen the look in his eyes sometimes after she'd opened her mouth. What was she always telling her son? *People gotta love you for who you are. Well,* she thought ruefully, *that applied less as you got older.* Truth of the matter was, a forty-year-old woman didn't get a lot of love either way, especially when she lived in a small town. And after a long series of failed relationships, she wasn't in the mood to give up on this one when it was still so new.

She examined Howie's face as he drove, hands positioned precisely at ten and two o'clock on the steering wheel, odometer nailed to the speed limit. His nose was a little beakish, brown eyes magnified by his glasses, thin lips. Not bad looking, though, and he had that luscious thick brown hair. A few times she'd reached over to tuck it back for him, and was secretly delighted when it immediately flopped down. It was, quite frankly, the only thing about him that was unplanned and unruly. When it came down to it, Howie really wasn't her type. She'd always gone for burly guys like Zach's dad, oil riggers, loggers, men who worked with their hands. She'd figured Howie would be a welcome change, that maybe that had been her mistake all along, falling for the wrong kind of guy. Unfortunately, by their third date they'd more or less run out of things to talk about, which was why she'd suggested they go see a movie.

"What do you want to do tomorrow night?" he asked, breaking the stillness.

Monica felt a rush of joy. He wanted to see her again. "I hear they're showing *2001* in the park. Figured we could go and you could explain how none of that actually happened."

He laughed, and Monica grinned in the darkness. She loved his laugh, it didn't appear often but when it did it was a hearty belly laugh, warm and full. "Tell you what. Next time I'll choose the film."

"Sure." Monica whacked his arm playfully. "But we gotta have some ground rules. Nothing with subtitles—I'm not going to the movies to read, for God's sake. And no documentaries, unless they're about polar bears."

"Polar bears?" He arched an eyebrow, glancing at her across the car interior.

"Sure, I just love those darn things." She continued chattering, her doubts about their relationship once again overwhelmed by her enthusiasm. Sure, they faced some obstacles, not the least of which was the long-distance thing once the case was over. But Zach was heading off to college soon anyway, and then she'd be free to move anywhere she wanted. And opposites attracted, right? As she watched Howie push the lock of hair from his eyes before setting his hand back into position on the steering wheel, the trace of a smile still on his face, she glowed. Even if it didn't work out, a little late-summer romance was just what she'd needed.

Nine

"Where are we on the interviews?" Kelly asked.

Monica shuffled through the papers in front of her. "Let's see—I've spoken to parole officers on my side of the state line, everyone with a taste for young boys has been accounted for, no one's gone off the grid, everyone's been checking in nice as you please." She glanced up. "Would help if we knew exactly when Randy Jacobs disappeared, though. Nothing to keep one of 'em from killing when he wasn't sitting across from his parole officer."

"I know. Unfortunately, Dr. Stuart hasn't been able to pinpoint the time of death any more exactly. Doyle, I don't suppose you've had any more luck?"

Doyle shook his head. "Nothing." He was oddly subdued, Kelly thought as she examined him. It was Friday, two days after their visit to Club Metro. She'd instituted nine-o'clock breakfast meetings for the unit to brainstorm, mainly because she'd quickly learned that if she didn't lock down Doyle in the morning, she'd waste half the day trying to find him.

"Too bad, 'cause there are a hell of a lot of sexual predators around here. Fifty level three's in this county alone, and those are the baddest of the bad," Monica noted. "Rapists, child molesters, you name it. Hell, we've got fewer than thirty high-risk offenders in our whole state. Must be something in the Massachusetts water."

Doyle rubbed his chin without responding, distracted.

"What's up?" Kelly asked after scrutinizing him.

He glanced up at them, seemed to deliberate for a moment, then held up a file. "I got some DNA matches back on the other bones."

Kelly held out her hand for the file. He paused for a beat, then reluctantly handed it over.

"What's it say?" Monica asked, standing to peer over her shoulder.

"Two more boys were ID'd, Brooks Ferrucio and Matt White." Kelly's eyes narrowed as she scanned through the pages. "Both in their late teens, both had prior arrests for solicitation and possession. Mostly here, but a few in New York and Vermont, too."

Monica let out a low whistle. "Lost hikers my ass. Jones was right, our guy targets gay hustlers."

Doyle grunted. "Doing the world a favor, you ask me."

"How enlightened of you," Monica said. "Maybe when we catch the so-and-so you can give him a medal."

"Looks like your lab did some good work here, Doyle," Kelly said grudgingly as she continued to peruse the files. "Bones were too degraded to give an accurate cause of death, but they've got a timeline for us." She turned to the whiteboard and erased the titles "John Doe #3" and John Doe #5," replacing them with the boys' names.

As she read aloud, she recorded the lab results below their names. "Brooks Ferrucio, age 19, last arrest May fifteenth in Williamstown, Massachusetts. Lab says he's been dead for at least three months, so he must have disappeared sometime around the end of May. Matt White was seventeen, last arrest was a year ago, lab says the bones look like they went through the winter. They're estimating he's been dead for six months to a year." Her cell phone rang, and she absentmindedly clicked it open. As she listened, she bent over and scribbled notes on a pad. "Got it," she said into the receiver. "We'll be there ASAP."

"What?" Monica asked as Kelly snapped the phone shut.

Kelly's brow creased. "Either of you know how to get to Cherry Plain State Park?"

"What, in New York?" Doyle asked, puzzled. "Yeah, that's a few miles across the border."

"Can you get us there?"

Doyle shrugged. "Sure. Why?"

Kelly gathered up her purse and grabbed her gun from the top desk drawer, reholstering it. "It looks like our killer has been busy."

"Thanks again for contacting us," Kelly said as she slipped on a pair of latex gloves and paper booties.

"Captain heard about your task force, thought the MOs might match up," the deputy said, then leaned in to her. "In all honesty, I think he's pawning them off on you. Our homicide clearance rate is nothing to write home about, last thing he wants is two more bodies on that list."

"Understood," Kelly said stiffly. At least it didn't look as if there'd be any jurisdictional issues here, which was a relief.

When she got the call that two more bodies had been found across the New York state border, she'd inwardly cringed. But as long as the New York authorities didn't throw up any hurdles, this might actually help her team. Two fresh bodies would offer a lot more information than the long-dead ones they'd been dealing with. Of course it meant she wouldn't be going home anytime soon, either. Still, she much preferred pursuing an active investigation to one where the trail had long since gone cold. Fresh victims meant that whoever they were tracking was still around. This was finally shaping up to be her kind of case.

They were in Cherry Plain State Park, just outside the small town of Berlin, New York. They had parked next to a small beach, more dirt than sand, on Black River Pond. A deputy had met them in the lot.

"How big is this park?" Kelly asked.

"One hundred seventy-five acres, give or take," The deputy said.

"Many campers?"

"A few. Honestly, we call it redneck camping, mostly folks who get too drunk to find their car keys at the end of the day and pass out on a picnic table. The highbrow crowd cross the border and pitch their tents off the Appalachian Trail."

"Who found them?"

"Park ranger. He's pretty shook up, I told him to stick around in case you wanted to talk to him."

"Great, thanks." Kelly held aside branches for Monica and Doyle as they marched into the woods off the parking lot. A hundred yards in she recognized an acrid tang in the air and held a finger under her nose. Just past a pair of nestled pine trees, two corpses were laid out perpendicular to each other, facedown on a thick carpet of pine needles. An older man in shorts and a sweaty T-shirt stood off to one side.

"That's our coroner," the deputy explained, jerking his head toward him.

"Smells pretty ripe, you sure they just got here?" Monica raised an eyebrow.

He shrugged. "Ranger said he went through here yesterday, this is his regular route. And they weren't here then."

"Regular route to what?" Kelly asked.

"Maintenance shed, back through the trees that way." He waved an arm vaguely off to the left.

"All right. On the off chance there are more bodies here, I'd like to call in our K-9 team, have them sniff around. It means keeping the park closed for a day or so."

"Not a problem."

"Why are they facedown?" Kelly asked.

"That's how we found 'em. Figured you'd want to see them that way before we moved them."

"That's awful considerate of you. See, Doyle? That's how it should be," Monica said.

"Stow it, Lauer," Doyle replied as he hunkered down over one body. "These been photographed?"

The deputy nodded. "Yep, and our crime-scene unit already went through."

"What was the cause of death?" Kelly asked.

"See for yourself," the coroner chimed in.

Kelly nodded for him to flip the first body. He eased the boy over, then stayed down on one knee beside him as he explained, "Rigor's already passed with this one."

"Eyes have been gouged out," Kelly noted. "Can you tell with what?"

The coroner shook his head. "Tough to say, but whoever did this really dug at 'em. Could've used almost anything, a knife, screwdriver…"

"What about the other marks?"

"You got everything from cigar burns to deep lacerations and puncture wounds. Looks like he was chained up, too, there's marks on his wrists. None of those were deep enough to kill him, though."

"They took his man parts," Monica noted, subdued. "And his throat's slit."

The coroner nodded. "That would be my guess for cause of death. I can tell you for certain after the autopsy."

All of which made the fact that the bodies were found facedown even stranger, Kelly thought. Removing the genitals indicated a sexual aspect to the murders. Usually in cases like this the victims were displayed faceup, posed to flaunt their vulnerability. "How long has he been dead?" she asked.

"That's where it gets weird," the coroner said, brow furrowed. "Based on the level of decomposition, I'd say anywhere from a few days to a week."

"But he just showed up today?" Kelly mused, puzzled. She bent to examine the wounds more closely. Someone had spent a lot of time hurting these boys, there was barely an inch of skin left unscarred.

"Would you mind if one of our guys sits in on the autopsy? We've got a forensic anthropologist on the team."

The coroner shrugged. "Hell, he can run the autopsy if he wants. It's my daughter's birthday, I'm already catching hell from my wife."

"What about the other vic?" Kelly asked.

"That's strange, too," he said. "He's fresher, and there's no sign he was ever chained up. No bleeding down there, so his privates were removed postmortem, thank God for small graces. Based on rigor and body temp, I'd say he's been dead for eight to ten hours."

As the coroner flipped him over, the deputy chimed in, "You might get lucky, it looks like your perp was sloppy. Found some loose change next to this one. We bagged it, maybe you'll get a hit on some prints."

Kelly and Monica exchanged a look. "Pennies?" Kelly asked.

"Yeah, I think so."

"How many of them?"

He shrugged. "Dunno. I can check for you, put in a call to CSU."

"What does it matter?" Doyle asked, eyeing her narrowly.

"Kelly, look." Monica elbowed her in the side.

Kelly directed her attention to the other dead boy. She caught her breath. Despite the damage, there was no mistaking him. "Let's go find Sommers," she said, jaw set as she turned back toward the parking lot. "I want to know how another of his 'boys' ended up dead in the woods."

"Easy does it…whoa, you gotta go easy on your old man here." He laughed as he tossed his daughter back over his shoulder, upside down. "Coming through with a sack of potatoes…hey, did you order potatoes?"

His youngest, Stephanie, rolled across the lawn on her back, gasping for air between peals of laughter. "No, Daddy!"

"Put me down!" Jennie squealed over his shoulder, pounding on his back with her tiny fists.

"No potatoes for you? Well, I guess I'll have to eat them all up myself. Maybe I'll make mine into French fries…

mmm, yummy." He pantomimed rubbing his stomach as he licked his lips.

"I don't want to be French fries!" Jennie cried over his shoulder.

"No? Are you sure?" He pursed his lips. "Because I sure do love French fries…"

His wife appeared at the screen door off the porch. She grinned at him and waved a phone in the air. "You got a call, sweetheart. Girls, time to come in and wash up for lunch!"

"All right, you heard your mom. Time for lunch." He winced as he lifted Jennie off his shoulder and eased her to the ground. The girls ran inside, still laughing.

His wife regarded him with concern as he took the phone from her. "Shoulder acting up again?"

He nodded. "Played nine holes the other day and forgot to ice it afterward." He took the phone with his good hand and kissed her on the cheek, then said, "Hello?"

She stepped behind him and massaged the injured shoulder with both hands as he listened. From that angle, it was impossible for her to see how his face darkened. After a moment, in a level voice he said, "Two of them? Huh, that's terrible. Well, thanks for letting me know, Chris."

"What was that all about?" his wife asked after he hung up.

"They found more bodies out by Berlin, in Cherry Plain Park."

"How terrible." She clutched at the pendant on her necklace. "I'm starting to think it might actually be safer back in the city!"

"It's starting to seem that way, isn't it?" he said pensively, gazing out across the lawn.

"Try not to let it get to you, honey. See, it's a mistake for me to go back during the week. I should stay here and take care of you," she chided. "Besides, the girls miss you."

"You know how hard it is for me to get work done when you're all here." He followed quickly with, "Not that I mind you coming up early this week. That was a nice surprise."

"Well, I thought we should take full advantage of the long weekend. Besides there's much less traffic when we leave on a Thursday. Remember last Labor Day, when we were stuck in it for six hours?"

"I remember," he said absentmindedly.

She shifted around to look him in the face. "Oh sweetie, you're so pale! I'll get you an ibuprofen, that should help with the pain." She took his hand and led him inside.

Ten

Kelly pounded on the door again, crossing her arms over her chest as she waited. Monica was already at the living room window, hands cupped over her eyes as she peered inside. "I don't see anyone. But man, someone trashed the place!"

"Really?" Kelly joined her at the window. Monica was right, the house looked like a tornado had ripped through it. Sofa cushions were strewn about, plants had been knocked over, paintings in broken frames were tossed to the ground.

"We better get in there," Monica said.

Kelly blocked her with one hand. "Not without a warrant."

"Really?" Monica paused. "But Sommers might be bleeding to death somewhere in there. I think we better chance it."

Kelly shook her head; she was already dialing the phone. "If Sommers turns out to be our guy, I don't want to lose the case on a technicality. There's too much at stake. Doyle? Jones here. Listen, how are we doing on that warrant?" She listened hard. "Call him back, tell him the place has been tossed. We really need to get in there ASAP."

"No luck, huh?" Monica asked. Kelly shook her head, lips pursed. "So much for those judicial connections he was bragging about," Monica snorted. "Should've known better. Now what?"

"Now we wait," Kelly said. "Five more minutes and we should have a warrant." She leaned back against the door frame. Monica plopped down in one of the wicker rocking chairs and tilted back, gazing up at the ceiling. She nervously tapped one foot on the floorboards. It was a quiet afternoon, the heat tamping down all noise. A squirrel crossed the lawn, reared up on its haunches to regard them intently, then settled back down.

"So. You do this, all the time? Chase these guys?" Monica asked, breaking the stillness.

Kelly nodded. "Pretty much."

Monica shook her head. "Don't know how you handle it. Those two today…I mean, I've seen plenty of bodies before. But not like that." She paused a beat before continuing, "You know, I got a boy about that age."

"Really?" Kelly said. "For some reason I assumed he was younger."

"Sure, 'cause I don't look a day over twenty-nine." Monica winked at her, and Kelly laughed in spite of herself. "I was pretty young when I had him. Things didn't work out with his dad, early on, and now he's on an oil rig in the middle of the Gulf somewhere. So it's pretty much always been me and Zach. I look at those boys, and I just cannot understand it, how anyone could be so cruel. I mean, they were just kids."

Kelly nodded. She almost told Monica about her brother, how he'd been even younger when he was murdered. But she'd spent so many years not talking about what had happened to Alex, to do so now felt wrong.

"So, you got a man in your life?" Monica continued after a pause.

"Not really, no," Kelly said uncomfortably. She never liked discussing her personal life.

"Really? Wow, that's hard to believe, a looker like you." Monica kept rocking, eyes shifting across the lawn, and asked, "What do you think of Howie?"

"You mean Dr. Stuart?" Kelly asked, suppressing a smile.

Monica shook her head. "I swear, I don't know what it is about glasses, they just get me every time. And I mean, the bigger the better. Give me a man with Coke-bottle lenses any day of the week."

"Seriously?" Kelly asked.

"Yup. Let me tell you, I spent the first half of my life chasing every boy that drove past on a motorcycle. And you can see how well that worked out for me," Monica said ruefully. "This time, I'm going after a guy with some brains. Nowadays I'd rather have someone I can sit and talk to without being afraid to use words with more than one syllable. You know what I mean?"

"Mmm." Kelly responded noncommittally. She had a tough time imagining Monica and Howard together, but stranger things had happened. "So, have you two…uh…"

"Haven't hooked up yet, but we're working up to it. He's coming over for dinner tonight, figured I'd see where it went from there," Monica said cheerfully. "But I tell you, I certainly wouldn't mind a little…"

Her cell phone rang, cutting off Monica, and Kelly silently heaved a sigh of relief.

Ten minutes later, warrant in hand, they were in the living room. "Well, no sign of him. But he definitely had some help with his spring cleaning," Monica noted drily.

Kelly nodded her agreement. They'd been through the whole house, but there was no sign of Sommers. The rest of the place was in the same condition as the living room: drawers overturned, furniture tossed about, walls ransacked. "Let's have Doyle put out an APB for his car. See if we can track him down."

"Sure. What do you want to do in the meantime?" Monica asked.

Kelly gazed around the house. "We got a warrant, right? Let's see what we can find out about our friend Mr. Sommers."

Eleven

He had two hours to find out what the hell was going on. Ten minutes ago his wife had left, taking the girls for a swim at the club so he could get some work done. He'd waited in his study until they'd pulled out of the driveway, just in case they'd forgotten a juice box or a toy or some other such nonsense. After a decent interval had passed he grabbed his keys and trotted to his truck. He'd stop by Berlin Pizza, just across the border in New York. There were always a few cops in there grabbing a slice during their shift. He'd have to be careful, though.

There wasn't any reason for them to suspect him, he reminded himself. *Ten fucking years!* he thought, pounding the steering wheel with his fist, then forcing his breathing to steady. And he'd always been so careful. Unlike that asshole Bundy, he took the time to bury them, and targeted boys that wouldn't be missed. Hell, he was doing a public fucking service, taking out the trash no one else had the balls to deal with. He'd bet that if they knew, most of the town would be thankful.

He couldn't understand how they had found the boy from the other night. He'd taken extra precautions, crossed another state line to a completely new location, had even dug the hole four feet deep instead of his usual three. No animal would bother digging that deep, not this time of year when there was plenty of food lying around the forest floor. And on the phone Chris had mentioned they'd found two bodies, not just one. So what the hell was going on?

A trickle of sweat snaked its way down his neck. He flicked a switch, powering up the car windows, flicked another one and a whiff of cold air seeped out of the vents. The Beemer had better AC, but he'd taken the truck to be less conspicuous. It was too hot, and there will still too many goddamn people around. He should've waited, held out until the last of the summer crowd had departed and there were fewer prying eyes. He sighed, running a hand through his hair, acknowledging the impossibility of that thought. There was no controlling the desire to take them. Once he'd chosen one, it was only a matter of weeks.

He flicked on his left turn signal and waited for a truck to pass before taking a slow, arcing turn into the pizza parlor parking lot, noting with satisfaction the police cruiser parked in the handicapped spot even though the rest of the lot was empty. Berlin Pizza was a victim of the 1960s obsession with space exploration. The building was all angles, bars jutting up to smack into each other, faded blue and silver planets splayed across the roof. The letters *e* and *a* were out on the neon sign. He met his own gaze in the rearview mirror and forced his expression to settle, features melting back into the complacent mask he wore for the rest of the world.

Inside, he ordered a "Galactic" slice, then leaned against

the counter, tapping his keys in a staccato. The cop was waiting for his order, hands crossed over his crotch. His face was lobster-red.

"Looks like you got some sun, there," he said conversationally to the cop.

The cop barked a short laugh. "You know it. Had one too many at a barbecue, woke up in a lawn chair three hours later completely cooked. Man, my wife was pissed."

"Damn, hate it when that happens." He laughed in agreement. "Was going to take the kids over to the Cherry Plain Park today, but signs say it's closed. You know what's up with that?"

The cop eyed him. "You live around here?"

"Nope, just across the border. Course, we usually go to Clarksburg," he continued hurriedly, noting the cop's skeptical look. "But that's closed, too. We got the long weekend coming up, and there's nowhere to take them to cool off." He let his voice ascend to a whine at the end.

The cop grunted. "Yeah, it'll be tough this weekend. You'll just have to dust off the sprinkler, 'cause from what I heard, they won't be opening either of 'em anytime soon."

"Damn, really?" He shook his head. "My wife'll be pissed. She'll be all over me again to put in a damn pool. Like I could afford that."

"Yeah, mine, too," the cop said, squinting up his blue eyes thoughtfully. After a pause, he continued, "Tell you what, you just let her know they found a couple of boys there."

"What, like a suicide?"

"Nope." He lowered his voice. "Murdered. Looks like it might be the same nut who killed those boys in Massachusetts."

"Damn." He let out a low whistle. "Who were they?"

"Couple of pansies—you know the type." The cop flicked a limp wrist at him.

"Were they shot?"

"Not so lucky." The cop paused, deliberating, then continued, "Nicked off their privates, dumped 'em right off the parking lot. Did a job on them, too, from what I heard. Tell your wife that, she'll probably never want to go there again." He chuckled.

"Yeah, I will. Thanks."

The pizza boy slid a slice with pepperoni and mushrooms on a paper plate across the counter toward the cop. "Thanks, Matt. Have a good day," the cop said, then headed out the door without paying.

Binoculars to his eyes, Dwight observed the exchange through the plate-glass window. He was parked across the street, his car tucked away in a line of vehicles shaded by an elm tree. He couldn't hear what they were saying, but he sure could imagine it. His lips curved up at the corners with delight. A minute later the cop left the pizza parlor, shoving the tip of a slice in his mouth, then wiping a greasy hand on the front of his uniform before opening his car door. Dwight watched as the Captain followed a minute later. As he exited, the Captain slid the paper plate holding his untouched slice into the trash can just outside the front door.

"Must've lost his appetite," Dwight chuckled to himself. The Captain got into his truck, a top-of-the-line Dodge, no shitty Tercel for him. He sat there without moving for a long time. Dwight checked his watch, counting off the minutes; four passed before the Captain finally turned the key, shifted into reverse and drove to the street. As the truck waited for a break in traffic, left turn signal on, Dwight twisted the focus knob on his binoculars, zooming in on the Captain's face. Dwight slapped the steering wheel with his free hand. "Damn, he looks *pissed*," he said jubilantly. Served the bastard right for telling him he'd never make the grade, humiliating him in front of everyone. Well, he'd discovered the Captain's dirty little secret. And soon enough, everyone else would know, too.

Twelve

"What do you think?" Monica asked, sounding worried.

Kelly shook her head. "Honestly, I'm not seeing it."

"Yeah, me neither. But I've been wrong before."

They were standing outside the interrogation room at the police station, peering through the smudged one-way glass at Calvin Sommers. He looked like hell, Kelly thought, a far cry from the well-assembled man she'd spoken with just three days ago. His face was smudged with blood and dirt, and his hair was greasy. He was working a faded trucker hat through his hands like it was a set of rosary beads. They'd seized his clothes for evidence, so he was wearing an enormous gray Berkshire State PD T-shirt and gym shorts. Doyle was storming around him. Every time he slammed a hand on the table, Sommers cringed.

Monica let out a low whistle as Doyle sent a chair skidding across the room, where it tipped over and landed with a clatter. "Why am I not surprised that he does such a great 'bad cop'?" she muttered. "I think you better get in there, see if the carrot works better 'n the stick."

Kelly nodded, picked up the envelope and opened the door. At her entry they both turned toward her, Sommers with a hint of hope in his eyes. She perched on the edge of the table at his elbow and waited a beat before speaking. "You're in a great deal of trouble, Mr. Sommers."

"I swear, I didn't do anything. I have no idea where Jim went after he left."

"And what time was that?"

"After midnight, maybe as late as one o'clock." Sommers paused, lowering his eyes. "I was waiting up for him. We had a fight when he got in."

"Right, you mentioned that. And then he left, and you didn't see him again."

"That's right." He nodded enthusiastically.

Kelly opened the envelope she had entered with. "But you went after him, didn't you?" She withdrew a baggie that contained a gun and held it up to him. "And you took this."

He didn't answer immediately. "All right, yes, I took the gun. But I swear I didn't use it."

"Where did you go?"

"I went back to where I found him." He paused. "There's a sort of flophouse down in North Adams. I went there, talked to one of the other boys—Danny. You can ask him, he said he didn't know where Jim was. So then I went home."

"Bullshit," Doyle snarled. "See, we talked to that kid, he claimed you had the gun shoved so far up his nose it scared the piss out of him."

Sommers examined his cuticle. "I just wanted—I needed him to tell me where Jim had gone."

"Because he'd stolen from you," Kelly said. "That must

have been upsetting. Anyone could understand why you'd be angry. Right, Lieutenant Doyle?"

Doyle shifted his jaw back and forth a few times before reluctantly responding, "Sure would piss me off."

"If Jim had needed money all he had to do was ask," Sommers said, almost to himself. "But the things he took, they're simply irreplaceable. I wanted to find out who he sold them to."

"Of course, because Jim would have to sell them through a middleman. He certainly couldn't handle that sort of transaction himself," Kelly noted.

Sommers nodded vigorously. "Exactly! See, I figured it probably wasn't even his idea, he wasn't sophisticated enough for that. Someone must have told him exactly what to take, because otherwise the chances of him stealing the most valuable pieces from my collection…"

"Just doesn't make sense," Kelly said, finishing his thought. "So there was someone manipulating Jim, forcing him to steal from you."

"Yes!" Sommers said, then dropped his focus back to the hat in his hands. "Jesus, if I'd only known. I was so angry with him, the things I said…" A tear snaked down his cheek.

"I'm sure Jim knew you didn't mean it," Kelly said sympathetically. "Where did you go after you left the flophouse? Danny must have told you where to find Jim."

"That's the thing," he said, rubbing his forehead with one hand. "I—I don't remember."

Doyle snorted. "I can't believe this crap." Kelly shot him a warning look.

"I swear! All I know is, I woke up in my car out by the dance festival. I started to drive home, and that's when the cops pulled me over."

"But you have no idea how you got there?"

He shook his head. "Not a clue."

"Were you taking any drugs last night, Mr. Sommers?" Kelly asked.

He shook his head vehemently. "No. At least—not last night," he concluded weakly.

"What about drinking?"

"Just a glass of wine at dinner."

"And you wouldn't mind submitting a sample to confirm that?"

"What, like a drug test?" Sommers hesitated, then said, "Sure, I wouldn't mind. But you should know, I might have had just a few hits off a joint, too. Not last night, but the night before. Would that show up?"

Kelly resisted the urge to roll her eyes. "I'll have you escorted to the lavatory, an officer will watch while you provide the sample. We're also testing your clothes, we need to determine if any of the blood found on them belonged to Jim."

"Right, okay." He looked down at the hat, which was still clutched in both hands. "Jesus, I feel like I'm losing my mind. This is such a terrible nightmare…."

"Mr. Sommers, thanks so much for your cooperation, we really appreciate your time. If you could just give us a few minutes, I need to speak to Lieutenant Doyle outside." Kelly motioned for Doyle to follow her. He grunted his discontent but joined her in the hallway. She waited until the door had shut behind them.

"Bastard didn't lawyer up," he complained. "What the hell are we doing out here? I swear, five more minutes with that pillow biter, I'll get him to confess to everything."

Kelly repressed a sigh; clearly sensitivity training was

something Doyle had opted to skip. "That's what I'm afraid of. You push too hard, when this goes to court the confession might get thrown out. I can pretty much guarantee Mr. Sommers will be hiring pricey legal counsel, and I don't want to give them anything to latch on to. I want Sommers to sweat it out while we wait for the test results. In a few hours we should have more to pressure him with."

"Yeah, okay," Doyle agreed begrudgingly.

"You've done such a great job getting the lab to expedite things so far, why don't you sit on them, see if they can push those tests? The sooner we get his tox screen results and the blood from his clothing typed and matched, the better."

Doyle mock-saluted. "I'm on it."

He shuffled down the hall. Monica stared after him, perplexed. "Is it me, or is Doyle going soft on us?"

Kelly shook her head. "Maybe he just decided to be a team player." Monica was right, she thought to herself. The past few days Doyle had seemed increasingly distracted. Hell, he'd been downright cooperative whenever she asked him to do something. "Whatever it is, I plan on enjoying it while it lasts. Did that kid Danny say where he sent Sommers?"

Monica shook her head. "The uniform that questioned him didn't think to ask. Want me to send someone back?"

"Definitely. I want to find out where Sommers was headed—might help us find the kill site."

"Good point, I'll have someone dispatched." Monica turned and looked back through the glass at Sommers. "I used to trust my radar for guys like this, but him? I don't know, seems like he couldn't hurt a fly. Are the really twisted serial guys just different?"

"Sometimes," Kelly said, watching as Sommers crushed

the hat to his face and inhaled deeply. *And sometimes it means we got the wrong guy,* she thought to herself.

Dwight awakened with a start, eyes automatically jumping to the clock. It was just before four in the afternoon. *Whew,* he thought, stretching languorously. Thank God he'd woken up in time for his shift. He'd been so exhausted when he fell into bed that he'd forgotten to set his alarm. Dwight sat up slowly, scratching the paunch that distended over the tops of his boxers then, in one fluid motion, he dropped to the floor and executed a series of push-ups. He got to fifty before he dropped to the ground panting. *Not too shabby,* he thought, pleased with himself. Especially considering he'd only started up again a few weeks ago. Another month of this and he'd be knocking out five hundred a day, no problem, just like he used to. He squeezed the roll around his belly and frowned. It might mean cutting out the beer, too. But better wait and see. No need for drastic measures yet.

Fifteen minutes later he'd showered, shaved, changed his bandage and was ready to go. On his way out the door he glanced at the clock, tossing his keys in the air and catching them. He could spare five minutes, he thought with a sly smile. After all, something had probably happened in the past few hours. Maybe it was already posted on one of the news sites.

As Dwight waited for his computer to boot up he suppressed a yawn. Damn thing was so slow, he really wished he could afford a new one. Man, he was tired. All this running around day and night really took it out of a guy. It was training, he reminded himself. When he finally got to Langley, they'd keep him up for days straight. This would help him get used to it. Hard to believe the Captain still managed to maintain this pace at his age. *Probably sleeps all day, though. Doesn't have to hold down a pissant job like the rest of us,* Dwight thought with a flash of anger as he tugged at his shirt collar, the polyester already making him sweat.

The *Berkshire Eagle* home page finally popped up. He let out a whoop at the first article—it was right there in black and white, Two Bodies Found In Cherry Plain Park. Dwight skimmed it quickly, eyes narrowing. Police were talking to a "person of interest" in the recent park killings, which was interesting, he hadn't seen that coming. Could they have caught the Captain already? Maybe his plan had worked too well. The report didn't say much else; he'd have to cruise down to Ace's Place after his shift, see if any of the local cops were willing to spill the beans over a brewski.

He scrolled down. There was another article below, an op-ed piece entitled, Prostitution In Our Community. The writer danced around the fact that it was gay hustlers getting killed, never saying it outright. But he suggested that the presence of such elements attracted danger to the community at large. "Amen to that, my brother," Dwight said aloud, nodding. Not that he minded hookers, he'd indulged in female company a few times himself. But little fag boys, that was different. He'd lived here his whole life, could remember back to when it was a nice place. Shame a bunch of homos had to come along and screw it up, just like they screwed up everything else. He'd heard straights weren't even allowed into Miami anymore. Thank God they still kept gays out of the military. His brow furrowed as it suddenly occurred to him that he wasn't sure what the official CIA policy was, but he shrugged it off. No way they'd hire a bunch of pansy spooks who'd never be able to maintain a cover.

Satisfied, he clicked off the computer and stood up, tightening the belt of his gun holster and clamping his hat on his head. The bosses didn't know that he carried. *But you gotta be prepared,* he thought. If some guy broke into a building he was watching, he'd squeeze off two rounds right in their chest. Dwight glanced at his watch again and frowned. To get there on time he'd have to blow through a few lights. Thank God his new radar detector had arrived yesterday. He grabbed it and tucked it under his arm. The screen door slammed behind him as he strutted outside.

Thirteen

Dr. Howard Stuart adjusted the viewfinder again and squinted through the microscope, brow furrowed. Raising his head, he turned to the open notebook beside him and furiously scribbled a few notes, then dropped his head back down and adjusted the dial again. A minute later he straightened, wincing, one hand reaching up to rub the crick in his neck.

"You okay?" the tech at the next table asked, eyebrow raised.

"Fine, thanks," he said with a smile. "It's always a challenge to adapt to new facilities." *And what a facility it was,* he thought as his eyes swept the room. Purgatory was more like it. His lab at the Smithsonian was strictly state-of-the-art; they had equipment there that wouldn't reach the marketplace for at least another year. The Massachusetts State Police Lab in Sudbury, on the other hand, appeared to have picked up most of their diagnostics at a rummage sale. He was gazing through a microscope that, for all intents and purposes, belonged in a public high school science class. And their vacuum oven...suffice it to say it left him cold.

Although the technicians themselves weren't a bad lot, he thought grudgingly. And the lab had proved a welcome escape from the increasingly aggressive attentions of Lieutenant Lauer. He'd begged off dinner at her house that night, claiming he'd reached a critical phase at the lab and couldn't handle the long commute back to the Berkshires. The truth was he was stalling; most of the work on the earlier remains had been completed, and Agent Jones was insisting he return the next morning to examine two new bodies.

Which meant an uncomfortable scene with Monica, he thought with a sigh as he gathered up the stack of papers he'd been working on, tapping them against the countertop to straighten them. He didn't have a lot of experience with women to begin with, and the intensity of her attentions was disconcerting to say the least.

One of the techs appeared at the door. "Dr Stuart, I have those results you asked for," she said.

"Thank you, Jamie," he said, taking them from her. Now she was more like it, he thought, taking in her slender form appreciatively. Quiet, subdued, nondescript. That was his kind of woman. Initially he'd been intrigued by Monica's attentions, and she did make him laugh. But the truth was something about her scared him. She was so loud, so different from the women he generally dated. He frowned slightly as his eyes fell upon the document in his hand. He flipped forward a page, checked the number, flipped through a few more. It was there on all of them.

"Jamie, have you double-checked these numbers?"

She rolled her eyes. "Of course."

"All right, then. Thank you." Still frowning, he picked up his cell phone and dialed. It was answered on the third ring. "Agent Jones? I've found something…strange."

* * *

"Looks like we got him!" Doyle chortled gleefully, slapping the stack of papers with one hand.

Kelly glanced up from her desk, then held out a hand for the papers. Doyle bobbed back and forth on his feet as he watched her, barely able to contain himself. "How sure are they that the blood on his shirt is a match?" she asked slowly. Monica crossed the room to peer over her shoulder.

"DNA will take another few weeks, but it's the same blood type. Jim Costello was A positive, which isn't exactly common," Doyle said. "And check out the tox screen."

"So Sommers had ketamine in his system," Kelly said. "I'm actually surprised they tested for that, it's not in the usual battery."

"I had them check for everything when the first test was negative," Doyle said. "And you know what ketamine does?"

"Gives you hallucinations," Monica said, then caught their glances. "What? I got a teenage son, I got to know this stuff," she said defensively. "Kids call it 'special k.'"

"It's big with the gays, too," Doyle interjected. "So our boy Sommers probably got pissed off when his little friend stole his shit. He drops a little ketamine, goes after him, does a job on him when he finds him, then passes out in his car."

"What, and forgets the whole thing?" Kelly said dubiously.

"Could be, actually," Monica said slowly. "They call it 'falling into a k-hole,' it's supposed to be like entering a dream state. And afterward they usually don't remember much."

"Or maybe someone drugged him to shift the blame," Kelly mused.

Doyle snorted. The lab reports had brought back his swagger. "I say if it looks like a duck and quacks like a duck, it's a fucking duck. We got the guy cold. We got the kid's blood on his clothes, and he admits to getting pissed off and going after him. We got motive, opportunity, and more than enough evidence to arrest this sicko."

Kelly looked at Monica, who shrugged. "Much as I hate to admit it, Sunshine here is right. We can link Sommers to two of the boys so far. Maybe he's hooked on this stuff and it makes him do bad things, things he doesn't remember after the fact. I say we charge him and see how it pans out."

"All right." Kelly nodded her agreement. "Doyle, since this is your jurisdiction, you get to do the honors."

Doyle smacked his hands together. "So I guess this is it, huh? Not much reason to keep the task force going if we caught the guy."

Kelly eyed him thoughtfully. She knew Doyle hadn't been a fan of the task force from the beginning, but he was practically pushing her out the door. Not that she'd mind getting out of here, but still. In part just to nettle him, she said, "Let's wait and see what happens. Have we tracked down Danny Smith yet?"

Monica shook her head. "No one was at the house when they went back. They'll try again later, after the shift change."

"Good. Meanwhile, let's have Mr. Sommers arraigned. But we say nothing to the press yet." She looked meaningfully at Doyle. "I don't want any leaks on this. If something goes wrong, all of our respective units end up with a black eye. So let's be sure we got the right guy before we start talking. Agreed?"

Monica nodded her head, while Doyle mumbled something that sounded like acquiescence. Kelly glanced at her watch; it was 4:30 p.m. the Friday before Labor Day weekend. The standard buzz outside their office was greatly diminished, most of the other officers having left early. *No reason not to join them,* she thought. Barring anything unforeseen, she might actually get three whole days off in a row, which for her was practically a record. She grinned and said, "Why don't we call it a day?"

Fourteen

He wiped the sweat from his brow with the back of his hand and dumped another bottle of bleach on the floor. Eyes watering, he almost choked on the fumes. He climbed up a few rungs of the ladder, stuck his head above ground, tore off his surgical mask and gulped in drafts of fresh air. He'd have to be careful, worst thing in the world would be for him to pass out and have his wife find him down there. He was a fantastic liar, a skill required by his life circumstances, but not even he would be able to explain away the room at the base of the ladder.

Taking a deep breath, he dropped back down and poured a good amount of clean water over the bleach, using a mop to swirl it around and toward the drain he'd installed in the center of the room. When he built the chamber he'd tapped into the sewer pipes so that everything would flow out to the septic tank. He made a mental note to call the service company to come and drain it. They'd just had it emptied a few months ago, so he'd have to come up with an excuse for why they were called back, maybe shove a few tampons down the toilet or something.

He turned on the hose and sprayed the walls and floor, the fumes abating as bleach circled down the drain. Pulling off his mask, he surveyed the room. He'd removed the chains and stowed them. Sometime this week he'd take them out on his boat and dump them in the nearest lake, along with a few other items that were too incriminating to dispose of through the normal channels. The only evidence now that the room was anything but a bomb shelter was the eyebolt embedded in the concrete. He could remove it, but he was loath to do that. It had been a pain in the ass to install in the first place, and he dreaded the thought of having to do it again. Besides, the cabinet he was going to set up for nonperishables would completely cover it. That, plus a few strategically placed cots, and anyone who came looking would have no reason to be suspicious.

Other than that, all that remained were his tokens. He eased the top off an industrial-size can of tomatoes, identical to a dozen others lined up next to it. He tilted it carefully so that a small glass jar slid out and into his waiting palm. A smile crept across his face as he took in the contents. Satisfied, he eased the jar back inside and pressed the metal top back down. He knew it wasn't the smartest thing in the world, keeping them around, but he couldn't bear to part with them. And besides, what were the chances anyone would come down here with a can opener, even if they did find the room?

Satisfied, he climbed the ladder, slammed the top back down, and dragged the industrial matting back over the trapdoor. He coiled up the hose and hung it back on the wall next to the truck. He methodically placed the parts of a motorcycle he'd been reassembling for years on top of the matting. His wife would make a fuss, but that was kind of the point, and it would be a lot of trouble to move anything.

As he wiped his hands dry on a rag, he surveyed the garage. Aside from the mess he'd just created on the floor, everything was immaculate and in its place, a testament to his usual type- A sense of order. He nodded to himself, walked over to the fridge in the corner, dug out a beer and popped it open. It had been a long day, and a revealing one, he mused with the first gulp. He caught a glimpse of himself in the corner of a chipped mirror that hung by the garage door to help his wife back out her car. He met his eyes: they were clearer now, calmer. He tested out an easy grin, then let his features settle back into their normal configuration. "Someone's fucking with you," he said to the mirror. *And God knows they are going to regret it,* he thought as he chugged another gulp of beer.

He felt fatigue tug at his brain and pushed it away. From here on out, he had to stay sharp, he reminded himself. He'd get through this weekend, hopefully without any further surprises. Then come Tuesday, when his family returned to the city, he'd go hunting. A smile tugged at the corner of his mouth as he pictured it. It would be different from the usual, and far more dangerous. But who knew? Maybe that would make it even more fun.

Kelly knocked again, shifting uncomfortably from one foot to the other as she tucked the bottle of wine under her arm and checked her watch. It read 6:35 p.m. She was pretty sure Monica had said to come at six-thirty; hopefully she hadn't been mistaken. She knocked one more time, part of her almost hoping no one would answer so she'd be able to go back to the hotel and eat by herself.

She turned and surveyed her surroundings. Monica lived on a quiet street that was a jumble of architectural styles, right next door to the liberal bastion of Bennington College. The neighborhood played testament to that, political signs in nearly every window advocated Green Party candidates.

Monica's house, a quaint cottage painted a fading but cheery yellow, was flanked by a neatly mown lawn. An enormous spiraling wind chime spun slowly in the evening breeze, spilling metallic notes down on an aging porch swing.

The door was suddenly thrown open. Monica was standing there, wild-eyed and covered in flour. She frantically waved Kelly inside, then dashed back into the bowels of the house, yelling, "Make yourself at home! Sorry, I've got a situation on my hands!"

Kelly found herself standing in a small but cozy living room. She set the bottle of wine down on a table, then picked it back up when she noticed a price tag on the side. She hurriedly scraped it off with her fingernail as she perused the room. Lots of plants everywhere, ivy tumbling down from the top of the TV cabinet, a potted palm hovering over a plush armchair in the corner. A flowered sofa facing the door was dappled with evening light, the same colors were matched by the swirling rug on the floor. Monica had good taste, which Kelly found somewhat surprising. She realized she'd been expecting something a little more eclectic, maybe an electric bull in the center of the living room and lots of horns on the walls. Everything was obviously inexpensive but well chosen. It was the kind of room you wouldn't mind spending a lot of time in.

Mentally Kelly compared it to her own spartan living room back in D.C. Aside from a bookshelf and a matched set of wing chairs inherited from her parents, the room was bare. Of course, it wasn't as if she spent much time there, she reminded herself. And she viewed that apartment as transitional anyway, the transfer six months ago had gone so quickly that she'd signed a lease on the first place she saw. Nearly everything she owned was still in boxes. It seemed a shame to invest in furniture when she'd be moving somewhere better the minute she found time to apartment-hunt.

There was a cry from the back of the house, and Kelly decided that despite her better instincts she should check it out. She passed through a small formal dining room with robin-egg blue walls and a table set for three, then pushed through a swinging door into the kitchen. It was large, twice the size of the living room. A center island dominated the room. At the moment, it was coated in an inch of flour.

"Crap!" shouted Monica, pulling her head out of the oven. In both hands she held the remnants of a pie, crusts smoking. "I can never seem to keep the damn edges from burning," she muttered, setting it on top of the island and waving an oven mitt to dissipate the smoke. She looked up and smiled. "Welcome, by the way!"

Kelly smiled faintly. "Thanks for having me."

"Hell, I'm just thrilled you could make it on such short notice." Her face clouded over and she looked away as she said, "Howie got stuck at the state lab, and I'd hate to waste the meal. I've got Zach out back working on the grill. Hopefully he's having more luck than I am."

"I thought he was staying at a friend's house tonight?" Kelly asked.

"He said his friend canceled." Monica put a finger to the side of her nose and winked. "Although my highly developed police instincts tell me he just didn't want his ma eating alone. He's a good boy."

As she said it, a door at the back of the house swung open and a tall, gangly teenager backed through. He was bearing a platter laden with a preposterous amount of ribs. "All right, I think they're finished. It's still hot as hell out there, though. Next time I vote we make gazpacho." He glanced up and saw Kelly. "Oh, hey. You must be the FBI lady."

Kelly laughed. "That's pretty much what my business cards say. I'm Kelly. You must be Zach." He definitely took after his mother, with the same unruly blond locks and blue eyes. He had a small cleft in his chin, dimples, and a smattering of acne. In his board shorts and ripped T-shirt, he looked like the prototypical all-American boy.

His face flushed red. "Ma's been talking about me, huh? Jeez, mom, I asked you not to do that."

Monica rolled her eyes. "Yep, that's how I spend my days, blathering on about you. Puh-leez, like I've got nothing else to discuss." She whacked him playfully on the arm.

"Watch it, you don't want me to drop these." He danced away from her, setting them on the one clean section of countertop with exaggerated caution. "Looks like we're having your world-renowned burnt-crust pie again."

"Nothing but the best for my baby." Monica pulled the cork on the bottle Kelly had brought. "Zach, grab some wineglasses from the cupboard."

"Three?" he said hopefully.

"Yeah right, three. You have a few birthdays I missed?" Monica snorted. "Two, unless you want to drink soda out of stemware."

All through dinner, Kelly watched them banter. They had

an easy camaraderie that dictated the rhythm of conversation, one built through years of shared dinners. She felt a twinge; it was something she'd never had with her family, at least not after her brother had been murdered. Her family had eaten in silence, seated in a row on the couch in front of the television set. In high school she had begged off family meals entirely, taking a plate to her room so she could eat while doing her homework. Her mother had initially raised a halfhearted protest but, in the end, gave in. Kelly suspected she'd privately been relieved.

She looked up to find them eyeing her expectantly, and realized she'd drifted off in a reverie. "I'm sorry, did you ask me something?"

They glanced at each other. "I was wondering where you're from, originally." Monica said.

"Rhode Island."

"Yeah? Do your folks still live there?" Zach asked.

Kelly shook her head. "They died a few years ago. It's just me now."

"Oh honey, I am so sorry to hear that." Monica touched a hand to her throat.

Kelly shrugged off the sympathy. "It's fine, really. I was too busy for them, even when they were alive. I've got to travel a lot, doing this…" She caught the look Zach and Monica exchanged, and forced some brightness to her voice as she added, "I've always been a loner, pretty much. My family was never close, not the way you two are."

"I suppose we are pretty close, aren't we, Beenie?" Monica winked and tilted her glass toward Zach.

"You promised not to call me that in front of other people anymore, Ma." Zach shifted in his chair, embarrassed.

"Oops, that's right. Sorry, sweetie." Monica tapped the last few drops from the bottle into her glass and took a swig, draining it. She wiped her mouth with a napkin, then leaped to her feet. "I'm going to grab the pie and some ice cream. Kelly, more wine?"

Kelly shook her head no; she was still nursing her first glass. She'd never been much of a drinker, and she'd driven here from the hotel.

There was an uncomfortable silence once the door swung shut behind Monica. Kelly racked her brain for something to say; she wasn't very good at small talk with anyone, never mind a teenager. She couldn't name a single current band, she realized, and suddenly felt unbearably old.

"My mom likes you," Zach noted, breaking the silence.

Kelly nodded, then realized that wasn't really an appropriate response, and said awkwardly, "Your mom's a great cop. She's been a big help in this investigation."

"It's been tough for her. She's not sleeping again, nights." Zach seemed to debate whether or not to continue. He cocked his head to the side, listening to the banging sounds coming from the kitchen, before continuing, "You know anything about this Howie guy?"

"Dr. Stuart?"

Zach nodded.

Kelly cleared her throat. "Not personally. He's supposed to be the best at what he does. But other than that…I mean, this is the first time I've worked with him," she concluded.

"Yeah, I figured as much. Thought I'd ask anyway." He scraped a fork absentmindedly across the tablecloth in front of him, organizing a few stray pieces of pasta salad into a mound. Kelly started to stand, clearing her plate. Zach jumped to his feet and grabbed it from her. "Here, let me get that. Mom'll be all over me if I let a guest clean up."

"Oh, okay. Thanks."

He vanished into the kitchen and Kelly took another sip of wine. She was sorry to hear that this case was affecting Monica so badly. It had been a while since one had gotten to her. Probably too long, she mused. She wondered if she was desensitized now, if she'd inadvertently handed over some of her humanity. Listening to the voices on the other side of the door, she was suddenly overwhelmed by a pang of loneliness so intense she had to set her glass down on the table and draw a few deep breaths. As the door to the kitchen swung open, she pasted a smile back on her face.

Dwight whistled a few bars of *The Farmer in the Dell* as he swung his nightstick in a looping circle, then grimaced. Damn tune had been stuck in his head for a few days now. He wondered if that happened to other people. For him, it was almost a daily struggle, one song or another winding through his brain on an endless reel. Some days were better than others, like the month his mind latched on to Eric Clapton, that was tolerable. But lately it had been the strangest scraps, things he couldn't even remember having heard recently. *I mean, what the fuck,* he thought, *The Farmer in the Dell? Where the hell did that come from?*

Dwight ran the nightstick along a length of boxes. The last few weeks he'd had the same assignment, working as a night watchman at the local cardboard box storage warehouse. It was a dream gig, no one to keep tabs on him, so he could duck out whenever he needed to. *Because who the hell was going to steal a bunch of cardboard, anyway?* He scoffed. He'd be sorry to lose the job once Mario got back from his triple bypass; after that it was back to answering calls from panicky residents whose cat tripped their fancy alarm system. This was a much better gig. Maybe he'd get lucky and Mario would kick. Then he'd get to hold on to this cushy assignment indefinitely—at least until his application to the CIA got processed. It was taking a hell of a long time, he thought, shaking his head. If he didn't hear from them this week, he'd make a few phone calls, make sure it hadn't got lost in the mail.

Dwight stopped in his tracks. There was a noise, sounded like it came from behind him, at the far end of the warehouse where he'd just patrolled. He deliberated; it was probably nothing, just a rat that had gotten in. He'd had to reset a few of the traps last week when he found some pellets in the break room. Dwight checked his watch; he was almost halfway through his shift. If he ignored the noise for another few hours it would become the day worker's problem. And he was really looking forward to the ramen soup he had waiting for him. He strained his ears, listening hard—there was a scrabbling noise about fifty feet behind him. He sighed. *Might as well check it out,* he thought, reminding himself that this was just the sort of dirty job he'd be expected to undertake once he got in the Agency.

He turned around and proceeded cautiously, treating this the way he would any other operation. The boxes were stacked in pallets that extended up to the ceiling, creating a labyrinth that shifted slightly from week to week, depending on deliveries. To conserve energy they kept the lights off, so he relied on a flashlight. He paused at one fork and squeezed his eyes shut, trying to remember which of these terminated in a dead end. That happened sometimes, one night he'd gotten panicky, he seemed to keep getting trapped in the same cul-de-sac. The air was thick with the smell of cut paper. But the maze hadn't shifted in a week now, he had it down. He turned right and edged along. In some sections the towers of boxes seemed to lean together, almost closing over his head. This particular passage got narrower and narrower, but if he remembered correctly it ended at the long aisle that spanned the back of the warehouse.

Dwight emerged from the aisle and drew a deep breath, calming his nerves. His hand was gripping the top of his gun holster, he realized with surprise, looking down. He debated for a minute, then shrugged and withdrew his weapon. Couldn't hurt to have it on hand, even if he was just on the trail of vermin. He edged forward, holding his Beretta in both hands. There was a strange chittering sound a few aisles down. He eased forward, keeping his back to the pallets, then whipped around a corner. Caught in the glare, a raccoon froze. Dwight squeezed off a few rounds as the animal regained its wits and scampered away. He charged after it, pausing at the spot where it had just been. His lips curved upward: blood, just a few drops but he'd tagged the little beastie. Now he could spend the rest of his shift tracking it down, maybe toying with it a little. It would be just like the other night, he mused. He'd thought it would be harder, killing the boy, messing with the body. He had speculated in advance that he might even get sick. All the other bodies he'd handled had already been dead, some of them for a long time. They were more reminiscent of the skeleton hanging in science class back in high school. But last night, man, that had been different than he'd imagined.

Dwight felt the same sensation in his stomach now as he

tracked the raccoon, wending back through the aisles, pausing periodically to note the tiny drops of blood. He tried to identify how he was feeling. It wasn't fun, exactly, it was something better than that. Maybe a little like sex, he mused. At the end, when he'd finished positioning the boys and had stepped back to examine his handiwork, he'd felt a thrill course through him like nothing he'd ever experienced before. Which is probably why the Captain did it, he thought. Not that he cared, really. For him this was just payback for one of the many wrongs done him over the years. Still, he could see where it could become a particularly satisfying hobby. Not that he'd need that, he reminded himself. Once the Agency accepted him, he'd pretty much have a license to kill, and wouldn't need to waste his time on ratty little boys. In a way he felt sorry for the Captain, having to settle like that. If you looked at things a certain way, he was doing him a favor.

The beam of his flashlight found a small furry lump at the edge of the aisle. Dwight was in the cul-de-sac he'd passed before, boxes towering above them on all sides. The raccoon was backed into a corner, dragging one leg, hissing at him. It knew it was trapped. Dwight smiled at it. He tucked his gun back in its holster and withdrew his night stick. "You and me, we're going to have some fun," he said in a low voice, swinging the stick in a slow circle and whacking it on his open palm. "Hell, we got all night."

Fifteen

"So what are you saying?" Kelly asked. "Were they all moved?"

They were seated around the table in the command center at the Berkshire State Police barracks. The building was quiet, even for a Saturday; all but a skeleton crew was off enjoying the long weekend. The four of them perched on the rickety chairs, sweltering in the heat. Dr. Stuart cleared his throat nervously and clenched the folder tightly with both hands. "I can't say that with any certainty. But based on the evidence surrounding the victim found in Vermont—"

"Randy Jacobs," Monica interjected.

"Yes, Mr. Jacobs." Dr. Stuart avoided her eyes as he responded. "If that truly was the dump site, the body had been left there quite recently, after the decomposition stages were almost complete."

"How can you tell?" Kelly asked.

"Insect activity. There was clear evidence of subterranean insect activity on the body, which differs markedly from what would have caused decomposition aboveground. In addition, there were traces of sand that differed markedly from the surrounding soil."

"So what does that mean?" Doyle demanded impatiently. Kelly cast him a hard glance. Since Sommers's arrest, he'd regressed to his usual surly self.

"I can't say for certain with all of them but, based on my examination, at least three of the bodies had been previously buried."

"Wait a minute—you're saying someone dug these boys up? Why?" Monica asked, running a hand through her hair. She looked tired, Kelly noted.

Dr. Stuart shrugged. "I'm afraid that determining the motivation behind that doesn't fall under my purview. All I can do is present you with the facts."

"Have you had a chance to look at the two more recent corpses?" Kelly asked. "I wasn't sure if they fell into your field of expertise…"

"Although I don't specialize in soft tissue, I am also a certified forensic pathologist," Dr. Stuart said.

"What's the difference?" Monica asked.

"One requires a Ph.D. and focuses primarily on skeletal remains, the other a medical degree and further training in soft tissue trauma," Dr. Stuart replied, a note of pride in his voice.

"Wow," Monica said. "Now I really feel undereducated."

"Finally, she admits it," Doyle snorted.

"This from someone who probably only has a GED," Monica retorted.

"Getting back to the latest two bodies," Kelly said. "What did you find?"

Dr. Stuart held up a folder. "There the pattern remains—

your John Doe was almost certainly previously buried, and showed signs of being shackled. His stomach contents were also negligible, he hadn't eaten in a few days. And there was something else…" He fumbled open the folder, dumping a stack of papers onto the desk. He sifted through them until he found photos that zeroed in on the wounds to one corpse.

"Is this our John Doe?" Kelly asked, leaning forward. She noticed Monica looked a little green.

"No, this is the other one, Jim Costello. Note the initial stab wounds, here, and here?" He pointed them out. "Hesitation marks. But if you compare them to the wounds found on your John Doe; which were almost identical, by the way, in terms of placement…" He pulled out a different photo and laid it next to the first. "No sign of hesitation. These were done decisively, by a practiced hand."

"So what are you saying?" Monica asked.

Kelly stepped back and crossed her arms over her chest. "He's saying we might have a copycat on our hands."

"Bullshit," Doyle said. He waved an arm dismissively at Stuart. "We got one killer, his name is Sommers, and he's a sick fuck. Case closed, time for all of you to go back where you came from."

Kelly gritted her teeth. "Lieutenant Doyle, I'll remind you these cases are still open. The district attorney hasn't even officially filed charges against Sommers."

"That's just because he was too busy planning his Labor Day barbecue," Doyle said. "Trust me, when he gets back in the office on Tuesday, that's the first thing on his agenda. The mayor told me so himself."

Kelly decided to ignore him and turned back to Dr. Stuart. "And was Jim Costello also previously buried?"

He shook his head vigorously. "Definitely not. Despite these two being found together, I'd postulate that they were murdered by different perpetrators."

"And is there any way to tell which of the killers is responsible for the original bodies found in the boneyard?" Kelly asked.

Dr. Stuart shrugged. "Based on the evidence we have, no."

"But if you had to guess?" Kelly pressed.

"I'd say most of them were the work of a more experienced killer," he acknowledged, pulling out another photo. "Particularly with the removal of the eyes, there's a marked difference. I suspect your second killer is a bit squeamish."

"Can't say I blame him." Monica shuddered. "Maybe Sommers had a partner."

"Yeah, and maybe I'm going to sprout freakin' wings. What's with you people? You got something against wrapping up a case?" Doyle slammed a palm down on the table. "It's Labor Day weekend, I got better things to do."

"Lieutenant, we're not quite done yet," Kelly said, but he stormed out of the room.

The three of them looked at one another. "How certain are you of this?" Kelly asked, turning to Dr. Stuart.

He shrugged. "Obviously not one-hundred percent, but I'd say pretty certain."

"And the John Doe, can you give me a time of death?"

"He'd been dead four days when you found him, give or take. Of course, I had to readjust my estimate based on the fact that he appears to have been buried, which slows the rate of decomposition dramatically. And since there was evidence of methamphetamines in his system, that would accelerate the life cycle of the insects—"

"But you'd say he died earlier in the week, on Monday or Tuesday?" Kelly interrupted.

"Approximately. Again, if we knew where he'd been buried first…"

"I doubt we'll find out," Kelly mused. "And no hits on prints for him, either, which is strange."

"I'm having the lab work up a facial reconstruction for him, if that helps," Dr. Stuart said.

"It should. We'll post it on the air, see if we get any bites. When will that be done?"

"In a few days. I assigned it to my lab at the Smithsonian. The Massachusetts State lab is still doing papier-mâché models," he said disdainfully.

"What do you want to do about this second-perp theory?" Monica asked. "I mean, I hate to say it, but the case against Sommers looks pretty strong. If Massachusetts decides to pull the rug out from under the task force, I'm not sure I can stop them. My captain wants to mark this one in the win column, too. We'll have to come up with more than hesitation marks to convince them to keep going."

"You're right," Kelly agreed. And she still had no rock-solid evidence that any of the boys had been escorted across state lines to turn tricks. She could try to claim the Mann Act at this point, asserting jurisdiction, but it would be a stretch. If any of the state police units balked she'd have a tough time proving her case, and it was clear Doyle wasn't ceding jurisdiction without a fight. Not that she was angling for one anyway, she reminded herself. In truth, she was tempted to stop arguing this. They had someone in custody who had a relationship with at least two of the boys, and he satisfied many of her profile's requirements. He was the right age, physically strong, and a longtime resident of the area. Not that Sommers seemed particularly outdoorsy, but then one never knew. Most agents would be happy to close the case and catch the next plane home.

Kelly sighed, sat down and kneaded her forehead with one hand. Something about it just didn't feel right. She was usually a good judge of people, and she pegged Sommers as a creep but not a killer.

"So what do we do?" Monica asked. Kelly looked up. Monica was standing on one side of the desk with her arms crossed over her chest. Dr. Stuart was standing on the other side of the room as far away as possible from her.

"I've more or less finished my analysis. If you don't need me anymore, I could catch the train back to Washington tonight," Dr. Stuart said after a pause.

Monica looked sharply at him. "Tonight? But I thought…"

Kelly came to a decision. Until told otherwise, this was still her case. And if she didn't feel as if it was finished, then it was worth investigating further. "No, Dr. Stuart, I need you to stick around for now. Monica, you and I will try to find Danny Smith, or one of the other boys. Let's see if anyone can tell us who Jim was stealing for."

Monica looked visibly relieved to hear that Stuart was staying, and Kelly felt a rush of sympathy for her. Clearly she wasn't as lackadaisical in her feelings for the anthropologist as she'd claimed. "You want to try the flophouse in North Adams again?" Monica asked.

Kelly nodded. "We'll start there. If we don't have any luck I'll call Officer Bennett and ask if he can think of anywhere else to look." Danny Smith hadn't been at the house when the units stopped by the day before, which was starting to worry her. If the case went to trial, he was the sole witness to Sommers's mental state the night of the murder. At the very least she needed to get an official statement from him.

"Maybe someone figured it was cheaper to off Jim than to share the cash. So they mimicked the other killings," Monica said, nodding.

"There's a flaw in that theory," Dr. Stuart pointed out. "The bodies were laid out side by side. Whoever was responsible had to know where the John Doe was buried."

"So that person would know if Sommers really is the killer," Kelly agreed. "All the more reason to find them."

Monica grabbed her purse off a chair. "Sounds good to me. I had nothing planned but a boring barbecue at my friend Syd's house today, anyway. Let's head out."

Danny Smith sank back against the wall and drew his knees in to his chest. The past twenty-four hours had been a nightmare. Cops were stopping by the house every couple of hours now, and it was becoming a huge pain in the ass to dodge them. They'd caught him unawares the first time, grilled him about Jim and the art guy. He'd told them the truth, that the guy had been crazy, waving a gun around, just enough to make them happy so they'd leave him alone. The fact that they kept coming back meant they were looking for more, and he knew better than to give it to them. One thing he'd learned over the years was to keep his head down and let the shit fly over it. There were people out there a hell of a lot scarier than the cops.

With the recent rash of murders most of the other boys had taken off early, hitching rides south to New York or even farther, to South Beach. *Pussies,* he thought to himself. You just had to have your head about you, stick with one of the old assholes you knew. You hooked up with some stranger, you deserved what you got. Not that he would mind being in South Beach right now, he thought wistfully. He'd never been farther south than New Jersey, but he heard Florida was amazing. He'd almost landed a ticket himself, had spent weeks seducing this one trick, only to have him fly the coop in a panic when the cops arrested his buddy. Danny sighed and scratched at his arms. He was jonesing, hard. And it was almost a week until the next Metro night, which would probably be his first chance to hook up with someone else.

Danny felt like shit. The meth had worn off, and he was fully sober for the first time in a few weeks. It was never his favorite state of mind, he preferred being too stoned to think. He was hungry, too, totally starving, and he'd bet there wasn't any food around. He ran a hand through his hair and slumped through the house to the kitchen, picking his way through a maze of stained mattresses, empty soda bottles and fast-food wrappers. He threw open the refrigerator and leaned in. The power was off, and a few empty ice bags had seeped water into the bottom drawer. There was nothing left but a bottle of mustard with a caked film around the top, and a jar of sauerkraut left over from a barbecue some trick had thrown for them a while back. He grabbed the sauerkraut jar and dunked his hand in, drawing out a clump of vinegary strands and stuffing them in his mouth, wincing slightly at the taste but swallowing hard to force them down. He finished the jar in three gulps and wiped his mouth with the back of his hand. That should tide him over until tonight, at least. Maybe he would make a few house calls, see who was left in town and feeling lonely.

There was a knock at the door. He cocked his head to the

side. Couldn't be Jordan, the only other kid left—he would never knock. Probably the cops again. He sidled over to the side window, the one that looked out on the street. There was a cheap sedan parked out front, it had *cop* written all over it. He ducked his head back and dropped to the floor, cursing under his breath.

He stayed low, out of sight of the front window, and frog-walked across the kitchen to the back door. Slipping on a pair of Vans, he eased it open as quietly as possible, just wide enough to slip through. He left it ajar and turned, ready to hop the fence to the neighbor's backyard, when a hand clamped down on his shoulder. He struggled and tried to jerk away, but the hand ground in further, pinching his flesh, and he let out a yelp.

"Easy there, boy. Keep your mouth shut," a low, menacing voice said in his ear. "You and me got some talking to do."

Kelly rapped again, then frowned. She'd sent Monica around back in case the kid tried to bolt through another exit. Maybe he was just hunkered down inside, waiting for them to go away. According to Tony, the bartender at Club Metro, Danny was currently without a sugar daddy, so he should be home. And what a home it was, she thought, cupping a hand around her eyes to peer in the front window. She'd seen crack houses that looked more inviting. The building itself was ramshackle. She hovered carefully on the only two porch floorboards that weren't on the verge of succumbing to termites. Inside, the place was a mess, the only furniture visible a cot mattress and an oily-looking couch that drooped to one side. A small TV console perched on an overturned milk crate in the corner, a wire hanger serving as its antenna. The interior walls were punctured with holes, and piles of trash were dispersed throughout the room like offerings.

Kelly bit her lower lip and debated. This was her last solid lead. If she couldn't track down someone who'd known Jim, she might as well disassemble the task force and head home. Maybe she'd get a chance to enjoy the long weekend after all. Glancing both ways down the street, she leaned in and tried the knob. Locked. "Damn," she muttered. She turned and picked her way to the edge of the porch, hands on her hips.

Monica reappeared and carefully hopped up the stairs. "Doesn't look like anyone's home," she said, stepping carefully past the rotting floorboards.

Kelly nodded but didn't answer. Her eyes were following a kid who had just turned the corner onto the street. His steps slowed when he saw them. With exaggerated nonchalance, he kept going, speeding up as he passed the house. He was good-looking but meth-head skinny, wearing a white tank top and torn khaki shorts. Kelly jerked a head in his direction and Monica nodded.

Kelly started walking briskly toward their car, parked down the street from the house. She saw him glance back over his shoulder as he heard their steps behind them. She kept her eyes down, making a show of sorting through her purse for car keys. When he was about ten feet away, almost at the corner, she broke into a run. "FBI! Stay where you are!" she shouted. Monica matched her step for step.

The kid tried to bolt, but in flip-flops he was no match for them. He got twenty feet before Monica took him down with a flying tackle. He landed with a grunt, rolled over and kicked at her. Monica flipped him facedown and expertly pinned his hands behind him. "Je-sus!" she said, panting a little. "Would you relax, boy? Give an old lady a break."

"The fuck do you want?" he snarled at them.

"We just want to talk to you." Kelly said.

"I don't know nothing," he said sullenly.

"Are you going to behave yourself if I let you up?" Monica asked, "Because honestly, I don't think I have another run in me today. You take off again, I'm just going to have to shoot you, understand?"

He nodded, and she slowly released him. He rolled to a sitting position and rubbed his wrists. "That hurt, yo. I'm calling my lawyer, suing for po-lice bru-tality."

Monica rolled her eyes. "God, am I tired of white kids talking like they grew up in the 'hood."

Kelly knelt down next to him. "Just relax. What's your name?"

He ignored her, picking at a scab on his leg.

She lowered her voice a register as she said, "Don't make the mistake of underestimating me. If you think I can't haul you in for assaulting a police officer, not to mention a federal agent, you are sorely mistaken. And once I get your prints I'm willing to bet I find out everything about you. So why don't you save me the time and trouble."

A corner of the scab came off and a thread of blood trailed down his leg. He rubbed it in with his palm, avoiding her eyes as he said, "Jordan Davenport."

"All right, Jordan. Were you at the house a few nights ago when Jim showed up?"

He shrugged.

"Might as well book him, it's the only way he'll talk," Monica sighed. "C'mon, kid," she said, grabbing one of his arms. "I'm sure you'll be able to find someone to bail you out, right?"

He yanked his arm back. "I wasn't there."

"Yeah? And why should we believe you?" Monica said.

"I got an alibi, guy named Steve. I can take you to his place if you want. I was with him all night."

"You met him at Club Metro?" Kelly asked.

The kid nodded.

"Did you see Jim there?"

The kid shook his head. "Nah, he didn't show."

"This is useless," Monica said. "And he looks like a minor. I say we take him in."

"Whatever." The kid sank lower into the sidewalk. "You won't find out what happened to the crap Jim stole, then."

Monica and Kelly exchanged a look. "You give us a name and an address, I'll not only let you off now, I'll give you a get-out-of-jail-free card for next time," Kelly said.

"Yeah? You can do that?" The kid looked up at her.

"Sure," she said. It was a lie, but she was desperate for information. And who knew, if they got something good here, maybe Doyle could be persuaded to hold up the deal in the future. It was doubtful, but maybe.

"Jim had a guy, someone he dated on and off. Lives over in Williamstown, on Cold Spring Road. Big fuckin' white house, you can't miss it."

"What's his name?" Monica asked.

"Sterling."

"Is that his first or last name?" Kelly asked.

Jordan shrugged. "Dunno. That's all Jim ever called him."

"How do you know that's who Jim sold the art to?" Kelly pressed.

"Danny said so. He was there that night when they met at the house. Said Jim got a shitload of drugs from this guy, and some cash, too." He scratched at his forearm. Raw red track marks dotted his arm from elbow to wrist.

"Where'd Jim go after that?" Kelly asked.

"Danny said he just took off. Figured he didn't want to share. Selfish bastard," Jordan muttered.

"And where's Danny now?" Monica asked.

"What, he wasn't at the house?" He looked puzzled when they shook their heads. "Well shit, I don't know. Maybe he got a date."

A woman approached wheeling a baby buggy down the sidewalk. She took in the scrawny kid on the ground and the two women standing over him, veered down the next driveway and crossed the street. Kelly examined Jordan; he didn't seem to be holding anything back. She debated arresting him just in case it turned out he was bullshitting her. But if she did, they'd have to drop him off at holding before they went to interview this Sterling character, and the paperwork alone would take an hour. "All right, Jordan." She held out a hand to help him up. He took it reluctantly and stood. "We're going to check this out. But if what you're saying turns out to be wrong, or if I find out you tipped this guy off, I'm coming back for you, understood?"

He nodded slowly. "Yeah, sure." He turned and trotted back in the direction of the house.

Monica shook her head. "Think we should have held on to him?"

"I don't think he'll be that hard to track down. Seems like these kids only have a few places to go," Kelly said. "Let's head over to Williamstown, grab some lunch on the way."

As they strolled back to the car, neither of them noticed a truck parked farther down the street in the shade of an elm tree. The driver sat low behind the wheel. He watched through a miniature pair of binoculars as Jordan entered the house, slamming the door behind him. The two women spoke for a minute, looking back toward the house, then got in their car and drove away. His fingers tapped along the steering wheel. He checked his watch, waited five minutes, then got out of the car, slinging a duffel bag over his shoulder as he approached the house.

Sixteen

Danny came to slowly. He was stiff, bleary-eyed, dizzy. He blinked a few times, trying to clear his vision. In the dim lighting, all he could make out was a sea of brown. He realized he was surrounded by pallets of cardboard boxes.

Danny heard a low chuckling and whipped his head around. Seated on a low stack of boxes a few feet away from him, eyes shielded by the bill of a baseball cap, was the creep who had nabbed him. He'd changed out of his uniform. Danny was still pissed at himself, if he'd looked closely he would've realized right away the guy was just a lousy rent-a-cop.

"Damn, you were out cold," the baseball-cap guy said, his voice low and conversational. "Gotta work on that dosage. I didn't figure on knocking you out for so long." He turned his wrist over, examining an enormous watch. "Still got plenty of time, though. Long weekend, so no one'll be here till Tuesday morning."

"Yeah?" Danny carefully eased to a sitting position.

Whatever the guy had given him, it dosed him good, he still felt hazy. His throat was parched, tongue enormous and swollen in his dry mouth. He forced a swallow, deliberating. "I don't do freebies," he said, trying to force some bravado into his voice.

The guy chuckled again, dipped his head lower so his whole face was in shadow. "You got me all wrong, boy."

"So what do you want?" Danny asked. He pulled himself up to a squat, stretching as though he was just trying to get comfortable. He glanced up, trying to gauge where the exit might be, but the whole ceiling was bathed in the same low light.

"Revenge." Baseball Cap said the word slowly, tasting it. Danny repressed a shudder.

"Dude, I've never even, like, seen you before." Danny coughed. "You got the wrong guy."

Baseball Cap shook his head. "I'm not getting revenge on you. You're just part of it. Understand?" He licked his lips. "Well, don't worry. It doesn't really matter either way."

"Yeah, right," Danny said, tensing his muscles in preparation. "Not to you, maybe." He drew in a deep breath and pushed himself off the ground, faking right and veering to the left, aiming for the narrow corridor by the guy's right side. He'd only got a few feet when an indescribable pain shot through him and he dropped to the ground, alternately going rigid and twitching uncontrollably.

Baseball Cap let out a holler. "Hot damn! That worked even better'n I thought it would." He held up an electronic apparatus in one hand. "Taser, police-issue. Just got it in the mail the other day. Damn! You should've seen your face." He laughed, left hand on his hip. "That was a hell of a lot more fun than the raccoon."

"You're not the guy," Danny gasped. "They arrested that guy, he's in jail."

"You're part right." The brim bobbed up and down as he nodded. "The guy they arrested—gotta be honest, I didn't see that coming. I shoved so much dope in him, I'm kind of surprised he survived it." He cocked his head to the side. "Guess since he was knocked out, they figured he done it. Pretty good setup, actually. See, I do that sort of thing without even thinking about it."

He sounded pleased with himself. Danny decided to press the advantage. "But with him in jail, if something happens to me, they'll know he didn't kill anyone."

"Nope, that's true, you got a point there. But I'm not after him. Sick son of a bitch deserves to rot, don't get me wrong, but he's not the big fish. Oh, no." He approached Danny, stopping at his shoulder. With a swift motion he yanked the taser up. Danny yelped as the barbs tore out of his flesh with a wet, ripping sound. He gasped for air, curling into a tight ball. "No, I got me bigger fish to fry."

"So what, you kill me?" Danny said with as much defiance as he could muster. "Go ahead. My life sucks anyway."

"That's 'cause you're queer," Baseball Cap said thoughtfully. "Ain't natural, you know."

"Fuck you," Danny said, kicking out at him.

The guy hopped away, agilely avoiding the blow. "You're a feisty one, ain't you? Not like that other kid, he was hardly any fun at all, too drugged up to feel a thing. Now." He settled down on his haunches and clasped his hands, meeting Danny's eyes. "You're going to help me figure something out."

"Yeah? What?"

"What he gets out of it." The guy picked up a length of cord from on top of the nearest stack of boxes. Danny twisted his head away and closed his eyes in resignation.

"One 'Mighty Mathias' and one...what do you want, Kelly?"

"The 'Richard Chamberlain,'" Kelly said, after perusing the menu.

"Good choice, I usually get that one myself. This is on me," Monica said, flipping open her wallet.

"Thanks." They were in a quaint deli in Williamstown named Pappa Charlie's. It was a student hangout, outdated posters by the door still announced games and dances from the previous semester. Stark wooden booths lined one wall, while opposite an enormous board listed dozens of sandwiches named for celebrities. The heat pressed in on the large plate-glass windows, engaged in a losing battle against the air-conditioning. Kelly ran a hand through her hair and closed her eyes, enjoying the flow of coolness on her skin. It was roasting hot outside. She had her doubts they'd be able to track down this Sterling character; anyone with common sense would be sitting in a pool or by a lake, waiting out the worst of it.

There was a whoosh of hot air as the door swung open. Monica glanced up from her wallet and broke into a wide grin. "Well, as I live and breathe, it's Sam Morgan. How the hell are you, Sam?"

"Hanging in there. How about this heat though, huh?" He smiled at Kelly. She felt herself flushing. "I thought it was supposed to be cooler up here in the hills."

"That's global warming for you." Monica shook her head. "Just gets worse every year."

"I suppose. How's the investigation going?" Sam asked. "I hear through the grapevine you've got someone in custody?"

Monica started to answer, but Kelly discreetly grabbed her elbow. "Sorry, we can't really say either way."

"Sure, I understand." He smiled at the girl behind the counter and said, "I'll have the 'Paltrow.'"

"Wife and kids still out of town, huh?" Monica noted.

He shrugged nonchalantly, but Kelly thought she detected a flash of something behind his eyes. "Swim meet. 'Fraid I'm on my own again this weekend."

Monica shook her head. "I dunno, Sam. Good-lookin' guy like yourself, I'm surprised your wife leaves you alone as much as she does."

He laughed heartily. "Easy, Monica, you're making me blush." His eyes slid along to Kelly. "I tell you, though, part of me misses tromping through the woods all day looking for body parts. It killed a hell of a lot of time. So what are you ladies up to this weekend? Kicking back a bit, I hope?"

"The usual, Sam. Big barbecue with my kid, nothing special."

"What about you, Agent Jones?" He smiled at her.

Nice eyes, she thought before catching herself. She shrugged with exaggerated nonchalance. "No real plans."

"Tell you what, you really need to check out the Appalachian Trail. I can point you to some sections that are absolutely unbelievable, if you have the time…"

His voice practically hummed with enthusiasm. Kelly smiled back at him in spite of herself. "That would be nice. I haven't been hiking in a long time."

Sam tilted his head to one side. "You look like you're about my wife's size. If you want I could lend you some of her gear. You'll definitely need a good pair of boots, and a pack—"

"Jones!"

Kelly swiveled automatically toward the familiar voice.

The figure standing in the doorway was silhouetted by the bright sun. She squinted slightly, then her eyes widened as she took in the man blocking the light. His face split into a wide grin as he strode forward.

"Jake?" She said. "What're you…"

"You're not an easy woman to track down," he said as he grabbed hold of her and spun her in a half circle. As he set her back down, she was uncomfortably aware of the others watching them.

She took a small step back and gestured toward him. "Monica and Sam, this is Jake Riley. We worked together on a case, about a year ago."

"Did you now?" Monica commented knowingly as she looked Jake up and down. "Must've been some case."

"It was. Nice to meet you," Jake said, shaking hands all around.

Kelly smiled thinly in response. It had been a hell of a case, the one that killed her partner. It still gave her nightmares from time to time—dark tunnels filled with the sound of beating wings. "How'd you find me?" she asked, raising an eyebrow at him. "I thought that since we canceled the trip, you were booked until mid-September."

"Dmitri decided to visit a…friend. And anything I could have done for him would have been redundant," he replied, measuring his words. Jake was the security chief for Greek shipping magnate Dmitri Christou, one of the wealthiest men in the world. Kelly knew Jake's verbal codes and guessed what he was referring to. Since his daughter's death a year earlier, Dmitri had become more involved in charitable causes. He'd spent the past year cultivating partnerships with various political circles to further his agendas. He was a close friend of the U.S. president, and frequently vacationed with him. What Jake was really saying was that with the Secret Service around, Dmitri didn't need any extra protection. "So I found myself with a little time on my hands. And since you were only a short drive away, I thought I'd surprise you. So here I am!"

"Yeah, but how did you find me here, at this sandwich shop?" Kelly asked, puzzled.

Monica nodded. "I was going to ask the same thing. You some kind of psychic?"

"That was just dumb luck. I was driving around looking for this little B and B I'd heard about, and decided to stop for lunch when I passed this place. Then I looked through the window, and recognized this gorgeous head of hair." He wound a finger through a coil of it affectionately. Kelly felt herself flush bright red.

Sam Morgan picked a bag off the counter. "Well, I should be going. Nice meeting you, Jake. Hope you enjoy your stay."

He looked a little crestfallen, Kelly noticed. She waved goodbye to him, then turned to find Jake eyeing her. "Wasn't interrupting anything, was I?"

Before she could answer, Monica chimed in, "Sam's a married man, you can relax about that. But looking the way you do, you probably don't waste much time worrying, huh?"

Jake laughed out loud. "I like your new friend, Jones. So Berkshire P.D. said you were off duty." He clapped his hands together. "How about we take the sandwiches and go have a picnic somewhere?" Monica and Kelly exchanged a glance. He rolled his eyes. "Based on that look, I'm guessing I was misinformed."

"We're on our way to question someone."

"Ah, I see. So that news piece I heard on the way over, about a suspect in custody—"

"There are a few more things I need to look into," Kelly interrupted him.

"I don't doubt it. You're nothing if not thorough," Jake said with genuine affection in his voice. "I hope it doesn't take too long, though. Driving through here reminded me a lot of Vermont. You remember Vermont, don't you, Jones?"

She flushed a deeper red and resisted the urge to whack him on the arm. Monica was grinning widely, clearly enjoying this exchange. Kelly cleared her throat and said, "Why don't you check into the B and B, I'll call your cell when we're finished."

He nodded. "It's a date." He bent down to kiss her. She turned her head so that it landed on her cheek, not her mouth. "That's right, you're on duty," he said, straightening up and sounding a little wounded. "I'll catch you later, Jones."

She grabbed the bag with their sandwiches and headed for the door with Monica in tow. The heat of the day hit her like a slap. Sweat trickled down her back as she settled into the hot leather interior of the car.

Monica turned the key in the ignition which, after a hot gasp, issued a stream of cold air. She shook her head as she looked at Kelly. "Damn. You practically set a land speed record running away from what is, if you don't mind my saying, a damned fine male specimen."

"We're friends," Kelly said weakly.

"Wish I had a friend like that." Monica chuckled. "I sure hope this Sterling character is at home. I wouldn't want to keep your Jake waiting."

Seventeen

He drove around idly, without noticing any of the tree-lined streets that swept past his window. He was back in a residential area, just across the state border in Vermont. He was supposed to be picking up lunch downtown, but had been too restless to go home and face his family. His wife would give him a look, but she knew better than to say anything.

This section of Vermont, south of Bennington, was pastoral, filled with rolling hills and farmland. He'd almost bought a place here years earlier, but the garage had been located too close to the house to suit his purposes. Vermont was a little liberal for his taste anyway, still full of tree-hugging hippies. Not that he had a gripe with them, he just preferred a different crowd, and his wife was much more at home with the country club set. He chuckled at the thought of her in Birkenstocks and a peasant skirt; no, they'd made the right decision buying in Williamstown and keeping their place in Manhattan so that the girls could get a decent education. And Massachusetts, Vermont and New York all shared a common trait that factored into his decision: the death penalty was still illegal in all three states. Of course, the recent involvement of the FBI threw a kink in the works. In retrospect, crossing state lines to dump the bodies had been a mistake. It left him vulnerable to the federal death penalty statute, which could override any state charges. Not that he planned on getting caught.

He slowed to a stop, took a right, changed his mind and executed a slow U-turn. His eyes were sore, he examined them in the rearview mirror: red and raw. He looked as worn-out as he felt, the past week had taken a toll on him, affecting his sleep. He'd tried napping earlier, but was too wound up, still enraged that someone was interfering with his hobby. It was hot outside, stifling, but his best ideas always came to him in the car. He slowed and motioned for a family to cross the street. They smiled and waved at him, and he mechanically flashed a grin and a wave in return. The kid with them was about eleven years old. He clutched a melting Popsicle, streaks of purple juice ran down his face and hands. The man's expression hardened as he watched the boy slurping away, his grip tightening on the steering wheel. Filthy little monster. His toe danced over the accelerator, tempted to bear down. He could say that it was an accident, that his foot slipped off the pedal for just a moment. He let his mind wander into the fantasy, saw the boy's startled expression as he hit the fender and glanced up into the windshield, saw his mouth open in a little O as he soared past, blood already pouring down the young forehead. He saw the lifeless body in his rearview mirror as he fixed an expression of horror and concern on his face and shifted the car into Park.

The boy stepped onto the curb to his left, breaking his

reverie. His lifted his hand in a small wave and drove on with a pang of regret. It wouldn't do, especially not now. No, he had to conserve his resources. He'd been racking his brain, trying to figure out who was messing with him, and why. Any good citizen would have simply reported him to the police, so he was dealing with something else, someone more like him. *No, not like him,* he thought with a flash of rage. He was unique, the things he did, the way he did them...he was an artist while all of his contemporaries were bumbling hacks. Which brought him back to his nemesis. Who had he pissed off, and pissed off badly enough that they'd mount this campaign against him?

He dismissed co-workers, both past and present; none of them had any imagination. Same went for most of the other people in his life, they were all dull to a fault. He ran through the roster of names over and over, but kept coming up empty. He turned right at the next corner and circled the block. The family that had passed him earlier was still walking down the sidewalk. The father wore one of those idiotic American flag shirts, all the more reason to eliminate his progeny, he thought with a sneer. Suddenly he froze, realization dawning. If he was right, he knew exactly who was exposing his hobby. A smile spread across his face as he backed the car into a driveway, flipped it around and headed toward town. He'd tell his family that he was late with lunch thanks to a flat tire. Later, after they'd eaten, he'd retire to his study to plan his revenge.

Sterling Evans leaned back against the door frame and regarded them idly. Dressed in a sheer cotton robe that swung open to reveal a tight, brightly colored designer swimsuit, he was all angles: pointy chin, sharp elbows, knobby knees. And yet somehow his movements were graceful, full of self-contained power. He reminded her of a cat, Kelly thought to herself, a lean Siamese. And truth be told, she wasn't much of a cat person.

The house was exactly as Jordan had described it, large and sprawling, a suburban version of Monticello. It was also located in Williamstown, not far from where Sommers lived, maybe a half mile at the most. This house was slightly smaller but no less impressive. Judging by the Maserati parked in the driveway, Sterling Evans had done well for himself. Air-conditioning leaked out the open doorway.

Evans yawned again and extended one arm up in a luxurious stretch. "Interrupting my siesta like this, y'all better have a warrant," he said in a limpid drawl.

"Don't see why we'd need one, Mr. Evans," Kelly said firmly, taking a small step forward across the threshold. "Your name came up in the course of an investigation. We're just here to confirm what we were told by a witness."

"A witness, huh?" he said, languidly eyeing her feet. "Well, if you're just here for a friendly chat, I don't see why those god-awful flats need to enter my foyer. One piece of advice, dearie," he said, leaning forward. "Those shoes just scream discount. Next time, get thee to Saks. I'll give you the name of my personal shopper. He can try to save you from yourself."

Kelly repressed a flash of rage. He smiled snidely at her, clearly pleased to have gotten under her skin.

"Well, aren't you something else?" Monica said. "A thief with an eye for fashion."

"I don't know what you're referring to, but if you want some style pointers, I'd be happy to oblige," he said with a sneer.

"You believe this guy?" Monica said. "Like he's anything other than a goddamn pusher."

He clucked disapprovingly. "Dear God, the two of you are just like Cagney and Lacey, aren't you?" He lowered his voice and leaned forward. "Here's the thing, ladies. One more nasty word out of either of you and I'm closing the door and handing you over to my lawyer. He's an awful prick, I'm afraid, and terribly inaccessible. Unless I'm mistaken he's in P-town for the long weekend. With this heat, who knows when he'll be back? And I'm betting you wouldn't want that, would you?"

Kelly gritted her teeth. "We just need a few minutes of your time, Mr. Evans. May we come in?"

He examined a nail, frowned and said, "I just had the floors done, wouldn't want them sullied. I'm sure you understand. Now, who gave you my name?"

"A young man named Jordan Davenport."

He tapped a finger against his chin and gazed toward the upper branches of the sycamore tree that sheltered his front lawn. "Lemme see now, Jordan…sounds familiar, but I just can't match it to a face."

"He claims you might know something about some stolen art," Kelly said, watching him closely.

His eyebrows shot up. "Did he now? Well, I'm sure I don't know any young men unkind enough to slander my good name."

"Really. This is a nice place you got here, Mr. Evans." Kelly arched her neck to peer past him. "When did you buy it?"

"Oh, let's see…a few years back," he responded, eyeing her cautiously.

Monica let out a low whistle. "Whew, at the height of the market. Must've set you back, what, a cool mill?"

"My mama always said only the poor discuss money." Evans waved a hand as if dismissing a gnat.

"So you were born with money, then?" Kelly asked conversationally. He didn't respond, instead examining a fingernail. "Mr. Evans, would you like another peek at my badge? Let me remind you that FBI means I can find out pretty much anything I want about you in under an hour, down to your favorite teacher in grammar school and how your first dog died." She lowered her voice another notch. "After all, we've received a tip that you act as a middleman for stolen artwork, which is frequently used as currency by arms dealers and terrorists. Perhaps you've heard of the Patriot Act? If you'd prefer, I could place a hold on all of your accounts while forensic accountants go over them with a fine-tooth comb to make sure there aren't any inconsistencies."

His lip curled up as he grimaced at her. "Well now, that's not very civil, is it?"

"It's hot out here, Mr. Evans. And I'm getting tired of standing on your porch in my cheap shoes. Either we come in and you answer a few of our questions, or I make it my personal mission to overturn every stone in your life." Kelly cocked her head to the side. "And by the looks of you, I'm guessing there's a whole quarry to deal with."

He stood defiant for another second, eyes darting across the lawn. Abruptly, he stepped to the side and swung the door open. Kelly breezed past, Monica following with satisfaction on her face.

The foyer was dark and cool. From it a hallway comprised of alternating blocks of black and white marble led past leafy ferns and artwork.

Kelly looked at it appraisingly. "There's some nice stuff

here. Of course you have the necessary papers of provenance, proving you acquired it all legally?"

He eased past them and shut a door on the left. "Somewhere," he said airily.

Evans continued down the hall. Kelly stopped and opened the door he'd just shut. He stopped dead in his tracks, hands on his hips. "Excuse me, missy, what are you doing?"

"Looking for the bathroom," she said with a small smile. The door had opened into a dining room. An ornate stainless-steel and glass table stood in stark contrast to the Colonial style of the house. Evans's taste ran to postmodern, she noted; the rug was a plush interlay of black and white circles, the candlesticks were straight steel rods, the lighting fixtures were a mass of tangled black wire.

"Bathroom is down the hall," he grumbled, pushing past her.

"Something you don't want me to see in here, Mr. Evans? The Mapplethorpe, maybe?"

He shrugged. "I don't know why you'd say that."

Monica rolled her eyes. "Man, you must have stock in the bullshit factory."

"Here's the thing, Mr. Evans." Kelly approached the photo and examined it closely. It showed a female bodybuilder in profile, flexing. A dark veil shadowed her features. "I have two dead boys, and I'm guessing they both knew you. This looks like the Mapplethorpe photo our first victim, Randy Jacobs, stole from Calvin Sommers. And I have a witness who saw you in the company of Jim Costello the night he died— making you the last person to see him alive. So I've got stolen artwork, drugs and arguments about money. As far as I'm concerned, you've pretty much made my case for me."

"If you could prove any of that, you'd already have arrested me," Evans responded sullenly. Kelly noticed his accent had evaporated. He now spoke in the hard flat tones of the Midwest.

"Honestly, Mr. Evans, I don't have to. I could haul you down right now, lock you up for the long weekend—did I mention the air-conditioning is on the fritz at intake?—and as you said, your lawyer is unreachable. You and I would have a lot of time to get to know one another. But I don't think that'll be necessary," Kelly said.

Monica leaned back against the wall, arms crossed over her chest, smiling slightly.

"Why not?" he said after a moment.

"Because though you're definitely a scumball, you don't strike me as a killer. You're the type that hates getting dirt under his nails," Kelly said pointedly. "So we're going to sit down and have a little chat about everything that happened the last time you saw Jim. And if I'm satisfied after that, you can get back to your siesta." She pulled a steel chair with a black leather backrest out from the table and settled into it, then looked up at him and arched an eyebrow.

He shifted from foot to foot for a moment. All his calm had vanished; now he was a bundle of nervous energy. He twitched once, then started to pull out a chair opposite her. Kelly held up a hand before he sat down. "You know, now that I think of it, I'd just love a nice tall glass of iced tea. Doesn't that sound good, Lieutenant?"

Monica nodded as she pulled out the chair next to Kelly. "That sure would hit the spot."

"Would you mind, Mr. Evans?" Kelly tilted her head to the side and smiled sweetly, easing out of her shoes as she did so and digging her bare feet into the plush pile of the carpet. "What a gorgeous rug. Silk?"

Without answering, he spun and stormed out of the room.

"You are a bad, bad girl," Monica said, shaking her head.

Kelly grinned back at her. "Hey, he's getting what he deserves."

"For the record—" Monica nodded toward her feet "—I like those shoes.

"Thanks." Kelly wiggled her toes reflectively. "I got them on sale."

Through red-rimmed eyes Calvin Sommers followed a fly's progress as it idly circled a strip of sticky paper dangling from a corner of his cell. It lit on the ceiling next to the strip, rubbed its tiny legs together then took off again, bobbing closer and closer to the trap. It landed a second time, a third…on the eighth landing it ended up squarely on the paper. The yellow strip fluttered slightly, the fly's exertions becoming progressively more feeble with each passing moment. As the movement stilled, Calvin squeezed his eyes shut and rolled over on his side to face the wall.

Jail had been exactly how he'd pictured it, back when his father threatened to send him there if he didn't stop his nasty proclivities. His parents had painted a vivid picture, and it was all there: the toilet—your most intimate moments exposed; the scrawny pallet that passed for a mattress; the cinder-block walls. The heat was stifling. The deputy who had delivered his breakfast had mumbled something about broken air-conditioning. The pile of mice feces in the corner was a nice touch, he ruminated, something even he couldn't have imagined.

Calvin had barely slept the night before, trapped in this Kafka-esque nightmare. He regretted every drug he'd ever

taken, every boy he'd invited home. He'd sat there at the ar-
raignment feeling the weight of all those eyes upon him—
people who were convinced he'd done horrible things to a
mere child. Consumed with guilt, Calvin had refused to allow
his attorney to petition for bail. Jim was in the ground because
of him, he reasoned. He deserved to be here, deserved to
suffer every single day. As soon as he could, he'd accept a
plea. He'd probably die in jail, he speculated, and wondered
how it would go down. Would he be pummeled to death by
scores of jeering inmates, or stabbed with a shiv as he stood
in line at dinner?

Calvin kept going over that night in his head, again and
again. In his mind's eye he could see the small trail of blond
fuzz over Jim's upper lip, the way his shorts hung low to
reveal the top of his hips. A tear trickled through his eyelids.
He'd cared for the boy, in his own way. Why was it that
everyone he cared for seemed determined to screw him over?

Jim had been so full of life, it seemed impossible that he
was dead. And somehow, Calvin himself had done it. He was
sure of it, deep in the recesses of his mind he caught fleeting
glimpses of Jim's dead eyes staring up at him. He had been
curled up in the back seat of his car, it was pitch-black outside,
and the radio was blaring some classic rock tune.

Suddenly, Calvin frowned and sat up. Why the hell had
the radio been playing that? Jim only listened to modern
bands, the names of which Calvin could never keep straight.
And he only played jazz. Strange. Had there been someone
else there? But who? Calvin closed his eyes and went over
what he did remember. He'd been angry. He'd grabbed the
gun, loaded it and gotten in his car. Drove directly to the
horrible place Jim had taken him to once. That's when he'd

asked the boy to come stay with him, because the thought of his blond Adonis in that hovel was too unsettling.

But Jim hadn't been there. Danny, the boy with the permanent sneer, said he'd already gone. It wasn't until the little shit was staring down the barrel of the gun clasped in Calvin's shaking hands that he'd given an address. He'd also offered a blow job or some drugs in exchange for not getting shot.

But had he accepted any drugs? Calvin shook his head, hard. He wouldn't have done that, he'd been too angry and would have wanted to keep his head straight. Calvin strained to remember more details. He recalled more driving, then he'd parked outside a house with darkened windows and a long driveway—a large, white house, one of the new ones built to look old. He'd snuck up, glanced inside...and then his mind went blank, it was as though someone had erased every other memory from that night. Except for the flashes of him, and Jim, in the car...

Calvin leaned against the wall and drew his knees up to his chest, feet on the edge of the cot. For the first time since this whole nightmare began, he felt a rising certainty that he might be innocent, that he hadn't murdered Jim in a drug-fueled rage. Like his lawyer had said, they hadn't found any signs of a struggle—none of his skin or hair was under Jim's nails. There was nothing other than Jim's blood on his shirt. But, in his entire life, he'd never been able to hurt anyone—even that time he hit a deer with his car he'd wept for weeks afterward. Plus he rarely took any drugs other than pot, the few times he'd tried one of the pills the boys were always offering he'd ended up nauseous and paranoid. No, he'd been drugged, and it had not been voluntary.

Calvin's jaw tightened with resolve, and he stood and

marched to the cell door. "Hey!" he shouted, loud enough for the cop down the hall to hear him. "Get my lawyer, I need to talk to him."

Doyle stormed down the hallway in a foul mood. He should've been on the deck of his boat right now, nice cold beer tucked into his hand. Hell, after the last few weeks he deserved it. He'd had that goddamn FBI bitch riding his ass until it was black-and-blue. Now they had the killer in custody, so there was no reason for him to be walking through the Berkshire State Police barracks. And yet here he was.

Doyle blew through a set of double doors, turned a corner, and nodded sharply for the guy inside the booth to buzz him in. He marched down the row and stopped in front of Sommers's cell. Hands on his hips, he glared inside. "The fuck you want?" he snarled.

The irritating old faggot stared at him calmly, hands clasped in front of his crotch. "I'd like to see my lawyer."

"It's a holiday weekend, numb-nut, there's not a lawyer in the world working."

"I believe mine will, at the rate I'm paying him," Sommers replied.

Doyle looked him up and down; this was a completely different person from the blubbering jerkoff they'd interviewed yesterday. All the panic and despair was gone, replaced by a preternatural calm. Doyle's lips tightened. "Nothing says I have to get your lawyer just 'cause you asked for him," he said, voice low.

"Maybe not, but I'd hate to file a complaint with the oversight board about the conditions here." He pointed to the corner. "After all, with mice feces, you never know. I could say the Berkshire State Police knowingly exposed me to the hantavirus."

Doyle tried to stare him down, but the guy wasn't budging. After a moment, he spun on his heel and stalked back down the hall. As he passed the booth again and waited for the door to be buzzed open, he rapped against the glass. "Call that dickhead's liar," Doyle ordered, deliberately mispronouncing the word. He hated lawyers, didn't understand how anyone could devote their careers to keeping scumbags out of jail. Hell, if he had his way the death penalty would not only be legal, it would be mandatory for all three-strikers.

Back at his desk Doyle threw himself into the chair and spun in a slow circle, rubbing his jaw with one hand. He'd just known this was too good to be true. In his gut he'd sensed that having a suspect in hand and the task force on the verge of being dismantled was too much to hope for. Now it looked like there was a wrench in the works. He ran a hand through his hair and chewed on the corner of his lip. It was nerve-racking, having those women always peering over his shoulder. Every day he showed up for work with his heart in his throat, convinced that they'd figured things out. These past few days he'd gotten a brief reprieve, but if Sommers got out of jail and they kept digging, it would only be a matter of time until he was discovered. He inhaled deeply, a trickle of sweat rolling down his face. He'd have to do everything in his power to prevent that from happening.

Eighteen

"You sure you don't want to take a turn?" Zach asked, holding up the spatula.

Jake waved his hands in the air in protest. "Absolutely not. One thing I've learned in life, you never mess with another man's grill."

Zach flushed slightly, obviously pleased that Jake referred to him as a man. Kelly noted it and smiled.

"Don't you burn mine, Beenie!" Monica called out from her post in a plastic lounge chair. "You know how I like it—"

"I know, I know. Knock off its horns and wipe its ass," Zach retorted.

"You don't say." Jake raised an eyebrow. "Sounds to me like there's a fellow Texan in the house."

Monica raised her margarita in a toast. "Yessirree, Amarillo born and bred. Yourself?"

"Austin."

"Ah, Moscow-on-the-Brazos." Monica nodded her head in satisfaction. "Nice town. You know if I hadn't met my husband, that's where I was headed myself."

"Really?" Jake grinned and crossed the lawn toward her.

Kelly watched as he settled into the chaise longue next to Monica and they compared notes on their Southwestern childhoods. She tilted a beer bottle to her lips and half closed her eyes. The heat of the day before had eased up. It was Sunday, and they were in Monica's backyard grilling burgers. The lawn was dotted with patches of wildflowers, all shaded by overgrown elms. Kelly inhaled deeply, relishing the smell of roasting meat and freshly cut grass.

A screen door slammed and their heads all turned. Dr. Stuart stood awkwardly holding a casserole dish. He gestured behind him with a thumb. "No one answered the bell, and the door was open. I hope it's okay that I came in."

"Howie!" Monica squealed, vaulting off her chair and striding forward to meet him. "You made it!"

"I brought a vegan casserole." He held up the platter. "I know everyone else probably eats meat, but I figured—"

"I'm sure it's delicious." Monica grabbed his arm and steered him toward the weathered red picnic table. "Here, let me grab you a drink. Beer or margarita?"

Kelly noticed that Zach was suddenly very focused on the sizzling burgers, a frown marring his features. She stepped forward and joined him. "Those look great. Can I help out?"

Without meeting her eyes he shook his head. She stood there awkwardly for another moment, uncertain what to say, then went to join Jake. He opened his arms, signaling for her to sit between his legs. After a moment's hesitation, she obliged. "You're sure this chair can hold both of us?" she said in a low voice, feeling the plastic weave strain under their weight.

"Hell, I'm not sure of anything." He nuzzled her hair affectionately. "But if it breaks I'm totally blaming you."

She punched his arm in retaliation. He grabbed her hand and kissed it, then pulled her in so she was settled against her chest. "I missed you, Jones," he murmured into her hair.

She sighed and let herself relax. "Yeah, me too."

"Yeah? 'Cause sometimes it doesn't seem like it," he said casually. "I mean, hell, we've been together for almost a year now. But your partner over there didn't know you had a boyfriend?"

"We agreed to keep it casual," she said in a low voice.

"I know. That's getting tough, though." He put a hand under her chin and gently turned her head so she was looking in his eyes. "I'm getting to where being half a world apart is too hard. I want to spend more than just a few days here and there with you."

"Can we talk about this later?" she murmured.

"Yeah, sure." He touched her cheek gently, then took a sip of beer and shook his head. "Jeez, you're right, I'm sorry. I don't know—I swear, something about being with you turns me into a chick."

"A chick?" She raised an eyebrow.

He held up a hand defensively. "I mean that in the best possible way, of course."

"Of course." She smiled.

"You two are something else. Miss Kelly, I still can't believe you never mentioned this hunk of a man you were hiding." Kelly turned and shaded her eyes with one hand, blinking. Monica was standing over them, margarita glass clasped in one hand. She was wearing a pair of khaki shorts and a Vermont PD T-shirt. Kelly noticed that today she'd taken the time to put on some makeup. If she wasn't mistaken, Monica had curled the ends of her hair, too.

"See, Kelly? Someone appreciates me," Jake said sotto voce.

Kelly ignored him. "Jake's not around very much."

"Oh." There was a moment of awkward silence. Jake cleared his throat. "So, Monica, what did you think about this Evans character?"

"You mean, did I believe his story?" She arched an eyebrow, and her eyes flicked toward Kelly. "I think Kelly's right, he doesn't have the cojones to have killed the boys. He'd let someone else do it, especially if it helped him out somehow. But I can't see him doing it himself."

"But saying that the boy was downstairs when he went to bed, then he woke up and the kid was gone…" Jake's tone was skeptical.

"I know." Kelly shifted uncomfortably. "It sounded sketchy. But what were we supposed to do?"

"You could've arrested him," Jake pointed out.

Kelly shook her head. "What, when we've already got another guy in custody for the same crime? Doyle would've blown a gasket if he'd known we were even talking to Evans."

"So what if he bolts?" Jake asked.

"I don't think he will, we didn't give him any reason to. And we'll keep digging next week, see if we can turn up anything else on him." When Jake raised an eyebrow, she bit her lip in frustration. "What, you think you could've gotten more out of him?"

"Oh, I have my ways," he said. A slow smile spread across his face, then halted when he caught her expression. "Easy, Jones, I'm just yanking your chain."

She pushed herself off the chaise longue with both hands as she muttered, "I'm going to get another beer."

"Have a margie, honey, you deserve it!" Monica called after her. "They're nice and strong, I made 'em myself."

"Burgers are done!" Zach called out.

"About time!" Monica clapped her hands together. "All right, everyone, help yourselves. Kelly, while you're at it pour me another, and make it a double."

The kid gasped as water seeped through the cellophane layers wrapped around his face, exposing only his mouth. The slow, steady stream of water coursed down, dribbling onto the board he was strapped to before landing on the concrete floor where it pooled in a filthy puddle. Dwight stood over him with a watering can, keeping one eye on his watch as he poured. When the boy choked, spitting up water, he eased up, slowing the stream to a trickle before abruptly stopping. The boy gasped for air between choking coughs. Dwight settled back on his haunches, surveying him with interest.

"What's the problem?" he said jovially. "You said you were thirsty."

The kid didn't respond. He'd stopped talking a few hours ago. It was interesting, watching him go through the stages, Dwight thought. For a long time he'd maintained an attitude, like he really didn't give a shit. Dwight had been impressed in spite of himself. For a little faggot, the kid was pretty tough. But once he started in with the phosphoric acid from the railroad hobby store, the blubbering and screams had finally come. In all honesty, he hadn't been crazy about that part himself. When it burned the kid's flesh it made a disgusting smell, and pouring it while wearing heavy rubber fishing gloves was tough. He'd come close to spilling some of it on himself. Plus he was a little worried about getting the stench out of the warehouse. He'd have to come up with a way to air the place out before Tuesday, when the day shift showed up for work. No, so far the water boarding had definitely been his favorite.

Dwight wondered if the Captain ever bothered with acid or anything like that. Despite all the hours he'd spent watching the Captain crawl in and out of the hatch, he'd never gotten a chance to see him in action; just saw the aftermath when he dug the boys up. And by that point it was hard to tell what had been done to them, they were such a mess.

He straightened and left the kid's side, strode a few feet to a small stack of boxes and picked up a sheaf of papers from on top. He shuffled through them, squinting to see. He'd brought in a camping lantern, which helped a bit, but the lighting was still dim for reading.

"All right, let's see," he said to himself, flipping the pages over one at a time. "Done that one there, and this one." He frowned as he read the next page, then glanced over at the kid and said conversationally, "They got one here about sodomizing with a baton, but I think you might like that too much. Kind of defeats the point." On the Internet he'd found a list of the different interrogation techniques used at military prisons for enemy combatants, like at Abu Ghraib. Not that he had anything to ask the kid, but it couldn't hurt to practice. That way, when he got to Langley and the higher-ups found out he already knew how to treat those damn ragheads, they might rush him through training. He kept flipping pages, then his eyes brightened. "Hot damn, almost forgot about this one."

He put the papers down, came back to the kid and bent over him. "You stay put, I'll be right back." He turned on his heel and vanished into the depths of the warehouse.

* * *

Danny waited, naked and shivering in just a pair of shorts. He was strapped to a board that rested at a forty-five-degree angle, so his head was below his feet. The water was frigid, droplets of it pooled on his sunken stomach. He listened, straining his ears. The cellophane wrapped around his face was horrible, smothering. He'd always been claustrophobic anyway, hated elevators, but this was so much worse. He couldn't imagine what the guy was going to do next, so far everything had been increasingly horrible. He tried to wriggle his hands and feet again, but they'd lost feeling a long time ago. His hands were bound together above his head, feet taped to the top of the slant.

Danny lifted his head up, flexing his stomach muscles, feeling the water run down his sides. The board rocked slightly as he did. He cocked his head to the side then, using his shoulders and hips, rocked to his right. The board followed his movement slightly, whatever the guy had propped it on wasn't very stable. He strained his whole body now, tilting from one side to the other, the board moving with him until with a heavy thud it slid off the support and he landed on his side, hands and feet still strapped to the board. He lay there, gasping. *Shit, if only he could see.* The barest trace of light filtered through the layers of plastic binding his eyes. *What now?* he thought.

He heard a sound in the depths of the warehouse and felt a ball of panic rush from his belly to his throat, further constricting his breathing. *Calm the fuck down,* he told himself. His shoulder sank a few inches into the puddle formed by all the water that asshole had poured over him. He groped with his hands, trying to feel for something that might cut the tape, but they were lashed to the board too high off the ground to reach anything. The puddle he was lying in felt pretty deep, though. Not that a puddle would do him any good, no chance the duct tape was just going to melt away.

Danny was overcome by a sense of futility. His whole fucking life had been nothing but a waste. And now, the end of it was going to be spent entertaining this sick fuck. He had no idea how much time had passed, it felt like days but the guy kept going on about how much time they still had, how much more he was going to do to him. And the asshole kept whistling the melody from Tom Petty's "American Girl"—the same refrain over and over like a skipping CD. It was driving him fucking batty.

Danny debated, lying there with so few options. His skin felt like it was on fire from the acid the guy poured over him, punctuated by cigarette burns, and his lungs hurt from coughing. He hadn't thought anyone could be as mean as his pa when it came to hurting him; turns out he'd been wrong. Fighting it any longer hardly seemed worth the trouble. By the end of this he'd be dead anyway, it was just a question of what would be done to him meanwhile. It wasn't like the movies, where he suddenly realized he had something sharp in his hand and could cut the tape and escape, or some shit like that. No, he knew for certain he was going to die sometime in the next few days, after this sick fuck checked off whatever else was on his list. When it came down to it, he really only had one option.

Making his decision, Danny leaned back, felt the board follow him, then strained his head forward with all his might until he flipped forward, the weight of the board pressing down, forcing his face into the puddle. His body fought reflexively for a few minutes, trying to lift his head out of the water, but the board forced him back under. Finally, his struggles stilled.

Dwight came around the tiers of boxes, talking to himself. "Goddamn, had a hard time finding this, stowed it away in a completely different bag…paid a hell of a lot of money for it, too, supposed to deliver more'n fifty volts…" His voice trailed off as he took in the scene. He darted forward, grabbed a corner of the board and lifted, flipping it back. The kid's mouth was gaping, the visible parts of his face already an unnatural color.

Dwight ducked his head down, listened for breathing, then dropped the board and sank back into a crouch. "Well, I'm not gonna give you CPR, you fuckin' faggot, if that's what you wanted," he muttered angrily. "Fuckin' waste of space that you are, couldn't even follow the goddamn plan." He raised the belt he was holding in one hand and spit out, "I spent a month's fuckin' salary on this, asshole!"

Dwight settled back so he was sitting on the floor, legs crossed. He glared at the boy for a few minutes. *Bet nothing like this ever happened in Abu Ghraib,* he thought, reaching into his pocket and drawing out three pennies. He proceeded to shift them through his fingers, one after the other, shuffling them with his thumb and middle finger until he felt himself calming down. *Nope, that's why you needed a full unit to deal with these bastards, going it alone was too tough.* He idly wondered how the Captain did it, and with so many of them. Of course, he had a better place to keep them, Dwight reminded himself. Wasn't like he was in a warehouse and had to keep stuff stored in bags all the way at the other end. Once, when the Captain was out of town, Dwight had snuck down to see the setup for himself. If he had a place like that, something like this would never have happened.

Standing, Dwight brushed off the seat of his pants and shrugged. "Fuck it," he said with resignation. "I got a barbecue to go to anyhow." He pointed at the kid. "I'll be back to deal with you later."

Nineteen

Simon Wentzel ducked low under some branches, stepping carefully to avoid the dry crackle of twigs snapping under his feet. It was in his sights now, just a few feet away. He shifted into a crouch, lowering himself down one inch at a time until he was settled on one knee. He felt his breathing slow as he zeroed in on his target. He'd been waiting years for this, it was hard to believe he was finally so close that he actually had the object of his obsession in his sights.

His movements were so measured as to be almost undetectable, like a plant arcing up to sunlight. Even though inside a voice screamed, *For God's sake, hurry up before you miss the opportunity,* he forced himself to maintain his composure, to raise the binoculars one millimeter at a time until they were finally at his eyes, to carefully shift his index finger over the focus button, twisting with infinite care until the zoom was adjusted and the picture suddenly leaped into focus. In spite of himself he let out a gasp. His gut had been right, he'd known it. On reflection, the day had felt special from the moment he awoke. En route to the park he'd seen a heron in midflight, silhouetted against the waning moon—an auspicious omen. Then his car was the first in the lot, always a good sign. And the morning air was already perfect, warm and laden with jasmine. The promise of a gorgeous sunrise lurked in the shades of crimson seeping up the tree branches.

Simon's chest swelled as he observed his prey. His body started to ache. Crouching in this position was hell on his artificial hip, but right now he didn't give a damn. He watched, riveted, as his target lowered its head, eyeing the ground carefully. He eased the binoculars back down, slowly, slowly, maintaining his focus as he did so. Pacing himself, he edged his right hand across his vest to the left side, holding his breath, issuing a silent prayer that he'd get to it in time. As he withdrew an item from his pocket, his pulse quickened.

Suddenly, with no warning, the bird launched from a branch and swooped upward. Simon followed its trajectory, scrambling and almost dropping the camera. He raised it to his eyes, focusing frantically as the bird rose above the branches, finally vanishing into the uppermost reaches of a leafy elm. He zoomed out, hoping to catch a flash of color again, breath snagged in his chest. Five minutes passed before he conceded that it was gone.

Simon sank to the forest floor, one hand absentmindedly rubbing his aching hip. He giggled, a stress reaction, the tension dissipating with the sound. He shook his head, a hint of a smile dancing around his lips, pleased as any girl with a full dance card. A goddamned genuine Kirkland's Warbler, this far east. If only he'd managed to get a photo! That bastard Glenn might not believe him, despite the fact that it was a code of honor among birders. Only the most craven would claim false sightings. Simon waved a hand in the air, brushing away the unpleasant thought. He'd submit the sighting to the state's Rare Bird Committee anyway, they all knew he adhered strictly to the ethics rules. Besides, when it came right down to it he didn't care who believed him. He'd seen it with his own two eyes, that was the important thing. He pulled a small notebook out of an inner pocket, wet the tip of a pen with a flick of his tongue, and scrawled: *Kirkland's Warbler.* He raised the pen from the page, considered, then added an exclamation point and underlined the entry. Above it were the other sightings of the morning, recorded in his precise cursive:

2 common nighthawks.
1 olive-sided flycatcher
1 hooded merganser
1 Cooper's hawk
3 bobolinks

Even before spotting the warbler, it had been an uncommonly productive day, Simon reflected, tilting his face up toward the treetops where his quarry had vanished. A glance at his watch confirmed the tale told by the brightening forest around him. Nearly seven in the morning. Soon the park would be swarming with sweaty hordes eager to spend the holiday gorging themselves on food before collapsing drunk on flotation devices in the lake. His lip curled at the thought, and he debated. Better to end on a high note? Or should he chance one more good sighting?

Deciding that on this of all days the gods were clearly on his side, he opted to stay. The roar of an engine nearby startled him, drove him deeper into the undergrowth. Simon edged forward slowly, binoculars swaying slightly like a pendulum as he crept into the interior, keeping the lake on his right. His eyes darted from branch to branch, dismissing the more common swallows and chickadees as too mundane to bother with. Unconsciously he furrowed his brow, already composing his next entry for newyorkbirding.com. He'd start by quoting one of his favorite poems, *Freedom* by George William Russell:

> I love the free in thee, my bird,
> The lure of freedom drew;
> The light you fly toward, my bird,
> I fly with thee unto.

Let Glenn put that in his pipe and smoke it, Simon thought, forcefully repressing a snort. Of course, as resident poet laureate at Hudson Valley Community College, he was expected to be more erudite than his cohorts, Glenn included. After the opening stanza he'd launch into a description of the morning. He began composing it in his mind: the sky cracked open like an egg at the horizon, milky light saturating his car as he drove to the park, the night trailing jasmine like a beautiful woman leaving a party. Wonderful imagery. Then an account of his slow march through the underbrush, the air caressing his skin, the palpable feeling that the Fates were on the verge of handing him another feather for his cap, so to speak. That was good, he liked it. The Listserv always went wild for puns, which he personally considered to be the currency of mediocrity. He hated stooping to it, but an entry like that would win over some doubters.

Distracted, he almost missed the raven perched less than fifty yards away. Not an uncommon sighting, but still noteworthy, he decided, freezing in place. They eyed each other

for a long moment. The bird had plainly seen him, its head
cocked to the side, and he cursed himself for not paying attention. If he reached for his binoculars now the bird would
vanish. He comforted himself with the thought that the bird
was close enough to count as a confirmed sighting regardless.
The bird regarded him calmly an instant longer and, in spite
of himself, a shiver ran down his spine. He'd never been a big
fan of ravens, to be honest. He knew a true birder was
supposed to love anything avian, but there was something
about them—the dead black eye, like a shark, always unset-
tled him. The bird seemed to sense his unease and hopped
down the branch, as though approaching him to ask a
question. At the last moment, the bough bent under its weight
and it startled away in a flurry of black wings.

Simon sighed with something akin to relief and withdrew his
notebook again. As he glanced down, he frowned. Something
jutted out from behind a bush a few feet to his left, the color
and shape discordant in this woodland environment. He took a
small step forward, peering around the corner of the bush. What
he saw made him suck in a big gulp of air, one that was released
in horrified pants as he tore back through the trees, binoculars
thumping against his chest in the cadence of a frantic heartbeat.

Kelly rolled over, yawned and raised her head off the
pillow, squinting at the clock. When she saw the time she let
out a groan and pushed herself to a seated position. "Gotta get
up," she grumbled.

"What? No." Jake reached an arm out and pulled her back
under the sheet.

"It's Monday."

"It's a long weekend, Jones. Learn to live a little, blow off

work on a holiday like all the normal people in the world."
He wrapped both arms around her. She struggled for a
moment, then went still. He lifted his head a few inches and
peered at her. "Don't think I don't see that."

"See what?"

"You got a squirrel in your head, Jones, and he's pounding
away on one of those little wheels, spinning like he's trying
to give himself a heart attack. You're just waiting for me to
let go so you can jump up and follow him out of here. Well,
bad news." He wrapped both legs around her, too. "Not going
to happen, not on my watch."

"Oh, really?" In spite of herself she grinned.

"Nope. Hell, I could stay like this all day." Jake rolled onto
his back so she was on top of him, facing away. "Yup, there's
few things I like more than a nice, soft Jones blanket. Perfect
for any time of year."

"You're nuts." She shook her head and relaxed back
against his chest.

"Maybe." He paused for a minute, then continued in a
more serious voice, "You want to talk some more about what
I said yesterday?"

Kelly stiffened. They'd managed to get through the rest of
the barbecue, and then last night…well, suffice it to say there
hadn't been much talking. Which seemed to be their pattern,
she thought with a sigh.

"Uh-oh, she's sighing. Never a good sign," Jake commented from below her.

Kelly laughed and spun so she was facing him. She
lowered her head and kissed the tip of his nose. "Did I ever
tell you, I really like your nose?"

"Yeah?" He rubbed the tip of it thoughtfully. "What part

of it? Because I have been told it's like something carved by Michelangelo…."

Kelly rolled her eyes. "You've obviously been living abroad way too long."

"Maybe. That's why I was thinking about moving back here." He watched for her reaction, ice-blue eyes steady on hers.

"Back here?" She raised an eyebrow. "What would you do?"

"An old buddy of mine, former Agency N.O.C., is starting a private security firm. Kidnap & Ransom recovery, that sort of thing, strictly high end. Asked if I wanted to partner up."

"Yeah?" Kelly plunked her elbows down on his chest and rested her chin on her hands. "Where would you be based?"

"Offices in New York and D.C. I'd go back and forth." He rubbed her chin with his thumb as he continued, "I'd be a hell of a lot closer than I am now, that's for sure."

Kelly nodded. "A lot closer."

He pulled her in and kissed her gently on the lips. "And that's a good thing, right?" he murmured.

Before she could answer, Kelly's cell phone buzzed along the top of the bureau. Jake groaned and covered his head with one hand as she leaned over and grabbed it.

"Hello?" she said, and listened for a moment, her brow furrowing. "I can be ready in ten. See you then."

She snapped the phone shut. Jake eyed her. "Let me guess. There's a work emergency."

Kelly was already pulling her hair back in a ponytail as she headed for the bathroom. "They found another body."

"Yeah?" Jake pulled himself up on an elbow and watched as she bent over the sink and splashed some water on her face. "So you were right, Sommers is in the clear."

Kelly shook her head as she squeezed paste onto her toothbrush. "Not necessarily. According to Monica, he made bail on Saturday." She brushed quickly, spit and rinsed her mouth.

"Huh. So where are you headed?"

"That's the bad part." She came back in the room and held up her suit, examining it for stains before draping it over the back of a chair and digging a bra out of her suitcase. "Monica's coming to get me. We're crossing the border again."

"What, to Vermont?"

"No, back to New York. Hopefully they'll be as helpful today as they were last week." She clasped the straps and pulled on a pair of underwear. Jake watched appreciatively as she bent over and pulled on a light pair of linen pants. She glanced up at him. "You'll still be here when I get back?"

"If you'll still be wearing that lingerie—" he crossed his hands behind his head and grinned "—I'll be right here waiting to peel it off."

She threw a hand towel at him, finished buttoning her shirt, grabbed her purse and left.

A half hour later she was bent over the body of a young man. Dr. Stuart knelt on the ground next to her; he'd been in the car with Monica when they picked her up. Kelly had found that fact interesting but hadn't commented. Frankly, she was happy that he'd be at the scene from the outset.

The boy was found facedown in the middle of a thicket, shielded from a nearby parking lot by a low hedge of brambles. This time they were in Grafton Lakes State Park, about ten miles northwest of where the last two bodies had been discovered. The ground was blanketed with a smattering of acorn husks and weeds that managed to survive on the scant light filtered down through the dense trees. All around them, crime-scene technicians were painstakingly chronicling the scene, setting numbered markers beside each piece of evidence.

"Got the pennies again." Monica nodded toward a small pile of change by the boy's outstretched hand.

Kelly's brow creased. "They're different though, scattered, not stacked."

Monica shrugged. "Maybe the guy who found him knocked them over."

"I'll ask him." Kelly pointed to marks on the back of the boy's legs. "What're these burns here?"

"Acid. Probably phosphoric, but I'd have to get a sample of the tissue to the lab to ascertain for certain," Dr. Stuart said with a creased brow.

"Yup, acid. That's exactly what I was gonna say." The coroner was standing awkwardly off to one side, watching Howard with unreserved admiration. It was the same guy from the earlier crime scene. Today he was sporting a ratty pair of cutoff jeans and a Jägermeister T-shirt. "You folks are taking this one, too, right?" His relief was palpable when Kelly nodded her head.

"How was your daughter's birthday party?" Monica asked.

"Good memory, Lieutenant," he said appreciatively. "It was great, brought in a clown and everything. The wife couldn't have been hap—"

"Have you established a time of death yet?" Kelly interrupted.

He rubbed his chin as he looked down uncertainly at the body. "Well, rigor is passing. In this heat, I'd say he died between twelve and thirty-six hours ago."

"That's a big range. Could you pinpoint it more exactly?"

He shrugged sheepishly. "Maybe."

Dr. Stuart cleared his throat. "I should be able to narrow it down considerably. You've already taken the body temp?"

The coroner nodded. "Soon as I got here. I wrote it down for you." He passed over a clipboard with a smudged form. "This is everything. So, if you're all done with me…"

Kelly nodded. "Please write your cell number on the form in case Dr. Stuart needs to get in touch with you."

"Yeah, sure. Absolutely." He nodded vigorously, scribbled a number down on the pad, and handed it over.

Dr. Stuart watched, his lower lip twitching with disdain as the coroner lumbered off through the bushes. "Honestly, it's criminal that coroners aren't required to be medical doctors. And they wonder why this country has one of the lowest homicide clearance rates in the civilized world."

Kelly waved over the deputy who was in charge of the site log. "Tell me more about this park," she said.

He scratched his nose. "It's pretty big, a couple thousand acres. Five ponds, there's decent fishing here, they've got rainbow and brown trout, perch, some decent-size bass—"

"Overnight camping?"

"Nope, day-hiking only. Lots of people come to swim."

"And I'm guessing it was pretty busy here yesterday."

The deputy nodded. "Yeah, the ranger said the place was packed."

"He found the body?"

The deputy shook his head. "Nope, it was some bird-watcher—nearly gave him a heart attack. I got him over at the picnic tables, if you want to talk to him."

"Thanks, I will." Kelly turned back to the body. "You got shots of everything?"

"Yeah, those were done a while ago."

"All right, then. Let's flip him." Kelly stood back as Dr. Stuart gingerly turned the body over. There were blank holes where the eyes should be, and his genitals were missing. The front of his body was even worse than the back, bruises and burns covered almost every inch of skin.

Monica let out a low whistle. "Damn. Someone did a job on this poor kid."

Kelly leaned down toward him. "It looks like Danny Smith."

"Shit, really?" Monica shook her head. "Man, these poor boys…"

Kelly frowned. On top of everything else this meant they'd lost the only witness to Sommers's state of mind the night Jim was killed. "We should pull in Jordan, see if he can make an ID. Dr. Stuart, can you take over here, make sure he gets loaded up?"

Dr. Stuart nodded briskly. "I think I'd better, there's no telling what these monkeys might do if left to their own devices."

"I just love it when he talks tough." Monica winked, and Dr. Stuart flushed bright red. "See you later, sweets."

He turned away without responding.

As they walked back toward the car, Kelly tentatively asked, "So, how is everything going with him?"

Monica shrugged. "Two steps forward, one step back, about par for the course with me."

"Yeah?" Kelly said uncertainly, debating whether or not to press the subject.

Monica stopped her with one arm. "Look, I know how he seems. Just trust that I'm not a fool, all right? I'm a big girl, I know what I'm doing."

"Of course." Kelly flushed, regretting that she'd opened her mouth. Monica was right, of course, it was really none of her business. She would just hate to see her get hurt.

"Good." Monica held a branch aside and nodded for Kelly to pass her. "Can I just say, though, that Howie is one hell of a kisser?"

"Really?" Kelly tried but failed keep the dubious tone from her voice.

"Trust me, honey, it's always the ones you least expect."

"You must be pretty goddamn pleased with yourself," Doyle said, glaring down at her with his hands on his hips.

Kelly almost choked on her coffee; he'd surprised her, coming up as she turned the corner toward the task force conference room. "Lieutenant Doyle," she said, raising an eyebrow. "I have no idea what you're referring to."

"Your goddamn task force. It was supposed to be disbanded this week, now you've gone and added another member."

"I did what?" Kelly stopped at the door to the command center, puzzled. Inside, a young man sat at the table flipping through one of the case files. A shock of red hair crowned a face covered with an amount of freckles that seemed almost obscene on an adult. That, combined with pale blue eyes and a tan that leaned more toward a sunburn, marked him as a prototypical Irish-American. When he saw her, he hurriedly pushed back his chair, knocking it over as he stood.

"Oh, crap, I'm sorry." He fumbled with the chair, then strode forward and extended a hand, grinning. "Lieutenant Colin Peters, BCI."

"BCI?" Kelly asked.

"Bureau of Criminal Investigation. Because there was another body found in Rensselaer County, the boss thought it would be a good idea to send someone to help out. But if you're already all set, like Lieutenant Doyle said…" His voice trailed off and he looked embarrassed.

"Nothing's set yet." Kelly said firmly. "Welcome to the team. Lieutenant Lauer will be here in a minute, we'll have a sit-down and get everyone caught up on the case. Lieutenant Doyle," she said, turning to face him. He scowled at her from the doorway. She meet his gaze levelly. "Why don't you grab some coffee and join us?"

Ten minutes later they were settled around the table.

Kelly crossed her hands in front of her and surveyed the room. "First off, what's our status with Sommers? I understand he made bail on Saturday."

"Pain in the ass," Doyle grumbled.

"Not when you consider that by leaving prison he might've lost his best alibi," Kelly pointed out.

"No such luck." Monica shook her head. "Just talked to his lawyer, and the guy's vouching for him. Says they drove to his house in Provincetown for the weekend, since Sommers's place is still a crime scene."

"Wow, that's some attorney," Kelly noted.

"Hey, for five hundred an hour, I'd take clients home with me, too," Monica said.

"Can't trust a lawyer," Doyle said.

"Not always, that's true," Kelly acknowledged. Doyle looked surprised that she was agreeing with him. "Doyle, dig into the lawyer's reputation, see if he's the type to cover for his clients. But until I hear otherwise, that clears Sommers, at least for our latest victim. Because of the holiday, prints might take a few days, but the vic has tentatively been identified as Danny Smith."

"Let me guess. Another boy toy," Doyle mumbled.

Colin looked at him sharply, and Kelly gritted her teeth. "Lieutenant Doyle, am I going to have to remind you again to tone it down?"

Doyle lowered his eyes and shook his head.

"Okay. So this is our third victim in two weeks. Since Sommers has been cleared for now, we need to focus on other suspects. There's a chance that we're actually dealing with two perpetrators."

"Working together?" Colin asked.

"Hard to say. They might be working together, or it could be a copycat. If they are colluding, this last killing might have been done to give Sommers an alibi so that we'd have to release him."

"Do you have any concrete evidence proving that there are two killers?"

"Not so far," Kelly said.

Monica said, "We found two of the boys at the same time, same place. One had been buried, the other hadn't, and we got an expert says they were offed by two different perps."

"Why was only one of them buried?" Colin's brow furrowed.

Kelly shrugged. "We don't know that, either. It looks like the earlier remains, the ones that were initially discovered in the Clarksburg State Park boneyard, had also been buried at one point."

"And what, someone dug them up? Why would anyone do that?" Colin looked horrified at the thought of someone running around digging up bodies. Kelly wondered what his experience had been, if he had the stomach for this kind of case. She'd make a few calls, see if she could get a copy of his file. Last thing she needed was another task force member who couldn't hold his own in the field.

Doyle snorted. "Because he's a sick so-and-so. And don't let the ladies fool you, son. I don't give a goddamn what any lawyer says, the guy doing this is named Sommers and he strolled out of here nice as you please last Saturday. Had a whole day to track down another of his little boy toys to kill." He jabbed a finger at them. "Mark my words, by Friday I'll have his bail revoked and he'll be on a fast track to Walpole."

"My, that kind of work ethic would be a welcome change," Monica said drily. "I hear they renamed Walpole, it's called Cedar Junction now. For you out of towners, that's the Massachusetts maximum security prison. Sounds a hell of a lot nicer than it is."

"Let's stay on topic, shall we?" Kelly said, repressing a sigh.

"What kind of MO are we looking at?" Colin asked, changing the subject.

Kelly cast him a grateful look before replying. "Pretty gruesome, at least from what we've seen with the latest three victims. Hard to say if the exact same MO was followed earlier, the decomposition of the bodies was too advanced. But on the fresh bodies we've seen clear signs of torture, everything from cigarette and acid burns to puncture wounds. The killer also gouges out the victims' eyes postmortem, and removes the genitals."

"Postmortem for that, too?" Colin asked.

Kelly shrugged. "We think. Again, a lot of this is supposition when it comes to the earlier vics. The ones we've ID'd so far all have records for solicitation, and they range in age from eighteen to twenty-four. Also, the last few victims had a stack of pennies next to them, which could be a sign that one of our killers was institutionalized at some point. But that could range from a kid who grew up in foster care to a former convict."

"So that's not really any help at all," Colin remarked. "And the suspect, what's his name...Summer?"

"Calvin Sommers. We've confirmed that he personally knew at least three of the victims and was, in fact, with one of the boys the night he died. He claims he doesn't remember anything that happened, and he tested positive for ketamine."

"Sounds pretty damning," Colin acknowledged.

"Damn straight it does," Doyle growled.

"But we just lost the only witness linking him to Jim Costello the night of the murder," Monica reminded them. "And we got that pesky alibi to deal with now, don't we?"

"For now. Let's see if we can start chipping away at it. Doyle, since you seem to be particularly motivated, why don't you dig into the lawyer's background, see what turns up," Kelly said pointedly. "Let's keep in mind that Sommers still has the best motive for killing Danny Smith, as far as we know, so let's stay on him. Lieutenant Peters, that's the basic rundown, but why don't you spend the morning going through the rest of the files, get more familiar with the details of the case. Let me know if you have any questions. Monica is going to try to track down a potential witness."

"What potential witness?" Doyle asked.

Monica and Kelly exchanged a glance; there had been no sign of Jordan at the flophouse when they stopped by on their way back from the park. In fact, the house now appeared completely abandoned. Since Danny had turned up dead, that was worrisome. Monica was going to sniff around the local scene, see if she could find out where the boys were hanging now.

"I'd rather not say just yet," Kelly said after a pause. "Peters, once you're up to speed, I have another stack of files for you to go through. I want you to cross-reference arrest records with addresses and missing-persons reports. Now that we have the extra manpower, I want to see if we can put a name to some of our other remains. ID'ing them might help us find a connection."

Doyle eyed the file box she was pointing to. "Who pulled those for you?"

"Officer Sayles has been working on this for the past week. I figured we should keep our options open in case Sommers was cleared."

Doyle grunted. "Sounds to me like you're assigning the kid busywork."

"I don't mind," Colin piped up. "I'm actually pretty good at this organizational stuff."

"And maybe with a fresh pair of eyes, you'll see something we've missed," Kelly said.

"So what're you going to do?" Doyle asked suspiciously.

Kelly answered, "I'm going to see if Mr. Sommers's lawyer is willing to meet for a chat."

"Who knows, maybe he'll tell you it was all a mistake, that he actually hasn't been babysitting Sommers. Charm him a little," Monica said.

"Stranger things have happened," Kelly said with a sigh.

"Not likely," Doyle said. "Don't know if you've noticed, but charm ain't exactly your strong suit."

"Doesn't seem to be yours, either," Kelly retorted, but felt herself flush red regardless and dropped her gaze. She straightened the papers in front of her, tapping out the edges on the desktop until they were aligned before tucking them back in a file. A corner still poked out, and she tossed the folder on to the table, aggravated. Avoiding everyone's eyes, Kelly grabbed her purse off the chair, yanked open the top drawer of the desk where she'd been storing her gun, and tucked it into her shoulder harness before leaving the room.

"What was that about?" Colin asked, looking between Monica and Doyle.

Monica had already crossed the room and was standing angrily over Doyle. He jerked out of his chair and stared her down. Despite the fact that her head barely reached his chin, she didn't back down an inch. "You're really pushing it, Doyle, you know that?" Monica growled.

"Hey, guys, I know I'm new here, but maybe we should all just calm down," Colin said nervously, stopping uncertainly a few steps away from them.

"What, you're pissed I said something nasty to your girl-friend?" Doyle said. "Get over it, blondie."

"I'm just sick of you always being such an asshole." Monica eyed him, inched a step closer. "What're you going to do, Doyle, you gonna hit me? 'Cause you got that look on your face."

"Sure you'd recognize it. Broad like you has probably been hit once or twice," Doyle said.

"Um, guys? I really think we should all just take a minute…"

"Stow it, kid. I'm leaving." Doyle cast one more glare down at Monica, then stormed out of the room.

Monica's gaze shifted to the floor and she swallowed a few times, hard, before slowly sinking into a chair.

Colin stood a few feet away, shifting uncertainly. "Lieu-tenant, are you okay? I could get you some water or some-thing, if you like…"

Monica laughed out loud once, sharply. She lifted her eyes to him before shaking her head. "That's sweet, but I'm fine, thanks. Just had a bad flashback is all. Funny, never realized till just now who Doyle reminded me of. Explains a lot."

"Yeah? Who?"

Monica shook her head again. "It's not important." She glanced at her watch. "Oops, it's getting late. I better get going." She clapped him cheerily on the shoulder as she left the room, saying, "Welcome to the team, kid. Chip away at those files—the sooner we solve this thing and get out of here, the happier we'll all be."

Twenty

He sat low behind the wheel of his wife's BMW. It was another blazing day, heat rising off the pavement in waves. He watched as Dwight left his house, door slamming behind him, headed for the decrepit Tercel parked in the driveway. A ragged bandage covered one arm—the moron had probably gotten another tattoo for some organization that would never accept him. The house matched the car in that both had seen better days; swaths of faded paint were peeling in strips, a broken window upstairs was covered by a blue tarp. *Probably had been there since the last big storm,* the man thought with a snort. *Disgusting, that people subjected themselves to these living conditions.* He shuddered to think of what the interior would be like if the outside was any indication.

He could've guessed at the condition of the house, though, based on what he knew of its owner. It was so clear to him now, he was surprised it hadn't occurred to him before. The problem was he'd credited his tormentor with more sophistication, when what he was actually facing was the peevish retaliation of a mental case.

He was parked up a short street that ended in a cul-de-sac and, thanks to the incline of the hill, it afforded a perfect view of the house through high-powered binoculars. He watched as the screen door banged open again, swinging against the side of the house as a woman burst forth. Dressed in a ragged dressing gown and—for God's sake, were those actually curlers?—a cigarette dangling from her lips, she engaged in a heated argument with Dwight about something. His mother, the man guessed. And from the looks of things, the apple didn't fall far from the tree. As far as he was concerned, Dwight Sullivan redefined "waste of space." It had been a while since he'd seen him, and on reflection Dwight's resentment of him made perfect sense. Their final confrontation had been such a trifling incident in his own life that he'd almost completely forgotten about it. Poor dumb Dwight and his delusions of grandeur. Always had some story about how he was waiting to be called up for the CIA or the Navy Seals, when in truth he was a sad sack pushing thirty whose most notable accomplishment was his ability to name a song in three notes.

As soon as he'd made the connection he'd driven over here and waited. Followed Dwight to and from work, discovered his lonely shift at the box factory. Had even sat high on a perch overlooking the warehouse floor, witnessing Dwight's clumsy, ham-handed attempts at mimicry. He winced at the memory; the clod couldn't even successfully torture someone to death. He was so incompetent his victim had managed to kill himself first.

He'd followed Dwight to a barbecue, watched from across the street as he drank himself into a state of advanced inebriation, then swerved back to the factory and loaded the body into his car. He hadn't even bothered to wrap it, the man had noted with disdain, just dumped it in the plastic-lined trunk of his junky Tercel. It was a miracle that Dwight had made it to the dump site and back without a routine traffic stop, which would have ruined everything. He wasn't surprised when Dwight left the body in a park adjoining his own property, the bumbling fool probably thought that was enough to implicate him. His daughters played in that park sometimes, he thought, seething. After what he'd been subjected to these past few weeks, he intended to make Dwight suffer. And then he meant to kill him.

Once Dwight left his dump site, he'd placed what was left of the boy in a special hatch in his truck and drove back to his workshop. It had taken the rest of the night to clean him up, removing all forensics evidence. In his stupor Dwight had even forgotten to gouge out the eyes, the man thought. Disappointing, really, to have attracted such a bungling nemesis. But at least it had given him an impetus to hone his skills further, kept him sharp when he'd been starting to get sloppy.

His face curved into a smile as he pictured Dwight's reaction to the news. As he watched through high-powered binoculars, Dwight stood on his front porch scanning the newspaper headlines. He had an eager expression on his face, like a kid at Christmas. The man shook his head slightly and set down the binoculars as he said aloud, "Don't worry, Dwight, they'll find your boy today. Just not where you left him."

Monica sighed. She'd been banging on doors all day, trying to track down this Jordan kid. She closed her eyes for a minute as she ran a hand through her hair, feeling sections that had stiffened with dried sweat. She flinched as an image of Danny's tortured body flashed across her mind. You'd think it would get easier, seeing the next victim, but it didn't.

She'd managed to track down Tony, the bartender from Club Metro, but he hadn't seen Jordan in a few weeks.

"Probably took off, to be honest," he'd concluded with a shrug. "Season ended early this year, because of all the...well, you know." He'd rubbed his muttonchop sideburns thoughtfully. "If he's anywhere around here, he's probably crashing at somebody's house." He'd given her the names of Jordan's past boyfriends, then grabbed her hand as she was leaving. "You know, these are good kids, mostly. Lost, but good kids. They don't deserve this."

"Hell, no one does," she agreed.

Now she was knocking on the door of the third house down the list. So far, the first house she'd visited was already sealed up for the winter. The caretaker who answered her knock said the owner had gone back to New York, and he had no idea if there was a young man with him. The second guy was in the middle of packing when she showed up. He was nice enough, said he hadn't seen Jordan in a few weeks; the good-looking kid helping him pack was probably the reason why. She had two other names on her list, then she was out of options.

It was another beautiful house, she thought as she gazed wistfully from the front porch down the sweeping expanse of lawn. Gabled, with fancy teak furniture scattered across the porch and probably even nicer stuff inside. Not that she minded her place, she reminded herself. It had suited them just fine over the years. In fact, once Zach left for college, it would probably feel huge to her. Part of her hated the fact that that day was rapidly approaching. Zach had his first real girlfriend now, a pretty little thing with dark hair and light eyes. In spite of herself, Monica felt a pang of jealousy when she caught the expression on Beenie's face as he gazed at her. That was the curse of being a mother, she reminded herself; they never stopped being the center of your life, but you sure as hell stopped being the center of theirs.

She heard footsteps and instinctively stepped to the side. The door opened, and a good-looking guy in his forties stuck his head out.

"Oh, hello, Officer," he said with surprise. "What can I do for you?"

She put on her most winning smile. "Sorry to trouble you, sir, but I'm looking for Jordan Davenport."

"Why? Did he do something?" He looked concerned and stepped forward, blocking the door with his body.

Monica shook her head vigorously. "Nope, nothing like that. Just turns out he might have some information for us, about a friend of his." She leaned forward slightly.

"Oh, okay," the man said uncertainly, then called over his shoulder. "Jordan! Someone's here for you."

Jordan slouched to the door a minute later. Monica had to resist the urge to throw her arms around him—all morning she'd been picturing him lying dead in a forest somewhere. "Well all I can say is thank God, Jordan. Honestly, I wasn't sure I'd see you alive again."

"What? Why not?" He scuffed his feet on the carpet. "What do you want?"

"Danny's dead, Jordan." She watched him. A shadow crossed over his eyes, but the rest of his face remained expressionless, a stolid mask. Her heart ached for this kid, what he must have suffered through to be so numb.

"I don't know anything about that," he said, surly.

"We're not blaming you for it, Jordan. I just need to ask you a few questions."

"Like what?"

"Like, did Danny ever make it back to the house after we left?"

Jordan shrugged and propped his body against the doorsill. "Dunno. I took off right afterward."

"And you haven't been back since?"

"Hell no. Got chased out of there, the owner showed up and said we had to clear out. Threatened to turn us all in unless we started paying rent."

Monica cocked her head to the side. That was odd timing. "Yeah? Who's the owner?"

Jordan avoided her eyes. "I don't know, some guy."

"You ever seen him before?"

Jordan shook his head. "I've only been crashing there since July."

"So who paid the rent for you all?" Monica asked, puzzled.

Jordan shrugged. "Some guy. I never met him before, it just gets set up every year."

"What, at the same house?"

Jordan nodded in response. "Yeah, the guy covers the summer, June through August, then we gotta clear out. I figured I'd try to catch a few extra days, you know, until I got a ride somewhere. But the owner said get out, so I came here." He glanced over his shoulder. His sugar daddy had disappeared into the depths of the house, but was probably eavesdropping from somewhere nearby.

"So let me get this straight," Monica said slowly. "Every year you guys show up, and someone's already paid the rent. You crash there all summer, then clear out come fall."

"Yup."

"Did anyone ever mention meeting this guy that's so generous?"

"Nope. I just figured it was one of the guys from Metro." Jordan leaned forward and dropped his voice. "The money some of these assholes got? You wouldn't believe."

"I'll bet," Monica said. "So what did the owner look like?"

"Good-looking," Jordan said appreciatively. "Not too old, maybe around your age. I offered to do him if he'd let me crash a few extra days, but he wasn't having it. I didn't get a vibe off him."

"Meaning what? You don't think he was gay?"

He shrugged again and slouched lower against the door. "Dunno. He was dressed pretty nice, but like I said, no vibe. Most guys, even if they don't want to fuck you, you kinda know."

"Okay," Monica said. "Any idea who Danny might've gone off with?

Jordan's lip started bleeding a little where he was gnawing on it. "He was freaked, said he wasn't going off with anyone he didn't know. Even said maybe he'd go home for a while, and Danny…he wasn't crazy about home."

"Can you give me a list of some of the people he dated this summer?"

"Yeah, but they mostly took off already," Jordan's eyes and voice both dropped as he asked, "Was it bad? What they did to him?"

"Yeah, it was real bad." Monica again fought the urge to pull him in for a hug. Standing there, he looked so alone and fragile. With his mop of blond hair, he reminded her a little of Zach. "So listen up. You trust this guy?" She jerked her head toward the house.

Jordan nodded slowly. "Yeah, he's one of the good ones."

"And he's going to take you with him?"

"He says so. We're supposed to bail tomorrow."

"Okay, I want a number where I can reach you. And here's my card." She paused, flipped the card over, and scribbled on it before handing it over. "That's my cell. If anything goes wrong and you need a place to crash, you give me a call, hear?"

"Yeah, sure." He examined the card for a minute, then tucked it in his pocket. "Thanks."

"No problem. Now go get me that number."

"Okay." He walked a few steps away, then turned back. "Did you figure out who the others were, the first ones you found?"

Monica shook her head. "Not yet. We're working on it."

Jordan stared at the floor, and said, "One of them might be named Freddy."

"Freddy what?"

"Freddy Robbins. I thought he just took off last summer, but then…usually you run into the other guys somewhere, you know? And I haven't seen him."

"Anyone else like that you can think of?" Jordan nodded. Monica spoke briskly, employing the same tone she used to get Zach to do something. "So write their names down, too. And send your friend out, I want to have a few words."

Dwight paced across his tiny bedroom in a panic. He felt the walls crumbling, his world coming down around him, and in desperation he was yanking at the remaining tendrils of hair that wound down his neck with one hand while the other rapped a beat in the air. In spite of himself he couldn't stop humming, that *Peter and the Wolf* song he'd loved when he was a kid. It was blasting in his head at top volume, so loud he couldn't believe his mother couldn't hear it.

Stupid bitch. She'd given him hell yesterday for coming home drunk. She was threatening to commit him again if he didn't stop, said she could see the sickness coming back. He wouldn't go, wouldn't lose another three years in that goddamn place with their goddamn doctors and goddamn arts and crafts. "Doesn't matter now, though, doesn't matter…" he mumbled as he turned again, took three steps, turned by the bed and headed back for the door. If the CIA found out what he'd done, they'd never take him. Weren't supposed to kill people until after you got in. He'd known that but had forgotten, somehow. He'd gotten distracted. It was all the Captain's fault—Dwight saw what'd been done to those boys and wondered what it felt like. It wasn't his fault, really. He'd explain that to them and they'd understand…

The broken shades were pulled closed. In the half-light that filtered through, the contours of the room were barely visible. The ceiling was low and composed of cheap tiles that hung just two feet above his head. A bed in the corner was a mass of tangled sheets; mounds of filthy clothing and dirty plates exuded a musty smell. The only clear illumination in the room came from a computer screen that glowed from a small desk set in the corner, one of those cheap pasteboard ones that were always on sale. A headline on the screen blared, Serial Killer Strikes Again In New York."

He rubbed his face with both hands and shook his head, trying to jar the song loose, but only succeeded in making it louder. He knew he had to do something but couldn't decide

what. Work started in a few hours, but he was afraid they'd
be waiting for him there. He'd cleaned up the warehouse as
best as he could, but maybe he'd missed something. He should
never have done those tequila shots at the barbecue, they'd
fucked him up. It still didn't make any sense. He'd been
hammered, but so hammered that he thought he dumped the
kid somewhere else? The whole point had been to leave him
right on that bastard's doorstep, so they'd take a closer look
at the Captain. Hell, he'd never even been to Grafton Lake,
probably couldn't find it sober if he tried. So what the fuck?

Dwight plopped down on the bed, exhausted. It occurred
to him that maybe the Captain was on to him, that he was
being played, too. Probably not, but if he had it figured
out…then Dwight was royally screwed, it would ruin the
whole plan. He scratched at the growth of beard on his chin
and deliberated. Finally, he stood and slapped on some
deodorant, then gave his uniform a sniff. A little rank, but it
could go one more day, he decided. He pulled it on, fastened
his holster, then dug around his closet until he found what he
was looking for. Either way, it was time to start the second
phase of his plan.

Twenty-One

"Agent Jones, would you mind taking a look at this?"

Kelly glanced up. Colin Peters was holding out a stack of files. He appeared concerned. "What are they?" she asked.

He hesitated before saying, "Suspicious death reports. When I talked to Stacey—she's new to records, just started last week—she mentioned coming across them and thought I might be interested since the deceased are all young males age eighteen to twenty-four. Skeletal remains."

Kelly shuffled through the files, brows furrowing as she did. "How far do these go back?"

"I haven't been through all of them yet, but so far—at least a decade. And then I came across this."

The outside of the file was stamped "Accidental Death." Kelly flipped it open, scanned the page quickly. "This one is five years old?" she asked after a minute, looking up at him.

"Yup."

"What does it have to do with our case?" Kelly asked.

Colin hesitated briefly then said, "I think it's pretty

apparent, once you read through it. Listen, I don't want to make trouble here. But check out the name of the investigating officer." He nodded at the file.

Kelly scanned down the page until she found the right line. Her lips pursed, and she said, "I'm going to hold on to these until I finish going through them myself, okay?"

"Yeah, of course. I've got a ton more to get through anyway."

"Great. Any more like these jump out at you, put them on my desk. And could you call the other lieutenants, tell them we're having a meeting in my office at three o'clock?"

"Sure."

"Don't mention why, okay?" she said, raising an eyebrow.

"Not a problem. I was about to run out for a coffee, can I get you something?"

"I'd love a tall iced coffee."

"Got it."

"And Lieutenant Peters—good job finding these. I'm glad you're on the team."

Colin flushed bright red. "You bet," he stammered before ducking out.

After he left, Kelly spread the contents of the top file across the desk and scanned through them, making notes on a legal pad as she went. As she read, she felt a hot ball of anger rising in her belly. It was outrageous that this information had been kept from her. She'd had a feeling from the beginning that something wasn't right in this case, that she was two steps behind and being denied critical information. The fact that she was right was small satisfaction. Especially considering the fact that if she'd had this information earlier, the most recent victims might have been saved.

Kelly inhaled deeply and released the breath slowly, eyes

closed. She needed to stay calm, figure out what her next step would be. She should run this new information by McLarty. There were political considerations here, and that wasn't her forte. If she had a choice, though, she knew exactly what she'd do.

"So what the hell is this about?" Doyle grumbled.

Monica regarded him quizzically. "Why, Doyle, you got somewhere you gotta be? There a crew-cut convention in town?"

Doyle ignored her. "What about you, kid? Don't suppose she told you."

Colin simply shrugged but appeared to wither slightly under Doyle's glare. "I—I think we should just wait for Agent Jones. She'll be here any minute," he stammered.

"Yeah, well, it's three-o-five now. She's got exactly one more minute before I leave and get on with my day."

"You've been assigned to this task force, Doyle. You got nothing else on your plate right now, so why don't you just sit back and relax," Monica said with annoyance. "You're not fooling anyone with that whole, 'I got a million other things to deal with' bull. Hell, more bodies popped up here in the last week than in the past year. If you weren't so goddamn lazy, you'd want to find out why. I got my boss breathing down my neck, and we've only got one body in the red column. Can't believe your captain doesn't give a shit about the five found on your side of the state line."

"He doesn't give a shit because we know who the killer is," Doyle retorted. "All I gotta do now is prove Sommers killed this last one to keep himself out of jail. And that won't happen if I'm sitting around here." He pushed his chair back and started to stand.

The door to the room opened and Kelly strode in carrying a box of files. She set it on the table with a thud as she said, "Afternoon, everyone—sorry for the late notice about this meeting, but something came up."

"What're all those?" Doyle said, eyeing the box.

"Old suspicious death cases." Kelly said as she removed the top file from the stack, whipping it down the table so it spun and landed in front of Doyle. "That one's from May, 2003, just after the first thaw. Remember it?"

Doyle leaned forward reluctantly and picked it up, turning to the inside page. He scanned it, then shrugged with exaggerated nonchalance. "Yeah, I remember. Turned out to be a lost hiker, so it got reclassified as an accidental death. So what?"

"Lost hiker, huh? What about this one?" Kelly tossed another one at him. "And this one?" She sent the files cascading across the table.

He dropped the first file and held up his hands. "Jesus, what's your problem now?"

"What's going on, Kelly?" Monica asked, looking puzzled.

"What's going on is we came in on this case about five years too late, didn't we, Lieutenant Doyle?"

"I don't know what the hell you're talking about," he muttered, standing. "And I don't need this bullshit."

"Sit down," Kelly said authoritatively. He kept walking toward the door. She raised her voice. "Take a seat, Lieutenant Doyle, or my next call is to Internal Affairs."

He paused, hand on the doorknob. "You got nothing," he said, still facing the door, but there was a trace of uncertainty in his voice.

"Oh, really? Because I think the local media would be intrigued by the fact that five years ago, the remains of a young male age twenty to twenty-two were found in Pittsfield State Forest. And that less than a year later, more human remains were found off another trail in the same park."

"These weren't the first bodies?" Monica asked, realization dawning.

"Not even close. I found four cases total, at two other parks within a fifteen-mile radius. Each time, the body was identified as a lost hiker who must have succumbed to the elements, and the death was categorized as an accident. And each time, the investigating officer was one Lieutenant William Doyle. Funny you didn't mention this earlier, Lieutenant."

Doyle had his back to the door. He crossed his arms over his chest and retorted, "Didn't see the point. Had nothing to do with this case."

"No? I think it would've seemed a little coincidental. Awfully handy, too, that the coroner agreed with your assessment, even though I couldn't find any reports detailing whether the bones were examined for evidence of foul play."

"We decided not to waste the lab's time. Lots of kids come here in the winter to go camping. They get lost in the woods, maybe meet a bear..." His voice trailed off.

"And I've got a stack of missing-persons reports here, all young males that went missing in the past decade. Ever think to have those bones submitted for DNA analysis, see if it matched any of these files?"

"DNA tests are expensive, missy. I'm sure as hell not going to waste the taxpayers' money..." He stopped short.

"On what?" Kelly said, voice lowering. "On a bunch of gay prostitutes?"

He looked away from her, chin set in defiance. Kelly examined his profile.

After a minute Monica spoke up, for once all levity gone from her voice. "You've just been burying these cases, Doyle? You've been letting this animal just kill these boys and get away with it?"

He didn't answer. Kelly watched him, then continued. "At the very least, Lieutenant, what we've got here is a case of gross incompetence. Honestly, I'd prefer to blame it on that than to consider the alternative. Because a corruption case right now would bring us to a standstill. All our files would be requisitioned by Internal Affairs, we'd have the press breathing down our necks even more than they already are… it'd be a mess."

"So what're you going to do?" Doyle asked after a moment. All the bravado had vanished from his voice.

"Why, you worried about your pension?" Monica said coldly.

He didn't answer.

"Lieutenant Doyle, I think you should step outside for a minute so the rest of us can make that decision together," Kelly said.

He opened his mouth and started to say something, then snapped it shut, yanked open the door and left the room.

There was a long pause. Colin stared at the table, picking at a chipped piece of Formica with his thumbnail. Monica's face was beet-red, her expression one of fury.

"You're not going to let him keep working this case, are you?" Monica asked, voice rising.

Kelly pulled out a chair and sat down. She would like nothing better than to kick Doyle off the team and watch IAD roast him. But McLarty had clearly outlined what needed to happen for the case to move forward. "Even though I'm sure we'd be lost without all the help he's given us so far," Kelly said drily, "I think we can probably spare the good lieutenant. But we're in an awkward position. We're already established here, at his home base, and I don't particularly relish the prospect of adding someone else from his unit to the task force. We don't know how many other homicide detectives were in the loop. So for now I say we keep him, technically. With the understanding that by and large he stays out of our hair."

"You really think he'll do that?" Monica said skeptically. "Hell, he's probably been working against us this whole time. That's why it took so long to get those damn lab results."

"From here on out, everything gets sent to either the FBI lab or to Dr. Stuart. I've already spoken to the people at the state lab in New York. Since the last three victims were found there, they've agreed to allow him to use their facilities."

"Why don't we just move everything over there, then?" Monica asked.

"I'd rather not—I still think our killer is local. If the situation changes and we need to shift locales, Lieutenant Peters said his captain wouldn't have a problem hosting us. So are we agreed?"

Kelly looked from one to the other of them. Monica paused, then said, "I'm not gonna pretend to be thrilled about it. I think Doyle should roast for this. But you're right, they start investigating him we'll get caught up in the net, and this guy'll get away with killing those boys. We got a fresh trail, we need to stay on it."

Colin glanced up from the table. "I got here pretty late in the game, so anything is fine by me."

"Okay. Right now the remains from these four "accidental death" cases are being exhumed, then they'll be sent to Dr. Stuart for analysis. With any luck, we'll be able to match them to one of these other missing boys." She gestured toward the box of files. "Colin, you're doing great work sifting through these. Keep at it. I also want you to check into any field cards about incidents around Club Metro in Northampton, even if they didn't result in arrests. There's a good cop there, Bennett. He can serve as your liaison."

"What am I looking for? Solicitation charges?"

"Solicitation, drug use, traffic violations, pretty much anything. Whoever our guy is, he probably tracks his victims for a while before grabbing them. Start with the past few months, see if any names pop up again and again. Monica, any luck tracking down Danny's former boyfriends?"

"I found two of them, still working on the other three. So far both claim they were out of town when he disappeared. I'm checking their alibis."

"All right, stay on that for now."

Monica hesitated before saying, "I'd like to look into one more thing first, if you don't mind. Jordan mentioned some guy chasing him out of the flophouse, claimed to be the owner. Apparently someone rents the place every summer, paying for the boys to crash there. I'd like to find out who."

Kelly tilted her head to the side. "Interesting. See what you can dig up, but try to get to Danny's other boyfriends today or tomorrow. It seems like everyone is leaving town. I want to know if they have alibis."

"Sure. I already got a call in to the local Registry of Deeds, they're digging up contact info on the owner."

"All right. Meanwhile, I got a call from Sommers's lawyer. He's got his client doing some sort of hypnotic regression therapy today and they want me to observe."

"Hypnotic regression?" Monica said, rolling her eyes. "What the hell is that supposed to prove?"

"Nothing, and it's not admissible in court. But I want to be there in case he slips and comes out with anything helpful. Maybe he'll cop to his confession again."

"Not likely," Monica snorted.

"No, but you never know." If Doyle's old accidental death cases turned out to be homicides, that meant four more bodies just got tacked onto their list. Add that to the other six from the boneyard, and the three fresh corpses found in the past week, and they were dealing with at least one major serial killer. *At this point I'd use a Ouija board if it got me a lead,* Kelly thought, frustrated.

"When are you going to tell Sunshine he's off the hook?" Monica asked, jerking her head toward the door.

"Let's let him sweat a little longer," Kelly said. "I've got a special assignment in mind for him after that."

Kelly ducked out a side door to avoid the media horde camped on the street in front of the police station. Once fresh bodies had started turning up, the vans multiplied to include the major networks as well as local affiliates. She despised dealing with the media, and had handed the daily press conferences over to Doyle's boss. The captain was happy to oblige. He seemed to enjoy standing on the top step of the barracks, rocking back and forth officiously as he droned on about how much progress "his" task force was making.

Kelly's hands clenched involuntarily as she thought of Doyle withholding information and burying files. She'd be lying if she claimed to be surprised. These days the budgets of many police departments were tied to their homicide clearance rates. So no one looked askance when murders were classified as accidents, particularly when there weren't any bereft family members demanding justice. Many serial killers targeted prostitutes and illegal immigrants for just that reason. And when you were talking about gay prostitutes it added a whole other layer, especially in a place with conservative views on homosexuality. She wondered how much the captain knew. That was always the danger of these task force assignments, you were thrown into a department and had to attempt to work within their structure, their codes, without ever knowing what that might entail. And in the end, you never knew who you could trust.

She felt a presence at her shoulder as she stooped to unlock her car door, and swiveled quickly, ready to go for her gun. The blond reporter, Jan, jerked back, holding both hands defensively in front of her chest. "Easy there, Agent." She laughed nervously. "I swear I didn't do it."

"I'm not going to make a statement," Kelly said, unlocking her door and sliding inside. As she reached to pull it shut, the blonde blocked it with her hand. She was surprisingly strong. Kelly raised an eyebrow at her.

"I understand another body was found today, across the border in New York," Jan said in a rush.

"Like I said…" Kelly smiled thinly, and waved her away from the door.

Jan pressed on, undeterred. She had hungry eyes, like so many of them. Desperate to get out of this backwater and into a network chair in a major city. And a serial crime case was just the ticket for that kind of career move. "I understand that Mr. Sommers, your prime suspect, has volunteered to take a polygraph clearing his name. Why wouldn't the district attorney allow him to do so?"

Kelly paused. The polygraph offer was a standard tactic

utilized by defense attorneys, who knew that ninety-nine percent of the time the test was refused because the results were meaningless. And then they could say that their client wasn't given an opportunity to clear his name. But the fact someone had leaked that offer to the press was worrisome. Had Doyle talked to the reporter? Or was Sommers's lawyer grandstanding to the media? One of the only reasons she'd agreed to sit in on this ridiculous hypnotic regression session was because she wanted to get a better sense of the attorney. "A polygraph is inadmissible in court," she responded, yanking her car door shut.

Jan leaned in the car window and dropped her voice. "You don't think Sommers did it, do you? Off the record."

Kelly leaned forward conspiratorially and matched Jan's tone of voice. "Off the record?"

Jan nodded eagerly. "Of course."

"I have no comment. But if I were you, I'd stop listening to Lieutenant Doyle. If I get the sense that anyone is leaking information from the task force, I'll make sure you and you alone are off the media list. It'll be hard to explain to your bosses why all of your reports take place on the steps of the local Dunkin' Donuts, don't you think?"

Jan snapped back from the window, her face pinching shut in a tight line. Kelly shifted the car into Reverse and backed out. As she drove away, in her rearview mirror she saw Jan standing there, hands clenched in tight fists, and felt a flash of empathy for her. It wasn't easy being a woman in either of their lines of work. She recognized that drive and ambition— she used to be the same way. As she turned the corner and Jan dropped out of sight, she idly wondered when she'd lost the desire to get ahead. Lately all she cared about was getting through cases. She no longer had the emotional attachment, the urge to gain closure for the families, that had once served as her impetus. Had she burned out like so many other cops and agents she knew, and was that just part of the job after a certain point? And if it was true, if she really didn't care anymore, why was she still bothering? She could go into a different line of work, spend less time traveling, maybe even start a family. Hell, she might even manage to take a vacation without getting interrupted by another murder. At the next stoplight she paused. It changed from red to green and back again as she sat, regarding herself in the rearview mirror. There were times these days when she didn't know who she was anymore, and that frightened her more than anything.

Twenty-Two

He watched as she waddled over to the next patch of weed-choked flowers, carefully aiming a hose at them with one hand while sucking on a cigarette with the other. The flowers shuddered under the force of the spray, flattening against the ground. After pummeling them for a minute, she nodded her head, satisfied, and dumped the hose on the grass where it created a rivulet of mud that wound its way down to the crack in the driveway.

Martha Stewart would be proud, he thought wryly as he observed her through binoculars.

It was half-past three on Tuesday, and no cars had gone by in nearly an hour. The house was set back from the road and the overgrown lawn and trees that lined the front of the property provided good cover. The next-door neighbor on the right had piled her squalling brats into a minivan an hour earlier with what looked like a month's supply of food and umbrellas; headed to the lake, no doubt. The single mother who occupied the ramshackle hut on the other side was working her day job at the diner. She wouldn't be back until after six, and the guy across the street was a contractor who usually pulled in late in the evening. He'd rung all their doorbells about a half hour ago and got no response, so he'd have to trust that if anyone was home they were too drunk or disinterested to check out a strange noise.

So far he seemed to have gone unnoticed; he'd switched cars once, using his wife's yesterday. The BMW was more noticeable than his truck, especially in a working class neighborhood like this one, but parking a car in the same spot three days in a row might draw more attention.

He'd rather do this at night, or without actually pulling into her driveway, but there was no way around it. He'd have to risk it. He'd smeared mud onto his license plate, concealing all but one number, and he'd painted the truck with washable paint; close up you could tell, but from twenty feet away it looked like a black truck. He took a swig of water, watching her totter into the house. He glanced at his left hand as he lowered the bottle; not shaky at all, which meant he was ready.

He slid on the work gloves, turned the ignition and pulled out of the side street. He cruised along slowly before turning into her driveway and parking. He strolled to the front door, the one they rarely used, holding a metal box in one hand. He glanced around and, as he'd suspected, from here he was only clearly visible to the house next door.

He rapped three times, a confident knock, nothing sneaky going on here, he thought. As she warily opened the screen door a crack, he flashed his most brilliant smile. "Afternoon, ma'am."

"Whadya want?" She squinted at him as smoke snaked toward her receding hairline. She was a tough-looking woman, all creases and folds, like a shrunken elephant. What remained of her hair straggled down the nape of her neck in wispy yellowing strands, too-red lipstick glared from her mouth. Her shriveled form was covered by an ancient paisley housedress that hung like a shroud.

To be honest, he felt a little badly for this woman who'd never done anything to him. But then he wasn't the one who had involved her. "I'm Russ, a friend of your son's? He said you had some pipe problems, asked if I could take a look. I was in the neighborhood, thought I'd stop by."

"You a plumber?" She squinted at the gray coveralls he was wearing, the name "Russ" emblazoned on his chest, red letters in a white oval.

"Yes, ma'am."

She regarded him skeptically. "Dwight doesn't have any friends."

He guffawed as though she'd just said the funniest thing in the world. "You kidding? Dwight and me go way back. I see him almost every night at Ace's Place. He's picked up the tab for me enough times, I owe him." He started to reach for the door handle, but she held on to it firmly from the other side.

"Nope, you're lying," she said decidedly. "I know my Dwight, he's too cheap to buy me a drink, never mind the likes of you. Go on and get off my property, now." She waved a hand, shooing him as if he were a gnat, and his smile vanished.

He yanked the door open with one hand as she raised both of hers in fear, backing away. "I really hoped it wouldn't come to this, ma'am."

She started to scream and he crossed the room in a bound, grabbing her head with one hand as he stuffed a cloth in her mouth with the other. With practiced precision he peeled a piece of duct tape off the back of his pants and slapped it over her mouth and nose, holding the cloth in place. She gagged slightly, eyes wide as she struggled to breathe. She tore at his arms, but her fingers slipped off the smooth fabric and he grabbed her hands in his, holding them tightly by the wrists as she flailed.

He watched for a minute, then said calmly, "If you stop fighting me, I'll take the tape off your nose so you can breathe. But you have to stop fighting me, okay?"

She nodded frantically. Her eyes were starting to pop a little, her skin already waxing pale.

"All right, then. Be a good girl," he chided. He eased back the tape around her nose, exposing her nostrils. She greedily sucked in air, wheezing slightly through her nasal passages.

She calmed down as she breathed. Her eyes focused intently on him. He had to give her credit, for an old bird she'd put up more of a fight than he'd anticipated. The important thing now was to keep her calm. "All right, Nancy, here's what's going to happen. I'm going to tape your hands together behind your back, and I'm going to tape your feet together. You and I are going to take a little ride. But if you do everything I say, no harm will come to you. Understood?"

A tear ran down her face, but she issued a slight nod.

"All right. Here we go."

Five minutes later he had her stuffed in the oversize duffel and stowed in the back seat of his king cab. He'd straightened up the kitchen, erasing any sign of a struggle, leaving no indication he'd been there. *Well, almost none,* he thought with a slow smile.

He could hear her rasping in the back seat. He shook his head at her naiveté; what did she think, that he was planning on holding her for ransom? One glance at her dump of a house told you she didn't have a pot to piss in. People were too trusting, when it came right down to it. Whatever happened to them was their own damn fault.

Twenty-Three

Kelly glanced up at the rap on her office door. Jake stood there, grinning, a white paper bag in one hand. "Excuse me, Officer, I'm looking for my girl. She's a good-lookin' redhead, about yay high?" He held a hand just under his shoulder and raised an eyebrow.

"Your girl, huh?" she asked.

"If you haven't seen her, I suppose I'll have to give this cheeseburger to some other needy soul." He peered into the bag quizzically. "It'd be a shame, though. Got one topped with brie, which I know she's a fan of."

"Brie? Yum." Kelly jumped up from the desk and crossed the room, reaching for the bag. He swept it away and held her back with one hand.

"Not so fast, missy. Gotta pay the kiss toll first."

She leaned in and let her lips graze his, then relaxed and probed a bit deeper. Suddenly self-conscious, she glanced over his shoulder to see if anyone was watching. He caught her look and smiled.

"Don't worry, looks to me like the rest of the office checked out for the day."

"They have? What time is it?" She turned over her wrist and squinted to see her watch face in the dim lighting.

"That's right, almost eight," he said when her eyes widened. "So much for our seven-o'clock dinner reservation."

She raised a hand to her mouth. "God, Jake, I'm so sorry."

He waved off her apology. "Don't be. You're on a case, I'm the one that dropped in on you. I figured this way at least we could eat together."

"Thanks." She gratefully took the bag and spread the contents out on the table in the center of the room. As she chewed the first bite, her eyes half closed. The burger was delicious, and she was famished. She realized that she hadn't eaten anything since breakfast.

"Little hungry, huh?" he said, bemused.

"Starving. What did you do today?" she said through a mouthful.

"Pretty great hike, actually, up the Appalachian Trail toward Vermont. Checked out a section of your boneyard."

"Yeah? I thought that was still closed," she said, her forehead creased.

"You need more than some stinking police tape to keep me out," he said. He caught the look in her eye and held up one hand. "Hey, I was just curious. Although I was seriously considering dumping a body there, thought it might get us a little quality time together."

She rolled her eyes. "Thanks, I've got more than enough bodies to deal with without any extra help from you."

"Anything so far?" he asked.

"Not really. Got an ID on one of the bodies we just

exhumed, it matches a ten-year-old missing persons case. But no real leads. I spent the afternoon watching someone get hypnotized, though."

"Yeah?" Jake chuckled. "Hey, don't bogart the fries, pass a few over here. How was that?"

"Interesting. Not what I expected." Kelly chewed reflectively. She'd expected the lights to be turned low and a couch to be involved somehow, but the therapist just had Sommers sit back in a leather armchair and close his eyes.

"Did you buy it?" Jake asked, raising an eyebrow.

"I don't know. He claims Jim agreed to come with him as long as Sommers didn't turn him in to the cops. Then they got pulled over. The cop got them out of the car, said he was going to bring them in. When Sommers had his hands on the car hood, waiting to be cuffed, he felt a pinch in his neck. After that, he doesn't recall much. Said he was in the back of a car, though, and saw Jim dead."

"Sounds guilty to me," Jake said.

"Maybe."

He looked at her. "You don't sound convinced."

She hesitated, then replied, "It's almost too obvious, you know? And Sommers has a decent alibi for Danny's murder, unless his lawyer is shadier than he seems. So far, his reputation checks out. He even testified against a client who tried to use him as a middleman to order hits from prison. That almost destroyed his practice."

"But you might be looking for two killers, right? So maybe Sommers is just one of them," Jake pointed out.

"Maybe. I don't know, I feel like this case is starting to bury me." She wiped the grease off her hands and took a sip of ginger ale. "I'm afraid I might be stuck here for months."

Jake started to clean up the wrappers, tucking them back in the bag. "Could be worse. I hear fall is nice here, leaves turning and all. Maybe we could find a place to rent."

"Maybe we could what?" she said, cocking an eyebrow. "What's up with you? Don't you have to go back to work?"

Jake shrugged. "I got some money saved up. And I got a call from Dmitri today. I guess his meeting last weekend went well, it looks like he might stay in New York for a while to set up this victims' foundation. It's not a bad drive up and back, I could probably even commute some days."

"You didn't get fired, did you?"

He grinned at her. "Oh ye of little faith. Nope, still gainfully employed. I'm just excited to be stateside for a while. Thought we could take the opportunity to spend a little more time together."

"Sure," she said uncertainly.

Jake stood and crossed the room toward the trash can. When he spoke, there was hurt in his voice. "Wow, that was a glowing endorsement. Thanks."

"I'm sorry, I just…I feel a little blindsided here," she said apologetically, crossing her arms in front of her chest.

"I've been trying to talk to you about this since I got here," he retorted.

"I know." Kelly glanced away. She didn't know why she always reacted this way whenever anyone tried to get close to her. But then she'd thought things were perfect just the way they were: they shared a few stolen weekends here and there, the rest of the time they got on with their respective lives and responsibilities. She'd assumed Jake felt the same way. "I'm sorry, I don't know what to say," she concluded lamely.

He gazed past her, toward the open door. "Listen, I know

it's tough for you to let yourself get close to people. I get that, believe me." He met her eyes and put his hand on top of hers. "And I'm trying to be understanding. But honestly, Kelly, I'm not a patient guy. There's only so long I will wait. Okay?"

She nodded and managed a weak smile. "Okay."

"All right, then. Can we go now?"

Kelly glanced back at the files. "I've still got a lot of work to do here…" she hedged.

"You might be stuck here for months, remember? Time to start pacing yourself." Jake cocked an eyebrow and said, "Besides, I checked the listings and there's something good on pay-per-view tonight. I feel strongly that we should watch it together."

"You want me to stop working so we can watch some porn?" Kelly said quizzically.

"Exactly. So chop-chop, let's get a move on." He clapped his hands together. "We don't have all night."

It took longer than usual to string her up. Despite her rangy appearance she was surprisingly solid and his shoulder still ached from last week. Just getting her positioned took some work. Usually the boys he worked with were long and lanky; they hadn't had a chance yet to gain any of the bulk age added year by year. Not her, though—a lifetime of beer nuts and boxed wine had given her fleshy arms and a protruding gut. His face twisted in revulsion when he stripped her down, he was half tempted to dress her again but that wouldn't do, even though she wasn't one of his typical guests there was a protocol to be observed.

The drugs worked like a charm on her, though, and she'd simply gazed at him blearily while he got things in order. He wondered if the dose needed to be adjusted for age, he'd forgotten to check. Not that it really mattered, in the end, but he was hoping to keep her alive for the completion of his plan.

Once she was shackled he stepped back to admire his handiwork; chains led from her arms to the wall, so that she was unable to lift them above her waist. No chance of her getting out of the manacles, so binding her legs was unnecessary, and at her age she was more likely to get sores than the boys. He usually kept them for six days, that left plenty of time for him to have his fun and to clean up. This time circumstances were somewhat different. He was using another location, on the off chance that Dwight was fool enough to go to the police. Not likely, but Dwight was a dumb shit, no telling what he might do when pushed. And because he wanted to extend the game a little longer than usual, he needed her off-site anyway.

He glanced around the room—it would suffice for his needs. Originally built by the Federal Civil Defense Administration in the 1950s at the height of the Cold War, the bunker was designed to house and shelter up to three hundred people underground in the event of a nuclear attack. Abandoned and boarded up during the sixties, it was still used occasionally by National Guard units for training. He'd checked, and no one had reserved it until the end of September, which left him plenty of time.

The bunker was a labyrinth of deserted, dusty rooms filled with forgotten items. He was holding her in the former bathroom. He'd managed to rig the shackles to an empty shower stall at the end of the room, out of sight of the door. Ten other stalls lined one side of the room, then an open archway led to a row of toilets. He held up an instrument that checked the air temperature and measured for any dangerous gases. No sign of carbon monoxide. At sixty-eight degrees she'd be chilly, but shouldn't go into hypothermia. Satisfied, he chucked her under the chin. "Be good for me, Nancy. I'll be back before you know it, and we'll get started."

He left, taking the lantern with him and casting her into shadow. Outside the bathroom was a former bunk room, with a few rusty cots strewn about as if a cyclone had swept through. He had stacked a series of duffel bags in the corner and surrounded them with rat traps to keep the vermin at bay; the last thing he needed was for rodents to mess with the tools of his trade. Thankfully he'd saved a few items during his purge last week. If he'd tossed them it would have meant a four-hour drive across three counties to repurchase them somewhere he wouldn't be recognized or remembered, and even then it was chancy. After all, it wasn't every day someone strolled in off the street and bought one of these, he thought, drawing a long, barbed hook out of the top bag, turning it so that it gleamed in the light. No, he'd been wise to hold on to this, it would've been a shame to have done without it.

A slight smile danced around his lips, then with a sigh he tucked it away. Not tonight, unfortunately. He had to get home, Sylvia and the kids would be back soon and they were all going to Tanglewood for a concert. It was one of his wife's favorite things to do. They'd set out a blanket and a picnic, enjoy chilled pinot grigio and listen to the Boston Symphony Orchestra while the girls chased each other around the lawn. Personally he found it a bit smelly and plebeian, but if he went she'd be placated, and he'd have more freedom tomorrow. It was inconvenient still having them here, but since the girls went back to school next week, Sylvia had decided to let them enjoy the last of their vacation in the Berkshires.

As he left, he snapped a kryptonite lock on a chain looped through the front door handles. The civil defense bunker was a little more public than he would've preferred, but under the circumstances it should suit his needs. Even if Nancy was found he'd taken care not to leave behind any evidence implicating him. Everything in the duffels was purchased with cash and little of it had been handled yet. The items he had used were soaked in bleach and alcohol for days. And, of course, he'd always worn his full suit every time he entered the bunker. He crossed the parking lot and ducked through the trees, removing the shower cap, the booties and the gloves as he went. By the time he emerged next to his parked truck, he looked like any other hiker enjoying the last gasp of summer.

Dr. Stuart squinted at the test results, flipped back a few pages, turned to the body in front of him and frowned. "It just doesn't make any sense," he said aloud, before setting the papers down on the table and removing his glasses so he could polish them.

"Why not?" Monica asked, crossing her arms over her chest.

"Just look here." He gestured for her to lean in as he hovered over a corpse laid out on a gurney.

Monica kept her eyes elevated. "Thanks, I've seen him."

"I know you've seen him, but have you examined him closely?"

Monica heaved a sigh and glanced downward. "You have any idea the kind of nightmares I'm having?"

"Actually, I do," he said, sotto voce.

Monica tapped him on the shoulder, her lips curving up

slightly with delight. "I swear, Howie, you're getting fresher every day. So what am I looking at here?" She forced herself to gaze down at the remains of Danny Smith.

His chest cavity had been peeled open, the skin held in place by enormous metal prongs. Howard probed the cavity with a wooden tongue depressor, pointing out elements as he went along. "I first suspected it when I saw the lungs were overinflated and filled with fluid, but that in and of itself doesn't prove anything. They would be the same in the event of a pulmonary edema, or even a drug overdose. The same conclusion could be drawn from the hemorrhages in his bony middle ear. They might be attributed to head trauma, or as a side effect of electrocution, both of which we know he was subjected to."

"You do dance around it, don't you." Monica sighed. She hated to admit it, since she knew this was his job, but the dispassionate way he was dealing with the kid's body kind of creeped her out. "What're you getting at, Howie?"

He beamed at her. "I'm saying that this boy drowned."

"He what? How is that possible?"

He shook his head as he said, "I'm afraid—"

She waved him off. "I know, I know, not your job to figure that part out, it's ours. Gotcha. Any idea where he drowned?"

He shook his head. "I'm still examining the fluid, but saw no sign of silt or other foreign matter indicating a lake or pond. It could possibly have been in a bathtub, or even a toilet. Further tests might show more."

"Jesus." Monica tilted her head back and rubbed her neck with one hand. "That's horrible. Poor kid."

"Yes," he said without conviction. "Anyway, now that I have all the remains consolidated here, I've made tremendous headway."

"Yeah, Kelly put the fear of God in Doyle, finally got him to play nice and share." Monica debated whether or not to tell him more. Despite her strong dislike of Doyle, there was a code among cops, you didn't rat one out to a civilian unless you absolutely had to. And Howie, though he was working with them, wasn't a cop in any sense of the word. She told herself that, knowing full well that the truth was she was half-afraid to find out what his reaction would be. If he didn't act horrified, just gave her that disconcerting stare, how would she handle that? Monica glanced across the room and re-pressed a shudder. "Honestly, Howie, I don't get how this doesn't wig you out."

They were in the center of a large room. Lining one wall were illuminated panels of X-rays, CAT scans, and MRIs; another held state-of-the-art computers and diagnostic equipment. Scattered about the room at odd angles were gurneys, each stacked with the remains of a different victim. Some of the carts held only a few bones, others nearly a full skeleton. The other fresh corpses were in cold storage.

Dr. Stuart shrugged. "It's my job," he said simply, looking wounded.

"I know, it's just…I can't help thinking of Zach when I see all these kids. Someone tossed them out like so much trash. It's just not right. Doesn't that bother you?" She eyed him expectantly.

He removed his glasses and began polishing them again. "In truth, Monica, it doesn't. If I let what people did to each other bother me, I'd never be able to do my job. I apologize if that bothers *you,* but it's how I am. It's not personal for me."

"Okay, so what else did you find?" she said after an awkward pause, changing the subject.

His eyes gleamed. "Now that I have them all in one place, I can say more definitively that you're probably looking for a pair of killers."

"Working together?"

"Doubtful. You see the burns here, and here?" He gestured toward Danny's legs. "On closer examination, it's sloppy work. Very different from what we found on the John Doe from last week. Those marks were deliberate, evenly spaced. Whoever did this had no idea what he was doing, while the other body underwent what I would call a very studied and thorough trauma. I'd compare it to cutting a lawn with a pair of scissors as opposed to using a lawn mower."

"Huh. Anything else?"

"Since most of the other remains are skeletal, it's difficult to say what they were subjected to premortem. But on the waist of the most recent John Doe, there's evidence of some sort of hook being applied through the flesh. Based on my research I'd guess he used something called the Algerian hook, a slow method of execution favored four hundred years ago in North Africa. Usually the victims were impaled through the waist by a suspended hook, and left dangling. Whoever inserted this one was particularly adept—he managed to avoid all major organs. In the end it wasn't the hook that killed the boy."

Monica shuddered. "That's horrible."

"Indeed. Apparently the hook was even used for such minor crimes as stealing a loaf of bread. Algiers was one of the safer cities in the world at that time."

Monica cast him a withering look. "Not that you support that kind of treatment."

"Of course not. Really, Monica, do you not know me at all?" He gazed at her quizzically.

Monica shrugged in response. "I guess I don't, not really. We haven't had a lot of those talks yet. Hell, I don't even know if you support the death penalty." She issued a short, barking laugh. When he didn't respond, she raised an eyebrow. "Jesus, really? The death penalty?"

He held up a hand. "Granted, in this day and age I think that sentence is applied too liberally for lesser offenses. But for certain criminals, when there's no doubt as to their guilt and no hope for rehabilitation…" He stared her down. "Are you saying that if the killer of these boys was caught and there was no doubt as to his guilt, you would want him to live?"

Monica eyed him levelly. "Absolutely. I don't believe in an eye for an eye."

"And if he killed Zach?"

"That's a terrible thing to say," Monica said, shocked. "How could you suggest that, even as an example?"

"I suppose we'll have to agree to disagree," Dr. Stuart said, turning from her to focus back on the body. His voice resumed the authoritative lecturing tone he was so fond of. "The eyes were gouged out of all the skulls. Based on the three found recently, we can determine that the genitals were removed, postmortem on two of them, premortem on the John Doe. And if pressed, I'd say two were killed by your novice. The ones that showed signs of previous burial were killed by someone else."

"So, what? We've got a copycat on our hands?" Howie shrugged and opened his mouth to respond, but Monica waved a hand impatiently, cutting him off. "I know, I know. Not your job. I'm just starting to wish it wasn't mine, either."

"Are we still having dinner this evening?" he asked after a pause.

"Can't, I have to track down a few more people," she said, turning to leave.

He caught her hand, but she refused to face him. "Let's not pretend this was ever anything more than it was, okay?" she said in a low voice.

He dropped her hand abruptly and she left the room, head down.

Twenty-Four

Doyle tilted his head back, taking another gulp of Gatorade. Another car drove past, a Volvo that barely held a family of five, water toys smashed against the rear window, canoe strapped to the top. As they drove past he caught a glimpse of a kid, mouth pressed up against the glass in a slobbery O. He snorted, glanced at the pad next to him and shook his head. "Not going to bother with that one, either," he grumbled.

The pad contained the license plate numbers of eight cars. Probably three times that had passed him so far, but Doyle hadn't bothered to write down every goddamn one of them. He had a sneaking suspicion that the second half of this assignment—tracking down the owners of those cars—was going to fall to him, too. It wouldn't hurt to lighten his workload from the get-go.

This was a bullshit assignment, anyway. Little FBI bitch was just trying to keep him busy, having him stake out Grafton Lakes State Park, the place where they'd found the last body. New York had refused to close off anything but the immediate area where the kid was found, which was probably smart. If another local swimming hole had been blocked off, people would've really raised a stink. Besides, no way in hell the killer was going to show up here again. He'd already jumped around to a couple different parks since they'd found his boneyard. In this neck of the woods he could pick and choose from another dozen without putting a dent in his gas tank.

Another car eased up the road, slowing to the five miles per hour speed limit when it spotted his cruiser. It pulled alongside and eased to a stop. The passenger side window rolled down. Doyle leaned forward and squinted to see the driver, grinning when he recognized him.

"How the hell are you, Sam?" he asked.

"Not bad, Lieutenant. You on duty?"

"Yup, undercover," Doyle nodded. He'd been given strict orders to stay out of sight, which he'd chosen to disregard.

Sam Morgan dubiously examined the patrol car. "Yeah? Guess I shouldn't trouble you, then."

"No, that's all right. I'm going nuts with boredom. See you got your girls with you." He nodded toward the two sets of blond ponytails poking up from the back seat.

"Thought we'd take a swim, cool off a bit. Unbelievable, this heat. Figured it would've broken by now."

"Yeah, well, I hear there's a storm coming. Probably hit sometime tomorrow," Doyle noted.

"Thank God. Hey, by the way, saw something kind of strange the other day, thought maybe I should mention it. The wife and I were coming back from dinner, a bit later than usual. Guy drove past us like a bat out of hell."

"C'mon, Sam, you know I don't handle traffic violations." Doyle said, cutting him off.

"No, I figured. Thing was, he turned in here. And then the next day, I read about that boy you found…anyway, it was probably nothing. Just figured I'd mention it."

Doyle rubbed the stubble that was already establishing a beachhead on his face. "You get a make or model?"

Sam shrugged. "It was a piece of junk, pretty old. It was definitely a sedan, though. A Toyota, maybe? Sorry, I'm not good with that sort of thing."

"Anything distinctive about it?"

Sam cocked his head to the side, thinking. "I'm pretty sure the hood was a different color, darker than the rest of the car. And one of the taillights was replaced with tape. Sorry I can't be more helpful."

"Well, don't worry about it. Probably just a bunch of kids looking for a place to knock back some beers."

"Yeah, probably. Well, have a good one." Sam waved and put the car back into gear, rolling past slowly.

Doyle waved in return, watched as the car rounded the bend fifty yards ahead. Wasn't much of a lead, but it was something. If he managed to solve this case on his own, without the help of the damned task force, he'd be a hero and Internal Affairs wouldn't be able to touch him. He'd sure as hell love to show up that FBI pain in the ass. He brooded for a minute, then picked up his radio.

"Georgia? Doyle here. Listen, honey, I need you to run a search for early model Toyotas and Hondas. I want you to look through the yearly inspections, find one with a different color hood. Check Massachusetts first, then Vermont and New York. Oh, and Georgia? Keep this between us and there's a steak dinner in it for you."

* * *

Jan clicked her fingernails angrily on the van hood. Her cameraman, Mike, stood off to one side uncertainly. She hadn't said anything since returning from the precinct's rear parking lot. Clearly she was in one of her snits again.

"Uh, boss? You want to stick around here a while longer, or should we—"

"Shut up and let me think, would you?" she snapped.

He raised a hand to calm her and stepped back, moving to the rear of the van.

The doors were open. Joe the sound guy was there, perched on the rear ledge, playing some sort of handheld video game. He glanced up as Mike approached. "How's the princess?" he asked in a low voice when Mike dumped the camera next to him.

"In rare form," Mike grunted in response.

Joe bobbed his head once. "Figures. Doesn't look like she's getting that scoop she was hoping for, huh? Hope she didn't actually put out for that bastard Doyle."

"Not that it would be the first time," Mike noted.

Around the front of the van, Jan stared off into the distance without seeing anything. She'd heard a rumor that one of the network bigshots had nailed an interview with Sommers, an interview that as a local should have been hers. Probably that bitch from CNN, the one who always looked so pleased with herself in her tailored Chanel suits. Jan tugged self-consciously at her skirt. It wasn't cheap, but it wasn't Chanel, either. No way she was affording that, not on her salary.

This case was supposed to be her big break, the one that would finally launch her out of this backwater into a major market. When she'd started in weather after graduating with her communications degree, she'd known it would be a hard climb, that not having attended a prestige school she was already at a deficit. But she'd worked hard, and had known enough to cultivate some of the right friends along the way. Those relationships had gotten her this far. It was time for the next step, though, *past* time. She was a pragmatist, knew that New York or D.C. was unlikely, but Boston was certainly within her grasp. And after a few years in the anchor chair there, once she'd paid her dues, who knew. Maybe a major morning show.

She stepped back to examine herself in one of the oversize side mirrors mounted on the van. The problem was that she was pushing her late twenties, and no one over thirty had ever managed such a major leap up the career ladder. At least, no woman had. Doyle had turned out to be a total wash, not worth the time and energy she'd invested in him. So far he hadn't told her anything that the captain didn't blather on about at the daily press conferences. And that goddamn FBI bitch... Jan's fists clenched and her cheeks flushed at the memory of her humiliation in the parking lot. She squinted, examining the slight creases at the corners of her eyes. If she didn't get a break in this case soon, she'd have to consider Botox. Her cell phone chimed and she glanced at the caller ID, not recognizing the number. She snapped it open anyway.

"Jan Waters here." She listened for a minute, her eyes narrowing shrewdly. She nodded as if the person on the other end could see her. When she spoke, her voice was saccharine-sweet. "Really? Why, Dorothy, I swear I owe you a hug and a kiss for that one. Or at least a big old margarita." She listened again, then laughed. "All right, then. Drinks on me next time. Bye now."

She clicked the phone shut triumphantly and marched to

the back of the van. Mike and Joe eyed her balefully. She assumed a false brightness and said, "Good news, boys, one of my contacts gave us a lead. Cops were at the Registry of Deeds today asking about a house where a bunch of the victims stayed. Let's head over there and check it out. Joe, get in touch with research back at the station, see if they can find out who the owner is."

She swiveled without waiting for a response and sashayed to the passenger side of the van, swinging inside and buckling up. It wasn't the best lead, but it was something. And she knew the other stations were completely in the dark, so if nothing else she had a scoop for the six-o'clock show. The station head would be pleased. As she waited for Joe to clamber into the driver's seat, she flipped down the visor and checked her makeup in the mirror. Looked like Botox could wait a few more months, she thought, smiling grimly as she applied another layer of lipstick.

Twenty-Five

Dwight paced back and forth. His hair jutted out from his head in greasy spikes that morphed into new formations every time he frantically ran a hand through it. His eyes were red rimmed and wild, and his chest heaved as he crossed the room again. "Motherfucker. Motherfucker!" he muttered, over and over again.

When he first got home he figured Ma must've left early for bingo to make sure she got the best seat in the house—she did that sometimes. He was halfway to his room when he turned, puzzled. Something niggled at his mind, telling him things weren't right. He'd turned back to the kitchen and there it was, a carton of cigarettes dangling on a wire strung from the overhead fan. He knew immediately what had happened. It was a nasty reference to a prank the Captain had played on him, the reason he'd sworn vengeance in the first place. During a training expedition, they'd gone deep into the woods, backcountry camping. He was the only one who had done it before; hell, without him, a few of them might not have survived the night. He'd gotten the fire started without using matches, dug them a latrine, showed them how to filter stream water through dead coals, strung up the food so that bears couldn't get to it. He'd gotten pats on the back; for once everyone seemed pretty damned happy he was along. He'd gone to sleep feeling like he was finally part of something.

Then the next morning Dwight awoke to find that they'd left him. Worse yet, they'd strung up his clothes and thrown the end of the line out of reach, so he'd had to shimmy up the tree in his goddamn thermals like some asshole. He'd been good and pissed when he caught up with them a few hours later. They joked around, patted him on the back, said it was all in good fun. He'd known better. Caught the Captain grinning at him, muttering to the others, and knew he'd been behind it. As Dwight had stormed away that day he told them they'd regret it, that someday he'd get back at them. And he was keeping that promise. It just hadn't occurred to him that the Captain might figure out the war before the final battle.

He compulsively rubbed his scalp again, sending tendrils of hair shooting off in new directions. Taking his mother—that was low. He might not always get along with her—usually didn't—but it was his mother, for chrissake. His first impulse had been to grab the twelve-gauge and dash out of the house. He was going to drive right up to the Captain and threaten to blow his head off if he didn't let her go. But halfway down the driveway he ground to a halt, throwing the car into Park. That was exactly what the Captain would be expecting. Deep down Dwight knew that when it came to thinking he was outmatched; the Captain always had a plan, he never did anything half-cocked. Hell, he was probably planning on laying all the murders at Dwight's doorstep. If he wanted to get his mother back, first he'd have to figure out what the Captain was up to.

His eyes squeezed tightly shut as he pictured what might be happening to her. The Captain wouldn't kill her, not right away. He never did, always kept them alive for some time while he played with them. Dwight had seen him coming and going through that hatch, popping up blinking and smiling, then descending again after eating lunch or taking the dog for a walk. "Sick fuck," he said, gritting his teeth. No, if he wanted to beat him, he'd have to try to think like him. Luckily he'd already had some practice doing just that.

"So you've never met him in person, then? I find that... unusual," Monica said, arching an eyebrow.

Gino Brondello shrugged as one hand scratched his belly through a stained undershirt. He was standing in the screen door of a duplex a few blocks away from the flophouse. "Listen, the guy paid cash. And that place was such a dump, figured I was lucky to rent it. It was empty for years after my dad died."

"So you inherited the house," Monica confirmed.

Gino nodded. Not surprising, Monica thought, taking him in. He barely looked as if he could manage himself, never mind multiple properties. "Yeah, money was always in my mailbox May first."

"What did he pay you?"

He examined the ground, seemingly distracted by a beetle scurrying across the peeling porch floorboards. "Thirty grand," he finally said in a low voice.

"Excuse me? Thirty grand for four months?"

He nodded again, looking painfully uncomfortable. Monica let out a low whistle. Even if the place had been a palace, that was at least twice the going rate for a summer rental in the Berkshires. No wonder Gino hadn't asked any questions, for him thirty grand was the equivalent of winning the lottery. It certainly explained the big-screen TV she could see dominating the living room behind him. Hell, he probably lived off that cash all year. "How long has this been going on?" she asked reproachfully.

"Dunno. Ten years, maybe?"

"Ten years is a hell of a long time, Mr. Brondello. You ever stop by the house, check in to see how the tenant was getting along?"

He shook his head. "That was part of the deal. I got a few complaints from neighbors sometimes, about parties there. Called the number I was given for emergencies and he said he'd take care of it."

"Who said that?" Monica pressed.

"Some guy. Didn't get his name."

"So let me get this straight, Mr. Brondello. You rented a house to someone who answered an ad you posted in the paper. But you never made him fill out a rental application, never even got his name or social security number, because he offered you a lot of cash to keep your mouth shut. That pretty much cover it?"

He glanced over his shoulder, as if help might arrive from the depths of the house. The TV blared in the background.

"You know, Mr. Brondello, at least three of the boys who were staying in that house have been murdered."

"I don't know nothing about that," he replied sullenly.

"I'm sure you don't. Still, I think you better come down to the station with me. I have a few more questions to ask you."

"Yeah? Like what?"

"Like where were you last weekend, Mr. Brondello? And have you been claiming this chunk of cash on your income tax forms?" Gino looked visibly uncomfortable at the accusation, and she knew she had him. Monica didn't think he was their guy. He didn't seem motivated enough to get off the couch to make a sandwich, it was doubtful he'd meticulously planned and executed multiple murders. But so far he was the closest link to their killer, so she kept her hand close to her hip holster as she said, "After you," nodding to her patrol car.

Gino paused for a beat, and she held her breath, wondering if she should have brought backup. He wasn't a big guy but he was thick, probably strong under all that fat. Reluctantly he shuffled past her. She followed him down the cracked-concrete path to the street, helped him into the back seat. Slamming the door shut, she heaved a sigh of relief. Gino settled into the back seat, arms crossed defensively over his chest, glaring at the grill in front of him. Clearly not his first time in a police car, she thought as she slid into the driver's seat. But his record was for minor stuff, check kiting, skipping court appearances, nothing that even qualified as a felony.

The number he'd been given probably matched a disposable phone. She'd run it anyway, but chances were it was already dead. She'd put Gino's photo in a lineup, see if Jordan could ID him as the guy who ran him off the property. Monica suspected it had been someone else, because Gino definitely didn't fit the description "good-looking." If she was right, they could sit Jordan down with a sketch artist, and with any luck might finally get a portrait of one of the killers.

Someone had rented that house from Gino every summer for the past decade. *It might as well have been a holding pen at a slaughterhouse,* she thought with a shudder as she pulled away from the curb.

Twenty-Six

She yelped in pain, fouling herself again, and the man turned his head away with distaste. It had been difficult rigging up the Algerian hook. Back home, he had an eyelet specially mounted in the ceiling for just such a purpose. Here, he'd had to rig a line from the shower pipe behind her. Instead of dangling them above, chains ran around the pipe and linked to the hook in her back. In order to apply the necessary pressure he'd wrapped a rope under her arms, and he intermittently gave it a tug, yanking forward so that her flesh strained against the hook. The stream of blood flowing from the wound gushed out when he applied pressure to the rope, slowing to a rivulet in between. He'd have to be careful, if she lost too much blood he'd have to give her a transfusion to keep her alive, always a tricky matter. At least inserting the hook so that it didn't penetrate any organs had been easier than with the boys; her skin was loose and flabby, and he'd pierced a roll of it no problem.

Initially she'd screamed and babbled, begging him to stop,

saying all the usual things. He'd ignored her; it seemed to distress them more when he did that. Speaking to them just reinforced false hopes for their survival. Better that he seem less human, that way they gave up far more quickly.

He had to admit, though, he wasn't enjoying this one at all. Perhaps he should've just started with Dwight. He could have dragged out the punishment for weeks, possibly even months with transfusions and antibiotics. He found torturing this old woman unsettling, even if she was partly responsible for the actions of her son. He took a deep breath and reminded himself of his objective: psychological punishment first, then physical pain. The wrenching guilt that Dwight was experiencing right now had to be intolerable. For most people, feeling responsible for injury to a loved one was far worse than getting hurt themselves.

In spite of that, looking at her now, face red, swollen, and tear-streaked, naked flesh blue and mottled with goose bumps, he was almost moved to pity. He eased up on the rope and she collapsed backward, groping until she reached the wall, trying to grab hold of something. She was gasping slightly, panting like a dog. She made no other noise. Her head hung forward in utter defeat. Looking at her, huddled and cowering like an animal, he decided to break his own rule.

"It's your son's fault, you know," he said in a low voice, conversational. "This wouldn't be happening if it weren't for him."

"What?" she gasped, after a moment. He saw a semblance of conscious thought return to her eyes.

"Your son, Dwight. He was very stupid, acting against me. He did some very bad things." He leaned forward so that she could see his eyes in the sparse light. "He killed those boys."

"You're crazy," she said after a moment, her breath evening out. "My boy never killed anyone."

"You don't believe me." He leaned in closer, speaking soothingly, as if to a child. "But you knew he was sick. It was you that sent him to the hospital the first time, wasn't it? You know what Freud said, blame the mother. Did you touch Dwight in bad places when he was a little boy? Maybe gave him long baths, had him share your bed after your husband abandoned you?"

"Fuck you." She spit with sudden and surprising vehemence. "You call yourself a man, beating up on an old woman. You're a disgrace."

He tilted his head to the side. "Thank you. You've made this much easier."

With a vicious tug he jerked the rope again. Caught by surprise, she lost her grip on the pipes behind her and flew forward until the hook caught with a ripping sound and she shrieked.

Kelly walked into the office holding up a file triumphantly. "DNA came back on another John Doe."

Lieutenant Peters glanced up. He had set the rickety table on its side against a wall, clearing a space in the center of the room. Now he sat cross-legged on the floor surrounded by stacks of files, regarding her blearily. "Which one?"

"One of the victims from the original boneyard, the one Dr. Stuart figured was between a year and two years old." She opened the file and held up a rap sheet with a mug shot. "Meet Richard Waters, aka Little Ricky. Couple of arrests in Massachusetts for solicitation and possession. He fits the profile of the other victims we've ID'd so far. Last arrest was two years ago, maybe that'll help us narrow down when he disappeared…" She glanced up to find Colin's face had gone ashen. "What's wrong?"

He held out a shaky hand for the file. "Could I see that, please?" he said unsteadily.

She watched as he opened it and scanned the page. Unless she was mistaken there was a tear in the corner of his eye. "Colin, did you know this kid?"

He nodded slowly. "He was my cousin. We grew up together."

"Oh, God. I'm so sorry. If I'd known…" She squatted next to him and awkwardly extended a hand to pat his shoulder. "Um, can I get you a glass of water or something?"

"No, I'm fine." He inhaled a deep, shuddering breath. "I kind of knew this was coming, but part of me hoped…"

Kelly cocked her head to the side. "Is that why you got assigned to this case?"

Colin nodded. "My captain didn't know about Ricky, he just figured I wanted to check out the task force."

Kelly thought for a moment. By getting involved with the case when he knew there might be a personal link, Colin had defied basic police protocol. But she couldn't really bring herself to chastise him, not when she understood exactly what he was going through. "Is there a missing persons file for him?" She asked.

Colin nodded. "Not here, though. It's in New York. "

"Okay." She rubbed her eyes with one hand. "Why don't I give you a minute to collect yourself. I'll call and get a copy faxed over."

Kelly straightened and looked down at him. He was examining the floor, looking completely bereft. She turned and left the room, easing the door shut behind her. She paused for a second with her hand on the knob, a rush of emotion causing her heart to thump uncomfortably against her rib cage. She felt that same horrible pit in her stomach, the ball of emotion that formed when she had found out her brother had been brutally murdered. She had wanted to scream and thrash but for some reason couldn't, despite the overwhelming emotions trapped inside her raging to be set free. Kelly swallowed hard and went to make that phone call.

Dwight squinted down from his perch in the crux of a tree. He was about fifty feet away from the Captain's backyard, observing it through swaying branches. In his full camouflage suit, he was pretty sure he wouldn't be noticed.

The Captain was running around, playing with his little girls like he didn't have a care in the world. Dwight's knuckles went white as he tightened his grip on the binoculars, jaw rigid with rage. Bastard had his mother tucked away in his dark hidey-hole, and was up here enjoying the late-afternoon sunshine. He shifted the focus to one of the little girls, the youngest. She looked about eight years old, blond like her daddy, hair set in pigtails and missing her two front teeth. He watched as she executed a clumsy somersault and came up laughing, tendrils of newly mown grass jutting out from her hair. He'd love to get his hands on them, he thought with a grimace. Show the Captain a little payback, make those little mouths scream and beg for mercy, maybe call their daddy to listen in while he worked on them. At the thought Dwight's mouth curled up at the corners. Not yet, though; first he had to get Ma out of there.

Over the past few hours he'd formulated a decent plan. An hour earlier the wife had driven away in her fancy Beemer, gym bag and racket in the back seat. Off to play tennis. He knew from previous months of surveillance that she'd be gone at least three or four hours. The Captain, on the other hand, was more unpredictable. Even if he did leave, taking the girls with him, it was hard to say whether they'd run out for a quick ice cream or go to the movies. Either way, once they left the house he'd have to chance it. No telling how long the sick bastard would keep his mother alive.

Dwight settled back and waited. The shadows started to lengthen across the lawn, the ghost of a wind whispered through the branches above him, cooling the air a few degrees. The Captain turned on the sprinkler and the girls dashed into the house, emerging a few minutes later in bathing suits. Dwight watched as they splashed each other, giggling. Another half hour passed. The Captain wrapped the girls in towels and helped dry them off, then ushered them inside. Fifteen minutes passed, then a door slammed. Dwight heard chatter from the front of the house. They rounded the corner. If Dwight twisted in his perch and craned his head to the side, he could just glimpse them strolling down the driveway. They vanished, blocked by interceding branches, and he waited, listening. A car door closed, then another, followed by the sound of an engine turning over and the crunch of gravel under tires. He peered intently through the foliage, waiting, marking the time on his watch. While he waited, Dwight knocked his knuckle against the tree trunk in time to the deafening roar of the song blaring in his skull. Five minutes passed with no sign of the car.

Carefully, he shimmied down the trunk and pulled off the tree branches hiding his pack. Slinging it over one shoulder he kept low, sticking to the tree line skirting the property as he came toward the house, headed for the garage. It was set a hundred yards back from the house, far enough away that even if they were home the wife and kids never heard the screams. Perfect planning, Dwight thought. No one ever said the Captain wasn't a smart so-and-so. Before the incident he'd actually admired him, tried to model himself after the guy. That was before he knew he was a full-fledged sicko, of course.

Like the house, the two-car garage was new but made to look old, gray shingles covering the exterior. The inside was spotless. One wall was lined with storage shelves and a work-bench, everything labeled and organized. A ride-along mower was parked against the back wall next to a row of hanging garden implements. The floor was covered in black industrial matting, a nice touch, Dwight thought, since it both covered the trapdoor leading to the hatch and protected the floor from any spills.

Motorcycle parts were strewn across one corner of the garage. Dwight frowned. Crossing the room, he kicked a few pieces aside, then dropped to one knee and grabbed one after another, grunting as he shifted the larger parts behind himself. He dropped the pack on the floor and dug a screwdriver out of it, inserting it into a crack between two of the mats to peel up a corner. Grabbing the edge, he hauled it the rest of the way up and tossed it aside. The door to the hatch was there, just a break in the concrete with a round handle set into it. Hurrying, he inserted his fingers into the ring and pulled until it opened.

It was dark down there. Dwight pulled the flashlight from his tool belt and flicked it on, tucking it into his mouth as he scrambled down the ladder. He paused at the bottom, groping around with one hand until he found the light switch tucked to the right. He flicked it, and an incandescent bulb cast the room in stark hyperrelief. Dwight clicked off the flashlight and turned, then frowned.

He'd only been in the room once before, but it had been dramatically different, like something out of a horror movie. Now it looked like your standard-issue emergency shelter, a locker against one wall, a cot on the other side stacked with old blankets and pillows. He crossed the room in two steps and threw open the locker: nothing inside but rows of canned food and bottled water. He grumbled something under his breath, then threw open the door at the end of the room. A smaller space, the size of a large closet, held a marine toilet and small sink.

His eyes wide, he tore his hands through his hair, barely noticing when he ripped out a clump of it by the roots. He bellowed once, then stormed out, leaving the trapdoor open behind him.

Doyle glanced at the phone again and rolled his eyes, then tapped the button that sent the call to voice mail. He hummed a little as he drove, head bobbing slightly in time to the Wayne Newton tune on his radio. He glanced down at the screen on the computer console bolted to the floor of the car, double-checking the address. Georgia had come through for him all right, almost too well. Ten cars in Berkshire County alone had different colored hoods. He'd managed to check out three so far: one belonged to an old Mexican guy, the other two to welfare moms. None matched the description he had, the hoods were all lighter than the body and the taillights were intact.

So that left seven. With any luck, he'd track down this guy by the end of the day. He didn't want to think about the alternative, if none of the names panned out. If that happened, he'd have to start crossing jurisdictions, and there it got tricky. Of course, even if he found the car Morgan had mentioned, it might turn out to be nothing, someone looking to grab a few nightcrawlers in the park. Doyle's grip tightened on the steering wheel. He was counting on nailing the guy all by himself. He pictured the headline, the look of fury and disappointment on that bitch's face when the governor handed him a commendation for catching one of the worst serial killers New England had ever seen. And there was no way a hero would lose his pension, not in this part of the state.

A minute later his radio crackled. He debated for a minute, then answered, "Go ahead, Georgia."

"Lieutenant Doyle? This is Agent Jones."

He squeezed his eyes shut and cursed silently, wishing to God he hadn't picked up. She sounded even pissier than usual, hard though that was to believe. "What do you want, Jones?" he asked after a minute.

"I want to know what the hell you're doing."

"Doing just what I'm supposed to be doing, sitting here taking down plates."

"Really. You realize the car you're driving is equipped with a GPS tracking system, don't you, Lieutenant?"

Doyle glared at the receiver. He'd forgotten the new squad cars came equipped with that. *Goddamn technology. Guy couldn't scratch his balls anymore without someone else knowing about it.* "Yeah, so I'm taking a break. So what."

"So you're treading on very thin ice, Lieutenant. Based on our conversation yesterday, I expect you to follow my orders."

He glared at the mouthpiece. Something about this woman made him want to spit nails. A decade ago, he'd walked out on the last female that had managed to piss him off this much;

it had been a toss-up between divorcing her or murdering her. Just as he opened his mouth with a retort, his eyes widened. Speeding toward him at about twenty miles over the limit was a battered Toyota, light silver with a dark gray hood. He swiveled as it passed, a grin spreading across his face. Flaps of torn red plastic covered the right rear taillight. He barked into the receiver, "Gotta go," before dropping it on the passenger seat, knocking the volume down so that he could barely hear the squawks of protest. Throwing the car in a tight U-turn, he flicked on his lights and sirens and gunned the engine, accelerating around the bend.

Jan tucked a stray strand of blond hair behind her ear and smiled winningly into the camera. She nodded briskly to Mike, who gave her a thumbs-up: camera rolling. "This is Jan Waters, Channel 6 News, reporting." She took a few steps to the side, gesturing to the house behind her with a sweeping gesture. "Through my sources I've discovered that at least two of the recently murdered boys were living here before they were brutally slain." She paused. When they edited this segment she'd have Mike insert footage of the interior of the house while her voice-over chronicled the chaotic scene. She repressed a shudder. It was horrible inside, through the windows they'd even gotten an amazing close-up of mice nibbling at a moldy sandwich. Her boss would shit himself when he saw that—it was exactly the sort of horror show that kept people from changing channels.

"The owner of the house, Gino Brondello, was unavailable for comment. According to his next-door neighbor, earlier today he was taken into police custody. Local authorities refuse to confirm whether or not Mr. Brondello is a suspect in the recent string of murders." Her voice was heavy with significance as she said this, and she slightly arched one eyebrow. Here they would splice in a sound bite from Brondello's neighbor, an obese woman wearing a sweatshirt despite the heat, who'd gazed nervously at the camera as she said that she'd always thought there was something funny about him. Not only that, but her cat had gone missing last year, a few days after he had complained about it shitting in his yard. They'd have to work on that bit, cut out the "shitting" part, but it was a perfect quote, got the television audience wondering about the guy. Hell, these days it wouldn't take much more than that to condemn a man.

"We spoke with residents on this block, who claim that for years this house has been occupied by groups of young men during the summertime." They'd insert another piece here, an interview with a blue-haired woman in her seventies saying she'd complained to the police repeatedly about loud parties at the house. Showed that the cops had known about the problem, but had done nothing about it. Jan considered keeping the second part in, where the woman said she was shocked that anyone would have rented to "that element," especially in a nice family neighborhood like this one, but decided against it. The prevailing winds had shifted, she could sense it. Folks were talking less now about how these boys were a blight on their community. The addition of fresh bodies to the death toll had suddenly shifted public opinion, casting the victims in a more sympathetic light. Before, folks could tell themselves, *Well hey, they deserved it, living that lifestyle.* But three dead boys in two weeks, not to mention the others found in the boneyard…at those numbers the collective guilt kicked in. *Those damn boys* became *those poor boys,* and that suited Jan just fine: made the human interest angle more compelling. She'd already spoken to her boss about expanding the piece into a series, tracking down a few boys who were still living on the streets, getting some of the heartrending back-stories on how they'd ended up there. Maybe she could even find one or two who'd become productive citizens. Hell, that was the kind of story that won Peabody Awards. And with one of those, she could write her ticket anywhere.

Jan assumed a serious expression as she concluded, "We have to wonder, were these boys being led like lambs to the slaughter? What were they compelled to do, in exchange for a roof over their heads? In the end, did it cost them their lives?"

She let that sink in, pausing before concluding brightly, "Once again, this is Jan Waters. We'll have more on this story tomorrow." She stood for another moment until Mike flashed the all-clear sign.

"What did you think?" she asked.

Mike shrugged. "Sounded good to me."

Jan rolled her eyes. It was easy to see why Mike had never advanced in this field. "Let me look at it, then I might want to shoot that last segment again. I think maybe I should look more upset."

"You're the boss," Mike said, turning away from her as he shuffled to the rear of the van.

Jan followed him, her face smugly confident. She was back on track, she could feel it. No other network had this story, and in a half hour it would be too late for them to catch up. She smiled as she pictured the expression on the face of that bitch from CNN when she found out she'd been scooped. Jan almost hugged herself. *Boston, here I come,* she thought as she climbed into the van.

Twenty-Seven

"What's with him?" Monica asked, jerking her head toward Colin. He sat slumped in the corner of the command center, a cold mug of coffee clasped in both hands. She and Kelly were in the hall just outside, speaking quietly so he couldn't hear them.

"The kid we just ID'd was his cousin," Kelly said shortly.

"No shit? That's a shame." Monica knit her brows. "Kind of a funny coincidence, him getting assigned to this case."

"Don't get me started," Kelly grumbled. "If he doesn't pull it together soon, he's off the team."

"Yeah? That's pretty harsh." Monica sounded surprised.

"Colin chose to get involved with the investigation. If he can't keep his personal feelings out of it, he's got no business being here," Kelly said forcefully.

Monica held up her hands defensively. "Jeesh, you're right, I get it. It's just that Doyle is basically AWOL, and if we lose Colin, too, it's down to just the two of us. Not that that's a problem, it's just that there are kind of a lot of leads to track down."

"Where are we with the owner of the house?" Kelly asked.

"I've got him in holding, but we don't have anything to charge him with. And he hasn't given me zilch on the guy he rented to, claims he never met him in person, never even saw him. The contact number for the tenant matched a disposable cell that's already been disconnected. I'm waiting for the IRS to get back to me on Brondello's tax returns. I'm guessing he never claimed the cash payments. Might be able to use that as leverage to help jog his memory. I've also included Brondello's picture in a photo array. A uniform is driving it over to the place Jordan is staying. If he confirms that a different guy chased him off, we can call in a sketch artist."

"Okay, let's hold on to Brondello for as long as we can. I also need you to find out more about the latest victim we ID'd."

"Colin's cousin?"

Kelly nodded. "See if he shared the same house, or knew some of the same people as the other boys. Start with that bartender from Club Metro—Tony. He has a good handle on the scene."

Monica took the file from her and flipped it open curiously. "Ricky Waters. Doesn't look much like Colin. First cousin?"

Kelly nodded once, sharply.

"Twenty-one years old. Such a shame." Monica glanced behind her toward the main open area of the station. A few detectives sat at their desks, muttering into phones or tapping away on laptops. "I'm actually kind of surprised that the homicide unit here hasn't tried to force a few more Doyles on us, what with all the fresh bodies pouring in."

"I'm guessing they're keeping their heads down and hoping all this blows over," Kelly said. "Which is fine by me since there's no telling how many were involved in the cover-up.

It's okay, if we need more manpower I can always have the Albany field office send in some agents."

"But you don't think we're there yet?" Monica asked.

Kelly shook her head. "Nope. We're still waiting for IDs on most of the bodies and, by and large, the summer crowd has headed south for the winter. I might have to go down to New York to interview them." Which would neatly solve her current Jake problem, Kelly thought to herself, adding, "Chances are this case is going to drag on for months, and I can't commit more Bureau resources unless I've got some solid leads."

"Well, Howie's pretty committed to this two-killer thing." Monica said.

"Yeah? What makes him so sure?"

"He says we got a pro and an amateur on our hands. Something about the marks on the bodies, how they were tortured." She shuddered slightly. "Honestly, the way he talked about it kind of gave me the creeps. Now I'm thinking this might not work out."

"I could've warned you about that," Kelly said, managing a small smile. "I dated a forensics guy once."

"Yeah? An anthropologist like Howie?"

"Nope, blood spatter analyst. We went out for pasta one night and he used the marinara to demonstrate a case he was working on." Kelly grinned. "Suffice it to say, I'm a cream sauce girl now."

"Yeah, well…" Monica kept her voice light, but her eyes stayed focused on the table in front of her. "Serves me right for getting my hopes up."

"Hey." Kelly impulsively grabbed her hand, then faltered as she realized all she had to offer were platitudes.

Monica's green eyes crinkled as she waited, then she broke

into a grin. "Thank God. For a minute there I thought you were going to say there are plenty of fish in the sea."

"Who, me?" Kelly smiled back at her. "Please, like I'm one to talk."

"You kidding?" Monica snorted. "I'd kill for a hunk of manmeat like Jake. And he's nuts about you."

Kelly examined the table, tracing a line across it with her thumbnail as she responded. "The question is, am I nuts about him?"

"Jesus, I wish I had your problems," Monica said with a snort. "Maybe I can snare Sam Morgan. Didn't you think it sounded like he and his wife might have split up?"

Kelly shook her head. "As long as there's a ring on his finger, steer clear. Learned that one the hard way, too."

"Did I miss something?"

They looked up to find Colin Peters standing in the doorway looking puzzled. His face was still drawn and white, but his jaw was set.

Kelly cleared her throat, embarrassed. "We were just discussing some of Dr. Stuart's findings."

"How you holding up, kiddo?" Monica asked with concern.

Colin shrugged. "I've been better. What's next?"

"I'm not sure I can keep you on this case," Kelly said cautiously.

A cloud crossed over his features. "Please don't boot me, Agent Jones. I know I screwed up, but even if you just keep me here going through files, please let me help. I've gotta do something. If you send me back to New York, I'll go nuts."

Kelly debated, then nodded her head once, sharply. "All right. Anything yet on those field reports?"

He looked visibly relieved. "I've been sorting them by

name. Seems to be the same few people popping up over and over. Nothing serious, mainly drug stuff."

"Anyone associated with the victims?"

"Not so far, but I'll keep looking."

"All right. Separate them out by age and stats. We're looking for men in their thirties and forties in good shape."

"Will do. It's a predominantly gay area, so a lot of guys match that description," Colin acknowledged.

"Speaking of which, I tracked down the last of Danny's sugar daddies, and it doesn't look like there's anything there," Monica said. "Most claimed they hadn't seen him in months, and their alibis are all pretty solid. Once I hear back from Jordan, I'll see about finding a sketch artist."

"The Bureau has sketch artists on call in most regions, let me know what turns up and I'll call one in," Kelly suggested.

"Great." Monica examined her watch. "Almost quitting time. What do you think, should we call it a day, or keep going on this?"

Kelly pressed her lips together as they watched her expectantly. "I don't have clearance to issue overtime—"

"Knock, knock!"

Sam Morgan stood there, eyeing them sheepishly. "Sorry to barge in like this, I'm looking for Lieutenant Doyle."

Kelly exchanged a glance with Monica, who wiggled her eyebrows. She repressed a laugh as she said, "He's out on the field. Something I can help you with?"

"I was just thinking maybe I should file a report on what we discussed earlier. Probably should be a record of it somewhere."

"What did you discuss?" Kelly asked.

"Didn't he mention it? Maybe it's really nothing." Sam looked puzzled.

"Why don't you tell me about it, anyway," Kelly said, leaning against the desk and crossing her arms.

Dwight gritted his teeth as he floored it. The cop had been behind him now for a few miles and was steadily gaining. "Piece of crap Tercel," he spit out. He should've traded it in for a motocross bike. Cops would never catch him if he had one of those. He could just take off into the woods and leave the goddamn bastards in his dust. His eyes flicked from the road in front of him to the rearview mirror. Fucking cops with their fucking timing. He'd been on his way to the tennis club, figured he'd grab the wife as she was leaving. The Captain wasn't letting the girls out of his sight but the wife, she was already off the reservation. Dwight was halfway there when the fucking lights appeared in his rearview mirror. He'd debated pulling over, but thought he could lose him if he made it across the border. He was going to take the Taconic Trail, which wound through Petersburgh Mountain and into New York. But another glance at the cruiser riding his ass told him there was no way. The cop was too close and Williamstown was coming up fast. Once he hit the traffic there he'd be fucked.

Making a snap decision Dwight flicked on his turn signal, eased off the gas and pulled over onto the shoulder. The patrol car stopped about ten feet behind him. He watched the driver in the rearview mirror—state police, and only one of them in the car. He shifted carefully, reaching under the seat until his fingers brushed against what he was looking for. Grabbing it, he straightened up, tucking it by his right side, glancing around as he did. He'd pulled over in the perfect spot. The bank he'd parked on dropped away into a gorge, black water haloed by a growth of algae. The ruins of an old sawmill perched above it. He remembered coming here back in high school to get drunk. The pit was supposed to be hundreds of feet deep.

The cop was getting out of his car cautiously, weapon drawn, edging forward. Dwight measured him with his eyes: just shy of six foot, probably a hundred-seventy, older, but tough looking.

The guy was hollering for him to put his hands on the steering wheel. Dwight complied, keeping the object tucked just inside his hand. He smiled as the cop approached. Didn't look like he'd called the car in, but it was hard to say. He probably only had a few minutes. As the cop came up to his window, barking orders, Dwight held up a finger of his left hand and gestured to the radio, which was blaring one of his favorite songs by Boston. The cop nodded, and Dwight reached over to turn it down with his left hand. As he leaned forward, his right hand shot underneath his left elbow and the barbs leaped forward. The cop jumped, body twitching, his gun exploding as he dropped to the ground.

Twenty-Eight

Jake fingered the ring in his pocket, feeling like an idiot. He'd been sitting on the same damn rock for over an hour, staring out at the placid pond. He watched as a series of ripples appeared, then with a quick splash a bass broke the surface, gulping at insects before diving back down. A good-size one, too, from the looks of it. He should've brought his rod. From the trail markers, he guessed this was the area where the hiker had come across that first arm bone. *Hell of a shock that must have been,* Jake thought to himself. His smile faded as he sank back into a reverie.

He'd purchased the ring on a whim. When he passed the store window in Zurich, it had seemed to propel itself toward him from a bed of velvet. Which was funny, because he'd never once in his life noticed anything in a jewelry store. As a rule of thumb he gave them a wide berth, especially when he was with a chick trying to steer him inside. Jake definitely considered avoiding precious stones to be one of his résumé skills. But there was something about that ring. The minute he saw it he thought of Kelly, how the rubies would match her hair. They'd never discussed it, but he didn't figure her for a diamond girl. The ring reminded him of her: it was traditional yet modern, elegant but warm. It had also cost a month's salary, but he'd had the girl box it up without even stopping to consider what buying such a ring might mean.

And that had got him thinking. When he'd found out Dmitri wouldn't be needing him for a week or so, Jake had decided to surprise her. He'd hoped she'd have some time off, but it didn't really bother him that she'd been working pretty much nonstop. That was the job—he'd been there himself in the past. When a case was fighting to get away from you, you had to chase it down. Hell, it was one of the things he loved about her, her single-minded tenacity when it came to her work.

But now he had the feeling she was deliberately avoiding him. The truth was he didn't usually have long, unbroken blocks of time to do nothing but think. And he wasn't enjoying it. He was an action guy, liked to be on the move, busy. Sitting around brooding like this wasn't him, but he couldn't seem to snap out of it. It was ironic. He'd spent years dodging the nets of the various women attempting to snare him. He'd finally met someone he could imagine spending the rest of his life with, and she just wanted to keep things casual.

"Jesus, I am turning into a chick," he said aloud. Another fish broke the surface of the water. He picked up a rock and tossed it sideways, sending it skimming across the series of ripples left in the fish's wake. He took out the ring, turned it over once, watching the light shimmer through it as it rested in his palm. It glowed like an ember. He closed his fingers around it, tucked it in his pocket and turned back toward the woods.

* * *

"Did Doyle check in yet?" Kelly asked the stout dispatcher.

The woman shook her head, avoiding Kelly's eyes. Kelly repressed a sigh. Clearly, the whole Berkshire State Police unit was colluding against her. Funny how that used to hurt her feelings back when she was a rookie—now it was par for the course. When the locals were cooperative it surprised her.

"Where's his car?" she asked.

The woman tapped her computer screen, then shook her head. "It'll take me a few minutes to track him down." She glanced up, her eyes almost completely concealed by folds of flesh.

Kelly stared her down. "That's funny, with your equipment it should come up right away. Why don't you try again."

The woman hesitated, then tapped a few keys. "Looks like he's just outside the city limits." She frowned. "It's a residential area."

"Color me shocked," Kelly said. "Radio him again, explain if he doesn't respond in the next five minutes I'll come after him myself."

Kelly stalked back to the command center. Based on his insubordination today, she had half a mind to march over to IAD with the files proving that Doyle had buried at least four murder investigations. She ran a hand through her hair, aggravated. They were coming up against a wall in this case. Monica's background check into the victims' ex-boyfriends wasn't eliciting anything new. Jordan had confirmed that Gino Brondello wasn't the guy who chased him off the property. However, he balked at sitting down with a sketch artist, said he didn't want to get involved and was leaving town that evening anyway. And the landlord didn't seem to know anything. The minor infractions Colin was tracking down had turned up the same plates over and over, most of them people they'd already investigated, regulars at Club Metro who had alibis or had already left town. The trail was going cold. Unless something major happened, she might just have to ride out the rest of the investigation knowing in her gut that the boys' murders would be relegated to the cold-case pile. Same thing had happened with the Tylenol Killer in the eighties, and a serial killer who had targeted young male athletes in Wisconsin just a few years ago. She was looking for one killer who had murdered almost a dozen boys and, if Dr. Stuart was correct, another who had taken the lives of two more. Three fresh bodies found in the past few weeks, and even then they hadn't caught a break. Both killers were careful to leave no trace evidence behind, just the puzzling stack of pennies. And there was no way to track those.

Kelly realized she'd read the same sentence over and over without processing it. With a sigh she tossed the file on the desk, tilted her chair back and put her feet on the table. At a tentative knock on the door, she glanced up.

It was the overweight dispatcher. She was wearing a uniform stretched taut at the seams and an expression of concern. "Agent Jones?" she said, a surprisingly kittenish voice issuing from her large frame. "I'm a little concerned about Lieutenant Doyle."

"Why? Because he hasn't called in all day?" Kelly asked, raising an eyebrow.

The woman paused, then said, "But that's just the thing. He had been calling in, to me, and then the calls just stopped…and his car hasn't moved for a while."

Kelly lowered her head and gave the woman a withering

look. The dispatcher's mouth quivered. Kelly considered up-braiding her, then decided it would be a waste of breath. "What did he say when you last spoke to him?"

"He was having me track down the owners of sedans with body damage."

"Really?" Kelly said, surprised. She was expecting to hear he'd been visiting a strip club or a bar while on duty, but this…it sounded as if Doyle might actually have been running down Sam Morgan's lead about the car. Colin had officially clocked out but was working on his own time, trying to compile a list of vehicles matching that description. Now it turned out Doyle had spent the day doing just that. And of course had opted not to share that information with her, she thought, fuming.

The dispatcher shrugged. "He didn't say why."

"So I'm guessing you've got an address for me now?" Kelly asked, arching an eyebrow.

The dispatcher flushed bright pink, walked forward and handed her a slip of paper. "I—I wrote it down for you," she said haltingly. "It's been in the same spot for at least three hours."

"All right, Officer. I'll look into it," Kelly said dismissively. The dispatcher waddled out, head down. Clicking open her cell, Kelly punched in Monica's number. "Hey, I've got a present for you. I need you to track down Doyle and give him hell."

"You know, I almost became a cop," Dwight said pensively as he wrapped another length of duct tape around the cop's legs.

The cop's response was a grunt muted by the tape covering his mouth.

"Yep, you're right, I would've made a good one. Sure as

hell got the jump on you, didn't I!" Dwight said, rapping him playfully on the shoulder before straightening to admire his handiwork. The cop was lying on his side on the cot, arms and legs bound behind his back. Dwight had parked the squad car down the street from the Captain's house. The wife had made it home from tennis and then went somewhere else with the kids. He'd watched as she'd piled them in the car and waved goodbye to the Captain, who drove off in his truck a few minutes later. Dwight debated following him, but the police car was too hot, he couldn't chance being seen in it. He should've just stashed the cop in the trunk of his Tercel, but he'd been unable to resist the lure of the police car. He'd spent his whole life dreaming of driving one.

It hardly mattered anyway. There were only so many places the Captain could be holding Ma, and Dwight felt confident that given a day or two he'd be able to sniff them out. After all, he'd grown up here, knew every inch of this county. In the meantime, though, he needed to keep the sick bastard away from her. And to do that, he needed a little outside help.

Dwight stepped back and surveyed the room. He'd pulled the locker away from the wall, revealing the hooks behind it. He'd also drawn arrows on the floor with a Sharpie, pointing out dead giveaways that this was a hell of a lot more than a bomb shelter. Now he bent to the level of the cot and looked the cop square in the eye. "Listen up, okay? The guy that owns all this?" He jerked an arm backward to illustrate. "He's the one you want. Son of a bitch killed all those boys. Me, I'm just a good citizen trying to help out. You got it?"

The cop looked pissed, he just glared back. Dwight examined him for a minute, then said, "You should've seen this place a few weeks ago, hooks coming out of the walls and ceilings. He killed them right here. I promise, you look around, you're gonna find something. Now, don't you worry, I'd never hurt a fellow officer." He glanced at his watch. "Kinda funny, though, that no one's come looking for you yet. Car's got GPS, right?"

He waited, but the guy didn't respond, just kept staring at him. "Huh. Well, once I get clear I'll call it in anyway. They'll be here soon enough. You just kick back and relax."

He gave a two-finger salute and climbed the ladder, covering the hatch with the mat and tossing a few of the motorcycle parts on top of it. That way, if the Captain came home early, he might not notice that his garage had been messed with. All Dwight had to do now was hike a few miles to where he'd stashed his Tercel. Then he'd drive to the pay phone outside the Burger King on Route 2. After that he could get down to brass tacks, start looking for Ma. If he was lucky, he might even catch the Captain with her.

Twenty-Nine

Kelly's phone rattled across the table. Jake rolled his eyes as she checked the number. "We're never going to get through a full meal, are we?" he asked, a hint of resentment in his voice.

Jake had insisted that they finally try to have dinner out at a nice restaurant, and in this neck of the woods Twenty Water Street in Williamstown was supposedly the best. So far, unfortunately, the service had been abysmally slow. It had taken almost an hour for their main courses to arrive, and there was still no sign of the bottle of wine they had ordered. Jake's leg bounced impatiently under the tabletop. This wasn't going at all as he had planned.

Kelly gave him a warning glance and turned her head to the side as she clicked her phone open. He raised both hands defensively. "I'm just saying, your food is going to get cold. If it isn't already," he grumbled, picking up his fork to poke disconsolately at gummy-looking ravioli soaked in pesto sauce.

She said, "Jones here."

"Kelly? It's Monica." Worry flooded her voice. "We've

got a bit of a situation on our hands. I got Doyle's car here, but he's nowhere around. And the front desk sergeant just got a crank call, some guy claiming he stowed a cop at the killer's house. The guy said we're going to have to work a little to find him, but that he hasn't been hurt."

"Crap." Kelly wrinkled her brow. "Where are you now?"

"At the address you gave me. And here's the weird thing, Kelly." Monica lowered her voice. "Doyle's car is parked in front of Sam Morgan's house."

Sam Morgan eased to a stop at the corner and waved across the elderly couple in the crosswalk, nodding and smiling at them. It had been a busy day. Sylvia had insisted they go out for an early dinner before she took the girls to the local cinema. It was hard to shake the feeling she'd been looking at him funny, ever since she discovered the trapdoor in the garage this afternoon. His grip on the wheel tightened and his teeth ground against each other when he pictured that clod violating the sanctity of his space. Sam had managed a quick lie, told her he'd only discovered the trapdoor himself that morning when he'd moved the floor mat to clean up an oil spill. He'd joked that now they'd have somewhere to go in the event of a terrorist assault on the Berkshires. She'd laughed with him, but as she slowly scanned the room he'd seen doubt in her eyes.

The Berkshire cops were truly useless, he thought disparagingly. In the past that had served him well, but now Sam found their incompetence annoying. How much clearer could he have made it for them? He'd gone so far as to deliver the tip about Dwight's car to the FBI agent as well, in case Doyle responded with his usual laziness and ineptitude. They should have had Dwight on the run by now, which would free him up from distractions for a few days. Even if Dwight was caught, Sam planned on hiring him a top-notch attorney once the heat died down. Owning a car that entered a park late at night wasn't enough to hold a man without bail, not on a first offense. And once Dwight was free on bail, Sam could punish him at his leisure. He just needed to buy himself a little time…

In a sudden flash of rage he pounded one fist against the steering wheel. So far he'd been going easy on Dwight's mother, but now that Dwight had made the mistake of infiltrating his inner sanctum…they would both pay, he'd make sure of it. He'd just gone and checked on the mother; she was holding up well, all things considered. For an old bird she was pretty hearty. She barely lifted her head when he came in, and her hands were bruised blue from the shackles, but her pulse was good and she'd probably last another few days. He'd considered escalating on her that night, revealing the next level of punishment, but truth be told he was a little worn-out. He'd had a long day playing with the girls, and would prefer to relax on the couch with a tall glass of Scotch and the early showing of *SportsCenter.*

As Sam turned the corner toward home, colored lights bounced across his hood and he frowned. He slowed as he approached the house—his driveway was filled with police cars. He watched as a few officers spilled out the front door and walked across the lawn. "Shit." He hissed under his breath. His mind raced. Had that asshole Dwight told the cops about him in some vain hope they might help find his mother? Would anyone believe that moron? It was his word against Sam's, after all. He was a pillar of the community, while Dwight was just a night watchman with a history of mental illness and delusions of grandeur. Sam kept driving, passing the house before taking a right down the next street. He'd been careful, hadn't he? He'd eliminated all traces of the hatch's real purpose. But it was possible that Dwight had taken something. Even he wouldn't be idiotic enough to call the cops without some sort of evidence. He shuddered involuntarily as he pictured the cans, their treasure sealed inside. All it would take was someone with a little too much curiosity…could Dwight have discovered his tokens?

Sam took another right. He had to collect his thoughts. He accelerated and turned on to the road back toward town. He could see the walls he'd carefully constructed around his life crumbling, the facade vanishing, the faces of his wife and children receding into the distance. He shook his head as he reviewed his choices. He could just keep going, head to Canada. But he literally had nothing but the clothes on his back, a small amount of cash and no passport. With the FBI involved, he'd have a tough time making it across the border. If he was going to get away, he needed time to get some things together, and he'd have to avoid the authorities until then. He had buried a box at the base of a maple tree on the perimeter of his first boneyard. In it was a gun, a stack of Canadian money and falsified papers for just such an emergency. He'd dig it up, grab some camping supplies and head north. Although it was always possible he was worrying needlessly. Maybe he should just hunker down and try to wait this out. He could stay at the civil defense bunker, call Sylvia from a pay phone to find out what the story was.

Sam thought again of the half-dozen black-and-whites parked at his house and knew that kind of wishful thinking would be his downfall. Game over, he'd been caught. If he didn't manage to escape somehow, he'd go down just like Bundy and Dahmer and all the rest of those incompetents. No, he'd have to head north while taking care to cover his tracks. And it probably wouldn't hurt to have some insurance, he thought as an idea dawned on him. Setting his jaw, he tapped the accelerator and spun the truck around. Bennington was out of his way, but if he got backed into a corner, he needed to have a final ace up his sleeve. And he knew just where to find one.

Thirty

"You want to tell her, or should I?" Joe asked in a low voice.

"Tell me what?" Jan snapped. She was holding a tray filled with plastic cups, ice cubes rattling. In a rare fit of largesse she'd offered to make an iced coffee run, partly to convince Mike and Joe to work overtime on the second segment of the series. After the 6:00 p.m. broadcast had wrapped up, they had driven down to Northampton. Jan was hoping to track down a few of the boys. Apparently most of them had already left town, but she'd gotten the address of a club that was a known hangout . If she could get some of them to sit down for one-on-one interviews, it would be quite a coup.

Earlier that evening the station manager had come down personally to watch the segment with her. He'd even proposed sitting her at the anchor desk tomorrow night for the follow-up. Jan glowed at the memory. Something in Joe's face, though, warned her that feeling might be short-lived. She watched as Mike and Joe exchanged glances. "What?" she demanded more insistently.

"The police-band. It's going nuts."

"Turn it up."

Joe ratcheted up the volume, and she heard the dispatcher request that all available units report to an address in Williamstown. Jan checked her watch: it was nearly half past eight, and they were an hour's drive away. "Fuck!" she exclaimed, slamming the tray on the ground. Coffee slush seeped into her navy pumps. Mike and Joe startled backward at the vehemence in her voice.

"So get moving!" she said, throwing her arms up. "Something's happening, and we're fucking missing it!"

Keenan Johnson strode home, backpack slung over one shoulder. He'd planned on spending the night in the library, but it was still so damn nice outside. His roommate had texted him about a "brews and blues" party that a few guys on the water polo team threw every Wednesday night. He'd gone to one of those parties last year and it had rocked. Keenan had spent the night kicking back on the couch, sucking down beer and taking hits off a spliff that was being passed around. The guys who threw the party were smart enough to invite the best-looking chicks on campus, and popular enough that most of them actually came.

The freshman crop had just arrived, and he had his eye on a cute blonde from Tempe. His roommate said she'd probably be there, and that had clinched it. *Screw organic chemistry,* he thought. It was only the first week of school anyway. No one seriously expected him to be studying yet.

He turned the corner onto his street and stopped dead. A truck idled by the curb, passenger door open. A guy was dragging a kid down the sidewalk toward it. Something struck Keenan as wrong, and he called out, "Hey!"

The guy swiveled his head toward him. Keenan was six-two and African-American, both of which made him stand out in Vermont. He'd grown up somewhere even more white-bread than here, but could play the street hood when he needed to. He slipped into his ghetto walk, chin up, stance aggressive as he called out, "Yo! What you playing at?" He pictured himself as the hero who saved some kid—that'd get the blonde's attention for sure.

The guy grinned and waved him off. "Nothing to worry about, just taking my kid home. Guess he snuck into some college party, had a few too many."

"Yeah?" Keenan examined the kid quizzically. He was definitely out of it, his eyes lolled back.

The man shook his head. He looked normal enough, like any dad. "Just hope I can get him in the house without my wife seeing him. She's the tough one in the family, you know?"

"Oh yeah, my mom's the same way," Keenan said with a chuckle. "Here, let me give you a hand."

He helped stuff the kid in the back seat, swinging his legs across as the dad pulled from behind. As they drove off, he waved. *Poor kid was going to have a hell of a hangover tomorrow,* he thought, grinning. A glance at his watch and Keenan realized he'd better hurry if he wanted to end up feeling the same way.

Thirty-One

Kelly turned in a slow circle. She was standing in Sam Morgan's living room, which looked pretty much as she would have pictured it. Either they'd used an interior designer or his wife had incredible decorating sense, the decor was ripped from a spread in *Better Homes and Gardens*.

"Wow. I didn't know serial killers had such great taste in TVs," Jake said admiringly as he examined an enormous flat screen that dominated one wall of the room. "This thing must've set him back a few grand at least. What'd you say this guy does for a living?"

"He's a stockbroker," Kelly replied.

"And he's the guy from the sandwich place the other day, right?" Jake eyed her. "Did you have a little crush on him?"

"Don't be ridiculous," Kelly said, but she could feel a flush spreading across her cheeks. "He's married."

"Thank God, because that would be too ironic. Kelly Jones, serial-killer-hunter-extraordinaire, attracted to the guy she was tracking. What would Freud say?" Jake teased.

"We still don't know if he had anything to do with this," Kelly said pointedly.

"Yeah, but let's be honest, it doesn't look good."

"The only reason I let you come along is because you promised to stay out of the way," Kelly said, lowering her voice. "You're just lucky the bed-and-breakfast was ten miles in the opposite direction."

"Hey, I'm out of the way. Just admiring the man's taste in TVs, is all." Jake raised both hands and flopped down on the couch. "Wow, this is comfortable. He's got great taste in couches, too—go figure."

Kelly turned away from him, aggravated. Monica was standing in the doorway looking concerned. "No luck?"

Monica shook her head. "I gotta say, I'm feeling a little guilty. I've been wishing for weeks that Doyle would just disappear. Maybe that voodoo doll actually worked."

"You checked the garage, too?"

Monica nodded. "Everywhere."

"What on earth is going on here?"

Kelly turned to find an immaculately dressed woman in her mid-thirties standing in the doorway, clasping the hands of two little girls. One of them turned in toward her mother, clamping on to a khaki thigh.

"You must be Mrs. Morgan," Kelly said, stepping forward. "We've got a warrant to search your house."

"What? Why?" the woman said, puzzled. Blond hair tied back in a neat bun, high cheekbones framing blue eyes. They must make a good-looking couple, Kelly noted in spite of herself.

Kelly dodged the question by asking, "Mrs. Morgan, where's your husband?"

"He's not here?" The woman peered around her, as if

doubting her word. "Well, he probably just ran out for something. I'm sure he'll be back soon, then we can clear this up."

"Sure, honey. Why don't you have a seat," Monica said, coming forward and guiding the woman to the couch. "Probably a good idea to send the girls up to bed, don't you think?"

The woman paused, then nodded in agreement. "Girls, go brush your teeth and get ready for bed."

"But Daddy said we could have ice cream when we got home," one of them whined, looking petulant.

Her mother cast her a warning look. "I mean it, Jennie. And make sure your sister washes her face, too."

The girl grumbled but stomped toward the stairs, leading her younger sister by the hand.

"So what's this all about?" Mrs. Morgan asked, gaze still focused on the stairs.

"Your name is?" Kelly asked, settling into the chair opposite her.

"Sylvia Morgan."

"Okay, Sylvia. I'm Special Agent Jones with the FBI."

"My husband was working with you," the woman said abruptly. "He helped you find all those poor boys. Weeks, he was out there."

"I know," Kelly acknowledged.

"So what could you possibly accuse him of? You know Sam, he would never hurt a fly."

"I'm not saying he did. But we received a report that an officer was being held here."

"Here? In my house? That's absurd," Sylvia said.

"Maybe, but the officer's vehicle is parked down the road. Is there anywhere else on the property you can think of where someone might have concealed him? Maybe some sort of duck blind, something like that?" Kelly watched her closely. She saw something flit behind the woman's eyes.

There was a long pause before Sylvia said, "Well, there's the bomb shelter."

"Where's that?" Kelly sat up straighter.

"Under the garage. Sam just found it today."

Kelly nodded toward Monica. "Send a unit to check it out."

They sat in silence, waiting while Monica spoke into her radio. Sylvia Morgan stared straight ahead at a Toulouse-Lautrec print on the far wall. A second later Monica's radio buzzed. She held it to her ear, then turned to Kelly and nodded.

Kelly leaned forward and said, "Sylvia?"

There was a long silence, then the woman responded, "He's there, isn't he."

"Yes, he is."

"What about Sam?"

Kelly shook her head, then asked, "Can you think of where Sam might have gone?"

"He's a good husband. A good father."

"Of course he is, honey," Monica chimed in, settling on to the couch next to her.

Sylvia suddenly twisted to face her, eyes brightening. "Maybe someone took Sam! They left the police officer, and took Sam. Isn't that possible?"

"Sure, that's possible," Monica nodded reassuringly. "So we better find them, huh? Anyone you can think of who might be after Sam? Maybe he's got a place he goes to get away?"

"That's what this house is," Sylvia said, irritated. "We live in Manhattan. This is where we come to get away."

"All right. I'm going to check on Lieutenant Doyle. Please stay here. I might have a few more questions for you." Kelly cut her eyes at Jake, and he nodded slightly in understanding. He wouldn't let Sylvia out of his sight.

Monica followed her from the room.

"How is he?" Kelly said in a low voice.

"They said he seems fine, just pissed as all get-out."

Kelly heaved a sigh of relief. An injured cop was the last thing this case needed, and despite her dislike of Doyle, she'd hate to have anyone hurt on her watch. As soon as she'd heard Doyle was missing she flashed back to last October when she lost her partner. That same cold feeling had settled in her stomach again. Now she felt it release. She wouldn't have to be calling anyone's families, not tonight.

"You think maybe someone really did take Morgan?" Monica asked, brow crinkling as they trotted down the front steps, headed toward the garage. Night had descended, and the heat of the day was dissipating under a cool wind that carried undertones of jasmine and dew.

"I think it's pretty doubtful."

"So, what? Sam Morgan is one of our killers? I've spent hours with the guy—he's as straight and narrow as they come. You saw in there, he's a family man."

Kelly shrugged. "So he defies the stereotype. Wouldn't be the first time."

"And what does that make him, our amateur killer or the pro?"

"Hard to say. Call Colin back at the office, have him start digging up everything he can find on Sam Morgan. I want to know how long he's lived here, when he got married, everything, down to parking tickets. Tell him to get people out of bed if he has to. I want phone records, too. With a cop found on his property, that shouldn't be too hard to get."

"Yeah, I'm betting we'll suddenly find the Berkshire State

PD ready to bend over backward for us," Monica snorted. She held up her radio and was patched through to Peters at base. Even through the radio the fatigue in his voice was apparent. He perked up at the news that Doyle had been located unharmed, and promised to get to work immediately on Sam Morgan's background.

They were coming up on the garage. An ambulance was parked kitty-corner by the open door. "So what's going on here? Killer A kidnapped Doyle and put in him Killer B's bomb shelter?" Monica asked, puzzled. "Why?"

"I have no idea," Kelly said. "But both of them are still out there."

Zach came to with a start. He was seated propped against a wall. It was pitch-black. He strained his eyes to see, but there weren't even the fragments of light that snuck in under doors and around the edges of window shades. His hands were clasped behind him, stuck together with something, and his feet were similarly bound. He reached back with his hands and felt around—tile, cold tile, like he was in a bathroom somewhere. It smelled horrible, too, like a toilet had backed up. He gagged at the stench, eyes watering.

There was a noise off to his right. He froze, stopped breathing for a moment, his blood running cold with fear. There it was again, something between a growl and a moan, like an injured animal. He flashed back on when their cat had been hit by a car and they found her hours later, curled under the porch, broken and bloody and dying. She'd made a similar sound. Mom had taken her out back, finished her off with her service revolver. He'd cried and refused to speak to her for a week afterward.

Where the hell was he, and what was in there with him? He edged away from the sound, but hit a point where his arms wouldn't follow, they were attached to something solid. He yanked at it, panicked, but couldn't budge. He was trapped, and with something horrible.

He tried to remember how he got here. That guy had shown up at the house looking for his mom. He seemed nice enough, and even looked familiar. Zach let him wait in the living room, said she was still at work, told him to make himself at home. Part of him had half hoped it might be a new boyfriend, the guy sure as hell looked more normal than Dr. Nimrod. *Not that that meant anything, obviously,* Zach thought, angry at himself. He'd been getting the guy a glass of water in the kitchen when he sensed someone behind him. He'd turned around quickly, and the guy was right there, holding up a syringe. Zach had dodged him, made it across the living room and almost to the front door, but for an old guy he was quick. The last thing he remembered was staring up at their ceiling, darkness creeping around the periphery of his vision, the room narrowing until it faded to a dot of black.

"Oh good, you're awake."

Zach winced as a blinding light filled the room. It took a moment for his eyes to adjust, then he saw that the guy had entered carrying a fluorescent camping lantern and a small bag. Zach jerked his head to the side to see what was issuing those terrible groans. It was an old woman, completely naked, skin hanging in pouches from her frame. She was filthy, covered with marks and welts and lying in a puddle that explained the overpowering smell of piss and shit. As he watched, she raised her head slightly and issued that awful sound again, a stream of dribble trailing out her mouth. She

gazed at him, eyes pleading for help. He'd never had anyone
look at him that way before. It was like he could see inside
her, to a terrible place full of desperation and pain. In a way
it was more revealing than her nakedness. He shuddered and
turned away, taking in the rest of the space. They were in a
bathroom. Their side of the room was lined with shower-
heads; a large open arch lead to the next room, where he
could see a few sinks.

"Please…" the woman croaked, her voice barely human.

"What's wrong with you, man?" Zach asked angrily, concern
for the woman making him forget his own dire situation.

The man was busy rooting through the bag for something.
He looked up at the woman. "Looks bad, I know," he acknowledged thoughtfully. "But it wasn't me that got her involved
in all this."

"She's an old lady."

"That's true. But then again, is that really a reason not to
hurt her? Does merely being old excuse you from punishment? I never understand that, when they release people from
prison early because they're old, or sick. If they did something
wrong, shouldn't they fulfill the terms of their punishment?"
he said earnestly.

The guy was obviously nuts, but in spite of himself Zach
felt lulled by his voice. He sounded so reasonable, like a
teacher or something, like he really knew what he was talking
about. "I'll scream," Zach said.

The guy shrugged. "Go ahead. She's been screaming for
days, it didn't help her."

"What did you do to her?"

"Ah!" The guy held up his index finger appreciatively.
"I'm so glad you asked. I tell you in some ways it's a relief,

finally having someone to explain things to. With the others, you see, I had to stay silent. Cutting off all human contact was an important element. But you now, you're different."

"Different how?" Zach asked. His teeth had started chattering, from the cold and from fear.

"Oh gosh, lots of reasons. You're an upstanding member of society. According to your mom you play soccer, might even have a shot at a scholarship. Even got a girlfriend, right?"

Zach sat bolt upright. "You didn't hurt Gina, did you?"

"No, of course not." The guy scoffed as if he'd said something ridiculous. "Please, I'm not an animal. Traditionally I'm very selective in who I choose. The two of you—" he gestured between them "—are obviously the exception to the rule." He let out a harsh laugh. "Otherwise I probably would have been caught a long time ago."

"You're the one that killed all those boys," Zach said, realization dawning.

The man nodded curtly. "I did them a favor. If they'd continued on that path, their torments in hell would have been far worse. Leviticus 20:13 says that if a man lies with a male as those who lie with a woman, both of them have committed a detestable act; they shall surely be put to death."

"What are you, like, a religious nut?" Zach asked.

The guy cocked his head to the side and said cheerily, "Nope. Sounds good though, doesn't it? A Bible quote really brings it home, could even get a few of the jurors teary-eyed." He started to speak in a singsong way that made Zach's skin crawl. "Or maybe my mommy was a drunk who beat me and locked me in the cellar. Or was she a whore who touched me in my naughty places, or was it an uncle who did that? I can never remember. Or maybe I just can't help myself, I was born this way. Or my daddy left, and I had no one to look up to. You know a little something about that, don't you? About daddies leaving?" He leaned in as he said this, uncomfortably close. His eyes gleamed white, reflecting the light from the lanterns. Zach shrank away from him. Seemingly satisfied, the guy squatted back on his haunches and observed him for a long moment. His voice was flat, devoid of all emotion when he said, "Or maybe I do it because it's fun. Hard to say, really."

He watched Zach for a moment longer, as if ascertaining whether or not he was paying attention, then straightened and crossed the room, back to the pile of bags he'd dropped by the archway.

With his back to them, Zach regained some of his courage. "So why us?" Zach jerked his head sideways toward the crumpled figure on the floor.

"I'm using her to send a message to someone else. Regrettable, but necessary." The man was drawing a series of what looked like tent poles out of the bags, twisting to tighten them together. At last he stood, brandishing a six-foot-long stick about an inch in diameter made of black metal. "And as for you, well, let's just say I need a little insurance for a trip I'm about to take. Figure if I have the son of a cop with me, I'm guaranteed safe passage. It's nothing personal. Behave yourself, I might even let you live."

Zach thought back on what his mother had told him about the cases. She hadn't said much, and her eyes clouded over when he brought it up. He'd never seen her so upset about work before. But she'd told him a little. "So if it's not a religious thing, why'd you kill those kids?"

"I'm a pragmatist. The boys aren't missed. I don't discriminate, illegal immigrants would suit me just fine, but they're tough to find around here. Plus some of them do actually have a family network, and it's hard to separate out which are which." The man tapped the tip of the rod against the palm of his hand contemplatively as he said, "No, a couple of fags turning tricks were just the ticket. Hell, they were practically begging to get in my car, I didn't even have to catch them. And if it came right down to it, nine out of ten people would thank me." He pointed the stick at Zach. "Most people around here didn't go to see *Brokeback Mountain.*"

"Seems like the boys are missed now," Zach pointed out.

"Through no fault of my own," the man muttered, face darkening with rage. "And that's why she's here."

"So why don't you just kill her?" Zach asked. In spite of himself, part of him wished the guy would just finish her off. At the sight of the stick, the noises she was making were becoming almost unbearable, accelerating gasps and moans as she scrabbled at the edge of her chains.

The man's voice shifted again, back to the conversational tone. "Because she hasn't completed the stations, we're only on stage five thanks to some…interruptions. Have you ever heard of bastinado?"

Zach shook his head, mesmerized by the slow swings the man was making with the stick as he advanced on the woman next to him.

"Bastinado is the Spanish word for caning, used throughout the world, but predominantly in the Middle East. It involves beating the soles of the bare feet with a cane. Very effective, due to the clustering of nerve endings there. From what I understand Uday Hussein used it to punish athletes who made mistakes during games." Without any warning he brought the cane back and whipped it forward. It hit the bottom of the woman's feet with a hard crack. She howled in pain, frantically drawing her feet underneath her. He chided her. "Now, Nancy, we've discussed this. If you take them away, I'll just have to strap them to a board, and it will only be worse for you. You know the rules."

Nancy cringed at his words. Hesitantly, she lengthened her legs back out toward him, trembling. The expression of resignation on her face was terrible to behold, and Zach started screaming as the man drew the cane back again. "Jesus Christ, stop! Please just stop!"

The man didn't answer. His movements sped up. In a frenzy he drew back the cane again and again, the sound of the pole pelting her feet and her howls reverberating off the walls until Zach was certain he was already in hell.

Thirty-Two

"So you never came down here?"

"Not before today." Sylvia turned in a slow circle. She'd slung a thin cashmere cardigan over her shoulders, top button done to hold it in place. Her arms were crossed in front of her chest as if she was warding something off. "These marks weren't there then. That man must have drawn them. What are you doing to find Sam?"

The three of them were standing inside the bomb shelter. Kelly could hear the crime-scene unit shuffling around at the top of the ladder, itching to get started before it got any later. They'd have to wait a little longer. Kelly wanted to confront Sylvia with what was inside, gauge her reaction to see if she was telling the truth, or if she'd known what her husband had been up to all these years. Sylvia Morgan was good at controlling her facial expressions, clearly she'd had some practice. Good, but not good enough; Kelly detected the underlying shock in her eyes.

"And Sam didn't know about this either?" Monica asked.

Sylvia shook her head. "He was as surprised as I was." She waved a hand around dismissively. "I mean, look at the place. No one's used it in decades."

Kelly shook her head. "I doubt that. Not a speck of dust anywhere. Don't you find that odd?"

Sylvia shrugged. "It must be well sealed."

"Not just sealed, but soundproofed." Kelly pointed out the padding on the bottom of the hatch.

Monica held up a can of beans. "And these don't expire for two more years. I'm pretty sure beans don't last that long."

Sylvia stiffened. "I don't know what you're implying."

"Yes, I'm afraid you do," Kelly said. "The hooks in the wall, and the rivets and drain in the floor; none of those belong in a standard bomb shelter. We checked with the previous owner, and he had no knowledge of it. I think if we ask around we'll be able to determine who built this for your husband, and when."

"Sam's a good man…" Sylvia said, but this time her voice betrayed doubt.

"Mrs. Morgan, we really need to find your husband so we can clear up some of these questions. Is there anywhere he might have gone? Friends, relatives?"

Sylvia shook her head. "Sam's mother abandoned him, he grew up in foster homes. He never discussed that part of his life, I don't think he liked to remember it. As far as friends…he has a lot of acquaintances, here and in Manhattan, but I can't think of anyone special he'd turn to for help."

Kelly had already asked the NYPD to stake out the Morgans' Manhattan apartment on the off-chance Sam showed up there. So far there was no sign of him.

"What about the other people in the search and rescue unit?" Monica asked.

Sylvia nodded slowly. "I guess of everyone here, he's closest to them. Chris Santoli would probably be your best bet, he's a day trader, too. They have a beer together and watch baseball games sometimes when I'm in the city with the girls…."

Her voice trailed off. Kelly recognized the look in her eyes, the sudden recognition that the rug had been yanked away and it turned out she was standing over a gaping chasm.

"Why don't you go on inside now, honey. We'll track down Chris Santoli," Monica said soothingly.

"Yes, I'd better see to the girls." Sylvia raised a hand to her forehead as if wiping away a memory, then slowly lowered it. "If you'll excuse me," she said faintly before mounting the ladder.

"She didn't know," Monica said, watching her go.

"No, she didn't," Kelly agreed, kneeling to examine the ridged floor canted toward a drain in the center of the room. "It's a killing room, that's for sure. I'm willing to bet that if he was careful enough to keep his wife from suspecting anything for almost a decade, we won't find much in the way of trace evidence down here."

"Probably not," Monica said. She started to set the jar back on the shelf behind her, then frowned. She rattled it slightly. Something shifted from side to side. "Hear that? Doesn't sound like beans."

They exchanged glances. "All these cans and no can opener," Kelly said thoughtfully. "Why don't we have one of the crime-scene guys run to the house, see if Mrs. Morgan wouldn't mind lending us one."

A few minutes later, a cop passed a can opener through the hatch. "She wants to come back down, find out what you're doing," he said in a low voice.

"Tell her we've sealed the scene. We can't let her back in until it's been processed," Kelly ordered.

He nodded and his head disappeared. Kelly and Monica looked at each other. "You want to do the honors?" Monica asked. Her voice was a little shaky.

"Honestly? No. But it's probably better if we know what we're dealing with." Kelly clamped the opener down and started to twist the handle. She steeled herself. Serial killers took all sorts of odd "trophies" from their victims, items that helped them relive the murder. Ed Gein, the real-life serial killer that the character of "Buffalo Bill" was based on, made lamps and a bodysuit out of human skin. Cannibal Stanley Baker carried the knucklebones of one victim in a special pouch on his belt. Sadist Lawrence Bittaker recorded his victims' screams as he tortured them. Chances were the can contained something horrible. It turned slowly, the metal top peeling back. When it was all the way open, Kelly peered inside. A smaller glass jar was nested within, the kind used for pickles and jams. She reached a gloved hand inside, careful to avoid the sharp edges, and lifted it out, holding it up to the light.

"Jesus," Monica breathed, falling back a step.

Kelly didn't say anything. Bobbing in a cloudy yellow solution were dozens of eyeballs, the roots still attached to most of them. As she stared at the jar, one with a blue iris rotated around to meet her gaze. She set the jar back down on a shelf. "Let's go back up," Kelly said abruptly.

They mounted the ladder in silence. Kelly gestured for the head of the crime-scene unit to come over. "I want photos and prints. Probably won't have much luck with trace evidence or blood spatter, but check anyway. And collect all the cans on the shelves, have the contents sent to the lab for DNA processing."

"DNA processing?" he asked, puzzled.

"You'll understand when you get down there," she said in a low voice. Sylvia Morgan was hovering just outside the garage, arms crossed over her chest. She had pulled on her cardigan despite the heat of the evening.

"Agent Jones? What's going on down there?" she called out.

Kelly ignored her. They watched as three crime-scene technicians slowly descended the ladder, hands reaching up to collect the equipment being passed down. The garage doors yawed open. Sylvia's car had been cleared out, and motorcycle parts were strewn across the floor like abandoned appendages. A cool night breeze filtered through.

"Agent Jones?"

"Go be with your daughters, Mrs. Morgan," Kelly said over her shoulder without turning to face the woman. "I'll be in touch if we find your husband."

Kelly felt the woman's rage hot on her back, then heard the crunch of gravel as she spun and marched back to her house.

"Jesus," Monica said again as the sound of her steps dissipated. "If I live to be a hundred, I don't think I'll be able to get that image out of my head."

"Me either," Kelly said, adding it to the grim catalogue of terrible things in her memory. She rubbed her eyes with a thumb and forefinger. Already, her dinner with Jake felt like it had happened months ago. And a long night still stretched before her.

"Do you think the other…parts…do you think he saved those, too?" Monica's voice was unsteady.

Kelly considered the question. "We'll know tomorrow when all the cans have been opened. Tonight, we need to focus on finding Sam Morgan."

Monica cleared her throat. "Yeah, you're right. I'll have a deputy get Chris Santoli's address. You want to call ahead?"

Kelly shook her head. "No, and I want a trained infiltration unit to go in first. If Sam Morgan is there, he might have hostages. I can't chance anyone else getting hurt. I'll arrange for a warrant."

"Okay. Can we get out of here now?" Monica glanced back at the open hatch and shuddered.

Kelly examined her. The fluorescent lights exposed the dark circles under Monica's eyes, aging her a decade.

"Why don't you head home?" Kelly said abruptly.

"What, now?" Monica said puzzled.

Kelly nodded. "You look like you could use some sleep. I'll have the tactical unit and Jake with me. If Sam isn't at the Santoli house, we'll just go down the list of other SAR unit members. It could take all night."

"And here I thought you needed me," Monica joked, but there was a touch of hurt in her voice.

"You kidding? I'd be nowhere on this case without you," Kelly said, awkwardly patting Monica's arm. "But Jake can watch my back. Hell, he'll probably insist on it. And something tells me Sam Morgan's too smart to stick around here, anyway. He's probably halfway to Canada by now."

"It's always the nice ones, isn't it?" Monica said, shaking her head. "And to think I was considering breaking up his marriage."

"Even if it turns out he's not involved, I wouldn't want to go up against Sylvia," Kelly remarked.

"No, you're probably right—those Junior League types are always scrappier than they look." Monica laughed, but it sounded forced. "I think I'll just stop home and check on Zach, then I'll catch up with you."

"Great," Kelly smiled at her, then glanced at her watch.

"Keep your phone on, I'm blocking all radio chatter because there's a chance one or both of them might be monitoring it."

"What about the other guy, the one who took Doyle?"

"I sent a sketch artist over to the hospital, and they dusted his squad car for prints. Maybe our guy is in the system and we'll get a hit. Otherwise it might take a few days to get an ID."

"Almost a good thing it happened to Doyle. Want to bet the lab takes half the time getting us the results?"

Kelly smiled wryly. "With any luck. I'll call you if we find anything. Now I better go get Jake, make sure he isn't trying to make off with that TV."

Dwight rubbed his eyes. He was tapped out, hadn't slept for more than a few hours in days now. It was true, you did start seeing things; just a few minutes ago he'd caught himself swatting at his windshield. Clear as day he'd watched an enormous purple dragonfly land on his dashboard, foot-wide wings pulsing slowly up and down as it regarded him with amber eyes. He blinked and it hovered for a moment before disappearing. Man, he had to hold it together. Unconsciously he tapped out the tune for today's song, Europe's "The Final Countdown," on the steering wheel.

He was running out of places to check. He'd been to all of their training sites, at least the ones they'd used during the short time he'd been with the unit. He'd gone through a few abandoned shacks in the woods that were pretty well-known. Nothing there but holes punched in graffiti-ed walls, bare mattresses covered with rat piss where horny kids got laid for the first time. The Captain was smart, even Dwight had to grudgingly acknowledge that. He wouldn't choose some-where too obvious, and it would have to be somewhere he

could visit undetected. Hell, he could have dug a hole in the
ground and just dumped her in there. Dwight gritted his teeth
at the thought and strained his mind, trying to figure out
where the hell the sick bastard could be. He wasn't at his
house. Dwight had a police-band radio, and had heard enough
to learn that before the airwaves suddenly went quiet. So,
they'd found the cop. At least now they'd be looking for the
Captain, too.

There was one more place he needed to check and he was
almost there. Then he'd have to find somewhere to lay low and
catch a few winks. He turned into a long concrete entranceway,
killing the engine and headlights as the car glided to a stop.

Zach blinked and sat up straight. It was dark again, and
silent. He didn't know what had happened, whether he'd
fallen asleep or passed out. At the memory of what he'd wit-
nessed his hands automatically reached for his ears, but he
was still tied up and they snapped back down with a clatter.
God, that was awful. He'd never imagined anything so
horrible in his entire life. He'd grown up on slasher films and
loved every one them, prided himself on the fact that when
his other friends had to look away from the screen, he could
still watch. Could eat popcorn, even. But what that asshole
had done to that poor woman… Zach started shaking uncontrollably. He wondered if she was still in here with him—if
she was still alive. His face was wet; he tasted a drop and let
out a little gasp of relief. It was tears, not blood. Just tears,
and he didn't even care that he was crying like a baby. Fuck,
no one would see him anyway. He was probably going to die
down here. The thought grew in his mind, taking on enormous
dimensions as the realization settled in. Earlier, he'd been so

disturbed by what was happening to the old lady that he hadn't considered his own fate. The guy said he wasn't going to "punish" him, but shit, he was clearly crazy. Zach's teeth started chattering, partly because it was cold, but also because he suddenly knew, deep in his core, that he was going to die, and it was going to be a slow and terrible death. He'd never see Gina again, or his mom. At the thought of his mother a sob escaped his lips and he began crying in earnest.

Kelly nodded, and the ram swung forward and crashed through the front door. She stayed to the side, waiting as the tactical unit swept into the house in front of her, weapons held at eye level, flashlight beams penetrating the gloom of the hallway. She was about to enter when Jake stepped in front of her protectively and proceeded down the hall. She repressed a twinge of annoyance.

"Do that again and I just might shoot you," she muttered so only he could hear. She knew him well enough that even from the back she could tell he was grinning. A chorus of "Clears!" chimed in from other sections of the house.

"Oh sure, and if I don't go in front of you I'll get an earful about how chivalry is dead," he responded in a low voice. "There's the man of the house now."

Kelly peered around him. They were at the doorway to the living room. On the far wall, a TV set that dwarfed the one in Sam Morgan's house was tuned to a Red Sox game. In front of a La-Z-Boy stood a man in a white T-shirt and boxers, mouth open, the bottle of beer in his hands tilted forward so that its contents dribbled down on the floor.

"Chris Santoli?" Kelly asked.

He nodded dumbly, mouth still agape. He was in his early

forties, with a weak chin and a shiny forehead chasing away sparse blond hair. A significant gut hung over his waistband.

"Is anyone else here with you, Chris?" she asked, shoving aside Jake with irritation as she stepped past him.

"N-no," he stammered, eyes sweeping the room, taking in the bulletproof vests and semiautomatics. The captain of the tactical unit issued a sharp nod. "House is clear," he confirmed.

"All right. Do a quick sweep of the grounds, make sure to check the garage in particular," Kelly ordered. "Mr. Santoli, why don't you have a seat?"

"Did you break down my door?" he said incredulously, still standing. "Jesus, what is this, fucking Baghdad?"

"You can file a claim with the Berkshire State Police Department, I'm sure they'd be happy to compensate you," Kelly said. "Now please, Mr. Santoli, sit. I need to ask you some questions."

Thirty-Three

"Zach? God, what happened in here? It looks like a bomb went off!" Monica called out with annoyance, hands on her hips as she perused the wreckage of her living room. He'd probably been wrestling with one of his buddies again. That happened at least once or twice a month—they'd start brawling over everything from video games to who was going to which college. Honestly, sometimes she wished she'd had a girl.

Sighing, she bent to pick up a chair tilted on its side, then caught herself. "Zach, get down here and clean up this mess!"

Monica cocked her head to the side at the lack of a response. "I mean it, Zach!" she said with less certainty. A minute later she stormed up the stairs and threw open the door to his bedroom. At the sight of the unmade bed and clutter, her eyes narrowed. She noted the time. "Oh, for Pete's sake," she muttered. "Of all the nights for him to break curfew, he had to choose this one."

Sighing, she snapped open her cell phone and started dialing.

* * *

Zach had finally stopped crying and now sat quietly, his back against the wall. He'd never been religious; his mom hadn't raised him that way. Now he kind of wished she had. It seemed like now would be the time to start praying, but all he knew were a few lines from a handful of prayers, and to just wing it felt wrong somehow. His mom had to be looking for him by now. She was going to be crushed—she'd never been good on her own. He'd already started worrying about what she'd do when he started college—he planned on applying to schools nearby so he could come home regularly. He figured that was why she'd hooked up with the nerd, because she spotted loneliness on the horizon. Zach had caught her crying last night, so she'd probably been dumped again. Even though he'd never liked the guy he still felt a little badly—maybe if he'd been nicer it would have worked out. Not that any of that mattered now.

He'd lost all sense of time and place. He could've been gone for days; it certainly felt like it. Part of him almost hoped the crazy guy would come back soon. Sitting down here, alone in the dark, he felt like he was starting to lose his mind. Every small sound was magnified. He stiffened at each one, trying to determine if it was another rat or something far worse.

Shafts of light suddenly appeared around the corner of the room, driving the shadows into corners. He went rigid. Was this going to be it? Zach started muttering under his breath, words of goodbye to Gina and his mother and everyone else he'd ever known. If this was death coming for him, he hoped it would be quick.

Light suddenly flooded the room, and Zach twisted his head to the side, blinking. He heard a sharp wail, and the brightness charged toward him. He cowered with fear, curling into as small a shape as possible, bracing for the blow. When none came, his eyes opened and he gasped.

The lantern had been dropped and lay on its side on the floor, casting a halo of light toward the ceiling. Next to it, a discarded backpack lay on the tile. A man knelt on the ground, a different man this time, larger and dressed in camouflage, a black knit cap on his head and a complicated tool belt strapped around his waist. In his arms he clutched the old lady. Her body was stiff, rigid; in the stark lighting she almost glowed like polished marble. She was dead.

The man raised his eyes to meet Zach. He was younger than the other guy, maybe in his thirties, unshaven and wild-eyed. At his expression Zach recoiled.

"Where is he?" the man spit.

"He's gone," Zach said. It took a minute to register that this was someone else, someone who could save him, and with that realization his words tumbled out in a rush. "Do you have a phone, could you call nine-one-one? My mom's a cop, they'll come right away. Can you get these chains off me? Maybe you can break the showerhead, bust a pipe or something."

The man watched silently as Zach babbled on, becoming increasingly frantic with every moment that passed. "Please, man, get me out of here. He could come back at any minute, we gotta go…"

"He didn't tell you nothing?" The guy's eyes narrowed.

"What? No. Listen, he's going to kill me, too. Please, get me out of here."

Seemingly satisfied at his response, the man turned back to the woman in his arms. Gently, he smoothed back a few strands of hair from her battered face. Carefully laying her back down, he dug something out of his pack—a dark sweater—and draped it over her, covering her head and upper torso. Digging into his pocket, he withdrew a handful of change and carefully stacked it in a tier by her outstretched hand. Zach watched, stunned into silence.

Abruptly, the guy stood and slung his backpack over one shoulder. Zach watched him, puzzled. "Are—are you going for help?" he asked after a moment.

The guy didn't answer. With his free hand, he picked up the lantern.

"Hey! Where are you going? You can't just leave me here!" Zach struggled against his chains, his breath coming in gasps as his panic mounted again. "What the fuck! Please, please call someone for help!"

The man didn't answer, just turned and left the room, the light sweeping out with him. As it faded to a point in the darkness, then vanished entirely, Zach started to scream.

Thirty-Four

"That's everywhere you can think of?"

Chris Santoli nodded. "Sam and I weren't really that close. I mean, hell, we had a beer every once in a while after training sessions, but that was about it. He was one of those guys kept to himself, you know?"

Kelly nodded as she glanced at her notebook. "Sure. But these are all of the sites where you trained?"

Chris nodded. "Yeah, far as I can remember. But I've only been with the unit a few years, since I left Morgan Stanley. Some of the other guys might be able to tell you more. Sam liked to mix it up, said it kept us on our toes. Ran it more like a military unit than a search and rescue. We trained a hell of a lot. Sam had us doing survival stuff out in the woods, obstacle courses and drills, that sort of thing. I was an ROTC guy myself, so I didn't mind, but some guys grumbled about it."

"All right, thanks." Kelly's phone rang, and she glanced at the number before saying, "Would you excuse me for a moment?"

Chris sighed heavily and flipped his hands palms up, aggravated. "Yeah, sure. You still need me, I'll be watching the game. Sox are down by three, they get another hit they could come back."

"Wow, when did we enter Neverland?" Jake commented. At the scowl on Chris's face he held up his hands defensively. "Hey, not that I'm one to talk. I'm a Rangers fan."

"Rangers suck," Chris said sympathetically. "But at least they're not the Yankees." As they started to rattle off stats and records, Kelly stepped out of the room.

"Morgan's not here." she said, keeping her voice low. "I've got units checking the other SAR members' houses. We're still hoping he'll turn up somewhere. Chris Santoli gave us a list of training sites they used, we're going to check those next."

"Kelly? I'm worried about Zach," Monica's concern was palpable.

"Why?"

"He's not home, and I've called all his friends and his girl-friend, and he's not there either. And his cell phone is sitting right here on the kitchen table. He never goes anywhere without it, it would be like him leaving the house without his head. I think something might really be wrong…."

Kelly glanced toward the living room. Through the doorway she could see the two men talking baseball, arms waving as the discussion grew more heated. "You're sure? He's a teenager, he might just be somewhere blowing off steam."

"My living room looked like a tornado hit it when I got home, and the door was unlocked. He forgets sometimes, but lately I've been so paranoid, he's been really good about locking it." Monica paused, then continued. "Kelly, I know this sounds like some stupid women's intuition thing, but I just know something is wrong."

Kelly pursed her lips. Could Morgan have taken Zach? But why the hell would he do that? It was completely outside his MO. "Does Zach have a car?"

"No, he only just got his learner's permit."

"All right. E-mail me a recent photo, we'll put out an alert. Why don't you stay at home, wait and see if he comes back?"

"I can't, I'll go nuts just hanging around. Howie is coming over, he'll call us if Zach turns up. Where are you going next?"

Kelly checked her pad. "The National Guard Armory in Pittsfield."

"All right, I'll meet you there."

Kelly clicked the phone shut, but almost instantly it rang again. She clicked it open with a sigh. "Jones."

"Agent Jones? Lieutenant Peters here." The young cop sounded excited. He was still back at the station, manning the command center during the search for Sam Morgan. "We got results back on the prints from Lieutenant Doyle's car, and one pair stuck out as unusual."

"Someone with a record?"

"Not exactly—he was printed by a private security firm." Kelly heard the sound of paper rustling through the receiver. "Looks like Lieutenant Doyle was abducted by one Dwight Sullivan, thirty-four years old. I pulled his license photo and he looks like a mean son of a bitch. Faxed it to the hospital for Doyle's confirmation, but I bet this is our guy."

"Excellent. Thanks, Lieutenant." Monica had been right, once one of their own was involved, the Massachusetts state lab had proved remarkably efficient. Kelly hoped that continued. "Let's put an APB out for his car. I'll head over to his house with a backup unit. I need you to make sure there's a warrant waiting for me there. Include detached structures, drawers, everything. And let's send photos of Sullivan and Morgan out to the media, start getting the public involved."

"You sure about that?" Colin said doubtfully. "We did that in a case I worked last year, the phone lines were tied up for days."

"I'd prefer that to getting blamed for not warning the public if someone else gets hurt. Send copies to border patrol in New York and Vermont, too. I think one or both of them will head for the border."

"Got it. Anything else?"

"Yeah, Monica's going to send you a photo of her son. Add it to the announcement."

Colin was silent for a minute, before saying, "Do I want to know?"

"It's probably nothing. We're just erring on the safe side." She snapped the phone shut and returned to the living room. "Mr. Santoli, do you know a Dwight Sullivan?"

"Bright Dwight? Sure, I know him." Santoli sounded puzzled. "Guy's kind of an asshole, he was in the unit for, like, a minute when I first joined up. Nickname's kind of a joke. He's not the brightest bulb in the batch, you know what I mean?"

"Any reason he might have a grudge against Mr. Morgan?"

Santoli chuckled and rubbed the back of his neck. "Yeah, you could say that."

"Could you elaborate?" Kelly asked impatiently.

"Dwight was a little off, you know the type. Nice enough guy, but obsessed with the training. Claimed he was waiting to hear back from the Navy Seals about joining up, then the next month it was the CIA. The CIA, you believe that? A few guys used to tease him about it, asked if he could do them a favor once he got in, get them Osama's phone number, stuff like that. I don't think he even got that they were messing with him."

"Sam Morgan one of those guys?" Jake asked.

"Nah, Sam's too nice. He just kind of nudged Dwight out of the SAR, said he should probably focus his energy on the application process. Dwight worshipped the guy, called him the Captain."

"All right, thanks."

"So we're done here?" When Kelly nodded, Chris plopped back into his chair with a sigh and picked up the remote, ramping up the volume. "Let yourselves out. I'll deal with the door after the game."

As they walked to the car, Jake asked, "So Dwight's one of your killers?"

"Looks like it. Apparently something happened when he was in the search and rescue unit that Sam Morgan heads. Maybe he developed a grudge against Morgan, and is trying to set him up by kidnapping Doyle and dumping him at his house."

"So Morgan might be the other killer, the more experienced one."

"Maybe," she acknowledged. "But for now we have to operate on the assumption that he could be another victim, possibly a hostage."

"But they're both in the wind, and Zach's missing, too." Jake shook his head. "Shit. I hate cases like this."

Kelly nodded. "I'm thinking you should head back to the bed-and-breakfast. I can have a unit drive you there," she said, staring straight ahead.

"No way," Jake replied.

"Jake—"

"Look around you, Kelly. You're looking for not one but two killers, and you're surrounded by what I'll politely refer to as yokels. And most of them have made it plain that they don't care if you leave here dead or alive."

"The situation has changed. Since one of their own was taken, they've become surprisingly motivated," Kelly noted drily. "Besides, I arranged for some other state police units to join us, and the Bureau is sending a hostage negotiation team."

"And we all know how ineffective they can be. This smells bad, Kelly."

"Should I have you hauled off in cuffs?"

He glared at her. "Don't do this, Jones. You need me here watching your back. You know I can handle myself. Don't make me spend the night sitting in a hotel room, wondering what the hell is happening to you."

Kelly was surprised by the vehemence in his voice. He was right, on all accounts. She didn't have a partner here to watch her back, and the situation seemed to be quickly spiraling out of her grasp. The added element of Zach's disappearance meant that Monica could no longer be relied upon, not in the state she was in. Having Jake accompany her was against Bureau policy, but she was unsupervised. *No one else had to know,* she reasoned, then caught herself. Funny, how lately she no longer cared about following procedure to the letter. After debating for a minute, Kelly turned back to the car. "Fine," she said. "But no more pushing in front of me when we enter a scene. And if you start to get in the way, I'm sending you home. And I do mean home, not the hotel."

Jake slid into the passenger seat of the car and turned to her. "Wow, you sure do know how to make a guy feel special."

"Don't push your luck," she said warningly. "I'm this close to changing my mind."

"Nah, you're not. I know you that well by now."

She didn't say anything, just stared through the windshield as she punched another address into the GPS system.

"Jones, you okay?" Jake asked, lightly stroking her cheek with one finger.

She shook off his hand. "I'm not losing these monsters," she said fiercely.

"Mr. Doyle? Mr. Doyle, I'm going to have to ask you to get back into bed!" the nurse said sternly as she rushed into the room.

Doyle didn't respond. He was standing unevenly, wires still dangling from strands of tape on his chest. He had disconnected the last few, sending the beeping in the room to an even higher crescendo. "Where the hell are my pants?" he demanded, glancing around.

"Mr. Doyle, the doctor recommended we hold you for observation." The nurse crossed her arms in front of her chest. "I'm going to have to ask you to lie back down."

"Screw that. I'm fine, just get me my damn pants," he muttered.

They stared each other down for a minute. The nurse started to say something else, then snapped her mouth shut and shrugged. "Fine, it's your life. I don't get paid enough to argue with you. Have a seat, I'll be right back."

Doyle remained standing, self-consciously holding the back of his robe closed with one hand as he waited. A minute later the nurse returned holding a plastic bag. "Your uniform is pretty filthy. Do you want me to me call someone, have them bring you some clean clothes?" she asked, eyeing him.

He shook his head and peered into the bag. "These are fine. I'm going back to work."

"All right. Stay here, I need you to sign a form saying that you're checking out against medical advice." As she closed the door, she rolled her eyes at another nurse coming down the hall and said, "Cops."

"Nothing?"

"Well, we got a confirmed crazy here, that's for sure. You should see some of his letters to Cheney, Santa probably gets fewer bold requests," Jake said, holding up a stack of letters. "This guy wrote to everyone—NSA, CIA, Army, Navy, French Foreign Legion. You gotta give him credit for persistence, that's for sure."

They were standing in Dwight's room. Despite his military aspirations, the guy was a slob. Dirty plates were circled by a smattering of flies, and piles of filthy laundry lined the periphery of the room. The tangled bedsheets gave off a rank odor.

Jake looked at Kelly. The circles under her eyes testified to her exhaustion. She'd pulled her hair back into a ponytail, and stray copper-colored strands danced around her face as she scanned the room, hands on her hips. She was wearing her bulletproof vest over a tailored blue camisole. Thanks to the heat, sweat stains were seeping down the sides. He'd seen that look in her eyes before, that grim determination in the face of long odds. He had to physically resist the urge to take her in his arms. "Monica call in from the armory yet?"

Kelly nodded. "Nothing there. They're going to the next site on the list."

"How many units are out now?"

"The one from Boston just got here, so four." Kelly pursed her lips. Chris Santoli had given them a list of twenty locations the search and rescue unit had trained at in the past few years, and one of the other members had added a few more sites. At the rate they were going, it would take the rest of the night to check all of them.

Jake examined her. "Nothing on the APBs?"

She shook her head. "No. They're supposed to call me if any stolen cars turn up in a fifty-mile radius."

Technicians were scattered throughout the house collecting evidence. Dwight's computer had already been removed by the lab techs, and other uniformed cops were poking through drawers and cabinets.

"What the hell is going on here?" a ragged voice said.

Jake followed Kelly down the dank hallway with its cheap faux-wood paneling to the kitchen. A rangy-looking woman was holding open the screen door, squinting at them. "Where's Nancy?"

"Who the hell is Nancy?" Jake asked, but Kelly held up a cautionary hand.

"You're a friend of Dwight's mother?" Kelly asked, stepping forward.

The woman eyed her warily. She was the wrong side of fifty. Years of smoking had hollowed out her cheeks and painted her teeth a shade of yellow that almost matched her dye job. Scrawny bowed legs poked out from spandex bike shorts, while her T-shirt proclaimed that Mohegan Sun had the loosest slots. "That's right. Supposed to pick her up for bingo."

"When was the last time you saw Nancy?" Kelly asked.

"Who the hell are you, anyway?" The woman looked her up and down. "Don't look like a cop, that's for sure."

"Special Agent Kelly Jones with the FBI." Kelly extended her hand. The woman acted as if it was something that had just turned up on the bottom of her shoe. "And you are?"

"Doris Greene. FBI? This about Dwight?"

Kelly weighed her words before responding, "Yes, it is."

"Yeah, he always said they'd have to do a background check before he joined up." The woman leaned forward and lowered her voice. "I gotta say, I'm surprised to see you. I always thought Dwight was bullshitting, didn't think the FBI would take a nut-job. Don't tell Nancy I said that, though."

"Sure, we'll keep that between us." Kelly pulled out a kitchen chair and gestured for the woman to sit. "So when did you last see Nancy?"

"We went down to Foxwoods the weekend before last. I won fifty dollars at blackjack," the woman said proudly. "Nancy is still pissed off about it."

"And you had plans tonight?"

"Yep. I always pick her up for bingo. She somewhere with Dwight?"

Kelly glanced at Jake, then said, "Do you know if they have any other family?"

The woman shook her head. "Nah, her husband took off when Dwight was a baby, and her sister died a while back. No other kids, neither."

"Anywhere else they might stay, like a hunting cabin?"

The woman barked a laugh. "You kidding? Nancy can barely hold on to this place."

"So you don't know where she might have gone?" Kelly asked.

The woman looked from one to the other of them. "Nancy is okay, right?"

Kelly rubbed the back of her neck. "Honestly, we're not sure. Any other friends who could help us find her?"

Doris shook her. "Nancy ain't what you'd call the social type, I'm pretty much it. She used to talk to Rose at bingo, but they got in a hissy fit a few years ago, haven't spoken since."

"What about a cell phone number?"

Doris shook her head again. "I've been telling her to get one. Took me an hour to find her once, casino security finally paged her so I could get the hell out of there and head home. She thinks they cause brain cancer."

Kelly smiled thinly. "Thanks for your time, Doris. Would you mind giving me your name and number, in case I have any more questions?"

Doris pushed back her chair and stood. "Sure. You call me when you find Nancy, all right? She's a mean old bird, but in a good way, you know?"

"Sure," Jake agreed, and stepped forward to guide her out by the elbow. Now that she was in the house Doris seemed reluctant to leave, probably sensing there was more going on.

She turned back at the door. "Hey, agent lady? You make sure to think long and hard before hiring Dwight. I've always thought that boy was trouble."

After she left Kelly surveyed the room. With one hand she reached out and batted the carton of cigarettes strung up to the ceiling fan. The carton swung back and forth before settling into an uneven pendulum. Jake watched Kelly follow it with her eyes.

"I'm guessing we won't be getting any sleep tonight," he said after a minute. "You hungry?"

Kelly shook her head. "Can't eat."

"What do you want to do? Want to catch up to one of the

tactical units? We could bust down some more doors, I know how you enjoy that."

Kelly cast him a warning look, then grinned in spite of herself. "Do not."

"Oh, sure you do. I've already decided to get you a battering ram for your next birthday."

She cocked an eyebrow. "Really? A battering ram?"

"Uh-huh. Thought you could use an extra."

Kelly's phone rang, chasing away her grin. She clicked it open and said authoritatively, "Jones."

Jake watched as her expression shifted, eyebrows knitting together in consternation. Without realizing it he held his breath.

"Where?" Kelly asked. "We'll be right there." She snapped the phone shut and looked at him "They found something."

"Zach?"

But she was already out the door.

Thirty-Five

After a ten-minute drive they pulled into a large semicircular driveway. Behind it loomed a hillside, blades of grass flashing red and blue in time to the silent strobes flickering from emergency vehicles. Kelly pulled to the curb behind an ambulance, and they got out without saying a word to each other. In spite of herself, she repressed a shudder. The cars parked at all angles to each other, the lights, being with Jake—it was all too reminiscent of a similar night about a year ago, the night when they returned to the command center to find her partner Morrow dead in a pool of his own blood...

At the point where the driveway curved back to meet the street, a concrete entrance had been carved into the hillside. Two sets of doors gaped open, the first glass, the next reinforced steel. Inside, an open metal lid sat to the side of a hatch in the floor. A spiral staircase led down.

"What is this place?" Jake asked, looking around. A dusty photo of Lyndon Johnson was mounted on the far wall next to a bare flagpole.

"Former civil defense bunker," Kelly murmured. "Let's get going."

At the bottom of the staircase they found themselves in a circular chamber composed of concrete. Another set of blast doors, then the room widened. Doors opened off it, like a rabbit warren, each leading to a dark corridor. They followed the sound of voices. Someone had set up emergency lighting, and huge floodlamps hunkered down on the floor, piercing the darkness with blinding triangles of light. In silence they walked through an enormous cafeteria, empty save for a few broken plastic chairs lying on their sides. The next room held a number of cots scattered around, tufts of cotton poking out of striped mattresses. Finally, a swinging door led to the bathroom. The outer room had sinks along one wall, toilet stalls lining the other. Monica sat slumped at the far end of the room, holding her head in her hands.

Kelly knelt down beside her. "Zach?"

Monica shook her head, then raised it to look at her. When she spoke her voice was completely flat, stripped of emotion. "He's not here, but there's someone else," she said, gesturing to the next room. "They think maybe Dwight's mother. But they found this." She held up her hand. Dangling from her fingers was a plain rawhide cord with a shark's tooth hanging from it. Her voice broke as she continued, "It was my Daddy's, always claimed he caught and killed the shark with his bare hands. Zach never took it off. Never."

Kelly examined the necklace, then took Monica's hand in both of hers and squeezed it. "We're going to find him," she said in a low voice.

Monica didn't answer, just dropped her head again.

Kelly stood and crossed to the archway that led to the

showers. A naked pile of flesh in the far corner glowed every time the photographer's flash strobed. The other techs stood to the side, waiting until he was finished, murmuring in low voices.

"What have we got?" Kelly said loudly, stepping forward.

They looked toward her. "A hell of a sick fuck, you ask me," one tech answered.

"Where's the coroner?"

"Outside puking, last I saw him," the same guy replied after a minute. He held a work case in his hand: fingerprint tech, Kelly thought to herself.

She repressed a sigh and turned to the photographer. "You almost done here?"

He nodded. "Two more shots."

Kelly waited, Jake silent by her side, as the photographer shifted and got shots of the corpse from a few other angles. When he stepped back Kelly pulled on a pair of gloves, a hairnet and booties. Skirting puddles of blood and excrement, she carefully edged toward the woman.

She was lying in a puddle of her own urine. Kelly's nose wrinkled as she eased off the sweater draped over her upper body. The woman's face was frozen in a rictus of horror, eyes gazing blindly up and to the right, mouth agape. There were bite marks on her face, the rats had already started on her. A chain still looped through a fold of flesh at her waist, fastening her to the wall. Her body was cold but still limp: rigor hadn't set in, so she'd probably only been dead a few hours.

At the signs of trauma mottling her flesh, Jake winced. "Sweet Jesus," he breathed. "I gotta second that emotion. Whichever of your guys did this, he's a sick fuck."

"Killer A," Kelly said with certainty. "These marks are too meticulous."

"You think? Because *meticulous* wasn't the first word that came to mind. I mean shit, just look at her feet."

Kelly carefully shifted toward the lower half of the body. The woman's feet were purple and swollen, almost twice normal size. A few of the toes had been broken and veered off in strange directions. Kelly pursed her lips as she stood. "Do your jobs, then leave her," she ordered the techs. "I want my guy to oversee transport. She's going to the task force morgue in New York."

Jake followed her back into the other room. She knelt by Monica again. "Monica, listen. I'm going to have an officer accompany you home. I need Howie here, to deal with the body. You go home and wait for Zach, okay?"

Monica shook her head and struggled against the wall, jerkily rising to her feet. "No, I'm okay," she snuffled, wiping her face with the back of her free hand.

"You're not. Go home," Kelly said.

"All due respect, I don't work for you," Monica said coldly. "That's my kid out there. I'm not going home until he's found."

Jake touched Kelly's elbow. "You should probably let her come along."

Kelly debated. It was a bad idea, taking part in a manhunt when you were personally involved. She knew that from experience. She'd done it herself last year after Morrow was murdered, and had nearly gotten killed because of it. But she also knew that there was no way in hell anyone would have been able to stop her. "All right, but you stay with us, no going off on your own."

Monica nodded and straightened her jacket. "Let's go."

At the top of the stairs, Kelly paused at the sound of approaching rotors.

"Did you call in a chopper?" Jake asked from behind her.

She shook her head. Through the front door, a spot of light grew, the circle expanding until it encompassed the entire raised concrete platform straddling the center of the driveway. Rotor wash kicked up the trash pooled along the curb, sending it spinning against the hillside. The three of them watched as a Massachusetts State Police helicopter set down. The door swung open and Doyle appeared, waving one arm. Kelly ran forward, keeping her head low.

"What the hell are you doing out of the hospital?" she demanded, shouting to be heard over the chop-chop of the rotors.

He avoided the question. "A few hours ago a guy matching Dwight Sullivan's description carjacked a lady at the 7-Eleven about a mile from here. He's heading up Route 91."

"How far from the border?" Kelly yelled back.

"They got about an hour to go," Doyle hollered. "State police almost had him, but another car got in the way and there was a pileup. They're trying to track him down now."

Kelly nodded and gestured to the others. "I'll ride up front."

Monica had already ducked under Jake's elbow, diving into the chopper. Doyle clambered in after her. The helicopter lifted off and swept into the night, its lights carving a hole in the sky.

Zach grimaced as the car went over another bump, sending him flying. The side of his head whacked the roof of the trunk and he swore. He tried to brace himself better, feet pressed against the spare tire; but with his hands tied behind him, every time they went over something he was thrown around again. He was wiped out from spending the first half of the ride frantically kicking the trunk hood and screaming when-

ever the car slowed, hoping to jar the lid loose, or that
someone would hear him. After a while he simply gave up.

He had no idea why this asshole was still carting him
around, and he still couldn't believe that other guy had just
left him there. What kind of jerk did that? He'd screamed
himself hoarse, begging for him to come back, to get someone
else, or at least to tell someone. But the guy just disappeared,
leaving him alone in the dark with a dead woman. He had
heard the first of the rats approach, the excited chatter, then
other small feet. Some of them had tried for him, nipping at
his bound hands, but he'd managed to thrust and kick them
away. They eventually let him be, drawn to the easier prey a
few feet away. It was a terrible sound, that gnawing.

And then the older guy came back, sending the rats scattering. He hadn't spoken, just pressed a gun against the base
of Zach's spine, marched him up to the car, then bound his
feet together again after stuffing him in the trunk of a beat-
up Volvo. Zach blathered away nonstop, asked the guy where
he was taking him, why didn't he set him free, was he just
going to leave the lady's body there? The guy didn't answer,
didn't say a word, which served to completely freak Zach out,
especially when he remembered that the guy said he'd never
spoken to the other boys. He avoided eye contact, too, which
Zach didn't think was a good sign. And he was pretty sure that
the object poking into his spine right now was a shovel.

The car slowed again, and the movement shifted. Zach
strained his ears. The highway sounds had drifted away, and
now he heard crickets and the crunch of tires on gravel.
That continued for some time, then the gravel disappeared
and the car shifted mightily from side to side, lumbering like
an ox. Zach struggled helplessly as his body was hurled

from one side to the other, issuing little grunts as his shoulder, chin, nose and knees rapped against the hard interior. He closed his eyes and gritted his teeth, trying to go limp and just roll with the car, the way he did when he was about to eat shit skateboarding. It didn't seem to make a difference.

At the bottom of one dip, the car suddenly stopped. When the trunk popped open, Zach's breath caught. Night air rushed in, cooling the beads of sweat rolling down his face. The man was silhouetted against the sky, a black form blotting out the stars. Zach craned his head to see over the lip of the trunk, but it was too dark to make out anything.

"Where are we?" he asked after a minute.

The guy didn't answer, just cut the tape off his feet and yanked them around so that they draped over the edge of the trunk. He pulled Zach to a sitting position, knocking his head against the hood. Zach winced and felt tears rising again. He squinted to see; it was pitch-black, no hint of a moon, just faint light from stars peeking through tree branches. They were in the woods somewhere. He could smell the pine, recognized the scrape of the guy's boots against dirt.

The guy reached past him to grab something, pulled it out and leaned it against the side of the car. Zach realized with a sinking heart that he'd been right, it was a folding camp shovel. The man unzipped his backpack, tucked the shovel inside, then slung on the straps. He pressed the gun into Zach's gut. His voice was low and threatening, different than it had been before, when he muttered, "You scream, you die. Now let's go."

The car was pulled off the road at an angle, front tires on the grass, hood lifted, emergency triangle propped in the street behind it. The rear of the car was jacked off the ground, a stray tire iron by its side.

"Blood and hair," Kelly noted, picking up the iron. "So it looks like Dwight caught another ride."

"Took them along this time, too," Jake noted, "which'll make it a hell of a lot harder to find him."

They were standing by the side of Route 2, a small road that branched off the main highway near St. Johnsbury in Vermont. Woods encroached from all sides of the two-lane road. A lone streetlamp served as sentry a hundred feet away. "Dwight knew that if he stuck to the highway, state police would grab him, so he decided to switch cars," Kelly said. "Pulling off here, he had a better chance of someone stopping to help him. Not a lot of traffic, especially at this hour. So probably no witnesses."

"Poor bastard. That's why I'm never a Good Samaritan," Jake said, lowering his voice as Monica trotted up.

She'd been down the way, talking to the state trooper who found the car. She jerked her thumb back toward him and said, "That cop says they're setting up roadblocks every fifty miles along the 91, and they got one on this road where it inter-sects the 15."

Kelly followed her finger, peering into the darkness past the streetlight. A state police car was parked ten feet behind her. Their chopper waited in a nearby field, rotors stilled. "Does he have a map?" she asked.

Five minutes later she was bent over a map of Vermont spread across the hood of the car. Jake held a penlight for her to see. "I'm guessing Dwight would know better than to go back to the highway. He probably cut up here, to the 15, then took the 16 north toward Canada."

"Yeah, but if he's that smart, he'll figure you've got border patrol on high alert. So how the hell does he think he's going to get across?" Jake asked.

Kelly poked the map at the top. "There, by Route 105."

Jake followed her finger and let out a low whistle. "He's going to hike in?"

"Both of these guys have lots of backwoods training, it wouldn't be a tough hike for either of them," Kelly pointed out.

"You think they're traveling together?" Jake asked. "Maybe offed Dwight's mother, then decided to make a run for it?"

"Maybe," Kelly said. "The woman who was carjacked only saw one man, but that doesn't mean Morgan might not have been waiting somewhere nearby. Or maybe he's a hostage, too, and Dwight stowed him somewhere." *Or Morgan's already dead,* she thought, but didn't say it aloud. Right now she had a lead on one of their killers. It was her responsibility to follow it and to try to prevent Dwight from crossing the border into Canada. If Morgan popped up on their radar, she'd divert some resources. As it was, there was currently a three-state manhunt in progress for both men. Chances were, sooner or later they'd be found.

"But what about Zach?" Monica asked. "Why did they take him?"

Kelly and Jake exchanged a glance. Both of them knew it wasn't likely the boy was still alive. It didn't make a lot of sense to bring a hostage on a run for the border, especially when your route required stealth.

"I'm sure he's fine," Jake said, trying to force assurance into his voice.

"Let's join Doyle in the chopper," Kelly said. "We need to cut Dwight off before he gets to the border."

* * *

Dwight wiped his mouth with the back of his hand. The radio was blasting to block out the pounding noises coming from the car trunk. He ran his hands along the leather of the steering wheel, pondering the fact that this was probably the nicest car he'd ever driven. Mercedes, and not some stinkin' C-series, either; the motherfuckin' S-class. He was surprised that the guy had stopped to help, that flat-tire routine had worked like a charm. Ironic, since a jerk-off in a Mercedes usually wouldn't give him the time of day.

"Shut up and play with your fuckin' golf clubs!" he roared after a minute. The pounding paused, then started up again even harder than before. Dwight grumbled to himself. He should've just bashed the guy's skull in when he took the damn car. Pain in the ass; he'd pull over now and do it, but he was so close he didn't want to risk stopping. Dwight had known as soon as he saw the kid in that bomb shelter that the Captain just couldn't stop himself from taking another one. Knew, too, that he'd be making a run for the border. And there weren't too many places you could cross these days that weren't being watched, not after 9/11. They'd talked about it around the campfire on that SAR training retreat. Nowadays border patrol didn't have the personnel to watch remote areas; hell, any bastard could wander down the old logging trail through Cold Hollow Mountain with an RPG over his shoulder. Wasn't an easy hike, but for Al-Qaeda guys who grew up in the mountains of Afghanistan, no pissant Vermont hill was going to stop 'em. Dwight had agreed with the rest that it was a damn shame. Had to carry a gun just to keep your family safe these days, goddamn government took your money and spent it on bridges in Alaska instead of hiring a few more guys to hunt Pakis on the border. He got back from that trip and promptly filled out his application for the border patrol. Still hadn't heard back from them, he mused. Well, it was too late now; Dwight was gonna be long gone. Maybe the Mounties would appreciate his talents.

An image of his mother, dead and lying in her own shit, swam before his eyes again. He squeezed them shut to force it away. His knuckles whitened on the steering wheel, and he shook it violently, screaming "Fuck!" as tears ran down his face. The car jiggled slightly but didn't swerve. The pounding stalled again. Dwight ramped up the speakers another notch, gritting his teeth in time to "Dream On." He'd wait until the Captain was distracted, maybe when he was working on the boy and had his back turned. "I'm gonna get him, Ma, I swear, I'm gonna get him…."

Thirty-Six

Zach tripped and fell again, bruising his knee. Wherever they were it was heavily wooded, and beech trees gleamed white around them. Over the years his mom had taken him camping pretty much everywhere in New England, so initially he'd tried to recognize the park. But the trail markers were faded, and the foliage could've been found in a dozen different places. He was pretty sure they were still in Vermont, though.

He tried to pick his way through the tiny beam of light projected by the guy's flashlight, but he kept swinging it across the ground from side to side, and time and again Zach's foot connected with a tree root and he went down hard. He was exhausted, too. The constant jolts of adrenaline, combined with the long ride in the trunk inhaling carbon monoxide, had left him headachy and sore.

The guy still hadn't said a word, just jerked him back to his feet whenever he fell by yanking a rope he'd strung through the handcuffs. He was strong for a guy his size. Zach was probably an inch or two taller than him, but the guy easily got him back on his feet. Each time it felt like his arms were being torn from their sockets. They'd been climbing steadily for a half hour or so, ever since they'd left the car. Zach wondered where the hell the guy was taking him—it didn't make a lot of sense to go up a mountain. *Unless you were going to kill someone and bury them,* he thought, his heart sinking.

The trees started thinning off to his right. With the next swing of the flashlight he saw the ground vanish on that side of the trail, trees balanced precariously on the edge, tipping toward the gully below. As the light panned back, he caught a glint of something red up ahead. Lifting his feet high to keep from tripping, Zach focused on that spot, praying the guy would swing the light past it again. He did, and Zach saw that he was right. A small wooden sign hung from a tree trunk up ahead, and the carved copper letters glinted in the flashlight's beam. An arrow pointed to: Jay's Peak, 3,861 feet. Zach's stomach leaped. He knew exactly where they were, he'd been here before with his Boy Scout troop. It was a park that straddled the Canadian border. They'd stayed at a ramshackle trail hut. It had to be around here somewhere. And unless he was mistaken, inside there was an emergency kit with a radio. If the guy got distracted enough, slackened his hold on the rope, he could make a break for it. Hell, at this point anything was worth a try. Zach tripped again and skidded down, heels scrabbling desperately for a purchase as his body slid toward the precipice. He felt the rope around his hands tauten, stopping his fall, and he gritted his teeth, tears of pain and relief rushing to his eyes. The guy was keeping him alive for some reason, maybe so he could hone more of his torture techniques. As Zach stumbled back to his feet, he felt his resolve harden. Before anything like that happened he was going to get away from this asshole, or die trying.

* * *

Kelly gritted her teeth as they circled. The helicopter had made a few passes now with no luck. The tree cover below was so thick it was nearly impossible to see anything.

"There!" Jake suddenly exclaimed. She jumped as his voice reverberated in her headset. Kelly shifted in her seat and followed his pointing finger. Half-hidden by the tree line, parked where a logging road dead-ended, she saw the top of a gray sedan.

She turned to the helicopter pilot. He'd been introduced as an old buddy of Doyle's, and had proved his worth, hardly blinking at the request to take them over the state line and out of his jurisdiction. Kelly hoped that having Monica on board would smooth things over with the Vermont State Police when their actions were reviewed.

"Can you set us down?" she yelled into her microphone.

The pilot shook his head. "Not there. Looks like there's a spot up ahead, open field about a half mile in. That's as close as I can get you."

Kelly nodded her assent and the chopper dove forward.

Dwight squinted through the scope. It had cost him a small fortune to buy one with night vision, but it was turning out to be worth every penny. Military issue, acquired through a guy who hawked the stuff via an innocuous-looking eBay site. The sales slip had listed the rifle as "Hummel figurines" on the sales slip, which Dwight found hilarious. Ma hadn't even blinked when she saw the box, he thought, a tear trickling down his cheek at the memory.

Dwight's finger twitched over the trigger, but he forced himself to wait and take a long, deep breath. He knew this park pretty well, had done some drills here on his own, getting in shape for Ranger camp. He'd parked at the gate next to a little-used access road, then humped straight over the hill to the other side. Below him was the trail that led to the border, about a half mile away. On the other side of the narrow trail was a downward slope clustered with trees, ending where the mountain slipped into a chasm. He was perched above a pasture, one of the few spots where the trees grudgingly ceded a few acres to grassland. Dwight could see for a hundred feet in either direction. Fifty feet below him was one of the long straight sections, where the trail wove between the field above and the trees below. Up ahead, the path segued into switch-backs. It was one of the only open spots for a half mile in either direction. Dwight knew that if the Captain was heading for the border, chances were he'd come this way. It was the perfect spot for an ambush.

He'd set up the tripod and hunkered down behind it, sprawled on a blanket. If anyone looked from down below, they would only see him as a rise in the hill. Dwight was gambling on the fact that the Captain would feel safe enough to take the main trail by cover of night. If he opted for one of the smaller paths, there was no way Dwight would ever find them. But, lo and behold, after an hour of waiting, two figures emerged from the tree line. Through his scope their bodies shimmered ghostly green. He'd had to repress a snort. The Captain thought he was so smart, but he turned out to be just as dumb and predictable as everyone else. A small part of Dwight was disappointed, he'd expected more of the man.

His jaw clenched as he tracked them with the rifle, follow-ing their slow progress. The kid was stumbling every few feet, dropping down and getting yanked back up. Dwight shook his head slightly. Sorry bastard never had a chance. It was a shame. He debated shooting the kid first, to put him out of his misery, but the Captain was a slippery so-and-so and he couldn't risk giving him a chance to get away.

Dwight tried to remember what he'd read in the sniper guidebook he'd found in a secondhand store. He regulated his breathing, three deep breaths in, three out. He focused on a point fifty feet in front of them, where there was a break in the trees and they'd be silhouetted against the night sky. It was hard to relax the way the book recommended. He felt a flare of rage just looking at the Captain, strolling along there, thinking he was going to get away with it. In a few minutes they were ten feet away from the spot. Dwight closed both his eyes, then opened just his right one. Five feet to go. Dwight inhaled deeply, felt his chest and rib cage lift off the blanket, then squeezed every drop of air from his lungs. One foot left, and his finger eased onto the trigger, cold metal drawing back toward him.

There was a shot, and Dwight jumped, surprised. His head jerked up reflexively, then he ducked down and fumbled for the scope, raising it to his eyes, praying he hadn't been seen. Both figures had turned and were facing away from him, looking back down the mountain. Multiple flashlight beams danced up the trail, and someone was shouting. He watched, lip curling back as the boy turned and bolted right, the sound of branches snapping as the boy vanished into the trees. The Captain dove after him, curses drifting through the night stillness. Dwight remained motionless, watching as lights burst from the trees on his right where the trail emerged. They bobbed for a moment before cutting right and dashing off in pursuit. He waited a full minute until the last of the clamor had subsided. A flock of bats, startled by the activity, swept up the slope. They passed a few feet over his head, wings beating frantically for shelter. After they vanished he sat up, letting the rifle tilt forward in its tripod, muzzle to the ground. He had an overpowering urge to scream, to beat his fists against something, but he couldn't let himself get caught. He pondered his options, then carefully tucked the blanket back in his pack and slung the rifle over his shoulder. Staying low, he jockeyed left, parallel to the logging road, heading toward the border.

Kelly swore under her breath as another branch lashed her face. She was tearing through the underbrush, brambles and low-hanging branches snatching at her hair and skin as she stumbled forward. They were racing downhill at nearly a sixty-degree angle; even if she wanted to stop she doubted she could.

The chopper had set them down a mile away, in a field right next to a logging trail. They'd hiked in toward the border, jogging when the terrain permitted it. Then Monica had seen the flashlight up ahead. She broke into a sprint, the rest of them hard on her heels. It had been too dark to see much more than the pinpoint beam that suddenly broke to the right, vanishing into the woods. Kelly could only hope they were chasing the killers, not some poor backpacker who had panicked at the gunshot. Kelly wasn't even sure who had fired. Back at the chopper landing site she had told everyone to keep their weapons holstered until it was clear they were needed. Obviously someone hadn't heeded her orders.

She could hear Jake tearing along beside her, and periodically Monica plaintively wailed out, "Zach!" Kelly was pursuing a shadow, trusting her ears more than her eyes, trying to dodge the worst of the brambles her flashlight picked out of the darkness. The helicopter suddenly swept overhead, following her orders to stay on their tail, and as its spotlight beam filtered down she caught a glimpse of a tall, slender man running through the trees. It was Morgan—she could tell by the set of his shoulders. He ducked to the right, vanishing into a clump of bushes. She veered to follow him, and saw Jake correct his trajectory, pulling in front of her.

Sam was having a hard time sucking in enough oxygen. His breath was coming in gasps and gulps, heart whacking against his rib cage as he ran. He was out of shape. Even after ditching the backpack it was hard going. He should have spent more time in the gym, but he hadn't anticipated getting chased through the forest. It was his own fault, he'd delayed too long in finding alternate transportation. He should have kept another car stored in a safe place for just this eventuality, that way he wouldn't have had to steal one from the bus station. Gathering that, plus his buried Plan B pack for the border crossing, had consumed a few precious hours, enough time for them to catch up with him. He was so close, too, less than a mile from the border. Sam kicked himself for loosening his grip on the rope and allowing the kid to escape. The whole reason he'd brought the boy along was to have a hostage in case they caught up with him.

He'd hiked these woods a few times before, and knew that the gully they were racing down soon dropped into a sheer chasm. If they pinned him down there, he was trapped. He heard a noise off to his left and cut that way, darting after a shadow.

Zach heard yelling from behind. He kept his feet high as he ran, legs pumping, trying to avoid fallen branches and roots. If he fell now he was done for. When he'd heard those voices behind him his heart had leaped, and for the first time in hours he'd felt hope. And then when he'd twisted and yanked forward, expecting to get snapped back by the rope, it had mercifully released and he'd dashed into the woods. He was holding on to it now as he ran, praying it didn't get tangled on something. The whomp of a helicopter was almost as loud as his own gasping breath. He could swear he'd heard his mom's voice, but was too terrified to stop. The worst thing would be to get caught again after experiencing this burst of freedom. He was so close now, he had to get away.

As he ran, the forest was intermittently illuminated from above, chopper rotors sending up squawks of avian protest in the trees. He heard another noise to his left, something smaller scampering through the bushes, and he veered away from it. The trees suddenly vanished and he was in a clearing, the slope canting forward. A few feet farther he realized why and tried to shift his weight, hurling himself in the opposite direction. The sudden weight change sent him spinning out. He landed hard and rolled on his side, tumbling downhill, howling as his arms were yanked up and his feet skidded down. His heels dropped over the edge, the ground giving way to empty space, nothing but yawning darkness rushing up to greet him. As he screamed, he felt the rope around his arms tauten. He gasped, both from relief and pain. Slowly, he was pulled back up to the edge of the cliff.

The voices nearby suddenly stilled. Glancing up, Zach saw a familiar form silhouetted against the night sky. The chopper cleared the trees, spotlight groping around the precipice until it fixed on the two of them. Zach winced in the sudden brightness. He could hear heavy breathing, wheezes that matched his own.

"Let him go, Morgan!" a voice called out. Female, but not his mother.

The man bent low over him. His voice was still raspy from running. "How awful, to have come so close," he said in a low murmur. His eyes glittered as he straightened, a small pistol digging into Zach's temples. "Don't do anything foolish, Agent Jones."

Sam Morgan sounded preternaturally calm as he held the gun to Zach's temples. Kelly felt Jake take a step forward and raised her arm to stop him. Just then Monica exploded out of the trees behind them, with Doyle hard on her heels. She came to a stop beside Kelly. "Jesus, Sam, don't hurt him!" Monica wailed, her voice choked and gasping.

"Sorry about this, Monica. I always liked you."

The crazy thing was, he sounded genuinely repentant. "Christ, Morgan, what are you thinking?" Doyle asked. With one arm Kelly impatiently waved for him to be silent. She edged forward, gun in one hand, flashlight in the other. "Look around you, Sam. There's no way out of here. Border patrol is mobilizing, we've got a chopper overhead. Drop the gun and let the kid go."

"What, and spend the rest of my life rotting in prison?" he sneered. "No, thanks. If you really think there's no way out, I might as well just kill us both." He jerked his hand upward, as if preparing to shoot, and Monica wailed. "Of course," he said pensively, "we are just a short ways from the border."

"I can't let you cross the border," Kelly said firmly.

"Why not? As you said, the border patrol is mobilizing. Might as well let them make the arrest. Either way you have me."

Kelly stared him down. In actuality, border patrol had said

it would take an hour to get anyone out there, and that had been forty-five minutes ago. The park wasn't an official checkpoint, so there would be no station, no guards posted to stop him. And she wasn't permitted to cross the border herself.

"Let him go," Jake murmured at her side.

"Canada won't extradite for death penalty offenses. If he crosses, we're not getting him back," Doyle said.

"Please, Kelly," Monica hissed. "Please, it's Zach."

"I'll be right on his tail," Jake said under his breath. "He's not going anywhere."

Morgan called out, "Some people would consider it rude not to be included in your conversation. I bet Zach thinks it's rude, don't you, Zach?"

The boy squeezed his eyes together as the pistol danced in front of them. Kelly watched as a tear slid down his cheek. "I love you, Mom," Zach said in a broken voice.

"Please, Kelly…" Monica begged.

"What do we do, Agent Jones?" Sam Morgan said.

Kelly debated. Bureau policy was very clear. In this situation, she was supposed to keep him engaged until a negotiator arrived, then cede control to them. The problem was she knew they didn't have that kind of time. She'd radioed for backup when they found the car, but those units were still at least ten minutes away. And Morgan was clearly not planning on sticking around for long. For now, they were on their own. She took another half step forward, keeping her gun steady, pointed at his chest. "Just stay calm, Sam. Let's talk this through."

"Are you still hitting on me?" He shook his head in rebuke. "Agent Jones, I thought I made it clear that I'm a married man. Why don't we start by getting rid of the helicopter."

Kelly glanced up. There was nowhere for the chopper to

land. At the moment, all it did was provide light. She decided there was no real harm in having it hang back. She waved for the pilot to retreat. They all waited as the chopper swung left, hovering over the woods a hundred yards away. She drew a deep breath as the rotor noise diminished. The pilot had warned her he'd have to leave soon to refuel—she just hoped he had enough to provide support until reinforcements arrived.

"All right, now why don't you just let the boy go," she said, the sound of her voice suddenly loud in the stillness.

Morgan cocked his head to the side. "You know, I think I will," he said. Kelly held her breath as he stepped toward Zach and bent down. It looked as if he was untying the boy's hands, then with a swift motion he jerked the rope up and away. She lunged forward as she realized what was happening, but it was too late. She heard Zach's scream reverberate off the cliff's walls as he tumbled backward into the void.

Thirty-Seven

Kelly rushed to the cliff edge, but Monica got there first, her shriek searing a hole in the air. Kelly leaned forward, peering down, but all she could see was a black pit. In the confusion Morgan had sprinted the twenty feet to the trees. Kelly looked around wildly, saw Jake and Doyle vanish into the woods after him. Monica was trying to scrabble down the cliff face. She'd turned and flipped over onto her belly, reaching down with her toes to find a purchase. She was muttering under her breath, "Mommy's coming, Beenie, don't worry, Mommy's coming."

Kelly had a split second to decide whether to continue the pursuit or to keep Monica from tumbling down after her son. She knew what McLarty would say: it was her job to stay on the suspect, she should have already raced into the woods after Morgan. Not doing so exposed her to disciplinary review if he escaped.

With one last glance toward the tree line, she tucked her gun in its holster and grabbed hold of Monica's arms, catching her before she continued her descent. Kelly leaned back with all of her weight and forced her voice to be soothing. "Listen to me, Monica, you can't go down there. I'll get the chopper back, we'll have him look for Zach."

Monica struggled against her for a minute, then went limp. Kelly straightened and snatched the radio from her belt, keying it to the band the chopper pilot was tuned to. "The hostage went over the edge. I need you down there, now."

The helicopter swept back into sight, spinning a hundred and eighty degrees so that it faced them as it descended, the spotlight panning the sides of the cliff. About twenty feet down the light picked up something, a lump of clothes and flesh. Kelly heard Monica catch her breath. "Is that him?" she asked in a small voice.

Kelly wrapped her arms around her, both to comfort her and to prevent her from trying to climb down again. "Let's just sit here and wait, help will be here soon."

Monica refused to move, staring down at the remains of her son.

As they watched, the lump suddenly shifted. "He's alive!" Monica cast about wildly. "Tell the pilot we need some rope, I have to get down to him!"

Relief flooded Kelly's chest. She braced Monica with one arm. "You're staying here. I'll have a rescue chopper called in. Don't worry, Monica. We'll get Zach out of there."

An hour later, Kelly was perched in the back of a forestry service SUV, frowning into her radio as she kept track of the manhunt. Monica and Zach had been loaded into the rescue chopper. Zach was in and out of consciousness and had broken several bones. She'd seen his face before they loaded him up, pale from shock and fatigue, small red scratches forming a complicated map of dried blood. Monica's forehead was creased with worry as she rubbed his uninjured hand over and over while murmuring to him. Kelly prayed he'd survive, but the paramedics didn't seem confident.

Doyle suddenly materialized at her side. A broken leaf jutted from his mustache and his cheeks were streaked with dirt. "Lost the son of a bitch," he said, shaking his head and avoiding her eyes. "Your boy's still on him, though."

"Who, Jake?"

Doyle nodded. "The other Vermont cops went in after him, but they had to stop at the border, too. A park ranger just showed up—he's helping them organize a sweep of the park."

"I doubt he's still here, apparently it's only a half mile or so to the border. My boss got in touch with the Canadian authorities. Mounties and border patrol will be on the lookout for him," Kelly said.

Doyle didn't answer, just shifted his weight from one foot to the other. "How's the kid?"

"Not good," Kelly said. "They think maybe internal bleeding."

"Bastard," Doyle snorted. "Goddamn Sam Morgan. I'd never have believed it."

Static burst from the radio, followed by chatter. They both tilted their heads to the side, ears cocked to listen. When it turned out to be nothing, Kelly sighed and dropped the radio back into her lap. "I think we might have lost him." A wave of exhaustion nearly overwhelmed her, and she dropped her head into one hand, rubbing her eyes. She felt something on her arm and looked up.

Doyle was awkwardly tapping her arm. "Not your fault," he said gruffly. "If I was on my game, he'd never have got away."

Kelly opened her mouth, intending to point out that if Doyle had come clean from the get-go it would have saved her a lot of time and they might not be in this situation, but she was too tired to argue.

He kicked at a stone near his foot. "You gotta understand, back then the homicide unit was short-staffed. When that first skeleton turned up, we figured it was probably just a lost hiker—no need to add another body to our workload. He was long dead, and it looked like no one was missing him. Then, when another body was found, if we'd admitted being wrong about the first one, it would've meant a black eye for the department. We were already facing budget cuts. It's not like we intentionally buried cases. Hell, we didn't even know they were gay."

Kelly regarded him coolly. "So, what you're saying is you don't think I should bother reporting this to IAD."

"I'm just saying, now that we know, does it matter?" Doyle shifted uneasily.

Another crackle of static, and she lifted the receiver back to her ear. It was Canadian border patrol. They'd found tracks that led to the main road, Route 243. They figured Morgan might have hitched a ride from someone.

"Shit!" she said, clenching her jaw.

Doyle spat on the ground. "Well, looks like Morgan is Canada's problem now. What about the other one?" he asked, voice overly casual.

Kelly shook her head. "No sign of Dwight Sullivan. They've still got roadblocks set up, but he might have hunkered down in the woods somewhere between here and the border. Or maybe he slipped across earlier."

"Yeah? I've been meaning to go camping myself," Doyle

said, working his jaw. "Maybe I'll take some personal time, check out the great white north."

Kelly eyed him. She'd never been a fan of vigilante justice, though she understood the impulse behind it. Hell, if she'd been given ten minutes alone in a room with the man who killed her brother, it's hard to say what she would have done. She liked to think she would have turned him over to the authorities unharmed, but far too frequently the worst offenders got off on a technicality. Kelly shrugged. "Suit yourself. Honestly, at this point it's not up to me. Unless something changes, all that's left is the paperwork."

"And we got Peters for that," Doyle said with a grin. "Anyhow, about the IAD…"

Kelly gazed at him levelly. "I'm a lot of things, Doyle, but I've never been a rat. You should know, though, that the way this has gone down, they're going to be going over the files with a fine-tooth comb. Your name is bound to come up. And you were captured by a man who you were tracking without backup, after not reporting in for hours."

"Yeah, I know. My captain said he'll back me on that."

In his eyes Kelly read the subtext, that his captain wanted the whole thing swept under the carpet in the hopes of keeping his department's name clean. She chewed her lip, agitated, thinking about all those boys whose deaths weren't investigated in the name of budget cuts and homicide clearance rates. Who knew how many other transgressions the Berkshire State Police department had committed? There could be an entire backlog of murder cases shelved as accidents, not to mention other crimes that weren't considered worth their time and resources.

But when it came down to it, how a department was run

was only her concern as long as she was working with them. And, as of this morning, she was done. "Then I guess your troubles are over," Kelly told him as she turned away.

Thirty-Eight

Sam Morgan checked himself in the side mirror of a parked car before entering the diner. He'd been lucky, an eighteen-wheeler had shown up before he'd been on the road ten minutes. The guy had pulled right over and offered him a ride. Thanks to that he was already halfway to Montreal. He figured in a big city, it would be easier to blend in. Soon as he got there he'd do what he could to alter his appearance, dye his hair darker, grow a beard. He wasn't worried. Canada had a terrible track record for tracking down criminals who fled across their borders, partly because their horror of the barbaric American legal system made them loath to get involved.

He'd wait a few years, until things settled down, then would send for Sylvia and the girls. He was confident she'd come; you don't live with someone for a decade without knowing them inside and out. She would understand that he would never hurt her or the girls, or anyone else that mattered. Deep down Sylvia was a woman more concerned more with social conventions than a moral code. As long as he kept his hobby to himself, and didn't take out any of their country club friends, he had the feeling she'd look the other way. Up here, it would be different. How much easier it would be having her onboard. For the time being he'd miss the girls, but there was no avoiding that.

The diner was a battered, converted metal trailer. A line of small booths on his left, a row of swiveling stools welded beneath a long counter to the right. A narrow aisle ran the length of the building. Noting that there was another door at the rear, next to the restroom, he nonchalantly walked the length of the building and slid into the far booth. He tugged the baseball cap he'd nicked from the floor of the truck cab further down over his eyes. At this early-morning hour there were only two other people inside. Both looked like truckers; one read the paper, the other stared into the steam from his coffee mug. The waitress came up and Sam ordered coffee, toast and eggs. He was ravenous, having had nothing but an energy bar since lunch yesterday. He patted his shirt pocket, thankful that his wallet had survived the flight through the woods. He had enough Canadian cash to get him through the week; after that he'd have to find an Internet café somewhere, arrange for a transfer from one of his offshore accounts. He wouldn't need much, it was smarter to rent a cheap apartment and live off the grid to avoid attracting attention. He'd check *craigslist* when he got to Montreal, see if he could find a sublet that didn't require a credit check.

As he devoured his breakfast, he outlined the next few days in his mind, going over the steps he'd need to take to settle into his new life. He was too preoccupied to notice the figure leaning against a tree outside the diner, scanning the room with a pair of high-powered binoculars.

* * *

Dwight ducked back behind a tree as the Captain strolled out of the diner. Son of a bitch looked like he didn't have a care in the world, Dwight thought angrily. Probably figured he got away clean, didn't count on ol' Dwight outsmarting him.

As soon as he realized the Captain had slipped through his net, Dwight had hit the road himself, crossing the border. Couldn't risk getting snared, after all. On the off chance that the Captain might somehow escape from the cops, Dwight camped out by some trees with a good view of the road. Soon enough he saw the Captain bolt from the woods, glancing back over his shoulder. He trotted down the road with his thumb in the air. When the truck pulled over to give him a lift, Dwight scrambled in the back, crawling on top of crates of Florida oranges. Popped open one crate and helped himself to a few. He had to say they were damn good oranges, or maybe everything just tasted better in Canada. An hour later when he felt the gears shift down as the truck slowed, he clambered out the back before it took off again.

His stomach growled and he frowned. He'd had an MRE, but the thought of toast and eggs had his mouth watering. He'd have to stop in for a bite when he was done.

The door swung shut behind the Captain with a tinkling of bells that were loud in the morning stillness. He headed through the parking lot, back toward the road. Dwight was lucky, the Captain was sticking close to the tree line, probably deliberately hovering near cover. And that route would lead him directly past the tree Dwight was hiding behind. Dwight checked the diner: the trucker at the counter had his back to the parking lot, the other was paying at the register. The waitress was focused on their transaction. He craned his ears:

nothing but birds chirping in the predawn light and the sound of the wind high in the tree branches. It didn't sound like any cars were coming. He'd have to chance it.

Dwight eased around to the side of the tree facing the road. The Captain was whistling, a tune he recognized but couldn't place. As the Captain's foot came into view, Dwight lunged to the side and jammed the taser directly into his neck. The Captain's eyes went wide before he dropped to the ground, twitching. The only noise he made was a sort of strangled gasp. Glancing sideways quickly to see if anyone had noticed, Dwight grabbed his heels and dragged him into the woods.

In the late morning Kelly conceded there was nothing more she could do at the border. More rangers and Vermont State Police had entered the park and were searching it for signs of either man. Morgan's and Sullivan's faces were splattered across every major newspaper and newscast within a three-state radius. She caught a ride to the hospital with a Vermont cop heading back for his shift change. His station was tuned to a talk-radio show, the chatter occasionally drowned out by the crackle of his police-band. She listened, leaning against the car window half-asleep, the heat from outside pressing against her forehead. People calling in to the show were outraged, professing shock and disbelief at the fact that not one but two potential killers had escaped and were now some-where out there among them. One woman with a particularly shrill voice said, "We'd be better off if our tax dollars got us guns to defend ourselves. Cops are goddamned stupid and incompetent. Who needs 'em?"

"You mind turning that off?" Kelly had asked, tired. The cop complied, and they passed the rest of the drive in silence.

Kelly steeled herself before pushing open the door to the ICU. Her badge had gained her entry with only a raised eyebrow. Now, part of her was wishing she'd been turned away. Monica sat in a brown plastic chair, her body slumped forward, head in her hands. Zach was a mass of tubes; what she could see of his face was pale and drawn. She walked forward, stepping quietly, and lightly touched Monica's arm. Monica started and looked up blearily.

"How is he?" Kelly asked.

Monica shook her head. "Too soon to say. He's had one surgery so far, he might need to have more. Both his arms and one leg are broken, one of his rubs punctured his right lung…"A tear trickled down her face. "The doctors say if he survives the next twenty-four hours, it's a good sign."

Kelly bent down and hugged her. Monica settled into her arms, and Kelly stroked her hair. "I'm sure he'll be fine. He's young and healthy, he'll heal fast."

"I hope so." Monica sighed and pulled back.

"Can I get you anything? Coffee, or food?" Kelly knelt next to the chair.

Monica shook her head. "I can't eat." Her voice hardened as she asked, "Did you get Morgan?"

"Not yet. They've issued a huge dragnet in Canada, though. They're working to get the public involved, posting photos of Morgan and Sullivan in the media. I'm sure we'll have them both in custody soon." Kelly tried to inject her voice with more confidence then she felt. The truth of the matter was that the Canadian government was already balking at pursuing two criminals who faced the federal death penalty if extradited. They were also not pleased that the U.S. government had allowed two serial killers to slip across their border. Amidst the waves of recriminations, it was hard to know what was actually being done to catch them.

Worse yet, she hadn't heard from Jake since he'd dashed off into the woods hours earlier. She tried not to think about it. Jake knew how to take care of himself. If he wasn't in radio contact, there was a good reason. "I still think Dwight might be holed up somewhere upstate. We've focused our efforts there for now. Vermont and Massachusetts are both devoting a lot of their resources to finding him."

Monica shook her head. "You'll never find Morgan. He's too damn smart."

"I've caught smart ones before."

"Maybe." Monica fell silent, gazing at her son's broken body. "I just feel so guilty, you know? Like I should have figured it out sooner. Then maybe Zach wouldn't be here."

"You can't second-guess yourself like that."

"No? Is there anything you would have done differently?"

Kelly thought it over. "Probably not. But I don't even let myself ask anymore. I lost a partner last year, and spent months afterward going back through the case in my mind, trying to figure out where I screwed up, what would have saved him. You can drive yourself crazy doing that."

"Yeah, well, parenthood is all about driving yourself crazy," Monica said mournfully. Her voice lowered as she continued, "If he dies, I don't know what I'll do."

"He's going to be fine," Kelly said, trying to sound reassuring. She pulled over the other chair in the room and sank into it, holding one of Monica's hands in hers, helping her keep watch over Zach. In spite of herself, her mind kept drifting back to Jake, and what she'd do if he didn't come back. Her heart clenched at the thought. She couldn't stop fixating on all the ways she'd brushed him off this past week, all the overtures she'd thrown back in his face. What was wrong with her? After all these years, she still pushed people away. She'd finally met someone wonderful, who really seemed to understand her. And now she might have lost him forever.

Thirty-Nine

"You ever get a song stuck in your head?" Dwight asked conversationally, as he bent his knees and dug his hands under a boulder. "Man, I do. Had 'We Are the Champions' playing over and over all night. Kind of funny, considering." He straightened his legs and struggled under the weight, huffing as he staggered a few steps until the boulder was hovering over the Captain. He relished the sight of Morgan's eyes going wide as he realized what was about to happen. He tried to speak, but Dwight had stuffed an old sock in his mouth and duct-taped over it. Dwight watched him struggle, straining fruitlessly against the ropes lashing him between two trees, head thrashing from side to side.

Dwight released his hands suddenly. The rock landed squarely on the Captain's chest. He watched as Sam writhed beneath it, screaming silently. Dwight slapped his palms together, brushing the grit off them.

"Pan-fort-eh-dirt," he proclaimed in mangled French. "Old-school torture. Figured you'd appreciate that."

He ducked back into the forest, scanning the ground. Fifteen feet away he found another good-size rock, not as big as the first one but perfect for pinning down an arm. He bent his knees again, careful to lift properly; he had miles to go after this, couldn't risk jamming up his back. As it was, the adrenaline was wearing off and underneath it he was dog tired. Good thing he'd been doing his exercises, otherwise he'd never have managed this.

After he was done with the Captain he'd try to hitch a ride and head farther north. He'd heard you could make a fortune on the fishing boats in the Gulf of St. Lawrence. Dwight lurched back to the clearing. They were about a mile into the woods, far enough from the road and the diner that he didn't think anyone could hear them. This was remote country, anyway, probably not a house for miles.

He dumped the rock on the Captain's right arm. Morgan went rigid with pain again, his head snapping back and forth. The boulder on his chest was making it hard for him to breathe, and he was wheezing through his nose. Dwight squatted beside him. "Huh. Gotta admit, I'm torn. I want this to take a while, but not long enough for someone to come by, you know what I mean? Maybe I'll switch this out for a smaller rock." He vanished into the woods again.

Sam Morgan straightened his right arm, locking out the elbow and flexing his muscles so that it lifted off the ground despite the weight of the rock. He struggled, straining at the ropes as he rolled his arm, trying to shift so that the rock slipped off. Veins throbbed blue. His arm muscles went ropy with the effort, and his breath wheezed harder through his nose. The rock yielded, moving a fraction of an inch, and he pressed the advantage, trying to shift it to the side. But after a long moment it dropped back into position, crushing his arm. A bone cracked, sharp and loud like a branch splitting, and his legs thrashed the ground in agony. His head arched back in a silent scream of pain. A tear edged out of his right eye and wound toward the dirt below.

Dwight reemerged from the woods. "Here we go!" he chirped, lifting a large chunk of granite over his head. "This one's for you, Ma," Dwight said before dropping it.

Kelly waited nervously. She wished McLarty would say something. She'd called to update him, fully aware that at this point he was probably getting better intel than she was. Since he'd originally asked to be informed of any changes, this was their third conversation of the day. A team of park rangers and Vermont State Police officers had found a Mercedes just outside the park on one of the back roads. The owner was stuffed in the trunk, dehydrated and bleeding, but more or less okay. They were waiting for confirmation on prints but, based on the description, the carjacker was Dwight Sullivan. Looked as if Dwight hadn't bothered to kill a final victim before leaving the States, which was the best news of the day so far.

"So we're pretty sure he also managed to cross the border," McLarty finally said.

"Yes, sir. Looks that way."

"I have to say, Jones, this is disappointing. You can probably imagine the crap I'm getting from our brothers in Canada. This is blowing up into an international incident."

"I'm sorry, sir. I believe I did everything I could." Kelly sat at the desk back in the command center. Despite his protests, she'd sent Colin home, haggard and exhausted. The room was unbearably stuffy, irritating her already pounding skull.

Fatigue caused her head to nod involuntarily, sleep dragging at the cusp of her consciousness. She just needed to get through this conversation, then she could lie down for a few minutes. The thought was so tempting she had to force herself to focus on the phone in her hand and the voice on the other end of the line.

McLarty sighed. "I wish that was enough. We're going to have to see how this plays out. Make sure you get that Sommers guy released ASAP, with our abject apologies. Hopefully he won't sue. If we can apprehend the two fugitives, I can probably mitigate the impact of this on your career. You followed procedure to the letter, right? Because this is one of those times that any cowboy moves will come back and bite you in the ass. So make sure all your paperwork is in order, double-check your warrants. You hear what I'm saying to you, Jones?" McLarty said.

"I hear you, sir." She had to remind herself that, nice guy that he was, McLarty was still a consummate politician—you didn't rise to his position without that skill. He was warning her to CYA, or "cover your ass." Meaning if everything wasn't in order already, she better get it there, and fast. She started to run back through the case in her mind, itemizing her actions. Then an image of Zach's face forced itself to the forefront and her eyes filled with tears.

"How's the kid?" McLarty asked, less gruffly.

"He slipped into a coma," she said flatly. She'd sat with Monica for hours, keeping vigil. When Dr. Stuart showed up, awkwardly balancing steaming coffee cups and a wilted bouquet, Kelly had excused herself. Easing the door shut behind her, she saw that Stuart had enveloped Monica in his arms and was rocking her gently.

McLarty paused again. "Sorry to hear it. What's the name of the hospital? I'll have my assistant send flowers."

She told him, waited as he scribbled it down. "Is that all, sir?" she asked after a moment.

He hesitated before saying, "Actually, Jones, I was thinking this might be the perfect time for you to take that vacation. The case is pretty much over now, probably be good for you to clear your head a little."

Kelly sat up straight in her chair, all traces of sleepiness banished. "Is this a vacation, or am I suspended?"

McLarty chuckled. "Don't be so paranoid, Jones. You're one of the best agents I've got, I'm not letting go of you that easily. The fallout from this is going to attract media attention for weeks. It probably couldn't hurt to wait things out on a beach somewhere."

"Is that better for me, or better for the Bureau?" Kelly asked.

McLarty paused again before saying, "Let's just say it's better all around, okay? For now, refer all media inquiries to me, and lay low. Take another day or two to wrap up the paperwork and loose ends, then get out of there."

Jan drew a deep breath before pushing open the door to the station manager's office. He was a bald guy, fat, who always let his eyes trail from her hips to her breasts before meeting her gaze with a slow smile. Not today, though. He frowned as he looked up from the desk and saw her standing there. Jan's heart sank at his expression. "Close the door," he snapped, and she slowly complied.

Not that she wasn't prepared. She'd taken the time to go home, shower and change. She'd devoted even more attention than usual to her hair and makeup, and wore her light blue suit, the most expensive one in her wardrobe. It had set her back almost a grand, but was worth it for the way it framed her tits. Saline drops had dispersed most of the redness in her eyes, though they still felt cracked and raw. She'd been up most of the night chasing the tail of the story with Mike and Joe, arriving at each scene only to discover to her enormous frustration that they'd just missed all the action. They'd been scooped by almost every other station, both local and national. All her hopes of yesterday were dashed. She felt like a fool.

The station manager swiveled in his chair and regarded her, face blank, absentmindedly scratching at something inside his ear. Sweat marks stained his armpits and he'd taken off his shoes and socks. The smell of feet mingled with air freshener and permeated the room. "We're going to be sorry to lose you," he said casually, knocking the wind out of Jan's lungs.

She struggled for a minute to remember the speech she'd rehearsed on her drive in. "But sir, there was no way to know…"

His eyebrows shot up. He listened to her, lips pressed in a smug line as she enumerated everything she'd done for the station over the years: all the good stories she'd dug up; how she'd poured her heart and soul into everything she did. She concluded with her best line, "If we can just forget these past twenty-four hours, I promise you I will be the best field reporter you've ever had. I'll work twenty-four/seven. I won't rest until I prove myself again…."

Jan's voice trailed off. The station manager just sat there, watching her with an odd expression on his face, as if he was in on some private joke. She was distracted by a movement over his right shoulder, her eyes drawn to his computer. An image danced across the screen. It was an animation of Marilyn Monroe in her famous white dress, but this time when the wind blew it up she didn't hold it down coquettishly, instead her arms waved in the air. And apparently she'd been unable to find panties. Jan looked away. Maybe she could get a sexual harassment suit going. It wouldn't be easy, not in this backwater, but times were changing. If she hired a good lawyer and lucked into a female judge…

"Twenty-four/seven, huh? That does sound tempting," the station manager said, rapping his knuckles against the armrests of his chair. His face split in a wider grin as he said slyly, "But you're not fired, Jan."

"What?"

"Nope. You've been called up. There's an open chair at WFXT—they finally decided to mothball the girl they had there. She had another kid, never lost the weight, I guess. Anyway, they want a fresh young face. And based on some of your recent reports—" he jabbed a finger at her "—they decided on you."

"WFXT? In Boston?" Jan's mouth hung slightly open. For the first time in a long time, she was speechless.

"Yep. An anchor chair, too. Just like you always wanted. It's the morning show, but still. Could work out well for you, play your cards right and don't fuck up again." He sounded almost jovial as he leaned forward and tapped her on a bare knee. "We're gonna miss you around here, though. Don't forget us little people, right?" He guffawed.

Jan recovered herself and smiled back at him, white teeth flashing as she joined in his laughter and said, "Forget you, Bob? Never."

Dwight scrubbed his hands in the diner restroom. He'd already ordered the full lumberjack breakfast: ham and eggs and sausage and toast. His mouth watered at the thought of it, he was starving. The Captain had a wad of Canadian cash in his wallet, more than enough to get Dwight where he wanted to go. The waitress said truckers came through pretty regularly, if he stuck around he could probably hitch a ride north.

It had taken longer for the Captain to die than he'd anticipated—the guy turned out to be pretty tough. In spite of himself Dwight felt a pang of admiration. He'd sat on a log and watched as the Captain's wheezing gradually slowed and stilled, the steady raising and lowering of his chest easing to a halt. The Captain's eyes gazed upward toward the trees. They'd been darting around all day and then, suddenly, they went blank. Dwight wished he could have taken longer with him, but out in the open it was too risky and he couldn't chance someone interrupting him. It had been slow enough, he figured. Ma would be pleased.

He splashed some water on his face and rubbed at the dirt on his cheeks, eyes squeezed shut. Keeping them closed, he reached out with his left hand, groping for the paper towel dispenser. His hand brushed something rough, and he squinted open one eye. Someone was handing him a paper towel. He twisted around, but the arm had already wrapped around his neck, locking him in a vise. He struggled, kicking back as his feet lifted off the floor and stars danced in front of his eyes, hands fighting to release the chokehold. After a minute he blacked out.

"Hello, Dwight," Jake said, releasing his grip and letting him drop to the floor.

Forty

"Where the hell have you been?" Kelly demanded angrily, arms crossed in front of her chest.

"Why, you miss me?" Jake leaned forward and planted a kiss on her brow. "I sure as hell missed you."

They were standing in their room at the B and B. Kelly had awoken from her nap to find Jake settled into the rocking chair in the corner, watching her. She'd forgotten to pull the shades before falling asleep, and night seeped in through the windows, the room lit only by a small lamp on the bedside table. She jolted to her feet at the sight of him, one half of her wanting to clasp him to her chest, the other demanding that she beat him senseless.

Kelly jerked away from his kiss. "I'm serious, Jake. You vanished, and stayed out of radio contact for almost a full day. What the hell happened?"

He shrugged. "Went after the bad guys."

When he didn't continue, she pressed, "And?"

He avoided her eyes. "And now I'm back. How's the kid?"

"Still iffy, but he's alive. I guess every hour he survives, his chances get better."

"I bet he'll be fine," he said reassuringly. "Now come over here, plant a kiss on me."

"I still want an explanation for why you went AWOL," she said firmly.

"Hey, you were the one who said I was only along in an unofficial capacity," he reminded her. "So technically, I didn't go AWOL."

Kelly's cell phone rang. She marched over to the bedside table and grabbed it. "Yes?" she said sharply. Her eyes widened as she listened, then she said, "Thanks for letting me know. I'll come by as soon as I can." Snapping it shut, she turned back to Jake. "Apparently Dwight Sullivan just turned up."

"Oh, yeah? Where?" Jake said with exaggerated nonchalance.

"Duct-taped to the hood of a car in the local impound lot. Whoever put him there knocked out the surveillance cameras first."

"Huh, that's strange. Lucky break, though, right?"

"What did you do?" Kelly's eyes narrowed.

"You heading over to the hospital? Why don't I jump in the shower, then I can drive us there." He pulled his shirt over his head and started to unbuckle his belt. "Man, I'm filthy."

"Jake…" Kelly sighed and plunked down on the edge of the bed. In spite of herself she let her eyes trail over his naked chest. "You know how I feel about that sort of thing…"

He knelt in front of her and rubbed her thighs. "I know. But sometimes justice needs a little shove in the right direction. I'm in a position to do that, and you aren't."

She didn't respond, just ducked her head. He kissed her nose, then headed into the bathroom. Steam began pouring through the doorway. He raised his voice to be heard over the shower noise. "Morgan had everyone fooled, huh? Some locals were even hoping he'd run for mayor."

"Who told you that?" Kelly asked, eyes narrowing.

"No one important. I just think it's nuts, that he almost got away with it."

"He did get away with it," Kelly said despondently. "He's probably hiding out somewhere in Canada right now, laughing at us."

Jake didn't answer. Kelly examined the swirls on the carpet. "The funny thing is, you talk to most serial killers, they think they're basically just like everyone else. They come up with all sorts of reasons for the things they do, blame the victims, God, their mothers... I think even the worst of them looks in the mirror every day and sees a good guy. People can justify pretty much anything to themselves."

There was a long pause. Jake cleared his throat, then called out, "Is this an amazing shower or what? I gotta say, that's my one requirement for our place in D.C. It must have good water pressure."

"Our place in D.C.?" Kelly asked, running her fingers across the pattern on the bedspread. The scratches on her face were starting to smart.

"Yeah. I'm thinking maybe a little town house in George-town. Supposed to be good schools there."

"What?" Kelly asked, alarmed.

"Schools. You know, for the kids."

Kelly launched herself off the bed and smoothed out the quilt. "What makes you think I want to have kids?"

"You're kidding, right? Everyone wants to have kids. It's an undeniable biological instinct."

Kelly straightened a stack of papers on the bedside table, then bent to pick up the clothes Jake had left scattered across the floor. She shook them out, then folded them neatly as she replied, "I'm a little old to be having kids."

"Please. You're what, thirty-seven? We've still got plenty of time. "

"I couldn't work this job with kids." She stacked the clothes neatly on the chair in the corner, eyeing the rest of the room. A glint on the carpet caught her eye.

"I've already thought of that. And since you're not exactly stay-at-home mom material, I thought maybe you could join our new business venture."

"What, work for you?" Kelly frowned as she bent to pick up the object, examining it. It was a gorgeous ring, rows of rubies set in a delicate platinum band. *Kind of surprising the housekeepers missed it,* she thought. She'd turn it in to the B and B's lost and found.

"More like partners. Or you could freelance, only take the cases that appeal to you. That sounds pretty good, doesn't it? And we'd pay three times what you're making now—for a hell of a lot less work."

"What makes you so sure this business is going to take off?" she asked idly as she set the ring on the nightstand.

"What, with my background and people skills? How could it not?"

Kelly fell back onto the bed and gazed at the ceiling with dismay. "You're nuts."

She heard the ancient knobs twist and the slap of water on tile stilled. Jake emerged from the bathroom, toweling off his hair. "Nuts about you," he said, cracking a grin. "Take your time, consider it. The offer stands." His gaze fell on the night-stand and his face blanched.

Kelly raised her head and followed his eyes. "Oh, that. I found it on the floor. We can turn it in to the front desk as we're leaving." She lay back down against the pillows. She was still exhausted. What she really needed was a long, uninterrupted night's sleep.

"Uh, no, we can't," he said, crossing the room to pick it up.

"What? Why not?"

"Kelly…" Jake said. At the shift in his voice, Kelly lifted her head. Jake was kneeling in front of her, towel hanging open, holding out the ring. "Not exactly how I pictured it, but…what do you think?"

Author Note

Sixteen years ago I worked as a development intern for Jacob's Pillow, a seasonal dance festival in the Berkshires. I learned a lot about myself that summer—first and foremost that I much preferred dancing to writing grants for dance companies. I also found out that I'm not much of a camper, and that if I spend too much time away from the ocean I become unpleasant. When I wasn't working (which was frequently—after all, my salary was only seventy-five dollars a month) I took full advantage of the opportunities the area offered, hiking the Appalachian Trail, swimming in limestone lakes, attending concerts on the lawn at Tanglewood and shows at the Williamstown Theatre. Festival interns were given room and board, and lived in cabins scattered across the grounds. As luck would have it I was assigned to a cabin far off the beaten track, set deep in the woods a mile from the main road. I was alone in my room one night when a storm knocked out our power. As I sat there in the dark, clutching my Swiss army knife and jumping at every noise outside my door, it struck me that this place would be a perfect, creepy setting for a murder. Sixteen years later I finally got the opportunity to use it.

I owe a huge debt to so many people who devoted their time, knowledge and support to this book. Dr. Doug P. Lyle answered the most scattered forensics questions patiently and promptly, and has been an invaluable resource for me as well as many other writers. FBI Special Agent Pamelia S. Stratton and Special Agent (retired) Mary Ellen Beekman offered ways to correct some of the more glaring inconsistencies in the narrative. Robin Burcell is not only a top-notch writer and Thrillerfest roommate, she also answered some important questions on police protocol. And Lieutenant Patricia Driscoll of the Berkshire State Police Detective Unit was kind enough to correct some of my terminology. It goes without saying that this book is a work of fiction, and in no way reflects the practices, procedures, or mindset of this fine law enforcement unit.

Barbara Volkle referred me to the delightfully named Tom Collins, birder extraordinaire, who described what the sighting of a lifetime would be in the Berkshires. And SF PC doctor Vernon Whitaker used what can only be described as modern-day voodoo to salvage all of my files when my laptop died a premature death.

All of my readers, Kalia Gibb in particular, made a huge contribution to the final draft of my manuscript. And Dorothy Sleeper is single-handedly responsible for the impressive sales of my first book, *The Tunnels,* in western Massachusetts. I can't thank her enough for her loyal and enthusiastic support.

My agent, Jean Naggar, has been a tireless advocate for my work. I also must extend a heartfelt thanks to everyone at Mira

Books, first and foremost my amazing editor Valerie Gray, who graciously responds to any request no matter how absurd, and whose notes produced a much better novel than the one I initially handed her. Heather Foy, Don Lucey, and everyone in the sales and marketing department are steadfast in their efforts to promote all of my books, and have been tremendously supportive throughout this experience.

Without the talents of my sister Kate, who sat with me for hours going over word choice, punctuation and plot points, this book would probably be unreadable. My other sister, Adrienne, and my parents have also always been some of my best readers, tempering their love for me with a clear-eyed view of what I've written and how it could be improved. It is said that writers lead a lonely life. Thanks to my friends, sisters, parents, husband and daughter, I can't say that I agree.

From the author of *Trust Me*

BRENDA NOVAK

Who was the real killer?

Romain lost his reason for living when his daughter was kidnapped and murdered. He used a cop's gun to mete out his own justice and spent years in prison. Once he was freed, he learned that he might have killed the wrong man.

And now Jasmine, a psychological profiler, believes the same man kidnapped her sister, Kimberly, sixteen years ago.

What happens next?

Jasmine knows Romain can help her...if he chooses. But searching for the man who irrevocably changed both their lives means they have to rise to a killer's challenge....

"Brenda Novak writes nonstop suspense at its very best."
—*New York Times* bestselling author Carla Neggers

MIRA®

Available the first week of July 2008 wherever books are sold!

MBN2460

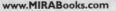

REQUEST YOUR FREE BOOKS!

2 FREE NOVELS
FROM THE ROMANCE/SUSPENSE
COLLECTION PLUS 2 FREE GIFTS!

YES! Please send me 2 FREE novels from the Romance/Suspense Collection and my 2 FREE gifts (gifts are worth about $10). After receiving them, if I don't wish to receive any more books, I can return the shipping statement marked "cancel." If I don't cancel, I will receive 4 brand-new novels every month and be billed just $5.49 per book in the U.S. or $5.99 per book in Canada, plus 25¢ shipping and handling per book plus applicable taxes, if any*. That's a savings of at least 20% off the cover price! I understand that accepting the 2 free books and gifts places me under no obligation to buy anything. I can always return a shipment and cancel at any time. Even if I never buy another book from the Reader Service, the two free books and gifts are mine to keep forever.

185 MDN EF5Y   385 MDN EF6C

Name _____ (PLEASE PRINT) _____

Address _____ Apt. # _____

City _____ State/Prov. _____ Zip/Postal Code _____

Signature (if under 18, a parent or guardian must sign) _____

Mail to **The Reader Service:**
IN U.S.A.: P.O. Box 1867, Buffalo, NY 14240-1867
IN CANADA: P.O. Box 609, Fort Erie, Ontario L2A 5X3

Not valid to current subscribers to the Romance Collection,
the Suspense Collection or the Romance/Suspense Collection.

Want to try two free books from another line?
Call 1-800-873-8635 or visit www.morefreebooks.com.

* Terms and prices subject to change without notice. N.Y. residents add applicable sales tax. Canadian residents will be charged applicable provincial taxes and GST. Offer not valid in Quebec. This offer is limited to one order per household. All orders subject to approval. Credit or debit balances in a customer's account(s) may be offset by any other outstanding balance owed by or to the customer. Please allow 4 to 6 weeks for delivery. Offer available while quantities last.

Your Privacy: Harlequin is committed to protecting your privacy. Our Privacy Policy is available online at www.eHarlequin.com or upon request from the Reader Service. From time to time we make our lists of customers available to reputable third parties who may have a product or service of interest to you. If you would prefer we not share your name and address, please check here. ☐

BOB08R

MICHELLE GAGNON
